of the

Apostate

D. R. Hill

CONTENTS

ONE

T he world was dead. It came during the night. Without warning and without mercy, the villagers perished before dawn ever came, and when Rhys awoke, he rose to the bleakness wrought by whatever curse had befallen his home. Now he stood there in the emptiness, in the silent ghostly streets, paralysed by grief, despair, and uncertainty. The Grey had come to Longford. All colour had faded. The air had soured and turned poisonous. Life had been quenched. The world was dead.

In the ashen skies above, the sun loomed pale and cold, its warming rays unable to penetrate the pervasive evil that settled across the land. It was mid-June, yet swathes of crumbling frost matted the ground and dagger-like icicles hung from the thatch eaves. The cold seemed preternatural in its ferocity; it was sinister and merciless, gripping Rhys with icy talons that sapped the warmth from his flesh, numbed his mind and senses, and pierced deep into his bones. It was suffocating; each lungful Rhys drew was shallower and sharper than the last, and what little air entered and escaped his lungs did so in frozen wisps of breath.

Time passed and clouds plumed from nothingness in the colourless skies above. Churning out of the venomous atmosphere they sank heavily into stifling fogs that drowned the streets of Longford. Through the dense murk came whispers of darkness: a darkness that drew inwards upon Rhys, towards the very heart of the malefic curse, all the while he stood silent and unthinking as he felt the life slowly draining from him.

Then he saw it. At first it seemed so faint that he thought it perhaps an illusion of the gloom, yet as his eyes settled upon it for a time, Rhys discerned the hovering glow that shone dimly through the darkling mists. It was mere yards away, but the near impenetrable veil of insidious haze that continued to effervesce around him blurred the white light beyond his perception. Yet as Rhys continued to gaze upon the glimmer, it rescued a portion of his mind from the abyss upon which it teetered, and for a fleeting moment, the grasp of the cold lapsed long enough for Rhys to shake himself free of the paralysis that had seized him.

Air flooded suddenly into Rhys's chest, and he realised now it had been some time since he had previously drawn breath. Though the air was noxious and stifling, it cleared his thoughts and rekindled vigour in his muscles. Lifting a benumbed foot from the ice-coated road, he stepped forwards and began to struggle through the throttling murk that pressed upon him. Each inch he battled forwards burnt into his last reserves of strength and brought him closer to death; but if Rhys was to die, he was determined to do so in the light. He fought on with outstretched fingers, and suddenly, the murk tore open. He stumbled forwards as the clasp of darkness released him.

He had pushed through a threshold, into a void in the gloom, where the air was clear and still held some warmth, where patches of colour remained, and where the aura of death was not so absolute. Gasping deeply, he sputtered and coughed up the last of the toxic fumes in which he had been drowning. He shivered violently as heat seeped slowly back through his skin. His eyes flared and refocussed, adjusting to what now was a blinding glare. The arcane shimmer dimmed to a gentle shine at the tip of an ebony staff etched with runic symbols down its length. The man gripping the stave revolved at Rhys's coming, as if his very presence had been sensed, and Rhys was suddenly met with a stare like none he had ever seen. Two bronze-flecked, golden eyes radiated from the stranger's dark face; his irises incandesced and swirled with vibrant magic that whispered of a hidden world beyond Rhys's wildest imaginings.

The stranger's mahogany skin and tall broad frame suggested he heralded from the south, though his rusting mail and tattered violet robes were hard to place. His matted hair was threaded black and silver and continued across his hirsute jawline to a short but unkempt beard. But every detail of the man escaped Rhys's notice, for his attention was fixed unwaveringly upon the supernatural glare that scrutinised every fibre of his being.

"Who are you?" the stranger demanded deeply.

Rhys felt his tongue immobilised by shock as he endured the man's gaze.

"Who are you!?" he repeated more forcefully with a narrowing stare.

"Rhys," he stuttered, finally able to summon words. "My name is Rhys North."

"Why…?" the stranger uttered coldly.

Rhys shuddered in fear and confusion as the man before him intensified his piercing stare.

"Why have you done this!?" the southerner hissed, his bulking form rippling with barely contained fury.

Rhys shook his head, almost ready to retreat back into the deathly gloom.

"Why have you invoked such wretched magic upon this place?"

"I haven't…" Rhys stammered. "You think I did this?"

"You stand amongst the dead, in a place where there is only death, and where only the dead lurk. I sense the darkness upon you."

"This was my home!" Rhys cried in defence before suspicion of his own began to emerge through his fear.

"I have walked these haunted streets and seen what wickedness has been summoned. The dead litter the roads; some lie cold in their beds having never drawn breath this foul dawn. None have survived. All have perished in the wake of this evil, and yet you emerge from this acrid murk barely tainted by the deathly malevolence that claims all and spares none. And you say you know nothing of what has transpired!? You think me so foolish to believe that you have not played a part in conjuring this curse?"

Rhys shook his head in defiance, fighting back acidic tears.

The stranger remained silent as he continued to study him.

"You arrived in the wake of this evil!" asserted Rhys accusingly. "*You* brought this wickedness with you!"

The man began to slowly encircle Rhys, dissecting him with his glare.

"Who are *you*?" Rhys demanded.

No response came.

"Why are *you* here?"

Still he was ignored.

"Answer me!" Rhys roared.

"You are wrong," the man replied after completing his circle. "*I* am not responsible for the curse that has desolated your home. I am here to discover its cause!"

"It is not me," Rhys growled.

"So you said," he returned. "Where were you? When the curse struck?"

"Here. In my home."

The stranger rubbed his beard forcefully, and through his fingers, he emitted a single word, "Impossible!" His leering gaze seemed to warm as the harshness that was there seconds earlier melted away.

"Who are you?" Rhys repeated.

"You need not fear me," he assured with a voice now devoid of animosity. "My name is Arlas."

Rhys nodded and felt somehow comforted.

"Are you alone? Have any others survived?"

Rhys shook his head as the haunting images of the dead flickered through his thoughts.

"Your family?"

"They were already amongst the dead," he voiced gravely.

"I see," Arlas nodded empathetically before pausing for a time. "We best leave here. You must come with me."

Rhys nodded in agreement as he looked upon the man with an inexplicable sense of trust. "Okay," he shivered. "Can I gather my possessions?"

"We are short of time," the man returned as

he glanced uneasily about in a way that suggested his eyes could penetrate the haze. He turned his stare back to the half-dressed and barefooted man before him. "You must be quick."

Rhys nodded once more. "This way," he said with a gesture, before leading the man in the direction of his house. He stepped forwards up the path and the stranger followed, and to Rhys's amazement, the walls of gloom drew open before them like parting curtains, as the refuge in the sinister fog remained centred around Arlas. Rhys tried not to peer beyond the veil of murk, yet wherever he turned his gaze, their vacant eyes stared harrowingly back at him. The dead lay within the streets in their hundreds. None had escaped.

"Here," said Rhys, when finally they approached the last house of the street. Once a quaint thatched cottage of stone in which Rhys had lived all his life, in the bleak gloom that now fumed around it, the building appeared more tomblike than homely.

Rhys pressed his palm against the door; it swung open on its heavy hinges. He stepped through into the dank hallway and made straight for the bedroom. Arlas remained within the entrance, glancing warily about the ruin.

Pulling a set of tattered leather boots over his frozen toes, Rhys then quickly donned his overshirt and coat, before strapping his father's knife to his belt. Exiting the room, he made haste for the pantry with a traveller's pack in hand, but before he could reach the door, Arlas spoke out with a newfound sense of urgency.

"We must leave now!"

Rhys said nothing as the two fled the cottage and briskly trekked out of Longford. When the final few houses passed them by, he looked back one last time and shuddered in horror at the fate that had befallen his village.

"We are headed to Oakton," Arlas explained as he led Rhys southward. "At a hard pace, it is little more than five days from here. I will answer your questions soon, but I would like to put some distance between us and this village—"

Before Arlas could finish his sentence, an ear-shattering wail pierced through the fog and raw unprecedented terror welled in Rhys's heart. He clapped his hands over his ears in an attempt to muffle the screech, yet the harrowing noise was unabated by his palms. As the shriek petered, the light atop Arlas's staff was snuffed out like a candle in the wind. The refuge in the fog collapsed and the veil pressed suddenly inwards upon them, bringing with it the noxious air and stifling chill that had been held at bay by the light.

Rhys locked eyes with Arlas to see the stranger shared his terror.

"Run," Arlas breathed.

The two men broke into a sprint, charging down the path towards the forest. The shadows of the treeline loomed faintly before them as Rhys drew steadily ahead, yet before either man could reach the woodland boundary, a second shrill cry sliced through the murk, far louder and infinitely more distressing than the first. Through the gloom, Rhys sighted a rippling shadow that darted amidst the fog, and the two men skidded to a halt.

"Get down!" Arlas commanded, forcing Rhys to the ground. The man gripped his staff tightly in anticipation, guarding Rhys against whatever evil lurked just out of sight. Ribbons of darkness continued to tear rapidly about the haze, yet always out of focus. Arlas thrust forwards with his stave, and from out of its tip spouted a tongue of black and purple flames. The fiery missile fizzled and sparked as it sailed into the gloom, vanishing momentarily before it flashed indigo through the murk as it exploded.

All fell silent. Rhys's heart throbbed. His eyes flickered about, scanning the haze ahead for any sign of movement. Then it appeared. Faint at first, a shadow steadily began to form out of the mist, darkening as it was birthed from the fog, before menacingly, it crept towards them. It was a spectre of shadow, hooded and cloaked, wreathed in flailing tendrils woven out of darkness. It drifted from the haze bent double, outstretching a ghostly skeletal hand of black bone wrapped in a thin mesh of translucent flesh. Clutched in its gnarled grip was a jagged dagger of wrought iron. As it drew closer, it hissed and whined in ear-splitting tones.

It lunged towards Rhys with unworldly speed, yet a second lash of violet fire spewed outwards from Arlas's staff, intercepting the spectre before the blade met Rhys's flesh. The jet of flame exploded around the phantom, enwrapping it in dark fire. It recoiled in anguish, emitting another shrill howl. Writhing and contracting, the shadows of its robes dissolved to ash and smoke, and in a matter of seconds, the phantasmal being had smouldered away, returning to the fog whence it came.

Arlas stooped over Rhys and extended him a firm hand. The sorcerer wrenched him to his feet, but as he did so, Arlas's eyes widened once more. Rhys span to glance behind him. Dread swelled in his gut as he sighted the darkling wisps of fog to their rear, each birthing a new phantasm of shadow.

"Get out of here," insisted Arlas, pushing Rhys away. "I'll hold them off!"

"But—"

"Now!" he commanded.

Consumed by panic, Rhys fled down the path towards the treeline as crackling violet flares began to explode behind him. The forest rushed up to meet him, and as he pierced the sylvan border the series of blasts subsided into silence. Rhys dared not look back. He sped on along the twisting bridleway, ducking under low branches and tearing through brambles grown across the path. Fuelled by fear, he raced deeper and deeper into the lifeless woods, urging his body to move ever faster in spite of his screaming muscles. His heart punched heavily in his chest as freezing air stung his eyes and swept frantically in and out of his lungs. Yards became furlongs and furlongs became miles as Rhys lost all track of time.

The path began to climb and narrow until it all but disappeared. Reaching the top of a verge, Rhys felt a root snare his ankle, wrenching his feet out from under him. Down he tumbled, slamming hard and repeatedly against the slope as he fell. When finally he struck the bottom of the dyke, his face smacked forcefully against the soil and his teeth sank into his lip. The metallic taste of blood swilled in his mouth. He spat. Rhys paused for a moment and watched as his blood trickled over the detritus that lined the bottom of the ditch: scarlet against the otherwise colourless ground.

Clambering up the far bank on hands and knees, he rose to his feet at the top. A clearing in the canopy revealed the horizon. The forest stretched on ahead of him towards the east, gradually progressing from grey to green as the reaches of the curse faded in the distance. Panting heavily, Rhys felt a sense of overwhelming relief. He turned to look back along the desolate path up which he had run. Nothing, nor no one was following. He was safe.

TWO

Pushing through the thicket, Rhys emerged into a glade carpeted in bronze and crimson leaves. Dew glistered in the rays of autumnal light that beamed through the thinning canopies of Oakwood. Rhys's lips curved upwards to a satisfied smirk as a rabbit jostled amidst the leaf-litter, its black eyes bulging in terror at the man approaching it. A hand clamped firmly across the base of its skull, whilst another gripped both of the creature's thrashing legs, tugging them backwards in a swift movement that with a soft click, dislocated its neck. Its marble-like eyes glazed over, its twitching nose relaxed, and its legs slumped limp in the man's grip.

Drawing his father's knife from the scabbard on his belt, Rhys cut the cordage of his snare pulled taught around the animal's hind leg. He draped the game over his shoulder beside two more lifeless coneys, securing them with a loop around his chest. Gazing west through the bare treetops, he watched the glaring orb of the sun begin to approach the brow of a distant hillock. The light would soon begin to die.

Disappearing back into the wood, Rhys returned to the road. Reaching the highway, he slid down the dusty wayside bank, patted himself off, and turned west. He stopped abruptly after but a couple of steps, raising his hand against the blinding dazzle of the sinking sun. Squinting brought the silhouette of a man centred in the mud track into focus.

Before him stood a scoundrel with clear intent, his appearance and demeanour as shady as any lawless vagabond that preyed upon travellers. His clothes were ragged and yet appeared to have once been expensive; most likely stolen, the garments were ill-fitting, not quite large enough for the bulk of a man they covered. His head was bald and black with grime whilst his brow bore an unsightly scar.

"Afternoon," Rhys greeted him warily, ensuring a distance remained between the two of them.

Unnervingly, the brigand licked his lips and took several steps closer towards Rhys. "Nice catch!" he grinned through a jaw full of crooked teeth grimed yellow and black with rot. A set of leering eyes greedily examined the rabbits that hung across Rhys's back, before finally his grotesque stare directed towards the coin-purse tucked under his belt.

"Not my best day—but it'll do," Rhys replied, his pulse quickening with every inch the highwayman drew closer.

The thug sucked a waft of air through his crooked nose as he took a final step inwards and leant in threateningly close to Rhys. "I'll take 'em off your hands... along with any gold you's got on yer," he wheezed in twisted satisfaction.

"Or—" Rhys began, taking a large stride backwards, "how about I give you two of these here rabbits, I hold onto my coin for the time being, and we both call it good business?"

"Funny!" the villain scowled as a grubby hand reached behind his back. The sound of metal scraping against leather chimed and the highwayman produced a rusted dagger, pointing it at Rhys's chest. "But I ain't looking to barter!"

"You seem a reasonable sort," Rhys said wryly as the footpad continued to edge nearer to him. "I am sure you are a busy man. Why don't I just head off on my way and leave you to... err... your business: the violent acquisition of other people's possessions, as it were—and we need not waste any more of each other's time."

The bandit contorted his face into an expression of furious impatience. He revolved the rust-coated knife in a series of small circles, bringing it to within inches of Rhys's heart. "Last chance!" he spat.

Rhys sighed heavily. "I take it negotiations have come to a close then? Very well." He fingered the drawstring of his coin pouch momentarily and the bandit issued a wicked grin in response, yet as the footpad lowered his guard, Rhys's fingertips nimbly darted for the haft of his blade.

The highwayman glimpsed the sleight of hand from the corner of his vision. Wrenching back his shoulder, he lunged powerfully into a stab, yet the rusty blade thrust only into open air. Instinct had seized control of Rhys, and without pause, he had leapt clean aside of the attack. With a single swift motion, he drew his dagger from the scabbard and swung the point of his blade in a downward arc.

Steel sank into flesh as blood gurgled from the bandit's outstretched forearm. The villain roared in agony and his weapon tumbled from his grip. Rhys's fingers locked around the footpad's throat as he wrenched the dagger from his wrist and pressed the incarnadine-painted blade against the brigand's neck.

"Please!" the bandit sputtered as Rhys stared into his bloodshot eyes.

"Why?" Rhys demanded intimidatingly. "Would you have shown me such mercy?"

"Yes...yes! Please let me go!"

"You liar!" Rhys scowled with narrowing eyes. He struck upward with a knee to the man's gut, before throwing him backwards to the ground by the scruff of the collar. "Get out of here!"

The wretched man scrambled back to his feet, clutching his arm as blood seeped between his fingers. But his terror quickly faded, when with a dart of his eyes, he glimpsed past Rhys's shoulder. A twisted expression of menace returned across his villainous face. "You'll get it now, you fuck!"

A snapping twig pricked up Rhys's ears. He twisted clumsily in desperate realisation of his fatal mistake. A second brute charged him from behind, brandishing an axe high above his head. The brigand roared as the axe-head cleaved downward at Rhys, giving him only time to flinch.

A flash of white erupted behind Rhys's eyelids with a thunderous clap. The light faded quickly to black. The gentle thrumming of his pulse grew steadily quieter. His breathing was deep and heavy. Slowly, his eyelids lifted. His vision blurred quickly into focus as he glanced about himself.

The axeman was sprawled upon the wayside bank, his eyes gazing vacantly upwards. A black cavity scorched from the side of his chest seethed with smoke, carrying the sickly-sweet stench of burnt flesh. Gripped with only confusion, Rhys stepped closer, inspecting the wound further. Gasping in disbelief, he peered into the hollow, catching glimpse of a smouldering froth that had once been a lung.

Staggering back in horror, Rhys swivelled to the rustling of bushes. The first highwayman had scurried up the bank in terrified retreat, fleeing into the woods and out of sight, leaving nothing but a speckled trail of crimson blood behind him. Rhys's throat tightened as his eyes scanned frantically about the treeline.

"Who's there!?" he cried out in frenzied panic. His eyes darted back and forth nervously in the silence. Not a moment passed before he turned and bolted west down the road, not daring to glance back.

Questions rushed through his mind, yet all were too fleeting in his scattered thoughts to have any hope of being answered. He sped on along the road without slowing until his legs ached, his chest burned, and the top of the sun faded behind the hills to the west. He halted at his body's limit, quivering as he tried desperately to suck air into his lungs. His pulse throbbed densely between his ears.

Clutching his side, Rhys looked back down the highway to the east, searching for any sign of a pursuer. He stood unmoving for some time, staring with a sharp alertness. When finally he was satisfied that nothing had followed, his heart had long since slowed to normal, and the twilight had faded to a dim dusk. Wiping the cold sweat from his brow, he continued on down the bridleway, leaving the woodlands behind him.

Shortly after moonrise, Rhys came to the village of Oakton. Set upon a crossroad, the village served as a rest point for many travellers and traders journeying across the northern reaches of Gwent, and further afield to the realm of Westverness. The final few merchants were finishing packing up their stalls when Rhys reached the market square. The ebb and flow of people through the darkening streets drifted mostly in the direction of the taverns and alehouses. Rounding a corner, Rhys arrived at The Smoking Oak, a large, thatched building resounding with cheers and laughter.

Rhys stepped through the open door and was greeted by a cosy warmth that contrasted the cool crispness of the dusk wind outside. The tavern was lit with an orange glow that emanated from lanterns and several hearths set around the wide interior. Drunken patrons, both regulars and wayfarers, shared stories and songs around tables, merry in each other's company. The owner Buckle was a plump and friendly man who would always find room for any in need of shelter. The tall innkeeper stood proud behind the bar as he polished a tankard with a wide grin that stretched between two rosy cheeks. Beside him stood his loving wife Martha, nearly half his height, yet just as warm as her husband.

Buckle winked at Rhys as he noticed him enter, before proceeding to pour a pint from a large barrel set behind the bar. Negotiating the crowded room, Rhys made his way to the bar and sat upon the stool opposite the tavernkeep, issuing him a gentle smile as he did so.

"How many today then, lad?" Buckle asked as he cut the flow from the keg and watched the last few drops of golden fluid splash into the tankard.

Rhys untethered the game from his shoulder, hanging them from a hook set above the bar. "I've had more successful days," Rhys admitted, "But it should cover what I owe you."

"Now, now. I told you not to worry yourself about that, m'boy," the innkeeper insisted, sliding the tankard across the oaken bar to Rhys. "You've got a living to make, son. Martha and I are doing just fine for the moment—business is great!" he gestured to the ram-packed tavern.

"No Buckle," he refused, loosening the drawstring of his coin purse, and sliding a copper over the bar in exchange for the drink. "I said I would pay you back by mid-October. I meant it."

"All right," the landlord agreed, reluctantly unhooking the game, yet sliding the copper back in Rhys's direction. "You're stubborn," he said wagging his finger half-jokingly. "Too stubborn some might say."

Rhys somewhat begrudgingly dropped the coin back into his pouch and refastened it about his belt. He raised the pewter tankard to his lips and savoured a long swig of the mead.

Martha took the game from her husband before shaking her head at Rhys with a beaming smile. "See that he doesn't try to pay for anything else tonight," she remarked, stretching on tiptoes to kiss her spouse gently on the cheek. "I'll get these to the kitchen." She turned and left through the doorway behind the bar.

"I don't need you to do this, Buckle," Rhys protested now, in Martha's absence. "I can look after myself."

"Really?" the man grinned. "If I remember correctly, when first you came through that door you were starved half to death, covered head to toe in filth, with nowhere to call home, no coin, and no story as to why or where you'd come from."

"I am grateful," he urged. "For everything. You took me in... put a roof over my head... and never did you ask for anything in return. But I am just trying to repay the kindness you and Martha showed me. I don't believe the world owes me anything. I'm trying to make my own way. I don't want you to be put upon."

"Okay," the tavern owner nodded in solemn understanding before his rosy cheeks pillowed into an infectious grin. "But those coneys—they make us even now!"

"All right," he agreed happily.

"Now, are you going to tell me what happened?" he asked insightfully with a subtle gesture to Rhys's wrist.

He glanced down to notice a maroon splattering of dried blood over the cuff of his jacket. "Oh, err..." he hesitated. "I just caught myself on some brambles."

"Hmm," Buckle muttered as he crossed his arms knowingly. "Well, I almost forgot: a young lad, probably about your age, stopped by here 'round noon. He was asking after you."

"Really?" Rhys pondered.

"I told him you were out—most likely in Oakwood."

"And then?"

"Well, he said he'd likely be back this evening, though I haven't seen him yet. Got the impression he went out in search of you. Strange fellow, he was. Definitely not from 'round these parts."

"Did you get a name?" Rhys queried, at a loss as to who the mysterious stranger could be.

"Called himself Thomas. Whether that was his first or last name, I can't say."

"I don't know," he shook his head. "Can't think of anyone I've met by that name."

"Well, I'll let you know if he comes through that door." With that, the barkeep dealt a swift wipe to the bar and left Rhys to his drink to serve the other patrons.

Rhys remained seated at the bar for the next few hours, talking to Buckle and those who came to order food and drink. One man spoke of a body aside the east road, with *'a queer burn on his side.'*

"Looked pretty fresh, he did," said another. "Couldn't for the life of me figure out what it was that killed him. I'd call him a poor sod, I would, but I'm pretty sure he were one of them bandits that have been plaguing the area. Looks like he got what he had coming to him, eh?"

At that moment, the tavern erupted into song, instigated by one table of very drunken traders. Buckle joined in as he always did, and encouragingly nudged Rhys from across the bar. Rhys reluctantly obliged, joining the discordant chant that blared throughout the rammed tavern. The song cycled through twice, and some even tried for a third round, but their attempts were short lived as their drunken bellows subsided into laughter and chatter once more.

With the quietening of the tavern, Rhys took notice of Buckle attempting to catch his glance from across the room. The innkeeper then darted his eyes to the door, from which Rhys felt a cool draft blow in. He glanced over his shoulder at the doorway in time to see a young man stride through.

The stranger stood little over average height, yet his upright athletic posture held a commanding presence. A tangled mess of weather-beaten hair swept in thick blond strands across his brow. His handsome face was cheerful, yet resolute, hinting at an assured determination. But of all his features, it was the stranger's eyes that proved the most distinguishing: a piercing blue that swirled and seethed with preternatural whispers. He examined the tavern with keen gaze, seemingly absorbing every aspect of the scene before him in impossible minutiae, and without realising, Rhys suddenly realised they had locked eyes.

Swivelling quickly back to his pint, Rhys bowed his head and sipped at the mead, hoping to avoid the traveller's intense stare, yet the footfalls of leather boots on wooden floorboards made straight for him, and within a moment, the man had seated himself on the stool beside Rhys. Peering up from his tankard, Rhys was relieved to see the stranger now paid him no attention. From the corner of his gaze, he examined the man once more; a set of weather-stained traveller's garments told the tale of a life on the road, their colours all but faded completely. Across the man's back was strapped a curious item: perhaps a staff or spear of some kind, concealed beneath a wrap of tattered cloth that appeared to have been stitched and re-stitched innumerable times in an attempt to hide or protect whatever item was hidden within it.

"What can I get for you?" Buckle asked him.

"A pint of your house ale if you will," he replied kindly. "And a room for the night if you have any spare."

"Coming right up," Buckle nodded, and made his way over to the largest keg behind the bar. Frothy amber beer spewed from the keg's tap into a tankard Buckle held beneath the flow, filling it quickly to the brim.

"Any news on North?" the traveller spoke out to him.

Buckle remained silent for a moment in wait to see if Rhys would speak up. "I'm sure he will make an appearance soon enough," he said finally as he set the beer down before the man. "I'll just go fetch the ledger," he added, disappearing.

"You are looking for North?" Rhys directed to the man before taking another gulp of his drink.

"You know him, I take it?" the traveller replied, turning to set his intense gaze on Rhys once more.

"Better than most." Rhys paused. "What business do you have with him?"

"He is the acquaintance of a friend. A friend who has been unable to make contact with him since they met this last summer," he said, averting his scrutiny.

"So, you don't know him personally?"

"I know *of* him. His general description, from where he hails. I have even saved his life, though I doubt he realises that as of yet. Now, if you are asking if I have ever met him, then my answer is that: I had rather hoped to be doing so about now. Alas, if he wishes to remain unknown to me, then that is his decision."

Rhys stared agape at the stranger who now seemingly ignored his very presence.

"Will you be wanting dinner sent up to your room, Mr Thomas?" Buckle asked jollily upon his return, setting the inn's logbook on the bar as he did so.

"If you'd be so kind," he replied rummaging through a pocket to produce a small handful of silver farthings embossed with the Crest of Westverness. "Will this suffice?" he asked, placing them beside the open ledger.

Briefly examining the foreign coinage,

Buckle nodded. "It's more than enough," he said moving to slide some of the farthings back in the man's direction, yet the stranger dismissed the notion with a silent gesture. Instead, Buckle produced a key, handing it to the man uttering, "Room eight. The end of the first-floor corridor. Your supper should be along within the hour."

"My thanks," the man nodded before looking to address both Buckle and Rhys. "Perhaps Mr North would care to join me in my room if ever he makes an appearance this evening." With that he raised his pint to them both and strode off in the direction of a narrow stairwell across the room.

"No chance he's figured out who *you* are," Buckle issued with light-hearted sarcasm.

Rhys shot the innkeeper a weak smile from the corner of his lips and rose. Leaving what was left of his drink, he made straight for the same stairway the stranger Thomas had left by, and climbed briskly to the first floor, following the corridor to its end. He paused for a moment of consideration as he stood silently outside the door, before finally he rapped his knuckles lightly against the wood.

"Come in," the voice called out from inside.

Hesitantly, Rhys twisted the iron handle and let the door swing open. The room was alight with a warm amber glow. The man had received the key to his room only moments ago, yet somehow every candle inside flickered with flame, whilst a moderate fire crackled in the hearth. Thomas sat comfortably in a chair by the fire, his hands crossed in his lap as he observed the licking flames dancing upwards from the kindling.

"Come in," he repeated at Rhys who stood silently in the doorway.

Finally, he entered, shutting the door behind him, yet he lingered still by it, not yet daring to approach the man. "That was you... on the east road this afternoon?"

"It was."

"What you had strapped to your back—concealed from others—it is a staff. And you—you are a warlock."

"Very insightful, Mr North," the man issued with a smile.

"Who *are* you?" Rhys demanded.

"Please, take a seat," he offered kindly, gesturing to a second chair clearly positioned with him in mind.

Rhys remained where he stood, awaiting his answer.

"You wish answers to a great deal many questions—who I am is far from the most pressing. At the moment, it is clear you do not trust me—which is understandable. If I am to gain your trust, it would help if we started at the heart of the mystery. Now, what is it you wish most to ask me?"

A long silence followed. "What happened? What happened on the twenty-first of June to the village of Longford—my home?"

The stranger took a deep breath. "A curse —one wrought from indiscriminate evil, rose up, quenching the very essence of all life throughout the village and the land that surrounded it. The resulting reek of death and despair enticed the arrival of wraiths: the fragments of tormented souls of those long dead, that through desperation, still cling to this world."

"But why?"

"I do not know. The wraiths are not responsible for the darkness that descended upon your home. They were merely drawn to the tragedy—to mass death on such a harrowing scale, similar as to when they are seen haunting battlefields in the aftermath of war. I have no inkling as to what could have brought about a curse as wicked and powerful as that which devoured your entire village. Nor do I have any thought as to why such malice was carried out."

"Then why are you here?"

"I am here on behalf of Arlas. He spoke to me of your meeting—of his discovery of the curse, finding himself upon the border of the dark magic by mere happenstance; his investigation that led him into the midst of the dark murk where hundreds of dead littered the streets; and of his finding of one man stood in the heart of it all, defying possibility."

"I don't know what you think—"

"What I think," he said rising, "what Arlas

thinks, is that there is a reason you survived that day. Now, it is my turn to ask a question of you. What is it that you know of magic?"

Rhys took a long moment of consideration. "The most important thing my father ever taught me, was to question everything. Accept nothing merely as it is. Until that day, I believed magic the stuff of myth and legend, and nothing more. I had seen no evidence for its existence in the world beyond the tall tales that people tell their children by the light of the fire. But now, its existence is all too apparent to me—as is its danger. Therefore, I hope you will forgive my lack of trust for you. If you are a warlock—in possession of the same power as Arlas—then you are dangerous.

"It would seem you saved me earlier today, and I do not wish to seem ungrateful. But I saw the speed with which the life was struck from that highwayman, and I witnessed first-hand the power Arlas can wield. I am afraid of you," he finished, with a solemn expression.

"You need not fear me," Thomas assured him with a tone of sincerity. The warlock took a seat and once again gestured kindly to the chair opposite him.

Rhys now, with great hesitation, braved stepping further into the room, and slowly and deliberately, he lowered himself into the chair.

"You are correct in many of your assumptions," the man continued warmly, "but not all. I am indeed a wielder of magic akin to

Arlas, but neither him nor I are mere sorcerers. I herald from an order both ancient and secretive: The Circle of Magi. We strive against the dark powers that seek to taint this land. We serve as protectors to the people of Cambria. The fate of Longford is our failure. That we could not spare you, and all of those that perished, from such a gruesome outcome weighs heavily upon the Order." He paused for a great while before finally saying. "I am Solomon Thomas, Acolyte of the Order of Magi. You may call me Sol."

Rhys's unease lifted. "My name is Rhys," he offered.

"It is good to finally meet you, Rhys."

THREE

R hys twiddled his thumbs as the all-seeing gaze of Solomon Thomas continued to examine him, the glow of his eyes seemingly peering straight into his very soul. It made Rhys uncomfortable, causing him to fidget in his chair through the prolonged quietude that had descended between them.

"You still haven't explained why you are here," he remarked, eager to end the silence.

"As I said," Sol began, "Arlas believes that there is a reason you were spared from the ill fate of the curse." The sorcerer's fingers moved for an item tucked under his belt, drawing a thin length of wood: a smooth dark walnut rod measuring just shy of a foot in length, narrowing to a tip at one end, carved into a handle at the other. The whole implement was lacquered and intricately patterned with the etchings of looped lines that formed decorative knots.

Rhys had never set eyes upon such

a fantastical item before, yet he knew both instinctively, and from his knowledge of folklore, that the length of wood Sol held lightly in his grip was a wand. With a twirl of his fingers the mage spun the wand so that its handle was pointed towards Rhys. A long moment passed before Rhys realised the man was offering the implement to him. Hesitantly, he reached forward and slowly curled his fingers around the stem. A subtle pulse ran down the implement's length as Rhys took it from Sol, and to his bewilderment, the wood vibrated with wondrous unseen energy.

"Magic throughout Cambria is shrouded in secrecy and legend. But all legends stem from some truth. The stories you have heard told and retold, spun as myths and fables by those who have never witnessed anything pertaining to the arcane: they are not birthed out of imagination, but out of history. Though over time these tales are warped through their telling, their details often altered drastically, they hark back to a single message of truth: that this world is not as it appears; woven deep beneath that which can be seen, is a fabric of energy, both arcane and mystical, that most can never hope to understand!

"The arcane arts are practised across the continent today, just as they have been since the origins of our people in this land. It was magic that brought about the ruin of your village, Rhys—and magic that delivered you from it."

"What do you mean?" Rhys questioned.

"What you hold in your hand is a wand: an implement through which one can exert their will over the magic that pervades this world," Sol explained. The mage gently nudged the candle upon the table between them, sliding it closer to Rhys. "Conjuring a flame is no trivial task. But extinguishing one is far simpler," he continued. "Clear your mind. Point the wand to the flame, and simply will it to die."

A medley of voices spoke up within Rhys's mind, protesting, making demands, and questioning everything that had crossed the lips of the man before him. Yet as he looked for the briefest moment into Sol's eyes, the man's commanding gaze quelled all resistance within him. Clearing his mind, Rhys inhaled deeply. Pointing the tip of the wand to within inches of the amber flame quivering upwards from the candle's wick, as instructed, he willed the light to go out.

They were plunged into immediate darkness with a whoosh of air that swirled softly throughout the room. The wand slipped from Rhys's fingers and clattered across the table as his eyes stared blindly about the dark. His vision adjusted slowly to the dimness, and his nostrils caught scent of the ribbon of smoke that climbed steadily from the candle before him. Yet the candle placed upon the table was not the sole flame that had been extinguished; every wick about the room that had been alight, and even the fire that had crackled within the hearth moments before, now smouldered, quenched by a simple fleeting thought from Rhys's mind.

He held his breath, closing and reopening his eyes, certain that his senses had betrayed him; yet the dark lingered still for several long moments before a sudden swell of heat relit the room into an immediate glow once more. The wand had found its way back into its owner's grasp, and it became clear that Sol had compelled the flames to rise once again. The mage's lips curled into a broad grin as his gaze still penetrated Rhys.

"A natural aptitude, beyond any that I have encountered prior," the mage breathed. "Magic— spellcraft, it is a learned art, one that can require a lifetime of studying and research. But what I neglected to tell you before I asked you to extinguish the flame, is that few ever possess the means to command magic effectively. What you have just demonstrated, is that you were born with a rare gift."

"But... I..." Rhys stuttered looking down at his hands as if they were those of a stranger's.

"Yet it goes further, Rhys," the mage continued. "There is a world of difference between the magic of witches and warlocks to that commanded by a mage. Witches and warlocks, the scholars of arcane learnings, they are capable of weaving spells and enchantments that can conjure light, heal wounds, alter perception, and even bring forth hexes and curses—yet this is the extent of their power.

"Among those gifted with the capacity to manipulate the arcane, is yet another group. There are those in this world whose innate gifts are so extraordinary, so uncommon, that there is thought to only ever be a few dozen of them in existence at any one time.

"I speak of magi: those born with such a powerful inclination towards magic that the elements bow to their will. They are capable of wielding magic as a weapon in and of itself. Their magic augments their physical prowess, sharpens their senses, and fortifies their constitution. Yet this power is latent and must be unlocked."

Sol arose from his chair and strode over to his bed, upon which was lain the staff wrapped in tattered cloth. The mage strew aside the ragged material and lifted from it a long stave of copper. At one end, the burnished metal forked into two prongs, each tipped with a small sphere, whilst roughly two thirds down the flawless shaft, the metal pressed flat into a clip-point-blade. Sparks of electricity zapped along the entire weapon's length and darted with discharging cracks between the conductive orbs at its head. Sol held the fizzling stave lightly in his grip, turning so as to allow Rhys to gawk silently at its unworldly beauty.

"Arlas is a mage—as am I. And I believe this power manifests within your blood as it does ours. It is for this reason that you survived the darkness that engulfed Longford. The power that lurks deep within you shielded you from the malevolence that consumed all else.

"I am here to ask that you leave this place, that you might join me upon my return to the Order of Magi on the morrow. I bid that you seek the destiny that has now presented itself to you—and learn what your power truly means!"

Rhys remained silent, his mindscape afire with bizarre notions that seemed both dangerous and seductive. All he knew, all he had ever believed true about the world, about himself, all now seemed shattered by the revelations that were unfolding before him. His thoughts soon became dizzying as a whirlwind of unanswered questions and unsated curiosity, mixed with wary scepticism and terror of the unknown, curdled in his gut, and overwhelmed his senses. But then a soothing quietness descended upon his mind, and finally his lips parted with speech. "Very well," he said calmly, yet in disbelief of his own words. "I will come with you."

Sol's expression flashed momentarily with surprise before a wide grin took form across his face. "Excellent," he issued excitedly. "We shall depart from here at dawn."

Silence set in once again whilst a wave of lethargy began to take a hold of Rhys. Seeing the man's sudden weariness, Sol set his staff back down upon his bed before turning back to Rhys to say, "Perhaps we should leave it at that this evening. There will be plenty of time to answer what questions have been unsaid. All I have told you is much to consider. I think it best if I leave you to dwell on what we have spoken of thus far."

Rhys nodded. "Okay," he uttered weakly as he arose on shaky legs.

"I will knock on your door at first light," he extended a hand to Rhys who shook it firmly. "Until the morning," he finalised, escorting Rhys to the door.

Troubled sleep eventually came to Rhys that night against the never ceasing torrent of thoughts that preyed upon his mind. Yet as his eyes sank shut through lassitude, they opened once more to the cold desolation of Longford. Choking fogs seethed amidst the greyness that soaked deep into the land and sky, whilst all essence of light suffocated in the smothering wretchedness of inescapable foul magic.

The shrill wails of wraiths pierced against the veil of murk, stabbing painfully at Rhys's ears, evoking frenzied terror that congealed his blood. The muscles of his legs snapped taught into a stumbling sprint that carried him desperately away from the pursuing phantoms, yet the ground pedalled slowly beneath him as if the air through which he struggled had thickened to treacle.

Rippling shadows darted amidst the gloom, the mist chilling as closer they drew, hunting Rhys by the stench of his life. A faint light glowed ahead shrouded by icy fog, growing steadily brighter with every inch he fought closer. With outstretched fingertips, he reached, struggled, clawed for the white glimmer that seemed ever beyond his grasp. Somehow, against the dreamscape, he succeeded. The curtain of gloom tore open and the phantasmal shrieks faded against the refuge in which he now stood.

The piercing light now shone clear from atop the black staff of Arlas. The man stood unwavering against the curse, studying Rhys with a gaze of glistering bronze and gold. Beside him Sol's fair complexion contrasted the dark features of the southerner, he too looking upon Rhys with the glow of azure irises.. Between the two magi there stood a third, slightly shorter in height than those beside him, and of athletic build. He was young, in his early twenties, his chestnut hair cropped short, and his jaw cleanly shaven. Rhys came to realise he looked upon a vision of himself, yet the man peered back at him with the eyes of a stranger. Emerald and malachite shattered together in ethereal storms that both sparked with violent energy and glowed with a tranquil hum, through a gaze that whispered of witnessed horrors, whilst speaking of deeply held unquestionable resolve.

The soft glow brightened steadily until a blinding whiteness seared at Rhys's eyes. He bolted upright and glanced about the dark. His vision focussed slowly through the dimness about him, to the familiar sight of his room. Sweat beaded coldly across his brow and his sheets clung damply to his skin as he swung his legs off the side of the bed. His toes curled against the wooden floorboards, and with a long exhale, Rhys shook the lingering images of the dream from his mind. Striding across the room, Rhys pulled open the shutters. A crisp swathe of air washed in through the window, and Rhys stared out to the graze of pink that crept up from the horizon with the impending dawn.

A final deep sniff of the twilight cleared his head fully, and Rhys quickly dressed into the traveller's garments he had lain out the previous night. When he finished buckling his scuffed and worn boots, there came a gentle knock. Rhys opened the door to see Sol ready for their journey, a pack across his back, to the side of which was strapped his concealed staff.

"Good morning," the mage greeted him.

"Morning," Rhys responded yawningly.

"Are you ready to go?"

Rhys nodded silently, retrieving his own knapsack from the foot of his bed and slinging its heavy straps across his shoulders.

"Come," Sol beckoned, turning down the corridor.

Rhys followed the mage quietly downstairs where the two men placed their keys upon the bar. Rhys noticed a fire crackling in the hearth, by which the innkeeper and his wife sat warming themselves.

"We came to see yer off, m'boy," Buckle said in a warm hushed voice as he rose from his chair. Martha too stood as Rhys moved closer to them. In her arms she held a wrapped linen bundle which she presented to him.

"Some food for the road," she explained kindly. "Just some bread and ham," she smiled.

"Thank you," Rhys beamed as he peeled back the cloth to peek at the contents. "—for everything."

Buckle put his arm around his wife. "It's been a pleasure son. Remember, you are always welcome here. Good luck." Buckle tussled Rhys's hair with his large hand.

"Stay safe," Martha added. With that, the two made their way back upstairs to their bedroom.

Rhys turned back to see Sol waiting patiently by the door. The man issued him a sympathetic nod as Rhys took a moment to gather himself. Taking one final glance around the tavern, he placed the food in his pack, and he and Sol stepped out into the dawn.

The sun was creeping up from behind a hill to the east as the cool morning air rolled around in a gentle breeze. A thin frost powdered the ground, glinting softly in the early light, whilst birds chirped in tuneful songs amongst the trees.

"We are headed for the town of Highshire; it is about twenty leagues west of here. I aim for us to arrive two days from now," Sol explained. "Today we look to cross the moor."

Rhys nodded silently as he realised they would be journeying further west than he had ever ventured before.

Sol pondered his expression. "Any second thoughts?" he asked warmly.

"Dozens!" Rhys laughed. "But chief among them being: should we have eaten breakfast before beginning a sixty-mile hike?"

Sol smiled widely. "A valid concern," he chuckled. "But fear not. We can stop along the way to eat," Sol promised, before setting off down the path.

Strolling briskly through the streets, they quickly departed from the village via the West Road, cutting a dead bearing through a coniferous wood that rose up in verdant totems either side of the mud track. The highway inclined steadily over the first passing mile and the morning light transitioned from scarlet to amber before clearing into sharp golden rays. The frost dissolved into a glistening dampness that seeped into the moist mud underfoot, whilst the cool edge to the breeze persisted, gradually swelling to strong bitter gusts.

The two men kept their silence as the woodland thinned until it dispersed completely, surrendering to rolling hills that gave form to the moor ahead. Scarlet bracken sprouted thickly across the hillsides, interspersed with a carpeting of golden-brown grass that clumped heavily in tussocks against the scouring winds that shaped the moorland. An emerald line of well-trodden pathway weaved its way through valleys and over brows, dictating the journey that lay ahead.

They marched out across the exposed wilderness as buffeting winds swept unhindered over the land, forcing Rhys to upturn his collar. With each passing mile the moor became more rugged and desolate. Weathered hillocks sprouted jutting tors of bare and craggy rock. Springs gurgled from beneath the soil and trickled as rills between jagged stones, flowing into valleys of sodden peat. Yet in spite of all its harshness, the bleak moorland held to it a stark beauty, the likes of which Rhys had never seen before.

Descending a steep bank, they came to a foaming stream where the two men paused for a moment.

"We should stop to replenish our water," Sol suggested, weighing his flask in his hand.

The two men knelt aside the runnel, refilling their flasks. Rhys reclined on the bank and loosened the straps of his pack. As he sipped several gulps from his waterskin, his gaze fell upon Sol's staff, the weapon having been partially unwrapped by the prevailing winds.

"Every mage possesses their own staff," Sol explained, noticing Rhys's intrigued stare. "Each utterly unique in its character and form. They are not designed or smithed, but forged through sacred ritual. It is said that a mage's staff is a physical manifestation of their very soul—an

41

expression of their will, shaped by their unique power."

"And yours... it can cast forth lightning?" Rhys asked, recalling the previous day's events upon the East Road.

"Chiefly, yes," the mage nodded. "Though I am by no means limited to such. Lightning—it comes most naturally to me, but all other elements are too at my command."

"Why did you remain hidden yesterday? Once you had killed the bandit?"

"Had I appeared to you there and then, there is no telling how you might have reacted," Sol explained. "You might have fled in distress, and I would have encountered great trouble in trying to speak with you. I thought best that I wait to approach you at a time when your mind was more at ease."

"Thank you...for saving me, that is," Rhys expressed after a time.

"It is fortunate I came upon you when I did," Sol conceded. "But up to a point, I felt you handled yourself impressively."

Rhys let out a half chuckle, not entirely sure how to interpret the compliment.

"We should get going," the mage said, corking his waterskin. "There are many more leagues to cover before the day's end."

Setting off again, they traced the winding path out over the hills, steering mildly northward as they climbed steadily out of a wide ravine to straddle a rude and lengthy ridgeway that rose up above the surrounding lands. To the south, the moor stretched endlessly, spouting dozens of tributaries that converged to birth the River Crann; whilst to the north, the moorland fell away to cultivated green pastures hedged to shape rectangular fields that sprawled out across the lowlands.

The sun crested the peak of its arc, beginning the second half of its voyage, drifting ever slowly down towards the west. Pangs of hunger began to strum and boil in Rhys's gut, thus the two men broke for lunch along the spine.

"I am sure there are many questions you wish to ask me, Rhys," said Sol as an apple crunched loudly in his bite.

"I do," Rhys nodded as he contemplated the raw wilderness that extended before him. "You speak of your order—the mages, as the protectors of Cambria. In what way? And who do you answer to?"

Sol smiled. "We are warriors, but belong to no army. We are servants, but to no king. We cannot be bought, nor hired. Our loyalty is to the code of our order; but there are ranks and positions of authority within the Order. I myself am an acolyte, a low-ranking member of the Circle, for I am only new to the Order. Arlas holds the rank of Archon; he commands the Order and is by far the most senior mage. Though he seeks the council of other Magisters within the Circle and will often make decisions based on the collective opinion of the Order, he holds the final say, and every mage answers to him.

"Our creed dictates that we must serve Cambria and its people for the greater good. We do not often concern ourselves with the politics of the realms, and seldom take sides in any war fought by man. We concern ourselves more with matters of the arcane. Cambria is home to all manner of creatures both malevolent and deadly, and ancient magic is woven into the land itself. Magic used for ill-intent and dark purposes poses the greatest threat to the people of this world, whilst monsters and creatures of darkness see mankind as their prey! We stand vigilant against these dark forces, defending the people with the gifts we possess.

"The Circle of Magi acts as the first and final line of defence against these perils. We seek out and investigate unusual magical occurrences and anomalies. We fight against the things no normal men could ever hope to face. We maintain the natural balance of this world."

"So, you concern yourselves with events like the curse at Longford?" Rhys asked, seeking clarification.

"Yes," the mage hesitated. "But the curse that struck your village, Rhys—such an event is not common. Nothing the likes of it has occurred since my time in the Order, and as I understand it, not for a great deal longer still. The threats we face are mostly simpler—perhaps no less perilous —but we seldom encounter anything as dark and mysterious as the magic that reaped Longford."

Rhys nodded sombrely.

"Since your meeting with Arlas, he has not rested in seeking answers to what happened that day. You will find resolution, Rhys; I promise you that."

"You said that there are likely only a few dozen people with the gifts of a mage in existence. How large then is the order?"

"The Order currently consists of twelve magi," Sol answered.

"I imagined there more," Rhys confessed. "I struggle to see how so few can protect the entirety of the continent—irrespective of the powers you hold."

"Our numbers are limited compared to the Order's past, yet they are growing. Not long ago in our history, there were far fewer mages in existence than even now."

"Why?" Rhys questioned, his curiosity sparked.

"An event referred to as the Purge," the mage explained. "Over two decades ago, our kind was almost cleansed entirely from this world. I know not how it happened, or what came to pass, but the Order was hunted and slain until there were few left. Of those few that survived, Arlas is the sole remainder. He never speaks of what transpired—the events are clearly too harrowing for his recollection. But he rebuilt the order—made it what it is today, and he continues to increase our presence throughout Cambria.

"Yet I fear irreparable damage was done during the Purge; centuries of our history were lost with the lives of those who fell. Thus, in some ways, the Circle may always remain a shadow of what it once was."

A silence followed.

"Come," Sol urged, rising to his feet and packing away the rest of his food. "Let us make haste. I wish to be clear of the moorland before nightfall. There is an inn that lies upon the border of the moor where I hope we may rest this evening. It will save us a night camped in these exposed hills."

"Excellent," Rhys sighed with relief at the idea of a cosy bed awaiting him at the day's end.

Continuing west, their pace hardened, following the bridleway that straddled the wending ridge. The crimson bracken thinned and faded till in its wake was left a thick expanse of bristling, brindled grass and swathes of prickling gorse. After several leagues, the winding ridge sank steeply to a shallow gully through which cut a gushing stream.

Breaking shortly to freshen their water again, they soon set off once more across the rugged hills. Black granite erupted through the tussocks in fractured teeth, specked with amber lichen and clumped with woolly moss. In places these stone formations stacked and piled into jutting tors that stood sentinel atop the barren hills.

The sun began to droop towards the western horizon as Rhys grew steadily wearier. His feet rubbed sore in his boots and the straps of his pack cut achingly into his shoulders. With the impending dusk, their brisk march lulled swiftly to a cumbersome trundle that dwindled still with each successive mile. Yet the mage Sol showed none of the signs of fatigue that plagued Rhys, his footfalls as light and energetic as when they had set out that morning. The man had merely slowed now to accommodate Rhys's exhaustion, and he could tell the sorcerer wished to press on.

A resurgence of vigour eventually found its way to Rhys with the coming of twilight, as the coarse moor broke against the greens of tamer lands. Now, blue slate walls lined the bridleway and livestock lay down about the grass. The first stars pierced through the violet dusk when eventually they drew near the inn.

Entering *the Saddlers' Meet*, they spoke briefly with the taverness, paying for the night's food and lodging before making for their room. The remote crossroad tavern seemed almost empty by comparison to the Smoking Oak, yet it was not without its charm. Upon entering their room, Rhys dropped his pack at the foot of his bed and collapsed back into the mattress. As he rested, he was ready to let his eyes weigh shut there and then.

Sol drew from his belt the wand to light the candles of the room, yet he paused for a moment of thought. "I have something for you," he said, rousing Rhys from a half-slumber. He rummaged through his pack and produced a leather-bound journal embossed with a hendecagram inside a circle, all etched with a gold finish. "A spellbook," he explained, "for your personal use."

Rhys flicked quickly through the pages before returning Sol a perplexed expression. "The pages are blank!"

Sol chuckled, apparently having not intended to play such a joke. "Yes, it is," he apologised. "I should perhaps have phrased it better; this is *to be* your spellbook."

"Okay…" Rhys replied, no less confused.

"Magic is not a universal art. Technique is tailored to an individual. Somatic components and verbal incantation are not specific to spells, but are dynamic depending on the individual caster," Sol explained. "What may well work for one spellcaster, will not necessarily work for another. Learning magic is a creative process, one driven by thought patterns that cannot be taught, but must be discovered for oneself."

"So, it is not strictly speaking something that you would study?" Rhys queried.

"More complex enchantments often require referencing the learnings and texts of other enchanters. They outline methods and techniques that can be applied to the reader's own castings, to build and alter the properties and effects of spells. Likewise, a number of more ritualistic enchantments and spells require complex iconography through the use of sigils, glyphs, and runes that do not change from caster to caster. But for the time being, these more extrinsic magical arts are irrelevant, and you need not concern yourself with them.

"This journal—this *codex* if you will, is for your own recordings on all you learn that you deem worth cataloguing for future reference. I suggest that for now, you use it for notations on any spells you discover, and the means by which you cast them."

"But I don't know any magic!" Rhys replied.

"You already know of *one* spell," Sol corrected him, handing Rhys the wand. "And by this evening's end I would hope you have learnt another," he smiled, reclining on his own bed. "Else we might be without any light this evening," he added, gesturing to the unlit candles about the room.

"Very well," Rhys sighed somewhat reluctantly, glancing down at the codex and wand in his grasp.

Sitting upon a deerskin rug, he positioned a candle on the table before him in the dim light of the room. Rolling the magical implement in his fingers he relaxed his aching shoulders and cleared his mind. Pointing the wand to the lifeless wick of the candle, he envisioned a fluttering flame rise up in a puff of heat. There he sat for several long moments, focussing gradually harder and harder until he strained his thoughts attempting to will fire into existence.

"Are you sure about this?" he directed to Sol, lowering the wand in defeat.

"Just relax," the mage advised. "Clear your mind and concentrate."

"All right," he exhaled, still somewhat resistant.

Rhys shut his eyes and drew an extended breath. His concentration turned to picturing a point of intense energy smouldering at the wick's end, yet still the candle remained cold and flameless. He tried tapping the candle's side, flicking the wand in its direction, and waving the wand in a variety of different motions, all of which failed to produce so much as a spark. He strived on to discover what combination of thoughts could conjure fire, yet all seemed futile, doing little more than work up frustration within Rhys. After several more minutes of failed attempts, Rhys closed his eyes in brief meditation to calm himself.

He raised the wand once more, this time imagining a jet of blazing heat spouting from its tip, enflaming the wick inside its scorching ray. A glowing ember grew from the wick's end, smouldering at first to expel a weaving twine of smoke that thickened to a spiralling ribbon. The ember sparked suddenly aflame, and Rhys stared on at the dancing amber light with disbelief.

Sol clapped his hands together, leaping to his feet and replacing the candle aflame with another in need of lighting. "Again!" he exclaimed, watching inquisitively.

The wand rose again in Rhys's hand as he repeated his last thoughts of a beam of burning heat. The second candle instantly birthed flame, and Rhys let slip a surprised smile.

"Now," Sol said with excitement, "the hearth!"

"Sure," Rhys laughed nervously, crouching before the grate.

Focussing upon the smallest log piled in the hearth, Rhys produced once more a ray of simmering thought. To his bewilderment, the bark of the wood began to furl and split beneath the heat, blackening slowly as a crimson glow welled up within the firewood. A torrent of white smoke hissed up into the flume, and within seconds, hot flames licked up from the embers. In moments, a full fire roared within the hearth, filling the room with crackling warmth.

"Well done," Sol beamed with admiration.

"Thank you," Rhys responded with a barely contained grin.

"Now," Sol returned, producing a quill and inkpot, "I suggest you write it down!"

FOUR

L eaving the refuge of the tavern the following dawn, the two men stepped out into a world of dense gloom. Heavy fog hung low in the atmosphere, casting a dark murk about them. Yet the mist, despite its potency, was utterly natural, lacking the wickedness and preternatural malice that polluted the gloom of Rhys's dreams. Regardless, it did not come welcomed, forming a veil their eyes could barely penetrate beyond a hundred yards or so. Had they not a path to follow, they surely would have lost their way.

Stiffness from the previous day twanged through Rhys's legs, but with the passing of the first mile, the tenderness faded along with the ache in his shoulders. The weather proved less relenting, worsening swiftly with the morning's progression. Sharp winds rose from the north, causing the fog to drift in heavy swathes across the land, and carrying forth frigid rain that drizzled miserably.

With every mile, the gales seemed only to strengthen until the rain swept in horizontal streaks. Before long, Rhys's clothes were waterlogged and dripping, chilling him to the bone. The rain then turned to sleet, and soon after the sleet to hail, stinging their skin as it pelleted the two men. By noon's approach the hail finally melted, descending once again in a fine spray that fell persistently across the misty landscape.

Sol was troubled less by the weather, but even his spirits were dampened. The bridleway carved straight along the flat, eventually entering a forest of conifers that loomed suddenly out of the gloom. The trees offered something in the way of refuge, sheltering them from the brunt of the winds, yet the sodden misery of the downpour was inescapable.

The path stayed west, deviating only to wind around the trunks of some greater trees whose tops seemed to vanish in the swirling veil above. Eventually the fog thinned and lifted to reveal the dreary overcast sky, though still the rains showed no signs of passing. They did not break for lunch nor rest at all upon their way, for the two men both knew the cold and wet would make setting off again too odious to bare. Instead, they trudged on across the muddy way, that with every hour, came closer and closer to resembling more a quagmire than a highway. The wetness maintained its hold through the late afternoon, with the rains only beginning to surrender at the coming of nightfall.

"We are making camp out in these woods tonight," Sol sighed as his feet squelched through the mud, uttering the first words that had been spoken between them for several hours.

Rhys had figured as much, but the words still seemed like a vexatious surprise.

"I see little point in struggling on against this weather," Sol continued. "If you see anywhere that is somewhat sheltered from the elements, we should make camp."

Rhys nodded weakly, his spirit as dampened and heavy as the sopping clothes that hung from his skin. Trundling on for a further mile, Rhys finally smiled in celebration at the sighting of an overhang between two elms that sat south of the road, serving as a sufficient barrier to the northerly sweeping rainfall.

"Perfect!" Sol exclaimed with relief, guiding them off the road.

They took refuge in the natural shelter: an archway of stone and earth retained by a great curving root system that spanned between the two trees. The moss beneath the overhang seemed the only patch of dry ground in the entire woodland. They sat below the roots and remained for a time in silence under the haven, whilst water trickled down from the ledge in dripping ribbons. After a while they reluctantly rose again to prepare the camp. Leaving their packs tucked under the shelf, they ventured off in opposite directions, in search of enough tinder to last the night. The task proved simple enough with the abundance of fallen limbs scattered across the forest floor.

In his search, Rhys came across a patch of edible mushrooms, gathering them for the evening's meal. Sol had already arrived back at the campsite by the time of Rhys's return, sat over a small pile of his own firewood, wand in hand. It took a few seconds, but he managed to ignite the damp kindling. The tinder smouldered with plumes of white smoke for several minutes before the heat finally desiccated the wood, giving rise to licking flames.

Rhys stacked the tinder he had gathered on the reserve pile and took a seat to warm his fingers by the fire. Urged by hunger, he rummaged for a pan in his pack. When the mushrooms were simmering above the fire, the downpour finally ceased entirely. Within the hour, the sky had cleared in patches, revealing fleeting scatterings of stars. Once they had eaten dinner, and washed the pan in a nearby stream, the two men sat beneath blankets, drying their clothes beside the campfire.

"When and how did you come to join the order?" Rhys asked rubbing his fingers together in front of the crackling flames.

"I am the newest to the Order. I was accepted into the Circle's ranks close to six years ago," he began. "As to *how* I came to join: my father was too a mage.

"Arlas recruited him long before I was born, and before he and my mother had ever met. He and Arlas became close friends over the years. My mother told me that she first met my father whilst he stopped off in Westport during a journey to the West Band: a vast forest in the northwest of Cambria.

"She joked that she hated him when they first met. *'An arrogant bastard that just wouldn't take no for an answer!'* she called him," Sol grinned to himself. "But my father wasn't the least bit deterred. I think he must have known then and there that he wanted to marry her, because after that, my father visited whenever his duties led him that way. Sure enough, they married two years later, and my mother quickly fell pregnant with me.

"She begged my father to leave the Magi so that he could help raise me. Arlas agreed to allow him leave of the Order, under the condition that he accompany him on one final mission beforehand. I believe they sought to kill a manticore: a terrible winged beast that possesses a tail tipped with deadly venom. The creature had slaughtered the inhabitants of a nearby village and was preying upon all travellers that strayed too close to its territory.

"The Circle's numbers were so few in those days, that every mage was needed to slay the creature. And so, my father agreed to Arlas's final request. But as fate would have it, he was wounded during the fight against the beast: speared by the venomous barb of the monster's tail. The venom of a manticore cannot be cured by any magic known to the Order—the wound was fatal. Yet Arlas managed to slow the course of the poison, giving him a few extra days of life.

"Arlas raced with my father on horseback across Westverness, and delivered him to my mother, arriving as she was in labour. He held out against the venom, longer than any would have predicted—long enough that he could hold me in his arms. But a few short minutes after my birth, he succumbed, passing away to leave my mother to raise me alone."

"I'm sorry," empathised Rhys. "That sounds truly awful."

"For my mother I believe it was, though she did well in raising me by herself. Arlas visited her and I a number of times throughout my youth. Unfortunately, my mother came to blame him for the death of my father, thus Arlas showed up on our doorstep more and more infrequently as time went on. Eventually, his visits stopped altogether—that is until years later; my mother fell ill to the Red Plague when I was seventeen.

"I'm still not sure to this day how Arlas found out, but he came to pay his respects to my mother before she passed. When she died, I had nothing left. Arlas stayed until after the funeral. He explained to me who he truly was, and what my father was. He spoke of the world that laid beyond the borders of my town, and the magic that suffused it.

"I passed the tests he gave me, demonstrating my capacity for magic. I figure he had known all along that I shared my father's gift for the arcane. Arlas asked if I would leave Westport with him. I agreed. A little over two years later, I underwent the Binding and became a mage."

Silence fell for a short time as Sol stoked the fire. "What of you?" the mage asked once he had finished. "I cannot begin to imagine whom and what you lost when the curse descended upon Longford."

Rhys nodded, quietly staring at the writhing flames, remembering back to when his life was irreversibly changed. "I lost every single one of my friends that day," he answered woefully. "And now... now I feel I can scarcely remember their faces. I feel so far removed from them, as if they died years ago. Yet what I fear most, is that the curse was not to blame for this."

"How so?" Sol asked gently.

"My mother died birthing me. I never knew her; in much the way you never knew your father," Rhys explained. "My father raised me by his lonesome and so seldom spoke of her that she is in almost every way a stranger to me; but I could not have wished for a happier upbringing. In his youth, my father had travelled across the realm as a trader, and ventured even further still. He was a learned man, and humble; and through his journeys he became very wise. Who I am today, I owe mostly to him.

"Almost a year ago, he was out by himself in the woodlands to the north of Longford, setting snares. Without realising, he wandered into the territory of a mother bear, who, protecting her cubs, savaged my father, mauling him to within an inch of his life. I'm not quite sure how, but my father managed to fend off the bear. He killed it, so I'm told, with nothing more than the knife I now carry.

"Miraculously, despite his injuries, my father managed to make his way back towards Longford and was discovered on the northern border of the village the next day. He was carried back to our house by the huntsmen that found him, and we treated his wounds as best we could.

"I cared for him in the weeks that followed as his injuries began to heal. But infection set in across one of his deeper wounds, and I was unable to prevent its spread to the rest of his body. He died late last year. He fought to his very last breath, but it was not enough to spare him from the fever that gripped him.

"After his passing, a darkness clouded over my mind: a despair that never seemed to lift. I shut myself away from the world. I hardly slept. I barely spoke to anyone in the village. I found trouble mustering the energy to do much of anything. And so, when the curse came, taking what little else I felt I had left, I was hollowed out.

"I fled the village, having lost everything. But in escaping the curse, finding myself looking back at the desolation wrought... It took me seeing the world devoid of all colour and life to truly appreciate how precious such things really are. Thus, when I found myself in Oakton, I was determined to survive, to live on, so that I could make something of my life—for all those who could not!" Rhys laughed uneasily as he rubbed a solitary tear from his eye. "It probably sounds ridiculous to you."

"Not at all," Sol replied sombrely, his intense gaze looking upon Rhys with only understanding.

Rhys managed a smile, his heart warmed by Sol's compassion. Sol then issued him a gentle nod and reclined back on his bedroll before lulling swiftly into slumber. Rhys was not so quick to drift off, yet after a time of gazing up at constellations viewable through breaking clouds, his eyes too eventually fell shut.

White hoarfrost layered the forest floor come dawn the next day, whilst the pooled and puddled rainwater had crusted with ice. Yet a ring of earth surrounding them had resisted the freeze, protected by the still smouldering fire, reduced now to embers, their reserve of kindling having run dry. Once breakfast was eaten and camp packed away, the two men ventured on west into the crisp morning. The woodland chirped and whistled with bird songs as amber sunrays cleft down through the barren canopies. Squirrels darted up and down bark whilst robins puffed out their scarlet chests at one another, squabbling in territorial disputes. Along the road they passed a huntsman and later a travelling merchant, exchanging friendly greetings on both occasions.

By late morning, the woods waned, opening to fallow farmlands bathed in warming sunlight that cast all frost and ice from the ground. Some way on, the road forked at a signpost that read '*Oakton 64 miles*' from the direction they had come, and '*Highshire 10 miles*' pointing onwards, due west. Yet the north-westerly route they embarked upon was unsigned and far less trodden. The cultivated fields sprawled on for miles, but steadily the borders grew wilder until untamed lands surrounded the bridleway once more.

Come late afternoon, Rhys sighted a sylvan treeline of feathered and spindling evergreens; the firs rose from beyond the horizon and sprouted endlessly northward.

"We are very close now," Sol told him as they veered from the bridleway to make for the woodlands. "They should be camped just inside of the woods."

Rhys remained silent as nerves and unease began to nag at him.

"Arlas awaits us!" Sol chuckled, pointing to the distant figure of a man stood by the forest's verge. "Why doesn't it surprise me that he knew when we would arrive?"

When they drew close, Arlas became clearly visible as he stood in waiting.

Sol hastened with excitement the final hundred feet, greeting Arlas with a firm embrace. Rhys stood awkwardly to the side for a moment before Arlas turned his attention to him.

"Rhys North!" he beamed. "It's good to see you in one piece!"

"I could say the same for you," Rhys returned as the two of them shook hands.

"You were right, Arlas," Sol smiled at Rhys, "he is certainly capable of magic. It would seem to come quite naturally to him."

"I had little doubt," replied the mage, clapping his hands together. "I trust Sol answered all of your questions as best he could?"

"I still have a few more," Rhys grinned, "but he has explained to me a great deal."

"I must apologise for leaving you on your own back in June, but I trust Sol has explained why it has been nearly four months since I saw you last."

"Err... I might have forgotten to mention it," Sol confessed.

Arlas raised an eyebrow to his fellow mage. "Then I had better explain myself. I'd prefer you not to think that I abandoned you without good reason.

"My intention was to lure the wraiths away from you, thus, once I believed you had made it to relative safety, I fled northward out of the village.

Alas, the curse that consumed Longford extended for some way in that direction, and the wraiths that pursued me did so unrelentingly. It was not until dawn the following day that I finally escaped them. I was forced east through the foothills of the White Mountains, with the intention of circling around the curse in hope of meeting with you in Oakton. Yet upon re-entering Longwood, I found myself in the territory of a fiendish hunter.

"I had come upon the fresh bodies of a travelling party that had been massacred in a bestial attack, and I quickly learnt that I had strayed into the hunting ground of a wendigo: a creature born from desperation and hunger when a man turns to cannibalism in the frozen wastes of the north.

"Never before have I encountered such a creature so far south of the White Range. They are fearsome and savage, and far too dangerous to be ignored. Thus, I was forced to abandon my plans of rendezvousing with you, Rhys, in order to hunt and slay the creature; to prevent any other unsuspecting travellers from falling victim to the beast.

"When I eventually arrived in Oakton, nearly a month had passed since our meeting. An innkeeper informed me that you had departed from the village but a few days earlier, and that he did not know when you might return. I was unable to stay and wait for you, for pressing matters required my investigation. So instead, when next I met with Sol, I instructed that he seek you out.

"I did not expect him to return so swiftly, but he sent word upon his arrival in Oakton that he believed you once more resided there. It would seem as if he were correct, for now here you are!"

"I am," Rhys nodded, uncertain how else to respond.

"You appear well," Arlas told him. "Many who witness horrors akin to what you have are left scarred by the experience. You do not seem to have suffered such effects."

"It took time for me to come to terms with what transpired," Rhys confessed. "I did not know what to make of what I had seen. I even questioned whether my senses had betrayed me, thinking that perhaps I had merely hallucinated the whole experience. I made my way back towards Longford, to prove to myself that it had all really happened. Sure enough, as I came within a few miles of the village, the colour faded from the land and a foul presence hung in the air. I dared not venture any closer. That was all the proof I needed. I imagine that is most likely the time when you arrived in Oakton to find me away."

"Unfortunate timing on my part. But you are here now, and you could not have arrived at a better time, Rhys," Arlas replied joyfully. "I have called for an assembly of the Circle: a conclave. It is not often the entire order find themselves gathered all in one place; it will be an excellent opportunity for you to meet everyone."

"Why is it you have called a conclave?" Rhys asked curiously.

"I feel we are due such an assembly; there is much of late that need be discussed and shared with the Order in its entirety, the destruction of your village included," Arlas explained. "And I wish to try and ease out some tension within the Order's ranks."

"Tension?" Rhys repeated in inquiry.

"Nothing you need trouble yourself with, Rhys," Arlas returned, casually brushing aside the remark. "Simply a few differences in opinion between some of us. But the chief reason I have summoned the Magi all to this place, is to discuss the curse that robbed you of so much, and other unsettling omens that I fear may not be so unrelated as first I thought."

"What else has happened?" Rhys questioned.

"Things of all manner of nature. Worrying rulings of earls and lords, to the queer behaviour of animals and beasts akin to the wendigo I slew. Something is stirring, awakening threats that once lay dormant. I fear it is all too coincidental to be happenstance. But beyond this, I cannot say. I must await the accounts of others at the conclave before I begin to draw any conclusions.

"But there is plenty of time to discuss these matters, Rhys. For the time being, your arrival is my main focus. Not all have yet arrived for the conclave," Arlas explained, "but you can meet those who are already here!"

"For whom are we still waiting?" Sol asked Arlas.

"Indus and Byron were south of the Virminter Mountains when I sent word to them. Last I heard, they were due to arrive on the morrow. Jack still has not yet returned from the West Band, where I sent him to investigate sightings of an ogre. I suspect he has been held up, as he would otherwise have arrived several days ago. And as you know, I sent Marus some months back to report on the war of the south. He should appear in the next day or so. But everyone else is already here."

"Then I think it is about time Rhys met them!" Sol insisted.

"Yes," Arlas agreed. "I am sure you are all too eager to get off your feet. We are camped not far from here. Come."

Arlas turned and walked through the treeline with Rhys and Sol strolling at his side. The dense woodland drew thick with shade around them. The boughs of the tightly packed firs hugged one another through interwoven layers casting an eerie darkness. Out of the sun, the air chilled quickly, and patches of mossy forest floor still clung to linings of frost that had not yet thawed. The trees seemed to press further and further inwards the deeper they delved into the woods, until Rhys felt they were squeezing between trunks to progress. But then suddenly the branches released their grip, and the thick forestry yielded to an emerald glade where the sunlight once more settled upon the ground.

Within the wide clearing were erected several canvas tents, centred around a large fire that crackled and blazed in the brisk autumnal air. Sat around the flames, upon bedrolls sprawled out across the cold ground, were three men that immediately looked up at Arlas, Sol, and Rhys as they entered the clearing.

"Gather around lads!" Arlas called out to them.

The men quickly sprung to their feet and made their way over to them.

Arlas looked at the three of them for a moment before scanning the rest of the clearing. "Where are the others?"

"They are off hunting deer, my friend," the eldest of the three mages explained. Seemingly older than Arlas, and likely surpassing fifty, he was both lean and muscular, despite his age. Time had been kind to both his face and physique, his demeanour as vigorous as any of the others' beside him. His dark hair was greying at the temples, and much of his rugged beard had already lost its pigmentation. From under a stern brow, pierced two eyes of stormy grey that spiralled with a magical aura like Sol and Arlas's.

"Very well," Arlas returned. "Everyone, this is Rhys North: the survivor of Longford. Rhys, this is Lawrence Swail," he added gesturing to the older man.

"Nice to meet you, Rhys," he welcomed gruffly, extending a hand to him.

"And you," Rhys replied shaking the man's hand with a firm grip.

"Seimon Wells," Arlas continued, now gesturing to a short man of athletic build. His long hair was knotted jet black and his eyes too were arcane in manner: two pools of effervescing silver. He was far younger than Lawrence, and likely only a few years older than Sol and himself.

"Welcome," Seimon said as he too shook Rhys's hand.

"And finally: Matthew Hault," Arlas finished, as he now looked to the last of the three men. He was likely of similar age to Seimon, but stood several inches taller with a slimmer frame. His hair and beard were a fiery red and his eyes a swirling mix of copper and bronze that too held the same effect of all the other mages present.

"Glad to see Arlas finally tracked you down!" he intoned, as he was the last to shake Rhys's hand.

Sol cleared his throat loudly, "I think you'll find that *I* was the one who tracked him down."

"Yeah, all right Sol… took your bloody time though!" the man quipped with a wide grin.

"Yeah, a whole week to travel twenty leagues and back to find one man whom I'd never met before. Whatever took me so long?" Sol returned, beaming with sarcasm. "Rhys, just ignore Matthew here."

"Don't let him poison you against me, Rhys," Matthew assured him with a smile. "Stick with me and you'll learn the ropes a heck of a lot faster!"

"Settle down you two," Arlas reproved, interrupting the banter between them. "Why don't we get Rhys down by the fire... maybe with something to drink? He and Sol have had a hard day's travel."

FIVE

Rhys laughed hard as he sat beside the warmth of the fire. Taking a long sip of hot mead from his mug, he continued to listen to Seimon talk.

"I tell you: his face went as white as a sheet! There he is, lying on his back, his staff is still up in the tree, and he is just staring in horror as the bushes begin to rustle. I'm thinking it's a dire bear, or maybe even a warg! We haven't seen it yet, just heard the farmer's description. Whatever it is, its growling something fierce. It sounds massive, and it is heading straight for Matt. I start climbing down the rock face, hoping I can reach him in time, but it's getting closer. Suddenly it bursts out of the bushes, going straight for Matt, and he just screams!"

"What was it?" Rhys asked.

"Matt... do you want to tell them?" Seimon asked, trying his hardest to keep a straight face.

"Not particularly," the man replied moodily.

"Oh, go on Matt!" Sol said, clearly having heard the story before.

Matthew Hault sighed loudly as he rolled his eyes. "It was a badger."

"A badger?" Rhys asked, confused for a moment. "Like a *dire* badger?"

"Nope… just a regular badger."

The group erupted into laughter.

"Why do you always have to tell that story?" he asked in annoyance, shooting a stern look at Seimon.

"Because it is hilarious, mate!" Seimon roared.

"Because it annoys you so when he does," Arlas said calmly, a smirk across his face as he quietly listened in on the discussion. "If you didn't let it wind you up so much, he would soon grow tired of telling it."

"Well…" Matt continued as he too was now struggling to hold back a wide smile, "that little bastard was ferocious! I still have scars from where he went straight for my—"

"Okay! That's enough information there, Matt!" Lawrence Swail said interrupting him mid-sentence.

"I'm just saying…" he continued once more, "that badger, he was as savage as any warg or dire bear I have ever come across! Also, I had been a member of the Order for less than a month at that point. Each of you have had similar things happen to you!"

"No one was judging you, mate!" Seimon laughed. "I thought it was a warg too! It's just a funny tale is all!"

"Surely a badger couldn't have done that to those farm animals... or killed the farmer's wife?" Rhys asked finally, curious to hear the end of the tale.

"That badger could of!" Matt declared loudly.

"It was a lycanthrope," Seimon explained. "No one less than the farmer himself! Poor sod didn't even know he was cursed."

"And what happened?"

"Well... we had to kill him," Seimon uttered solemnly.

"Kill him? But it wasn't his fault!" Rhys protested.

"There is no cure for lycanthropy Rhys," Arlas sighed. "The man was no longer human. He had already killed once and would do so again."

"But he wasn't to blame for the curse!" Rhys disagreed. "He didn't want to kill his wife! Surely there was something else that could be done for him?"

"Killing a man is never easy Rhys; but if it could save countless others then it need be considered. The man was a danger to everyone for miles around. Even if he had isolated himself in some remote forest, he would have eventually come across some traveller that would fall victim to his blood lust. At first the curse acts only under the full moon, but eventually the werewolf form of a lycanthrope becomes the dominant body, taking form whenever the sun sets. The savagery of the beast mind seeps into the human brain until there is nothing truly human left. To let him live would have been the eviller of the two options."

Rhys remained quiet, unsure how he felt about the matter.

"Sometimes you can't save everyone, Rhys," Sol said putting a hand on his shoulder.

After that, the conversation became light-hearted once more until the sun had completely set and the sky grew dark. As the discussion lulled for a moment, Arlas's eyes widened and his ears seemed to prick up.

"Stanton, Robert, and Ethan are near," he asserted, rising to his feet.

Rhys glanced around the dark edges of the clearing, but he could neither see nor hear any sign of the three men approaching. A minute or so passed until Rhys eventually heard the snapping of a twig on the far side of the glade, before finally the branches of the pine trees parted, and three figures emerged from the darkness. Between two of them hung the carcass of a stag, tied to what appeared to be one of their staves.

"Look what we killed!" the third man called out to the group.

When the three men drew closer, they were illuminated by the glow of the fire. Slumping the dead stag upon the floor, they each stood to face the others.

"Sol," the largest of the three men said as he noticed the young mage. "Didn't expect to see you back so soon," he uttered in a distasteful tone. "Is this him then?" he asked, glaring intimidatingly across the fire at Rhys.

"Yes," Arlas confirmed, patting the man on the back. "Ethan, this is Rhys North."

The hulking man nodded sternly at Rhys before turning his attention back to their kill. He was a tall and burly olive-skinned fellow with an accent that was difficult to place. Drawing a knife, he effortlessly cut the strappings that bound the creature to his staff: a knotted and gnarled length of wood with what appeared to be a shard of amber embedded in one end. Without pause he then stabbed under the animals hide and proceeded to begin skinning the stag.

"Rhys this is Ethan Hall," Arlas said, looking disapprovingly at the man who was no longer paying either of them any attention. "This is Robert Kwesi," he continued, turning to the second mage, a man of the south, possessing the region's characteristic mahogany skin and matted black hair, with churning eyes of chaotic amber. He was lighter in complexion than Arlas, far leaner and at least a decade younger too.

"Hello," the man said in a deep booming voice as he nodded to Rhys. He planted an angular staff of wrought iron firmly into the ground and took a seat by the fire.

"And this is Stanton Grey," Arlas said, looking to the final man who still lurked far enough away from the flames that he was partially obscured by the darkness.

When he stepped forwards, his spectral appearance loomed white against the blackness of the air. He was an albino, his skin ghostly pale, and his hair a snowy white. Against his pasty complexion, two blood red irises shone with an eerie, arcane aura. His torso was bare in spite of the frigid clime, revealing his gaunt yet chiselled frame. A skirt of hide tassets hung from his waist, and his forearms and shins were bound in fur wraps and greaves.

In his hand he clasped a staff that appeared to be made solidly of ice, around which the air plumed in the same manner as does a man's breath in the cold of winter. The mage stepped towards Rhys giving the fire a wide berth. The very air that surrounded Rhys chilled as he approached, dropping several degrees in temperature.

"A pleasure to meet you," he uttered somewhat distantly as he extended a hand to Rhys.

Standing, Rhys shook the man's icy palm, replying, "And you."

The strange mage stared blankly at Rhys for a moment, examining him. "My condolences," he added after a time.

"Sorry?" Rhys asked, fuddled for a moment.

"Your village—my condolences for what became of it."

"Oh... err, thank you," returned Rhys, not quite knowing how to respond.

Stanton nodded quietly to him, before turning and seating himself away from the others in the dark, where he remained for some time.

An uneasy silence fell upon the camp of magi as Robert Kwesi and Ethan Hall butchered the stag. Once they had skinned it and cleaved the meat from the bones, Lawrence placed a pot over the fire and began the process of creating a stew from the venison.

A discussion arose once more after a time, though it was somewhat more sombre now that the other three mages had returned from their hunt. A sense of unease was spread amongst them, that even as a newcomer to the group, Rhys could detect.

"Rhys," Sol began, rising to his feet, "would you care to help me gather some water?"

"Yeah, sure," Rhys nodded as he briefly glanced around at the others.

Sol handed two empty wooden pails to Rhys, picking up another two for himself, and led Rhys through the trees towards a nearby stream.

"As you might have deduced," Sol spoke quietly, "that is a glimpse of the *'tension within the Order'* Arlas mentioned earlier."

"I wasn't going to say anything," Rhys said. "What is causing the discontent?"

"Well..." Sol began, not knowing exactly where to start in his explanation. "Aside from the fact that there are a couple of magi within the Order that are just down right bastards..." Sol smiled with a frustrated chuckle. "None of the oaths sworn in joining the Order ever say you have to like the other magi, or even pretend to do so. Many of the dictates we follow are not set in stone, but are determined by the reigning Archon. Some of the magi, myself excluded, disagree with a number of the principles to which the Order currently abides."

"I can hardly say I felt welcomed by either Robert or Ethan," Rhys replied.

"In truth, I imagine you shall find that neither of them are that bad," responded Sol. "Neither are particularly friendly, yet I cannot say I have any personal qualms with them, regardless of any differences in opinion we have. Now Indus on the other hand... He is who you need to watch out for. Him and Byron—though Jack and Marus aren't much better. But I won't say anymore. You can make up your own mind whenever you meet them."

"What is the problem with them?" Rhys asked.

"I won't go into their beliefs... you'll hear enough on those when Arlas holds the Conclave," Sol explained. "It is one thing for individuals to hold different opinions, but Indus has taken it a step further. He undermines Arlas, at times going against the creed of our order to employ his own methods—that are often both ruthless and reckless. Yet worst of all, he is very charismatic. I fear he has sown seeds of disloyalty in the minds of several of the other magi. He would see himself as leader of the Order, bringing drastic change to how we operate. In a way, some of the magi answer firstly to him before Arlas."

"Does Indus no longer answer to Arlas at all?"

"He still somewhat begrudgingly honours Arlas's authority. There is no question as to Arlas's leadership. If nothing else, Indus respects power; he still sees the man as his superior, despite his insurgency. But the result of this, is the rising friction between some of the magi."

They soon reached the banks of the stream where the fast-flowing water gushed loudly in the still night air. Rhys and Sol carefully filled their pails from the icy flow and returned back to the camp carrying the sloshing buckets through the darkened wood. Upon their return, Lawrence was seasoning the pot of steaming stew above the fire. The smells melted into the air, stirring up a fierce hunger in Rhys. Adding the final touches, the man called out to his fellow magi and began serving the meal into wooden bowls.

"Here," Sol said handing Rhys a piping-hot dish.

Rhys sat by the fire once more with Sol, Matthew, Seimon, and Lawrence, listening to the cheery conversations they held as they ate. Stanton, Robert, and Ethan sat amongst themselves on the opposite side of the glade, clearly happier in each other's company, rather than mingling with the rest of the group.

"Where is Arlas?" Rhys asked after a time as he realised the mage was nowhere to be seen.

"He will be nearby," Lawrence said, spooning a tender piece of venison into his mouth. "He spends more time by himself these days. I believe he takes solace in his own thoughts."

Another hour or so passed as they sipped hot mead around the fire. Arlas eventually emerged from the trees, greeted by Lawrence, who offered him a bowlful of the stew that he had been saving.

"Thank you, my friend!" Arlas beamed as he seated himself down by the flames. "I had almost forgotten that I had not yet eaten."

"Anytime old friend. Anytime."

"Rhys," Arlas said as he quickly finished his meal. "I think we are imminently due for a talk."

"I think you are right," Rhys nodded.

"But I understand you are more than likely exhausted."

"You can say that again," replied Rhys as he felt a wave of weariness wash over him.

"Then, we will speak in the morning," Arlas said rising. "We have much to discuss."

SIX

R hys bolted upright, suddenly awoken. Looking around himself, momentarily disoriented, he realised where he was. The early morning light glowed dully through the canvas of the tent. Sol still slept undisturbed beside him, rolling over with a low murmur as he dreamt.

Rubbing his eyes, Rhys reached for his waterskin. He was wide awake, and not entirely certain why. He lay down once more, trying to drift gently back into slumber, whilst attempting to recall what had awoken him; yet try as he might, Rhys could not fall back to sleep. Eventually he dressed, cautious not to waken Sol, and left the warmth of the tent, stepping out into the crisp morning air. A heavy frost coated the floor of the glade and a light mist hung in wisps above it. The sun had not yet risen, yet the half-light diffused enough to softly illuminate the sylvan clearing. Embers smouldered in the base of the firepit. All was still.

Looking ahead, Rhys saw Arlas stood watching him from the tree line. The mage issued Rhys an intriguing look, before turning and silently disappearing through the foliage. He wanted Rhys to follow.

Rhys slowly approached the trees and pushed his way through the branches, briefly catching sight of Arlas ahead of him. He was leading Rhys in the direction of the stream. He continued to follow, hanging back slightly until the rushing of water became audible and the runlet came into view. They had come to a point further downstream than from where Rhys had collected water the night before. Here the brook flowed shallower and wider. The trees receded to form a second clearing. Thin sheets of ice extended from the mossy banks, crusting over the edges of the water. Arlas strode briskly over a set of steppingstones, crossing the brook, centring himself in the glade on the far side, before finally turning back to face Rhys.

Hopping across the stones less gracefully than the man he followed, Rhys approached the mage, rubbing his hands together in the brisk air.

"I am sorry to have awoken you quite so early, Rhys," Arlas began, "but I wish for this discussion to be private."

"All right," Rhys said cooperatively yet slightly perplexed. "What do you wish to talk about?"

"First, we must speak of you," he posed.

"What of me?"

"You possess the aptitude for magic; such is clear. Had you discovered this dormant skill by happenstance, then it is likely you would have one day become a powerful warlock—should you have chosen to pursue it. But such was not the case. Your induction to the world of the arcane was through me—through the Order. Thus, a new possibility presents itself: it is feasible that you may be no mere warlock. It is entirely possible—that the latent power of a mage lies within you."

"You think I'm a mage?"

"No. To become a mage, one must undergo the Binding: a ritual of old that awakens inner power, binding one's soul to a staff: an instrument of will. But I do believe you possess what is required to *become* a mage."

"And you want me to become one?"

"That I do," Arlas returned. "But it is not simply a matter of unleashing the esoteric energies dormant within your blood. Such power must be respected, for it holds many dangers. The magic a mage wields is more powerful than any weapon crafted by man. A mage is capable of bending the elements to his will: summoning fire from nothing, conjuring lightning down from the heavens, and causing the very ground to quake. A mage wields the potential to distort the very fabric of the world around them. This power, if used for ill purposes, is devastating!

"It is far too dangerous to be bestowed on simply anyone. It is for this reason, that the Circle of Magi exists. The creed of the Order is to use magic only to serve and protect Cambria, never for personal motivations. One must put all others before oneself. Only those who swear fealty to the Order are allowed to undergo the long and arduous journey towards becoming a mage and joining the ranks of the Circle of Magi.

"One does not swear this oath of servitude lightly. In doing so, your life is forfeit to the Order's cause. All that you are, the man that you were, dies, and in his place is born a loyal servant of the Circle.

"Rhys, if you are to join, you must know that it is not a decision to be taken lightly. Your mind and body will belong to the Order—now and forever."

"Is this you asking for my oath?"

"This is me telling you, that if we are to proceed any further, that you must know what is expected of you. You must be prepared for a lifetime of service to the Order and to the protection of Cambria."

"But I barely know anything about you or this order! How can I be asked to make such a promise when I know the least bit of what it entails?"

"You stand at the beginning of a path. It is not until its very end that you will be asked to pledge your life in service. You are free to change your mind at any point from now until you take the oath, at the time of the Binding Ritual. Yet if you already know that you are unwilling to offer your life to our cause at the end of this road, then there is no need for us to speak any further. I ask you not yet for your life, but whether it is something you are willing to give?"

Rhys sighed heavily as the weight of the decision pressed down on him. "The goal of the Order at this time is to determine who or what is responsible for what happened to my village?" he asked.

"It is but one of our goals. But it is chief among them, yes."

"Then I need no other motivation. I must discover why such a fate befell my village! Should the time come where I need to swear my life to your order, I will be willing to do so."

"I am glad to hear it," Arlas beamed warmly.

Rhys nodded in the prolonged silence, before asking, "What comes next?"

"Now begins the path to your joining, which ends with the Binding Ritual carried out at the rising of the sun on the winter solstice.

"When normally an individual is believed to have the potential to become a mage, and desires to join the Order as you do, over the course of the following two years, they are trained in both the schools of magic and the art of combat. Throughout such time, the most senior members of the Order determine the perspective initiate's loyalty to the Circle and its cause, and also whether or not the individual truly possesses the potential to become a mage. This is achieved by subjecting the perspective initiate to a series of tests. Their results in these tests are used in making a decision as to whether they should be allowed to undergo the ritual."

"What happens if they lack either the loyalty or potential required?"

"We bid them farewell and allow them to return to whatever life they had before they met the Order."

"But what if someone is deceitful in their word? What happens then to one who swears the oath with no intention of holding true to it, simply to attain the power that a mage holds?"

Arlas chuckled. "The Circle's magisters are for the most part wise enough to see the true intentions of men. Should an individual however, succeed in deceiving the Magisters and turn rogue, using their abilities for personal gain and pursuit of power—as rare as such an instance is, they are from that point forth declared an enemy of the Order: an apostate. Perceived as the highest of threats, they are hunted down by the Circle. For an apostate, little chance is stood against the rest of the Order united."

"My assumption would then be that they do not exactly live long enough to act upon their true intentions," Rhys suggested, smiling slightly.

"Then you are accurate in your assumption. Throughout the millennia in which the Circle has existed, it would be foolish to believe that such has not occurred; but it is hardly commonplace. Most men are not capable of hiding their true motives for the time that would be required to carry out such a deception."

"Very well. When do we begin?" Rhys asked.

"Soon," Arlas replied, "but there is more we must discuss first." The mage paused for a moment before his tone became all of a sudden solemn once more. "Rhys, what I am about to tell you is knowledge that a potential initiate is forbidden to know."

"Then why are you about to reveal it to me?" Rhys questioned in both suspicion and confusion.

"I wish to make a request of you—a decision which I believe would be unfair for you to make unless you know what I am about to reveal. The reason for these tests is not to weed out those less capable, but to weed out those less likely to survive the binding."

"*Survive* the binding? You mean the ritual can kill you?"

"That is exactly what I am saying. Very few users of magic actually possess the capacity to become a mage. Those that do not possess the vigour required, perish during the ritual. Instead of their soul binding to the staff, it is completely and utterly destroyed."

"So, the tests you carry out to decide whether someone should undergo the binding ritual... they allow you to be certain someone has the potential to become a mage?"

"No," Arlas answered solemnly. "There is no way to determine for certain; none except the ritual itself."

"Then for what purpose are the tests you subject these people to?"

"The tests can hint as to someone's chances. Though they are in no way conclusive, they provide slight indications that allow for the decision of the Circle Magisters. Throughout the history of the Order, the tests have spared the lives of many who would otherwise have died had the ritual been carried out."

"Yet some still do?"

"Yes. More than half of all men to undergo the ritual succumb to it. For women, that proportion becomes substantially higher. It is for that reason that the Order no longer permits women to join its ranks. Women did once serve in the Order of Magi alongside their male counterparts, but we now consider the risk to female initiates to be too great, for their binding is more often a death sentence than an initiation."

"And yet you will happily send men to this fate?" Rhys protested.

"No. We do not send anyone to this fate. They choose it on their own accord. It is true that they do not know of the inherent risk the binding ritual holds, but by such a time, they have already sworn their service to the Order. In swearing the oath, one pledges their life, whether that be a life given in service, or a life lost to the binding.

"It is expected of each and every one of us to willingly give our lives in the line of duty. Some merely make such a sacrifice earlier than others. We do not sentence men to death by tricking them into undergoing the ritual. We offer them a new life, one of purpose with a cause worth dying for.

"It is easy to judge the workings of our order Rhys, without seeing the good it does. We understand that the world in which we live is harsh and dangerous. In order to protect the many, the few may suffer. The risk of the binding ritual is a price we must pay. With every life lost to it, many more can be saved. This is the most fundamental belief we hold!"

"I'm sorry," Rhys apologised. "I hadn't considered that standpoint."

"It is quite all right Rhys," Arlas replied calmly. "It is healthy to debate such ethics; especially when dealing in matters of moral ambiguity. It prevents us from becoming set in our ways and following preconceived beliefs blindly."

"Then why keep the dangers of the binding ritual a secret?"

"Do you now not have second thoughts? The prospect of a lifetime of service is one thing, the prospect of death is another. Men go to war knowing that in war men die; yet do they ever really consider that it might be *their* life that is lost?

"Men justify the risks they face in war and

battle by believing the laws of this world apply somehow differently to them. Not knowing how or when death might come to you, creates the illusion that the risk may be lower than it is. Yet when presented with the very same odds in a situation where the threat is known, such as the binding ritual, the risk seems substantially higher —too high for most to willingly accept!

"The binding ritual would be seen by most as betting their life on the roll of a die, or the toss of a coin, whilst perceiving their chances of surviving in the line of duty to be somehow far greater, when in truth the risks are far more similar than they seem!

"The Circle is like an army, in that we need warriors to fight our war. The reason we keep the nature of the binding ritual a secret, is that in knowing the truth, far fewer would ever be willing to undergo it. The Order does not deceive men about the risk they face in joining, but rather they deceive themselves!"

"But then why did you reveal it to me?" Rhys demanded.

"The tests perspective initiates undergo take the form of three rites. First is the Rite of Blood, the second is the Rite of Ash, and the third is the Rite of Stone. The Rite of Blood determines the potency of magic within a warlock's blood, and can only be carried out on the day of the spring equinox. The Rite of Ash can determine a warlock's affinity for elder oak: the wood from which all staves are forged. It can only be carried out on the autumnal equinox. The final of the three rites, the Rite of Stone, is carried out on the summer solstice and measures one's capacity to conduct magic through sarsen.

"There is however a fourth rite, known as the Rite of Reckoning. This rite can be carried out under a blood moon, an event that proves to be a rare celestial occurrence, and only if none of the other three rites have yet been performed.

"The Rite of Reckoning combines aspects of the Rite of Ash, the Rite of Blood, and the Rite of Stone. The results of the test can be difficult to interpret, and it is therefore often inconclusive. Moreover, if this ritual is undergone, it will distort the results of any of the other three rites should they be performed subsequently. For these reasons, and due to the rarity of the blood moon, this ritual is seldom carried out. In my time as a mage, I have seen it performed but once."

"Why does it even exist?" Rhys asked. "What benefit is there to this ritual over the other three?"

"If the results of this ritual manifest strongly, then this test can prove more indicative than the other three combined, and more importantly: it need not be carried out in conjunction with any other rituals.

"Both the spring and autumnal equinoxes, and the summer solstice, have already come and passed this year. But in less than a week, a blood moon is set to occur. Rhys, I explained that the reason why I am revealing all of this to you, is that I wish to request something of you. I believe if you are to make this decision fairly, you deserve to know what risks you face!

"To survive the curse that took your village from you, you must be latently endowed with powerful magic. I believe that you have the vigour required to survive the binding and to become a mage, Rhys. That you still live is testament to that. You have already survived against the odds once; I have little doubt that you will do so a second time.

"What I ask of you, Rhys, is that you forgo the Rites of Blood, Ash, and Stone, opting instead to be tested by the Rite of Reckoning—I wish for you to undergo the Binding Ritual this winter solstice, two months from now."

"Why?" Rhys asked. "Surely it would make more sense in light of everything to wait until next year and carry out the other three rites? Should the results of the Rite of Reckoning prove inconclusive, there would not be any way to determine if I could survive the Binding. What then? I would be left to either undergo the binding without any indication as to my chances, or choose not to join the Order at all. It seems like a needless risk to take!"

"I am afraid that if we were to wait until next year, it may be too late!" Arlas explained. "I have mentioned briefly the omens that have occurred recently. I believe Cambria is upon the precipice of change. Ancient magics that have long stayed dormant are awakening. For these reasons, delaying your joining may prove a mistake.

"The Order is in a weakened state. It has not yet recovered from past conflicts, and our numbers are low. Should a time of turmoil be arising, we would have urgent need of you, Rhys! You may be more important than you know. I do not pretend to understand the full extent of what is happening, but all I know of magic and this world urges me not to delay your initiation to the Order.

"I wish to perform the Rite of Reckoning with you on the coming blood moon. If the results indicate you possess the vigour required to survive the binding, we can make plans for your pilgrimage this winter to the Northern Circle, where we will perform the Binding ritual. By this year's end you could be a mage—*if* we pursue this course of action.

"I do not need a decision from you now. I will give you until the eve of the blood moon to consider my proposal. And should you desire to forgo the Rite of Reckoning, electing instead to be tested by the other three Rites, then I will respect your wishes and we shall wait until the winter solstice of next year. But I do urge you to consider, for I would not request this of you if I did not think it necessary!"

"Alright," Rhys agreed after a period of silence. "I will give it some thought."

"Thank you, Rhys," Arlas replied. "Now we must address the matter of your training. Regardless of whether you choose to undergo your binding this year or next, it makes sense to begin your training immediately. You must learn both the techniques of spellcraft and the skills of fighting. From today onwards, I will instruct Lawrence to train you in combat during the day. During your evenings, Sol will aid you in grasping the basics of magic."

"As you wish," Rhys nodded.

"Come, let us wake the others for breakfast."

SEVEN

L awrence Swail seated himself beside Rhys and presented him with a hot bowl of porridge.

"Thank you," Rhys smiled as he ladled a spoonful into his mouth.

"Arlas tells me I am to start your combat training today."

Rhys nodded, realising the porridge was far too hot as it scalded his tongue and lips.

"We shall begin as soon as you've eaten," he divulged, bemusedly watching Rhys trying to suck in air to cool the porridge in his mouth. "First thing we need to decide is what school of combat you would best be suited to."

"What are the options?" Rhys returned, cautiously blowing the next spoonful of porridge.

"When you become a mage, your staff will be the weapon through which you cast all your offensive spells. This will likely be the main weapon with which you fight. Most members of the Order, Arlas and myself included, fight purely with a staff, wielding it in two hands, both to cast spells from afar, and as a quarterstaff up close in melees. This discipline is by far the most dynamic, allowing for a wide variety of spells to be cast whilst granting the greatest manoeuvrability.

"There are a few magi of the Circle who choose to equip a shield. This more defence-orientated school of combat is utilised by Byron and Jack, and by Ethan whom you met last night. Whilst some spells can just as easily be cast from a staff when it is wielded in a manner similar to a spear, there are those which require a second hand to produce. Moreover, whilst a shield offers excellent defence, and can also be used as a weapon in its own right, its weight can stifle your movement.

"Finally, two of the current members of the Order fight with a companion weapon. Robert Kwesi uses a staff at range in much a similar style to me. Yet when he finds himself in close quarters, he falls back on his skill as a swordsman. He equips an arming sword about his belt which he draws when close quarters combat is called for. He does so because he was trained with a sword long before he joined the Circle, and thus never truly needed to master the quarterstaff discipline.

"The other mage who makes use of a companion weapon is Marus Stone, whom you still have yet to meet. Whilst originally, I taught Marus in the school of quarterstaff fighting, he has since adopted a more unorthodox technique. Marus's stave is somewhat unique, in that it is shorter and more compact than a typical mage's. He has thus chosen to equip a second weapon in his off-hand. As I understand, it is currently a war-axe," Lawrence chuckled. "I personally cannot see much benefit to him doing so—I imagine he would find a shield far more advantageous. Yet the accounts of some of the other magi who have witnessed him in combat of late assure me that he is proving... proficient. I am told he fights with unreserved aggression and speed, and has bested even Jack in sparring."

Rhys stared blankly at Lawrence. "And, which would you recommend for myself?"

"Well," he pondered, scratching his beard as he looked Rhys up and down. "Though you are in good physical shape, I cannot imagine you are the strongest of men. You are small in stature and likely lack the raw physicality of someone with a frame like Ethan or Byron's. A shield proves heavy and requires a considerable amount of strength and endurance to be used effectively.

"I am personally opposed to fighting with a weapon in each hand such as Marus does; there are no martial disciplines that I have ever encountered that suggest there is much advantage in doing so. But admittedly, I have not seen Marus's technique first-hand. Robert's manner of fighting however, certainly has its merits. Yet I do not believe you have received any form of sword training prior to now, and so once again, I see little advantage in it for you.

"My recommendation, Rhys, would be for you to train in the school of two-handed quarterstaff combat. But ultimately the decision is yours."

"And you can teach all of these techniques?" Rhys asked as he finished the last of his breakfast.

"Before I became a mage, I was a soldier. Long before I ever held a staff I fought with a sword and shield. My swordsmanship is not as sharp as it could be—yet I am perhaps better with a sword now than ever I was in my military career. I can say much the same for usage of a shield."

"And why is your preference to forgo a sword and shield?"

"For the very same reason I do not don heavy armour as other members of the Order do: I like to be light on my feet whilst I fight."

"I'll defer to your judgment," Rhys acceded. "Train me in the school of quarterstaves."

"Excellent!" Lawrence exclaimed, taking Rhys's empty bowl from him, and discarding it in the camp's pile of washing up. "If you will follow me." Lawrence stood and led him to one of the tents, before asking Rhys to wait outside. Disappearing under the canvas, Lawrence emerged a moment later with a pair of wooden quarterstaffs and a set of leather hand wraps.

"Here, put these on," he insisted, handing the wraps to Rhys. "You will need them."

Rhys wound the leather strappings tightly around his hands and wrists, tying them securely. Lawrence then led him to the edge of the glade, through the trees, to the very same clearing where he and Arlas had spoken but an hour earlier. Crossing the steppingstones, Rhys followed Lawrence to the centre of the grass, where the mage handed him one of the two quarterstaffs.

"I thought it best if we trained away from the others to start off with."

"Thank you," Rhys offered appreciatively, immediately feeling more confident now they were in private.

"Are you right or left-handed, Rhys?"

"Right."

"Very well, that will make things easier for the moment. Hold the weapon with your left hand positioned at the end and your right at the midpoint of the staff."

Rhys observed as Lawrence demonstrated with his own weapon and attempted to mimic him.

"Loosen your grip slightly... excellent. Now first of all, when fighting with a staff, you should aim to keep your opponent at a medium distance to you. Your staff is primarily a ranged weapon; your best chance is to pick off your foes from a distance with spells. When enemies are in near proximity, there is also an array of spells you can use to ward off surrounding foes, should they get into close quarters. These range from spells that explode outwards, or create a wall of energy between you and your foe. Regardless, sooner or later, you will find yourself in a melee.

"Though you will often find keeping a distance from your foe the most effective tactic, there will always come a time where a hand-to-hand combat is unavoidable. And since we cannot practise magical attacks with you as of yet, it is with close quarters fighting that we shall begin your training.

"Now, you will come up against all manner of opponents throughout your time as a mage. They will likely wield every type of weapon from swords and axes to lances and spears. If you are fighting an opponent with a sword or an axe, the length of your weapon gives you the advantage of greater reach. If your opponent gets in too close however, the length of your staff quickly becomes a disadvantage."

"Right," Rhys responded, signifying that his instructor held his full attention.

"The next thing you should know, is that when you are attacking, you need to not focus only on dealing blows to your opponent's head or torso. The head, chest, and gut may seem like the most obvious targets, and it is true that a direct blow to such areas will prove deadlier, but it is important to attack your foe's body as a whole. The hands and feet of your opponent may not seem like the most obvious targets, but if you can deal a successful blow, you can cripple your adversary.

"If you can wound a limb of your enemy, they will likely be unable to continue fighting, or at the very least will be somewhat hindered by their injury. This in turn will allow you to dispatch your opponent with greater ease."

Rhys nodded as he continued to listen intently.

"The first moves I am going to teach you are three simple blocks or *parries*. First there is a low block." As he spoke, Lawrence held his left hand at about head height and his right hand slightly lower so that the staff pointed to the ground in front of him.

Studying Lawrence's stance, Rhys mirrored the man's positioning.

"Next is a middle block," he continued. Lawrence moved his hands to waist height, so the staff was now pitched horizontally.

Once again Rhys copied his instructor.

"And finally, there is the high block." This time Lawrence raised his right hand so that his weapon was pitched upwards.

Rhys too altered his staff's positioning to match.

"That is good. Just shift your left foot so you are stood a little more side on."

Following the instructions, he quickly corrected his footing.

"Excellent! Let us try a few of those now. I will try to strike at you, and you decide which block is appropriate. I'll start slow and get faster."

Lawrence lowered his centre of gravity and adopted a side on stance to face Rhys. He swung his staff slowly in a low loop towards Rhys's leading foot. The two staves tapped gently as Rhys moved his into the position of a low block. The second swing, as slow as the first, was aimed for his head. Wood met wood once again as Rhys blocked high. The next swing was slightly faster, aimed for his torso, and was met with a centre block. Lawrence's hands gathered momentum as his staff continued to accelerate through the air.

The attacks that followed were swifter, yet Rhys seemed to keep pace with ease. His eyes followed Lawrence's hands, quickly judging from which direction the next blow would come. As the speed increased further, the two quarterstaffs began to clatter loudly as they struck one another with considerable force. The strikes kept coming, Lawrence continuing to move his stave ever faster until Rhys was struggling to keep pace. Suddenly, a low arc caught Rhys off guard. The staff struck him across the heel and took his feet out from under him. He hit the ground hard and felt the wind knocked out of him. He groaned in discomfort, wincing on the grass. Lawrence outstretched a hand and hoisted him back to his feet.

"Take a moment to catch your breath," he offered. "Forgive me, but I needed to gauge your natural speed and dexterity."

Rhys nodded. "And?" he wheezed as he tried to speak through short sharp breaths.

"You definitely possess some natural talent. Your eyes and hands are both keen and quick—factors which cannot be taught. Once you have undergone your binding ritual, your senses and speed will be heightened by the magic in your blood. That you show such finesse now, before your full potential has been tapped, is promising. But natural flair and dexterity are not enough to be deadly on the battlefield. One must also master technique and discipline. Now—are you ready to continue?"

"Yes," Rhys puffed as he took a last few deep breaths.

"Then we shall go again. The same as last time."

Rhys once again adopted his defensive stance. Starting with a slow arcing swing for his chest, Lawrence once more increased the pace with which he struck. The speed of the attacks quickened more and more until again they were faster than Rhys could react. Lawrence's quarterstaff struck him suddenly across the temple. Dropping his weapon, Rhys recoiled from the blow. It was clear that Lawrence had pulled the hit at the last moment, not wanting to injure Rhys, yet he had still been struck with considerable force. His head rang for a moment as he rubbed the rapidly bruising skin.

"Are you okay, Rhys?" Lawrence asked.

"Yeah," Rhys mumbled as he shook off the blow.

"Then pick up your weapon and let's go again!" Lawrence ordered in a sharpened tone.

Rhys picked up the staff and readied himself. The swings quickened. Rhys kept pace for the first few seconds, until Lawrence feigned a low strike, jinking out of the faint with a quick thrust for Rhys's chest. His skin stung as the wood made contact, but he ignored it, readopting his defensive stance.

"You must watch the whole of your opponent, Rhys, and not be fooled into simply watching his hands and weapon."

"Okay," Rhys nodded, his heart pumping forcefully. "Again!" he uttered, this time determined not to fall for the same trick. Lawrence began more quickly this time, but Rhys was ready for him.

"You are doing well so far," Lawrence assured him as their weapons clattered loudly against one another. "But simple blocks alone will not defend you in a fight!"

The mage launched another swipe at his foot. Rhys intercepted it with a well-coordinated block, but quickly sliding his weapon up the shaft of Rhys's staff, Lawrence swatted his hand. Rhys cried out as his grip recoiled, causing his staff to tumble to the ground. His fingers throbbed violently from the blow. He feverishly shook his hand to try and quell the pain.

"When blocking, it is not enough to merely intercept your opponent's attack. You must also deflect it and move out of the way of his next strike. Stagnant blocking seldom occurs in true combat—intercepted blows are repelled and redirected with parries. Always look to deflect the momentum of your foe's attack; it is not enough to simply stop a blow dead, for you leave yourself open to disadvantageous weapon binding —your opponent will either obtain control over the movement of your weapon, or they might gain an opening by sliding theirs along the length of yours."

Rhys trapped his hand between his legs and waited for the pain to subside before retrieving the quarterstaff. His benumbed fingers now clasped the shaft more clumsily.

Another series of swings were directed towards him. Rhys deflected each successfully, ensuring his interceptions parried away the incoming strikes. All of Lawrence's attacks were knocked clean aside, save for the very last: a glancing blow to the shoulder.

"Excellent!" Lawrence applauded. "Next, I want you to start moving your feet. Your opponent will constantly be trying to outflank you—as should you him. You must move with your enemy to prevent him doing so and to try and best position yourself for a counterattack."

Taking their stances again, Lawrence dealt a long series of sweeps, each met by Rhys. The two men circled one another. Lawrence advanced forwards and Rhys retreated in response, maintaining a constant distance between the two of them as they shifted back and forth, strafing both left and right.

"Very impressive, I must say. You are light on your feet for someone that has had no previous training. You may find that this proves your most valuable asset. In combat, positioning is everything. If you can move faster than your enemies, you can both dodge their attacks and outflank them."

"Understood," Rhys nodded, heeding the advice.

"We shall take a few minutes break," Lawrence declared. "When we begin again, we shall move onto attacking and countering."

With that, Rhys walked to the edge of the clearing and sat back against a tree. He unwrapped the strappings from his right hand to find his fingers were stiff and bruised. He cringed as he massaged them in his other hand. Lawrence offered him his flask of water from which Rhys took a swig. Rewrapping the strappings, he climbed back to his feet and wiped the sweat from his forehead.

"When you block a swing from your opponent, you want to deflect their blow and move their weapon into a position that favours your next attack. Take a swing at me," he instructed.

Rhys swung in a low arc at Lawrence's front foot. Lawrence intercepted the blow and forced Rhys's staff upwards and away from him.

"From this position, I have the advantage!" Lawrence insisted, pausing halfway through the motion. "Your arm and your torso are open—vulnerable to my next attack."

Lawrence slowly slid his staff along Rhys's to show the possible strike he could make to his grip, and also gestured the motion of attack he could make for Rhys's ribs.

"If you were to find yourself in this position," he continued, "there are a few things you could do. You can attempt to strike with the reverse of your staff to intercept your opponent's counter..."

The two of them slowly enacted the manoeuvre.

"You could attempt a kick to your opponent, to set them off balance in the hope they are unable to complete their next attack. Or, you could sidestep your way clear of their blow."

Without warning, Lawrence cleft his staff down hard and fast towards Rhys. Reacting instantly, he leapt clean aside without a moment's hesitation. The staff rushed close to Rhys's face and clattered against the soil where he had stood an instant earlier.

Instinctively, he slammed his foot down hard on Lawrence's weapon, jamming it into the ground and obstructing any further attack. With his own staff, he lunged for Lawrence's chest, yet before he could complete the arc of his swing, Lawrence wrenched free his own weapon, in turn pulling Rhys's feet from under him once more. Rhys tumbled to the grass. He rolled over to see Lawrence's staff pointed inches from his chest.

"Good!" he exclaimed as he grabbed Rhys by the arm, pulling him up off the grass. "A great instinctive reaction, regardless of the outcome. When you are in combat you must take every opportunity your opponent offers you.

"Sparring and fighting for real are two very different situations. There is no chivalry or honour in a fight to the death. There is merely survival. Do not be afraid to fight dirty. Take any advantage you can, and be wary of any trickery or subterfuge your opponents might throw at you.

"Your mistake was your lack of awareness. You were so utterly focussed on landing your blow that you neglected to consider your precarious footing. What you thought to be your advantage, quickly became a vulnerability that in turn became *my* advantage. Always remain completely aware of both your opponent and the environment, and do not consider your foe defeated until after the finishing blow has been dealt."

"Noted," Rhys grumbled, rubbing the side of his hip where he had struck the floor.

"Do not be disheartened, Rhys," Lawrence assured. "It was an impressive tack. With training, you will learn to execute such manoeuvres without fault. Now—shall we attempt everything we have learnt thus far, all together?"

"Alright," Rhys agreed calmly, eager to impress.

The two men backed away from one another momentarily and took their stances. Rhys instantly launched himself at Lawrence in an attempt to catch the man off guard. Despite Rhys's lack of hesitancy, his attack was met with a swift deflection at the last second. His haste proved successful none-the-less, for he had as it turned out, somewhat surprised Lawrence, leaving the mage with not time enough to counter the assault.

Unhindered by the lack of a riposte, Rhys was able to quickly lunge for a second blow in short succession. This attack was met more confidently, parried effortlessly away. Rhys threw a kick directed to Lawrence's thigh, though the mage stepped clean aside with ease and Rhys drove his boot instead at empty air. He stumbled forwards off balance. Catching his footing, he spun awkwardly with just enough time to raise his staff in defence, intercepting Lawrence's next strike. His feet were still not fully set, and as Lawrence brought his staff down hard, the force staggered him backwards.

Lawrence descended upon him yet again, this time dealing a glancing blow to the back of Rhys's hand. The strappings offered little in terms of protection and pain fired up his wrist. He winced, keeping hold of his staff, and parried the next incoming blow much as he had been shown. To his surprise, the swift manoeuvre succeeded, leaving Lawrence momentarily open to assault. Changing direction, Rhys rapidly unfurled his body, whipping his stave at Lawrence's gut. Yet once more, the swing met only wood as the mage defended himself easily.

Lawrence dealt another series of quick strikes, which Rhys successfully matched. Changing tactics, the mage took a powerful swing at Rhys's waist, leaving himself exposed. Rhys leapt hard away, throwing himself out of range of the swing. The quarterstaff sailed inches past. Rhys thrust a powerful jab into the opening Lawrence now presented, certain this time he would land the blow. But to his dismay, it was knocked clean aside with little distress from Lawrence. Off balance again, Rhys realised his mistake too late. Lawrence drove a shoulder into his side, toppling him back. Somehow managing to remain on his feet, he stumbled away in a last-ditch attempt at defence. Yet now he lacked all composure.

A gasp of pain expelled from Rhys's lungs as the shaft of wood cracked across his forearm. His staff slipped quickly from limp fingers as he seized woefully at the injury with his other hand. Agony thumped up and down his wrist, Rhys now cradling it with gritted teeth.

Lawrence laid down his weapon and walked slowly over to him. "Let me see it," he insisted, looking at Rhys's hand as it began to swell and bruise.

Reluctantly, Rhys released his grip of his throbbing forearm and allowed Lawrence to examine the injury. Slowly, the mage removed the leather wrappings and gently pressed his fingers along the bones. Rhys grimaced in discomfort.

"It's okay, it isn't broken," he assured. "I can fix it." Lawrence drew from his belt a wand of polished ebony. He pressed the tip against the reddened skin and suddenly Rhys felt a surge of energy flow through his limb.

The wrist seared in pain and Rhys watched it swell and turn black with bruising. Soon after, it returned once more to normal size and the dark purple contusions began to rapidly fade. The discolouration of his skin turned to blue before becoming a yellowish hue, until, after little more than a minute, the bruising had all but disappeared. When Lawrence released Rhys's hand, he was left with little more than a dull ache from an injury that felt as if it had been given weeks to heal.

"Wow," Rhys gasped involuntarily as he studied his wrist in amazement. Flexing his fingers, the last remnants of pain from the trauma subsided.

"Healing a sprain is somewhat more difficult than a laceration, but it is far easier than a break. Had you fractured the bone it would have taken longer to heal."

"How much longer?" Rhys asked.

"Only a day or so. But the methods I'd use

would be different. We would likely have splinted the arm and applied a salve overnight. It *is* possible to repair bone in the manner in which I healed the bruising, but it requires a deft hand for healing magic which not I or many possess."

"Thank you…" Rhys exhaled. "But you could have pulled the blow!"

"I did, Rhys," Lawrence returned stoically. "Had I struck you with full force, your wrist would have shattered."

"Oh…" Rhys murmured, unsure whether to be impressed or concerned. "You still could have been gentler though."

"Pain is as much a part of your training as any technique or manoeuvre I show you. You must learn to both embrace it and to fear it. Fear and pain make you stronger. They push you to fight harder and to move faster. You must learn to harness them both, for in battle, it is they that will keep you alive.

"In order to avoid pain in this training you must avoid mistakes! Pain is the acknowledgement your body makes of its failures and limitations. You must learn to overcome them!"

"All right," Rhys said, not quite so eager to continue.

"Are you ready to go again?" Lawrence asked sternly.

Rhys nodded hesitantly.

Lawrence's staff lanced immediately

towards him before he had any time to prepare. The wooden quarterstaff pummelled his ribs.

"Are you ready, Rhys?" he asked again, more forcefully.

"Yes!" Rhys shouted as he deflected the next strike.

The two of them practised in this way for the entire morning. Rhys failed to land even a single glancing blow to Lawrence, whilst taking the brunt of several hits himself, though none were enough to cause serious injury. As time wore on, the frequency of the strikes became greater in number as Lawrence pushed him harder and harder.

"Let us break for lunch," Lawrence offered finally, as he helped Rhys back upright, having moments before dealt him a blow powerful enough to throw him clean off his feet.

"Okay," Rhys wheezed.

"Do not be dismayed, Rhys. You are making good progress, even if you have yet to see it. This is but the first day of months of training, and you have an entire lifetime ahead of you to both refine and master your technique." Lawrence paused and looked at Rhys. "I will bring you something to eat."

EIGHT

Soreness twinged in every one of Rhys's muscles and joints. His fingers flexed numb and awkwardly. The broken skin across his knuckles wept as Rhys rinsed his hands in the frigid stream, the blood swirling away in crimson wisps through the crystal water. He tongued his bulging lower lip, tasting the stinging flavour of iron where the flesh had split. Wetting his face, he washed away the sweat clinging to his brow and sipped water cupped in his hands. As he quenched his thirst, the glimmering reflection of the sky above darkened with a silhouette, and Rhys suddenly felt a sweltering heat surge across the nape of his neck.

"Stand... slowly!" a deep menacing voice commanded from behind.

The scorching heat burned greater before a blade of glowing metal nicked his skin. Rhys recoiled from the burn, clasping a wet hand across the raw singe.

"Stand now!" the voice repeated.

Heedfully, Rhys rose to his feet and gradually turned to face the man threatening him.

Lifted to his throat simmered a blade, the blazing steel crimson with heat, jutting from a staff of charred wood that cracked and glowed orange like embers. The weapon was clasped in a hand of melted skin that seemed almost to have been scarred by the very staff it gripped. The burns knitted up the forearm of a tall and dark mage that glared at Rhys with fiery eyes of raging amber, deep set beneath a furrowed brow. Rhys gazed into the mage's menacing stare, suffering against a torturous unease that welled from the emptiness within his impossibly dark pupils. He averted his gaze to realise the mage before him was accompanied by three others; like a pack of wolves, they fanned out, pressing inwards on Rhys's flanks as he backed right up to the bank of the stream.

"Why do you trespass here?" the mage hissed, rotating the blade pointed to Rhys's throat.

"I'm not!" Rhys refuted with a confidence he did not feel.

"You dare lie to me!?" he sneered through gritted teeth.

"Indus!" the low voice of Arlas boomed with anger. "Leave him alone!"

"We caught him lurking here on the outskirts of the camp!" Indus snarled, neither lowering his weapon nor averting his gaze.

"And you did not stop to wonder if he is

intended to be here?"

"*Is* he?"

"He is. So, lower your weapon from his neck or I will raise mine to yours!"

"As you wish," Indus sniggered, issuing Rhys a twisted smirk before slowly lowering the heated blade.

"Indus, this is Rhys North. He is training to become an initiate of the Order," Arlas explained, his voice still tense. "Rhys, you have just met Indus Mark."

Arlas emerged from behind Rhys, stepping out from beyond the limits of his peripheral vision so that he drew into view. The senior mage shot Indus a disapproving gaze before turning to look at the other three mages stood beside him. "This here is Byron Lance," he said gesturing to the man who was by far the largest of the four.

He was clad in a full hauberk of plated mail, standing nearly seven foot tall. The behemoth of a man was built with the frame of an ox, as unusually broad as he was tall. Matted brown hair sprouted from his scalp and a bristling beard from his burly jaw. He did not nod or smile at Rhys, but instead glared at him with the same intensity as Indus, from a pair of dark cavernous eyes.

"Here also is Jack Ironwood," Arlas added, directing his attention to the third figure. He was a handsome man, staring at Rhys with a piercing blue gaze more forgiving than the others'. His short-cropped hair was golden brown, sweeping down across his jaw into a well-kempt beard. As he stood silently examining Rhys, his countenance gave nothing away.

"And lastly, Marus Stone."

Rhys looked to the fourth man. His heterochromatic eyes leered narrowly back; one a deep green and the other a shimmering blue, glinting against his ashen complexion. His lips coiled subtly into a grim smile that hinted at a deep and wicked malice. Dark hair tangled into a greasy fringe whilst his chin and neck were smoothly shaven. Holding himself in an upright posture, standing shorter than the others beside him, he was a near identical match in height and build to Rhys.

"A pleasure," the mage articulated with a well-spoken tongue that sounded almost condescending in nature.

Rhys nodded to the four men silently as he looked across their faces. They each continued to leer at him, conjuring in Rhys a feeling of disquiet; his presence was not welcome, and these men intended to show it.

"Indus, I want to speak with you—in private. The rest of you can make your way to the camp," Arlas uttered, dismissing them with a curt gesture.

"As you wish," Indus sighed reluctantly as Arlas led him away through the trees on the far side of the clearing. The other three magi strode off in the opposite direction, towards the campsite, disappearing through the foliage.

Rhys was left alone in the clearing once again. Wiping the rest of the blood from his knuckles, he slowly edged towards the far side of the glade where Indus and Arlas spoke just out of sight. Rhys listened quietly as the two magi argued in harsh tones.

"I believed he was intruding!" Indus hissed.

"And that justifies you holding your staff to his throat!?" Arlas scorned. "It is in violation of the creed of our order to do such a thing! You revealed yourself to a stranger and threatened him! All because he was near the outskirts of our camp!?"

"I had little intention of harming him!" Indus contended. "I merely intended to scare him from this place!"

"And what if he *had* been a random commoner out in the woods? Do you think he would have simply fled, never to return? If he breathed word of our presence, he might have returned with a hoard of peasants wielding torches and pitch forks to drive us from these woods!" Arlas reviled. "What then? Would you have driven them away with fear too?"

"If it were called for," Indus replied smugly.

"This cannot continue, Indus!" Arlas growled. "Consider this your last warning!"

"Before what?" Indus demanded. "Are you going to kill me Arlas?" he pressed derisively. "You do not have the power over me that you think! I do not fear you, nor do I appreciate you summoning me from my duties elsewhere!"

Suddenly, Rhys felt a hand on his shoulder, startling him. He gasped silently as he spun to face Lawrence. The man issued Rhys a suspicious look, all too aware of his eavesdropping.

"I brought you some food," he remarked knowingly, passing an apple and a cob filled with salt pork to Rhys.

"Lawrence..." Rhys whispered nervously, "I was just..."

"Minding your own business?" he smiled jestingly.

"No... It's not—"

"Come," he said warmly, "let us leave them to their discussion. There is still much to learn today."

They sat and ate quietly by the flowing water, out of earshot of Arlas and Indus. Eventually the two men emerged from the trees as Rhys was finishing his apple. Indus strode passed with a smug expression, shooting Rhys a grim smirk before nodding coldly at the man beside him.

"Good to see you, Lawrence," he uttered snidely as he passed them.

Arlas paused before Rhys and Lawrence watching Indus as he strode through the treeline towards the camp. The senior mage sighed heavily as he shook his head disapprovingly.

"He is merely protesting, Arlas," Lawrence proffered cheerily. "He does not like authority. It irks him that he must abide by your commands—he is merely attempting to assert himself. Do not lower yourself to his pettiness and you will feel all the better for it!"

"I hope you are correct, old friend," Arlas exhaled, "but I cannot help but fear the anger that he holds in his heart."

"His frustration will eventually be conciliated with time."

"I can only hope you are right," Arlas sighed again.

"You worry too much, Arlas!"

"I worry for his sake," Arlas replied solemnly. "Should he venture too far down the path he is on, there is no way back for him. I do not wish him to suffer the same fate as others before him!"

"Do not worry yourself with it," Lawrence assured. "And let us not concern Rhys with it either; he does not need to be bothered by such things."

"Perhaps he does," Arlas posed thoughtfully as he examined Rhys intently with his gaze. "Lawrence speaks highly of you," he remarked, changing the subject. "He claims you have natural talent."

"An exaggeration, I am sure," Rhys replied, struggling to believe Lawrence had said such things, his bloodied knuckles and split lip speaking to the contrary.

"Maybe so," Arlas shrugged, "but if such is

the case, you have done well to convince him otherwise."

"There *is* room for improvement," Lawrence commented.

"That is him giving you praise, Rhys," Arlas smirked. "Don't let his sternness fool you!"

"If you say so," Rhys returned, looking at the stoic, yet warm expression on Lawrence's face.

"Well, I will leave the two of you to it," Arlas beamed, before striding off in the same direction Indus had gone, leaving the two men to begin sparring once more.

The afternoon's training proved tougher than the morning's. As Rhys grew weary his reactions became dull. Blow after blow he took to his hands, legs, and torso. Finally, as the sun started to descend, they ended the day's schooling.

"You did well today," Lawrence declared, patting Rhys firmly on the back.

Battered and bruised, both bodily and in self-esteem, Rhys remained silent.

"We will resume first thing tomorrow morning. Now come, let us warm by the fire at camp."

Whilst the sun sank between the trees, Rhys sat huddled by the warmth of the campfire, nursing his beaten hands.

"How was the training with Lawrence?" Sol asked, planting himself down beside Rhys.

"Painful," Rhys replied coldly, not averting his gaze from the flames.

"It is tough... I won't lie," Sol began, "Lawrence is not afraid to push you. But I am surprised that your training began so soon, and that your first day was quite so... intensive."

"I guess Arlas is just eager to induct me into the Circle."

"What do you mean?" Sol asked, bemused by Rhys's statement.

"Nothing," Rhys lied.

"Right," Sol returned quizzically, before changing the subject. "Well, Arlas has asked me to train you in the basics of spellcasting."

"I know," Rhys sighed in exhaustion.

"I understand that you are weary from your day's training," Sol sympathised. "I personally thought it would be best to alternate your days of combat training with days of schooling. But as you clearly are aware, Arlas seems eager for your training to be somewhat—accelerated, and so we are to carry out our lessons in the evenings."

Sol drew a wand and presented it to Rhys. It was carved from hazel, etched with interlaced arcane symbols along its length. "I managed to procure this for you," he announced.

"Thank you," Rhys replied, admiring the beauty of the instrument as he turned it over in his bruised fingers.

"Let us start with something you will find useful. Give me your hand."

Rhys hesitantly extended his arm towards Sol. Drawing his own wand, Sol aimed it at the most swollen of Rhys's digits. The finger grew hot as Sol focussed upon it, and the flesh steadily inflamed. A moment later, the swelling relieved itself, and the pain faded in the seconds that followed, allowing Rhys to flex his finger once again without discomfort.

"Now you try," Sol instructed as he began to rummage through Rhys's pack. He quickly produced Rhys's codex and laid it open in front of him. "A healing spell does not repair damage to flesh and bone, but instead hastens the body's own healing processes. For this reason, many a mortal wound cannot be healed by magic. That is not to say that you cannot save a life by way of healing magic, for if the cause of death from a wound would be blood loss or infection, repairing the damaged flesh can prevent such from occurring.

"The limits of healing spells lie within the body's own capacity for self-repair. One cannot heal a stab to the heart or trauma to the brain, nor rid an infection that has already taken hold. A lost eye cannot be regrown, and a severed limb cannot be reattached. Wounds will scar, and some damage proves permanent. The school of restoration merely distorts the passage of time through which an injury endures. That said, it is perhaps the purest and most useful of all schools of magic."

Over the next few hours Sol instructed Rhys in the basic arts of healing. Though Rhys's initial efforts proved futile, as Sol helped Rhys in discovering the correct thought patterns, he later found himself able to reduce both the swelling and bruising of several of his fingers, whilst also forming fresh skin over a number of abrasions to his knuckles. When it was time to eat, Sol took over, healing the remainder of his injuries, returning him to full fitness. Utterly exhausted, sleep came instantly to Rhys that night.

He awoke at first light and ate a quick breakfast before he and Lawrence parted from the rest of the circle to train in the glade by the stream. They picked up where they had left off the previous day. For the duration of the morning, the two men circled one another attacking and countering.

In the first hour, Lawrence landed a series of strikes to Rhys. His attacks were swifter, more powerful, and far harsher than anything he had issued the day before. It was all too apparent that Lawrence had been significantly holding back previously. What was not clear, was how much Lawrence had held back. Was the ferocity with which the mage fought now the full extent of his speed and strength, or had Rhys yet only glimpsed but a fraction of Lawrence's capabilities? Regardless, Rhys was being pushed hard, and taking a battering. He was very far from landing a blow to his opponent. Every action he made had already been anticipated by Lawrence before Rhys even began to move.

They continued throughout the morning without rest. Rhys slowed from exhaustion as time wore on, his body taking more and more blows as a consequence. His entire anatomy suffered some form of pain or another, ranging from bruised fingers to aches from the previous day's exercise, all of which were affecting his morale.

A clever counter from Lawrence suddenly sent the quarterstaff flying from Rhys's grip.

"Can we break?" Rhys panted heavily.

Lawrence responded with a stoic nod. "Keep it up, you are making good progress!"

Rhys was doubtful of the notion.

"Here, take a sip of this," Lawrence offered, passing him a flask as Rhys nearly collapsed when lowering himself to the ground.

As Rhys uncapped it, a sweet aroma rose from inside. Bringing the flask to his lips, he inquisitively sipped the syrupy fluid. It tasted potently of honey and spices, and though the flask had not been heated, the liquid seemed hot to the taste. When he swallowed, a soothing energy washed over him. His soreness was alleviated and a new wave of energy buzz through him; all from one sip. He looked at the flask in astonishment before passing it back to Lawrence.

"What is that?"

"We call it amrita, though others have different names for it. It is a simple stamina draught. Revitalises—gets you back to fighting condition. It is easy to make and proves effective."

"It is amazing!" Rhys exclaimed, feeling invigorated as he stretched out his arms.

"Everyone reacts to it slightly differently —some experience greater effects from it than others. It acts to replenish the energies expended through vigorous exercise."

"What is it made from?" Rhys asked in wonder.

"Mostly simple herbs. There is some honey in it as well. The key ingredient though, is fig sap.

"Fig sap?" Rhys repeated.

"Yes. Normally it is poisonous and can even burn the skin. But when purified through alchemy, it has properties that can invigorate the body and mind."

"Is there a downside to using amrita?"

"If used frequently, it becomes less efficacious and the body becomes resistant to the benefits. Aside from this, fig trees are only indigenous to the very south of Cambria. Their sap is an ingredient that proves somewhat hard to come by."

"Well, I am glad to feel the effects!"

"Does that mean you are ready to continue?"

"Yes."

Rhys retook his stance and the two engaged once again. Half an hour or so passed without Rhys taking a hit as the new-found energy surged through him. Though as the day wore on, he began to feel the effects of fatigue once more creep in, and in the last hour of their training, Rhys was on the receiving end of more blows than the entire day before combined. Finally, a swift thrust from Lawrence struck him square in his chest, throwing him backwards to thump heavily to the ground. As Rhys gasped for breath, the mage stood over him with a sense of pity in his eyes.

"I think we should finish there today," he uttered flatly, helping Rhys to his feet.

Not pausing to wait for him, the mage turned away and abruptly departed, leaving Rhys wheezing cold and alone in the glade as he slowly caught his breath. When finally he'd recovered, he issued a slow, solemn sigh, making his way back towards camp by himself.

NINE

"**G**et up Rhys!" Lawrence barked as he stood over the man.

Rhys wheezed heavily as he tried to force air back into his lungs. A sickening feeling twisted through his gut from the blow that had just winded him. Crawling across the ground, Rhys curled his fingers around the shaft of his quarterstaff once more. Slowly, propping himself up with the weapon, he rose to his feet. Spitting blood, he flourished the stave, readying himself again.

Lawrence quickly lunged for him. Rhys deflected the blow. Yet before he could react again, a second swing struck the side of his thigh. His leg crumpled momentarily from the pain, and as he dropped to his knee, a successive strike knocked his staff clean out of his grip.

"Again!" Lawrence yelled, commanding Rhys to pick up his weapon.

Reluctantly, Rhys retrieved the staff and

prepared himself for another blow. He parried the next few incoming swings, before a high jab cut clean past his defences, striking him to the ground for another time.

"Come on, Rhys. Hit me!" Lawrence advanced again, unleashing a flurry of blows, several of which struck their target until the last disarmed Rhys again.

Rhys wearily recovered his quarterstaff one more time and Lawrence re-engaged.

"Hit me!" the mage roared as he broke through Rhys's feeble counter to pummel him another time.

Another flurry of exchanges resulted in a long arc clouting Rhys across the temple.

"You aren't even trying, Rhys!" Lawrence growled in frustration as Rhys dazedly rubbed the rapidly swelling lump on the side of his brow.

It was true; Rhys had given up on attempting to strike Lawrence hours earlier, electing instead to adopt a purely defensive strategy. It was damage control. Rhys had realised he was unlikely to ever land a successful blow on Lawrence, and so far, every attempt he had made had simply left himself vulnerable to counterattack. Rhys had grown wearisome of taking blow after blow from Lawrence over the past week. All he wished now from the training was to avoid injury as much as possible. But thus far, his plan had not proved successful. Lawrence had keyed into Rhys's idea the very moment he had first conceived it. The mage's response was to come at Rhys with unrelenting ferocity, bludgeoning him into submission in an attempt to force him to fight back.

"I can't!" Rhys retaliated in anger. "I can't," he repeated shaking his head.

"You can't what?" Lawrence demanded.

"I can't hit you."

"So, you won't even try? You are giving up?"

"No… But I can't go on like this!"

"Do you need a break?" Lawrence asked unsympathetically.

"Yes! I need a break from being beaten the shit out of!"

"You cannot expect to win a fight Rhys if you don't fight back! You can only win if you are willing to give everything you have to do so! When you fight for real, it will be to the death! Your enemies will not show mercy or restraint. There is no code of honour between foes. The war we fight is bloody and brutal. The only way to survive is to fight with all the might you can muster. Anything less, and you are already dead." Lawrence stood in silence for a time, looking down at Rhys. "We are done for today," he exhaled in a disappointed tone as he turned and left.

Frustrated, Rhys tore the leather wraps from his hands, casting them aside. Kneeling on the bank of the stream, he rinsed more blood from his knuckles before drawing his wand, attempting to heal some of his injuries.

'What am I doing here?' Rhys thought to himself. He had spent an entire week being beaten with a stick, and for what purpose? He barely knew anything of the Order of Magi, and many of them seemed if anything, hostile towards him. What motives did he truly have to join their ranks?

"It is tough, I know."

Rhys looked up startled. Arlas was sat before him, perched on a rock across the stream. "I didn't hear you approach," Rhys confessed as he returned his attention to attempting to heal his bruises.

"It was not my intention to sneak up on you," Arlas assured warmly. "It is easy to forget that those who have not undergone the joining ritual lack as keen a sense of hearing as a mage. I should have announced my presence."

"No, it's quite all right. You just surprised me is all."

"I came to apologise," Arlas admitted after a period of silence.

"Apologise? What for?"

"I have asked a lot from you, Rhys," the mage explained. "I have given you a lot to question without providing much in the way of answers. Lawrence has been pushing you harder than any of his pupils before. There are two reasons for this."

"What are they?"

"The first is quite simply that he sees in you great potential. I too have observed you as you trained, from a distance. He is not wrong in this judgement. There is no doubt that you have the beginnings of a skilled fighter!"

"And what is the second reason?" Rhys pressed impatiently, sick of hearing praise when by his own judgement, he seemed only to be failing in his training.

"The second reason, is that I asked Lawrence to push you as hard as possible."

"Why?" Rhys shrugged in exasperation.

"For the same reason I have asked that you undergo your joining ritual this year. I believe that you must be prepared for what is to come, and the time in which we have to ready you is short."

"But you have yet to explain what for!" Rhys protested in frustration.

"You are right," Arlas conceded, turning his back on Rhys. He stood motionless and silent for a time before finally he began to speak in a solemn tone. "I have kept things from you, Rhys, that I now realise I should not have done. What happened to your village—such a curse is unlike anything I have ever witnessed before. Or at least it was... the first time I saw it."

"What do you mean?" Rhys demanded apprehensively.

"Longford was not the first village to suffer the curse which befell it. On the day I met you it was the fourth time I had seen such dark magic!"

"You have seen it before...!?" breathed Rhys in realisation.

Arlas issued a singular nod.

"But you still have no idea what it is?"

"I have some suspicions," Arlas confessed. "We refer to it as the Grey. I know that the magic used to create such a curse must be fuelled by blood. I know that it is an ancient and dark magic which should have been long forgotten. And I believe that the reasons behind it are far more sinister than to simply cull an entire village in one fell swoop.

"I first saw the curse nearly two years ago. A small hamlet had fallen victim to it in the northern reaches of Westverness. Its effects had all but faded, for my discovery of the settlement was long after the curse had reaped the lives of its inhabitants. I could not figure out what had slain an entire settlement—many months or perhaps several years had passed since the curse had been conjured. All that remained were the sinister whispers of the faded black magic.

"When next I came upon this reaping of life, it was little more than a year ago. A village in the foothills of the Virminter mountains by the name of Blackruth. I came upon the cursed ruins of the village but a few days after the spell fell upon it. This time, the effects of the dark magic were there to see.

"I studied the nature of the Grey to find I knew nothing of it. It is a blood ritual that speaks traces of the most ancient of magics. Alas, I was no nearer to discovering the cause. I needed to witness the curse taking form in order to learn more.

"The next village to succumb to the Grey was located on a small island just off of the eastern peninsula. I heard rumours of it from a number of merchant sailors. They spoke of the isle of Glenontauch that had turned dark beneath the sunlight. Few ships pass close enough to ever see the small isle, and even fewer ever land upon its shores. I manage to barter passage to the isle to discover it too had been reaped by the Grey, though it had happened months before I arrived.

"When next I came across the dark curse, it was the fall of Longford. Each time this curse has struck, it has been a village both small and inconspicuous. The settlements targeted are those so seldom visited by traders and travellers, that their fall would likely go unnoticed for great lengths of time. And each and every time the curse has struck, not one person has survived... But then you walked out of the mist!"

"What are you saying?"

"I did not simply walk into the heart of Longford. I cast upon myself dozens of magical wards to protect me against the evils of the curse. Had I not, I imagine I would have succumbed to its effects and been killed in a matter of minutes. Even still, I could feel it clawing at me, sapping the very life from my being. It weakened me considerably. Yet you were stood amidst the ruin without any protection whatsoever.

"No being, be they witch, warlock, or even a

mage, could survive the effects of the Grey without some form of magical protection. When first I met you, I thought that you must be responsible. Surely, I had found the man I hunted: the man responsible for all the death and destruction I had seen thus far! Even now a small part of me still suspects that you might be responsible for what happened. But then why would you have agreed to come with me on that day? Why would you have journeyed here with Sol? And why would you be here now?"

"What *do* you think now?"

"I believe what you say. I believe that Longford was indeed your home and that you know even less of the Grey than I. But I do not know how or why you survived. You should not be alive!"

"So, you have no answers?"

"No. But I believe that you are the key to finding them!"

"What does that even mean?" Rhys protested.

"You survived for a reason Rhys; and I believe that the best way for the mages to discover what is truly happening, is with you in our ranks. Whether we understand it or not, you are somehow connected to everything that has transpired, and it may even be that you have a part to play in stopping it!"

"But how can I be important in all of this when I know less of it than any of you?"

"That has yet to be revealed," Arlas returned.

"That is no answer! You don't know. How can you be so sure that you will ever even find out?"

"I have been a mage for a very long time, Rhys. I understand the way this world works better than most. If experience has taught me anything, it is that we have witnessed but the very beginning of what is unfolding. We have seen but a glimpse of the whole picture, more of which, I have no doubt, will later be revealed. You are but one piece in the puzzle that has only begun to take shape. Just because we cannot yet see where you fit into all of this, does not mean that you do not have a place within it."

"But then why is it so urgent for me to undergo the binding ritual? Why do you wish for me to become a mage by the year's end?"

"The frequency with which the Grey is arising is becoming more regular. Between the first and second time it struck, nearly two years went by. Yet, between the second and third time, less than a year came to pass. The next occurrence —Longford, fell even sooner after that!"

"It is happening more and more often!" Rhys realised.

"Now you understand why we cannot afford to bide our time. We must be ready for when next the curse strikes. *You* must be ready."

"All right," Rhys agreed after a long pause.

"What do you need me to do?"

"The blood moon is set to rise but a few hours from now. I must press you for your answer Rhys; will you undergo the Rite of Reckoning?"

Rhys stared silently at the man as he endured his intense gaze, contemplating everything he had been told. "Then you have my answer:" he said finally, "yes. I will undergo the Rite of Reckoning."

"Thank you," Arlas breathed with a sense of relief. "The blood moon will rise with the setting of the sun. There is a place several miles north of here that is a suitable location to perform the Rite. We will begin preparations shortly and leave within the hour."

"Okay," Rhys nodded.

"But before we go, I must ask one more thing from you."

"What is it?"

"That, for the time being at least, you keep all that we have discussed to yourself. When the time is right, we will reveal all to the others. But I wish for there to be absolutely no doubt before we do so."

"Of course," Rhys agreed, not questioning why.

Arlas nodded in gratitude, rising to his feet. "I will begin to gather the components needed for the ritual. You need only bring water for the short journey. Until we leave, I suggest you do your best to heal any injuries you have sustained during the day's training."

"I will," Rhys nodded, rubbing a now prominent lump on the side of his brow.

Rhys returned to camp, and as Arlas had suggested, attempted to heal his injuries to the best of his ability. Sol joined him by the fire and aided Rhys in reducing the swelling of his temple.

"I think we should begin something new this evening," Sol began, producing his own codex of spellcraft and flicking through the worn pages. "I was thinking something along the lines of minor illusions."

"We will have to skip tonight's lesson," Rhys explained.

"Why so?" Sol asked curiously.

"I'm... running an errand with Arlas tonight. We are set to leave shortly."

"An errand?" Sol's eyes narrowed with intrigue. "What kind?"

"I'm not entirely sure," Rhys lied. "He hasn't really explained anything to me. You know how he is—all mysterious and such!"

"Yeah... I guess so," Sol shrugged, not investigating further, though Rhys suspected the mage had not entirely bought his deception. "Okay," he said, "no problem, we will pick it up again tomorrow night." Sol glanced past Rhys for a moment. "I think he is waiting for you now."

Rhys peered back over his shoulder to see Arlas stood watching him and Sol from the edge of the clearing. "I shouldn't keep him waiting."

"I will see you later," Sol nodded.

Rhys rose to his feet, gathering up his wand, flask of water, and overcoat before striding over towards Arlas.

"Are you ready?"

"I am," Rhys confirmed, glancing back at Sol to see him watching the two of them from beside the fire, before following Arlas northward through the trees.

"You will not need to keep this from him for long," Arlas assured, as if he had read Rhys's thoughts. "Should the Rite prove successful, we will reveal to the others that you will undergo the joining this winter upon our return."

They continued along their northward bearing through the pine forest as the sun grew low in the sky and the light of day dwindled. After nearly a couple of hours, they had covered two leagues, and arrived at the foot of a hill, up which the forest appeared to thin. As they climbed the hillside, the canopy above them opened up, revealing a ring of deciduous trees that had already shed their leaves, encircling the brow of the hillock before them. When they neared the top, Rhys studied them more closely. Twisted and gnarled, appearing far older than any of the pines that surrounded them, Rhys immediately understood through some unknown intuition that the great trees stood sentinel across the hilltop were ancient by any standards. Their trunks were smooth and white, contorting high until they split into boughs of enormous girth that divided further and further, forming a vast network of branches. The limbs of the primeval trees were both twisted and straight, some knotting together whilst others rose upwards cleanly in shoots of fresh growth.

"These are elder oak trees," Arlas explained as they summited the hill. "They are among the oldest trees in Cambria. It is said that their lifetimes can span millennia. Some are believed to be more than ten thousand years old!"

"They are incredible!" Rhys exclaimed as he looked upon the magnificent sentinels.

"They can only grow along the ley lines of Cambria; where magic is at its most focussed."

Rhys stepped between the ancient trees to the foot of a perfectly round grassy knoll that sat upon the flattened hilltop. On the grass were arranged a series of grey stones in a circle. Rhys counted eleven, each irregular in size and shape, matching the equal number of elder oak trees that surrounded them.

"These stones are sarsen," Arlas explained as he knelt beside the larger of the rocks measuring just over a foot in height. Running his fingers gently over its lichen-covered surface, he spoke once more. "When arranged in a circle such as this, they can channel magical energies inward. Ideal for performing rituals."

"Who made this?" Rhys asked.

"I was the one who laid *these* stones, years

ago now. They are set in a manner similar to the Northern Circle, but this ring is rather makeshift when compared to the henges that exist throughout Cambria. It is but a down-scaled replica, yet it serves its purpose for basic rituals such as the Rite of Reckoning. The magical energy that needs to be focussed for such a ritual is minimal."

"What do we need to do?" Rhys asked as he looked to the west where the sun had just dipped below the horizon, streaking amber and red across the sky.

"You can rest for a few minutes. The moon will not rise for another hour or so, and before the ritual can begin, I must make some preparations.

TEN

Twilight blended into night as Rhys watched Arlas finish the preparations for the rite. Within the stones, he had arranged a circle of candles, each now aflame, casting an orange glow over the sarsen. Within the centre of the candles was lain a bone dagger, a large chip of wood, and a splint. The mage was now walking the perimeter of the circle, touching his wand to each of the eleven stones in turn, murmuring a few words under his breath each time he did so.

"The moon is rising," Arlas declared as he looked to the east.

Sure enough, the lunar disc was emerging from behind the dark horizon, though it was not its usual ghostly white. The moon's surface shone with an incarnadine lustre: the colour of blood. Rhys had never before seen such an unusual astronomical sight, and stood speechless, in awe at the moon's eerie beauty. Slowly, the scarlet orb crept above the land until the full disc hung low in the sky, casting its crimson light across the forest.

"The time is now, Rhys," Arlas announced as he rested a hand upon his shoulder. "Step into the circle."

Following Arlas's instructions, Rhys stepped slowly between the stones, towards the ring of candles, before cautiously striding over the flames to take his place in the circle's core.

"Kneel before the blood moon."

Kneeling upon the ground, Rhys glanced up at the crimson moon before gazing down at the items before him.

"Draw the blade across the palm of your hand," Arlas instructed from outside the ring.

Rhys took the bone dagger, gripping it tightly, and slowly pulled its edge across his palm. As he sliced carefully at his flesh, blood pooled from the wound.

"Now, place the fragment of elder oak in the blood on your hand."

Careful as to not spill the blood seeping from the cut, Rhys set the bone knife down and took the chip of elder oak, resting it gently in his bloodied palm.

"Now light the splint."

Rhys took the splint in front of him and held it within the flame of one of the candles until it caught alight.

"Light the elder oak."

Hesitating for a moment, Rhys brought the flame close to the fragment of white wood in his palm. Holding the flaming splint against the elder oak, the wood quickly began to smoulder until it too caught aflame. Ribbons of smoke twirled upwards from the flaming wood as the fire simmered across its surface, burning hot in Rhys's bleeding palm.

"Finally," Arlas said deeply, "smother the flame in blood!"

Rhys looked up at Arlas in hesitation, then to the crimson moon in the sky ahead. The moon now seemed impossibly large, its scarlet light bathing the entire world beneath it.

Taking a deep breath, Rhys slowly began to curl his fingers around the scorching flame. A wind rose sharply, swirling around Rhys with tremendous force. The candles flickered intensely, their flames rising high into the air. The fire in Rhys's palm snarled hot, searing his flesh, before suddenly his fingers clamped shut. At that second, the candles were extinguished all at once, and the wind fell still. All was quiet as the light from the moon slowly faded from incarnadine to the purest of whites. The pain in Rhys's hand vanished. Slowly, he uncurled his fingers.

A white and silky ash poured from Rhys's palm. The lump of elder oak was now nothing more than a silver dust that dissipated in the gentle breeze. When the last of the ashes were washed from his skin by the night air, Rhys looked down at his hand in amazement. The cut across his palm had fully healed and there was not a single trace of blood on his skin. Stunned, Rhys slowly looked up at Arlas.

"The signs are clear," he breathed softly. "We shall go forward with the joining ritual this winter solstice!"

Rhys rose steadily to his feet, still staring at his palm. "What now?" he asked after a period of silence.

"The night has only just begun, for the Conclave of Magi is set to take place at midnight—I would like for you to be present."

* * *

"Put this on," Sol said, handing Rhys a set of white hooded vestments.

Rhys looked upon the fine garments under the light of the moon, admiring their quality. He passed the garbs over his head, allowing the flowing robes to descend to the ground. Sol too adorned a set of the vestments, though they differed slightly from the pure white robes Rhys wore, hemmed with a dark blue trim.

Sol raised the large hood of his robes and Rhys too lifted his. His feet were quickly growing numb as he stood barefoot upon the icy ground. Sol gestured for him to follow, leading Rhys from the glade, through the trees, in the direction in which many of the other mages had already headed.

They walked for nearly half an hour through the darkness of the wood. Stepping carefully across the forest floor, Rhys constantly drew breath in pain a sharp twigs and roots underfoot barbed the soles of his feet; on one occasion, he stubbed his toe against a large stone with enough force to make his eyes water. Sol however did not seem to be suffering from such troubles. Whether the mage merely avoided the same stumbles that ailed Rhys, or whether the mage was simply more tolerant of the pain, Rhys could not tell.

After a time, they came to the edge of the trees. Before them, sparkling brilliantly in the moonlight was a wide pond that mirrored the entire night sky above. Within the waters, stood waist deep, most of the other magi gathered in a large circle that was not yet complete. Behind each of them, set in the floor of the pond's basin, standing vertically, were each of the mage's respective staves, forming a second incomplete ring that encircled the magi.

Sol led Rhys to the water's edge and began to wade in. Hesitating for a moment, Rhys realised he was expected to follow. Taking a deep breath, he slowly dipped his right foot into the gelid water. His already numb toes cried out from the cold as he stepped fully into the pond, and goosebumps prickled across his entire skin. Shuffling forwards, the water quickly rose to his knees, and as it reached his waist he began to shiver violently.

Wading out to the centre of the pond, Sol planted his own stave into the mud beneath the surface, taking his position within the circle. Rhys placed himself beside the mage and looked around at the other men who stood silently in the water. Their faces were shadowed beneath their hoods and Rhys could only identify who was whom by the staffs set in the water behind them.

Each of the men's garments were white, though they differed in the colour of their trims. Several of the magi, the Circle's acolytes, adorned robes with the same blue hems as Sol's garbs, whilst a number of others bore green trims symbolising the rank of paladin. Finally, three magi were decorated with scarlet trims: the magisters of the Circle.

Rhys stood shivering in the icy pond whilst the remaining mages emerged from the forest edge, wading into the water to take their places in the ring. The final man to appear was garbed in black, purple trim lining the hems of his archon's cassock. If his iconic dark vestments had not been enough to identify him, the ebony staff in the mage's grip clearly distinguished Arlas as he strode through the freezing water, waves rippling across the surface of the pond in his wake. Finally, Arlas planted his staff into the mud of the pond bed, completing the circle, before taking his place in the ring of mages.

Suddenly a line of flame erupted from each of the staves set in the outer ring, licking upwards from the surface of the water. Each trail of fire began to inch inward towards its respective owner, before halting a foot or so from their back. At that moment, each track of fire forked into two, tracing outwards until meeting the flames emitted from the staffs adjacent. Within moments, the thirteen men were encircled by a wall of flame several feet high, floating off the water's surface. They were not only trapped within the burning ring, but separated from their weapons.

"Brothers!" the deep voice of Arlas called out. "I have summoned your presence for the Conclave of Magi. We are gathered to discuss matters of both the Order and all else. Speak freely within the circle, for here the voice of any can be heard! What say you?"

A moment of silence followed in the still night.

"There is one among us who is not of our order!" the unmistakable voice of Indus protested. "His presence here is forbidden!"

"As Archon of the Circle, it is within my power to grant audience to any I so choose. Rhys North of Longford is here under my authority. For tonight, he shall be treated as an initiate."

"Arlas," the cold voice of Stanton Grey spoke. "This is most irregular. Can you explain why you would have an outsider bear witness to our discussions?"

"Several hours ago, Rhys North underwent the Rite of Reckoning!" Arlas proclaimed.

A sudden hubbub of mutterings broke out as the hooded heads of the surrounding mages turned left and right, each of the men glancing about to gauge the reactions of their brethren, before, as silence once more descended, each and every one of them turned their gaze upon Rhys. Though their eyes were shrouded by the darkness under their hoods, Rhys could feel their stares upon him.

"For what reason would you subject him to the Rite of Reckoning when you know full well it rules out the use of the other three rites?" Indus's voice cut through the silence.

"As you are all aware, Rhys North is the sole survivor of the curse that consumed the village of Longford. I myself was only able to enter the village to investigate the curse through the use of several powerful wards. Without such safeguards, I believe I would have quickly succumbed to the effects of the curse and suffered a fate the same as all who lost their lives that day. Yet Rhys survived without any shielding whatsoever!

"I took this, combined with his aptitude for quickly grasping basic spells and enchantments, as evidence enough that he was a suitable candidate for the joining. I did not perform the Rite of Reckoning this evening because I wanted to determine if Rhys could undergo the Binding Ritual, but to affirm the beliefs I already held. The results of the Rite were as conclusive as they can be. Therefore, this winter, Rhys and several of us will undergo the pilgrimage to the Northern Circle, enacting the binding ritual on the solstice!"

"Arlas, regardless of whether your hunch was correct, do you not think these actions were somewhat reckless? Why have *you*, the man who preaches patience and caution above all else, suddenly decided to do away with the traditional practise of induction?" Indus chastised. "Why do you seem impatient to carry out the binding ritual on this man before the year is out? It would seem as if there is more you have not revealed to us; which begs the question: what other decisions have you made without consulting the Circle beforehand?"

"Is it reckless to pursue a course of action where you believe there to be little risk? What do we benefit from delaying? The Rite of Reckoning can prove difficult to interpret, but when the results are as clear as they were tonight, then they are more indicative than the Rites of Blood, Ash and Stone combined. I do not need to justify my actions, for the results of my actions speak clear!"

"Yet you know that had you consulted the rest of the Circle on this, not all would have been in agreement!" Indus challenged, raising his voice in an attempt to rally the other mages against their archon. "This is why you chose to delay this conclave until tonight. You would not have left this decision to debate, for you feared the majority would not condone such actions. Instead, you kept the rest of the Order in the dark, presenting your case only after you had acted!"

"It is within his rights as your superior for Arlas to make such decisions!" Lawrence rebuked, attempting to quell Indus's outburst.

"And so, a different set of rules apply to Arlas than the rest of us?" Marus Stone quarrelled.

"I am still bound to our laws and code, Marus. But as Archon, I have the authority to make decisions concerning the Order without first consulting the Conclave. You may question my actions, but you lack the decades of wisdom and experience that I hold as Archon. If one day you should ever rise to become the leader of the Order, then you will be free to make such decisions as you see fit!

"But this topic of discussion is not the reason I called this conclave! There are many issues to discuss, and if we ever hope to do so before the night is done then we cannot squander time with such petty debates over the distribution of power throughout the Order!"

"Then what are we here to discuss?" Robert Kwesi asked, speaking for the first time.

"Though several of you are already aware of what I am about to reveal, most of you have yet to learn the full extent of the curse we call the Grey. The events that happened in Longford were not unique. The same curse that struck Rhys's village reaped at least three others before it. The settlements targeted by the curse were isolated communities, suggesting that the perpetrator behind all of the events is attempting to go unnoticed for as long as possible. But these events have not gone unnoticed, for *we* have uncovered them!

"I know very little of the curse's true nature beyond what I have already discussed with each of you previously. It is clear that it is an ancient blood magic ritual, the purpose of which still proves illusive. But this curse, the Grey, is not my only concern.

"Several months ago, I found myself in the territory of a wendigo south of the White Mountains, in woodlands very similar to these we find ourselves in now! To the south, the Orc are becoming more hostile and organised than they have been in nearly four centuries. To the east, Lord Wargrave, Earl of Iarbhaile, is building an army for a purpose we have yet to determine. And each and every one of you has in this last year seen and reported of events and phenomena as equally bizarre and unworldly as any of these!

"My friends, it is all too clear that the very fabric of Cambria seems to be changing. Something has perturbed the natural order, and I am willing to bet that it is in some way connected to the Grey. Thus, it falls to us to ascertain what exactly is causing these events, and to put a stop to them! We must plan our next steps in tackling these objectives, for I fear what we are seeing now may well be just the beginning of what is yet to come!"

"Arlas is right!" Stanton agreed. "I too have seen happenings which I find most peculiar. This year alone, I have seen flocks of ravens in numbers so vast they blotted out the sun, flying in no direction, but circling vast areas without landing for days. I have seen a roving band of hobgoblins and bugbears raid a village in broad daylight, and entire hectares of crops laid waste to blight. Such occurrences are each not only rare, but the darkest of omens!"

"These events are likely mere coincidence!" Jack Ironwood argued. "The Grey alone is what we should be focussed on. We would be foolish to worry ourselves with other concerns! That these affairs have occurred all at once does not mean they are related. There is no evidence to suggest there is any connexion between them other than the time in which they have taken place!"

"We cannot afford to ignore the signs, Jack!" Seimon Wells insisted in disagreement. "You are right in saying that we lack proof of some connexion between these occurrences, but the probability of all these events occurring simultaneously without any link between them is insurmountably small!"

"Then what could possibly be causing such rare happenings?" Robert Kwesi questioned.

"What of the Occult?" Ethan Hall asked.

"No," Lawrence returned, dismissing such a notion. "Their order strictly forbids the use of blood magic. Besides, they are spread far too sparsely throughout Cambria these days to coordinate any magic that could have effects like what we have seen."

"I would not be so certain, Lawrence," Arlas refuted. "The Occult still holds power over Cambria despite their decline in the past few centuries. I have spoken with the Grand Cleric, for the Occult was too my first suspicion. It is true that they have a deep understanding of certain magics that in many ways exceeds our own. But in order to cast such vast ripples across Cambria that could create omens like those we have seen, they would need to gather in mass to perform a ritual unlike any before it.

"Their Grand Cleric assures me that they have not held an assemblage in decades, and I am inclined to believe her when she says she has no knowledge of the Grey. It may be possible however, that a rogue coterie of the Occult may be using blood magic as a means to overcome their lack of numbers."

"But to what end?" Sol asked.

"I do not know. Nor do I think it likely. The Occult is quick to root out any members within their order that turn to the dark arts. If the Occult is to blame, then I believe it could only be a splinter group of their order that have somehow come upon the resources required to cause such widespread effects. Thus, the Occult's involvement does seem improbable, but cannot be ruled out until we know more."

"Then what do you suspect, Arlas?" Indus questioned.

"I have not yet enough information to postulate. I believe it is necessary for our order to set itself the goal of investigating all these strange events. I am therefore issuing you all new instructions. From this point forth, each of you must abandon what pursuits you previously held, and instead turn your attention to discovering the cause of these happenings. Our greatest priority is in discovering the root of the Grey and bringing whomever or whatever is responsible to justice.

"I am giving you each free reign in which to do so, provided you act within the codes of our order!" Arlas declared, glancing at Indus from under the shadow of his hood. "Use every investigative technique and method at your disposal. Listen closely for rumours and leave no stone unturned. But most importantly, we must conduct our search with the utmost discretion.

"It is most likely that the individuals responsible for the Grey intended to keep their actions secret from *us* above all others, knowing that we would oppose their actions. Should they discover that we are aware of their conduct, they may throw caution to the wind in desperation. We cannot afford for them to learn of our investigation, for it may result in them targeting far more, and far larger settlements than they have done so thus far.

"The entire circle is working together on

this, and so it is important we remain in contact. I therefore suggest we meet once more in these woods in the final days of the year to share what we have each learned. Until then, venture forth and gather as much information as you can. I will leave it to each of you to decide where to begin."

"We will not let you down, Arlas," Seimon assured him after a period of silence.

"Finally, to bring the discussion full circle, there is still the matter of Rhys's binding. Seimon, Matthew, Robert, and Sol; I request that the four of you accompany Rhys and myself on the pilgrimage to the Northern Circle for this year's winter solstice. I therefore would ask you to return to Highwood for the second week of December to allow us enough time for the journey."

ELEVEN

O ver the next few days, most of the magi departed from the camp in Highwood, setting off in every direction, each with their own ideas of where to begin their investigation. Indus Mark, Byron Lance, and Marus Stone were the first to depart, setting out before dawn the morning after the conclave, without so much as a word to any of the others before leaving. Arlas informed the rest of the circle that he believed they had ventured west towards Iarbhaile.

Seimon Wells and Matthew Hault were the next to head off, bidding the others a kind farewell, explaining that they meant to travel eastward to see if they could uncover anything from the wreckage of both Longford and the isle of Glenontauch.

The following day, Sol said his goodbyes to Rhys as he left for the south with Stanton Grey and Robert Kwesi. Jack Ironwood and Ethan

Hall seemed to slip away that same day almost unnoticed, though Arlas explained they had discussed with him their intentions of journeying to the south to investigate Orc activity.

The last man to depart was Arlas himself. He neither revealed his plans nor his destination as he said farewell to Rhys and Lawrence.

"I am leaving you in Lawrence's very capable hands," he explained to Rhys. "You will continue your training until my return in just over a month's time. He will teach you everything you need to learn, and then some. When I return, I expect that you will be more than ready to make your pilgrimage."

"There is a lot to cover," Lawrence made clear, "but I believe he will be very skilled in no time!"

"Good," Arlas smiled. "Take care old friend, and the same for you Rhys." With those final words, Arlas departed, leaving the two men in silence.

In the weeks that followed, Rhys continued his training with Lawrence. Since the night of the conclave and the Rite of Reckoning, it was as if something had changed within him. He now trained with a new determination. For the first fortnight, they continued their usual routine of sparring with quarterstaffs throughout the daytime. Rhys still did not come close to ever striking Lawrence, though he himself took far fewer blows. As they continued to practise, Rhys became evermore proficient. His manoeuvres and tactics steadily grew more precise and refined, whilst he fought and moved with a raw flare that from time to time proved unpredictable to his mentor, catching him off-guard on several occasions; though still the decades of experience that Lawrence held over him proved unmatched.

During the evenings, Lawrence took over Sol's role, teaching him in the ways of enchantments and spells. They covered topics quickly, and Rhys soon became adept in spellcraft from all manner of schools of magic. His healing spells quickly progressed in their potency. He learned several illusory incantations, allowing him to cast magical light from his wand and to hide and obscure arcane markings from sight. He learnt to produce spells that could both enchant objects to heat up and cool down on their own accord, and how to carve magical glyphs that could act as rudimentary arcane traps for hunting. Rhys soon filled a good half of his codex with scribblings and jottings. Had he not made such scrupulous notes, he believed he would never have kept track of all he was taught.

When mid-November came, Lawrence took up a shield, instructing Rhys how to both attack and defend against it. The mage seemed no less skilled in this discipline than he did at quarterstaff combat. His training as an infantryman in his life before the Circle was all too apparent.

Though it was a jarring change of pace

at first, under Lawrence's instruction, Rhys soon managed to adapt his technique appropriately, and he quickly learnt the skills required to take on such foes. But the instant Rhys grew comfortable with the change in drills, Lawrence mixed things up again, switching weapon sets to a training sword, and days later an axe. The mage did not stop there, brandishing all manner of weapons, throwing everything against Rhys to prepare him for any and all circumstances.

When December's first week began, Lawrence took Rhys deeper into the woods, teaching him in the arts of tracking various magical creatures, and how to hunt them. Rhys learnt a wide array of magical snares and tools to allow him to both follow and kill his quarry, from a glyph that exploded into flame when trodden upon, to a rune that allowed its caster to hear everything within earshot of it.

The time that Rhys spent learning from Lawrence seemed to both drag on and blur by. Though his mentor pushed him hard, and could both be stern and unsympathetic at times, Rhys found a deep respect for the man and quickly grew to consider him a friend.

When the time drew near that several of the other mages would return, ready for the pilgrimage to the Northern Circle, Lawrence adopted his quarterstaff once more.

"Same as before," he urged. "I want you to try and land a blow on me. When you manage that, then there is nothing more for me to teach you!"

"Then this will be over quick, old man!" Rhys jested as he readied himself for their duel.

Lawrence did not hesitate, immediately lancing forward with ferocious speed. The weeks of training had not been in vain however, as Rhys effortlessly stepped aside having anticipated the strike. An upwards swing from Rhys was quickly met with a powerful counter from the mage, but Rhys hastily retaliated with a riposte of his own. The two men exchanged a rapid flurry of blows, matching each other's advances with well-practised blocks. As they circled one another, they both shifted back and forth, testing their opponent's guard for any possible opening.

Nearly an hour or so passed as the two men sparred. Quarterstaff stuck quarterstaff with loud crack after loud crack rattling through the air. Lawrence came at Rhys with greater speed and agility than he had ever done so before. It was clear to Rhys that only now was his mentor finally unleashing everything in his arsenal, yet Rhys avoided the man's assailment with a similar level of skill. Finally, after nearly two months, Rhys seemed to prove a match for the man.

Eventually a glancing blow grazed Rhys's shoulder, but he quickly responded with an onslaught of his own attacks. Lawrence took a swing for Rhys's head, which was met by a strong block. Before Rhys could counter, Lawrence threw his shoulder into him. But this time, Rhys was ready, twisting sharply away to Lawrence's flank. Lawrence had lost his footing. The mage was left open and undefended.

Rhys exploded from the mark, and with all his speed and might, brought down his staff across Lawrence's back. To Rhys's disbelief, he watched as the quarterstaff made contact, whipping powerfully down onto his mentor's unguarded shoulders. The mage was bludgeoned to the floor by the force of the blow, and suddenly, everything fell quiet.

Lawrence sprang back up from the ground with a stern look across his face. He stretched out his hand. Rhys stared at the man in shock for several seconds before finally he shook it. Lawrence's expression rapidly dissolved to a broad grin as he patted Rhys firmly across the shoulder.

"Perfect!" Lawrence came out with. "A better move than I could have pulled."

"I doubt that," Rhys returned as he could not help but also smile. A sense of pride welled within him, but it was humble; he knew he was still years away from Lawrence's level of skill.

"No, I mean it!" Lawrence continued. "You have come a very long way in such a short time!"

"Only because of your teaching."

"You are too modest," Lawrence refused. "You have exceeded all other pupil's I have had to date Rhys. I pushed you far harder than I have any before, and in less than two months you have learnt what would take most years! I am proud of you."

"I don't know what to say…" Rhys uttered as his heart warmed. "Thank you!"

"That is all you need to say," Lawrence smiled. "Now…" he said, retrieving his quarterstaff from the ground, "again?"

Rhys did not manage to land another blow to Lawrence that day, though such could almost be said for his opponent. The mage did graze Rhys once or twice, occasionally landing a glancing blow, but put simply: he had trained Rhys too well. They continued to spar until late in the afternoon, when from the trees behind them, Rhys heard an all too familiar voice.

"He's got you on the run Lawrence!"

"Sol!" Rhys exclaimed as he revolved to catch sight of the mage.

"It's good to see you," Sol sighed as he stepped out into the clearing and removed the heavy pack from his shoulders. "I can see the two of you haven't been taking it easy since last I saw you!"

"That would be putting it mildly," Rhys smiled as he greeted the mage with a firm handshake.

"How goes the hunt?" Lawrence asked as he too welcomed Sol.

"Not well," Sol replied with an agitated expression. "I have had little luck in chasing down all my leads," he explained. "I've been in search of a couple of ex-sisters of the occult that the Grand

Cleric has grown suspicious of. She believed they might be practising dark arts.

"Alas, I have travelled from town to town, always several steps behind them, only to have the trail go cold. It may be worth picking up the hunt for them again at the start of the new year, but from what I have gathered, their goals and motives are petty. I have begun to doubt whether they have any connexion to the Grey. I'll tell you more about it later," Sol huffed as he slumped to the ground in front of the small campfire, groaning slightly as he did so. "But first I need something hot to drink. Where are the others?" he asked looking around.

"You are the first to return," Lawrence explained.

"I figured I'd be among the last! But then again, our order is not exactly known for ever arriving early."

"I thought you were travelling with Robert and Stanton?" Lawrence inquired.

"We split up a couple weeks back. The two of them wanted to pursue a lead in Orthios. We heard rumours that a black-market merchant had somehow acquired writings on what he believed to be an ancient blood magic ritual. I do not yet know what they found. It seemed too important to ignore, but we still did not want to give up the chase of our apostate occultists. So we divided in hope of investigating both leads. Hopefully they had more success than I."

"Let us hope so," Lawrence agreed.

"You must be hungry," Rhys said changing the subject.

"I am famished!" he declared.

"Then let us get a meal on the fire."

Night fell as Rhys prepared a stew from the last of the venison that he and Lawrence had hunted almost a couple weeks earlier. The meat was frozen in the crisp, late autumn air, but Rhys had already prepared it some days ago, and within the hour the warm smells from the simmering pot melted through wisps of rising steam.

"Is it ready yet, Rhys?" Sol joked impatiently. "I don't know how much longer I can last!"

"Nearly," Rhys assured him as he tasted the broth. "Another half hour by my reckoning."

"Ugh! That is ages!" Sol groaned clutching his gut in an exaggerated manner.

"I hope there is enough for all of us!" Seimon Wells called out as both he and Matthew Hault emerged from the dark woodlands surrounding them.

"I should have known that the two of you would arrive just in time to eat our food!" Lawrence laughed heartily.

"We are half an hour too early it would seem! I was rather hoping you'd have dinner ready for the moment we arrived!" Matthew replied as the two of them approached the fire and were illuminated by its warm glow.

"Well, if you don't send word of your coming beforehand, then you can hardly expect a meal on arrival!" Lawrence teased, embracing the two men one after another.

"Sol, Rhys," Seimon greeted them as he sat holding his hands up to the crackling fire.

"Yeah, good to see the two of you. Shame I can't say the same for you Lawrence!" Matthew jested.

Lawrence responded with a friendly jab to the arm. "Well, it's a shame that there isn't enough stew for you then isn't it, Hault?"

"Hey!" the mage protested. "That's not fair."

"Is there enough for me?" Seimon asked, rubbing his chest to warm up.

"Plenty—just not enough for Matthew here," Lawrence responded.

"Fine!" Matthew grumbled, sniffing the flavours that hung in the air. "I'll go catch my own deer and cook my own stew."

"By which time we will have already eaten and be warm and asleep in our tents," Sol smiled, to which Matthew sighed heavily.

"Please can I have some?" he asked begrudgingly.

"There might be some scraps left at the bottom of the pot," Rhys grinned.

"I've got a full wineskin. I'll trade you some for a bowl!"

"What else have you got?" Lawrence asked.

"No!" Matthew refused. "I've got a long time north of the White Mountains coming up. I am saving it!"

"And Rhys and I have been alone in these woods for nearly two months with nothing but water to drink," Lawrence argued, trying to persuade the mage to part with whatever he had stashed in his pack.

"Fine! But you can't have all of it; just a few sips." Rather disgruntled, the man rifled through his pack and produced a small pewter flask, handing it to Lawrence.

The older mage uncapped the flask sniffing the contents. "You always get the good stuff, Matt," Lawrence chuckled before taking a large swig.

"Just a few sips!" he reminded Lawrence, though the man ignored him.

Exhaling with a deep satisfaction, Lawrence capped the flask before tossing it across the fire to Rhys. "Here you go, lad," he issued as he did so, before licking his lips. "You've earned it!"

Tentatively, Rhys unscrewed the pewter cap and gently sniffed the flask's contents. The peaty scent of whisky swirled up from the neck of the flask, and as Rhys sipped the spirit, it swilled hot down his throat. Ensuring he did not empty the flask, he savoured several more mouthfuls before capping it and returning it to its owner.

The five men enjoyed the hot stew, and afterward there was still plenty to spare left in the pot. They chatted late into the night, catching up with one another before finally retiring when the half moon was high above them.

TWELVE

R hys drew back the canvas of the tent and was greeted by a wall of chilling air. The once verdant glade had been bleached white by a shallow powdering of snow through which only the tips of grass blades protruded. Yet Rhys's attention was not focussed upon the transformed scenery, but instead drawn to Arlas; the mage knelt poking the embers of the fire pit with his stave, rekindling flames from the ashes.

"Good morning," the southerner greeted him without returning Rhys's gaze. "By which I mean to say: 'Hello.' Whether it is a good morning or not is a matter for debate," he added looking around at the snowy ground. "I personally do not mind such weather, but I know many a man who despises the cold."

"It is fortunate that I am not one of them," Rhys replied as he took a seat beside the mage.

Arlas chuckled as if Rhys had said something funny. "Oh, you will… soon enough."

"What do you mean?" Rhys asked.

"We are about to travel north of the White Mountains. I presume you have never done so before."

"No, I haven't," Rhys confirmed.

"Then you will not fully understand when I tell you that you do not yet truly know what the cold is."

"The winters were harsh enough in Longford," Rhys replied. "It is after all, among the most northerly of villages in Gwent—and in all of Cambria, as I understand it."

"That it is," Arlas agreed. "But most consider Cambria to end where the White Range begins. Instead, it stretches much further northward, for hundreds of miles, before you finally reach the Frozen Sea. Beyond the White Mountains lies the barren Carparth Tundra: league after league of frozen wasteland that stretches far beyond the horizon in every direction. There are reasons why so few have ever made it their home.

"At night, the winds grow cold enough to freeze a man's blood in minutes. Blizzards can descend from clear skies, and flesh can turn black with icy rot. At this time of year, there is not a harsher nor more dangerous place in all of Cambria. This pilgrimage, Rhys, is not merely a journey to the Northern Circle. It is in itself a trial you must survive before you can join the Order."

"Of course! Because there's just no fun in it if you aren't literally risking life and limb is there?"

Rhys laughed, though somewhat nervously.

"Well, we wouldn't want to make it easy for you, would we, Rhys?" Seimon's voice called out as the others began to emerge from their tents.

"Arlas!" Lawrence gleamed, greeting his friend.

"Hello Lawrence," Arlas replied warmly.

"Robert has not yet arrived," Lawrence warned.

"I believe he will within the hour," the Archon assured. "I saw a man journeying this way at first light whom I suspected to be him. He was several miles behind me, but that was nearly half an hour ago now."

"Then are you to wait for him?" Lawrence asked.

Arlas remained silent for a short time as he looked at Rhys and the others. "We shall," he declared finally. "I believe he will arrive within the next hour, but if not, we shall delay a while longer. We should make ready to leave now, however; to spare any further lost time should he arrive later."

"Then I'll ready my pack," Rhys announced.

Over the next hour, Rhys, Sol, Seimon, and Matthew dismantled the camp, readying their bags for the long journey northward. Rhys was forced to unpack and repack his knapsack several times, for each time he thought he'd finished, he realised he'd failed to fit some portion of his rations or equipment inside his bulging pack. Robert Kwesi arrived just in time for breakfast, when they were readying to eat one final meal before their departure.

"Forgive me, Arlas," he apologised as he first emerged into the clearing, "I did not give myself enough time to travel back here from Orthios. I underestimated how long it would take."

"No harm done, friend," Arlas reassured, resting a hand on the mage's shoulder. "You are here now. That is what matters—and just in time for breakfast."

"He's got better timing than you two!" Lawrence smirked turning to look at both Seimon and Matthew.

"Seems a little *too* convenient if you ask me!" Matthew uttered loudly as he too came up to welcome the man's return.

"Hello Matthew," Robert greeted him very formally.

"Robert, how many years have we known each other?"

"Nearly ten now," Robert Kwesi replied with a perplexed expression.

"And in that time, how many times have I told you—call me Matt!?"

"I'm sorry... Matt," the man apologised, fearing he had offended.

"You have never told *me* to call you Matt," Rhys remarked jovially as he choked the drawstring of his bulging knapsack tightly.

"Well, perhaps you should read something into that!" Matthew uttered disdainfully as he turned to leer at Rhys.

Fooled for a moment, Rhys fell silent until Matthew cracked a smile.

"Relax, North, I'm just messing with you!" he chuckled looking back to Robert. "Both of you! I'm just trying to get you to lighten up a bit, Robert."

The leftover venison accompanied by a serving of beans made an adequate last meal before the pots and pans were cleaned and packed away. Heaving taught the straps to his bag, Rhys fastened quick the buckles and stepped back in trepidation, fearing the seams of the pack might split open at any moment. But in spite the swollen contents, the stitching held out and Rhys now faced only the trial of lifting the luggage on to his shoulders. For a moment longer he was spared the task as Lawrence approached him.

"I have something for you," he announced.

"I seriously don't think I can get any more into this bag... and I know I have already said those exact words on more than one occasion this morning, only to be proven wrong; but I think it may be true this time!"

"Here," Lawrence presented Rhys with a thick wolf fur cloak. "I think this may prove more useful outside your pack anyway."

"Thank you!" Rhys exclaimed gratefully as the mage wrapped it over his shoulders, allowing the pelt to drape down over his back and chest. The fur had a faint musty smell to it, but was plush and soft to the touch, and relieved Rhys of any sense of chill.

"You are going to need it." Lawrence shifted suddenly to a more sombre tone. "It is fiercely cold on the Carparth Tundra. Not many can survive its conditions this side of autumn. The journey itself will change you, Rhys. Making it as far as the Northern Circle will require you to give all that you have. Do not lose faith, and do not succumb to winter's grasp."

"Thank you, Lawrence," Rhys breathed, wrapping the pelt now more tightly around himself, his gut knotting anxiously.

"Good luck." Lawrence shook his hand, offering a final warm but grave smile, and turned to walk away. His back was turned, but Rhys could read his mentor nonetheless; the man clearly had doubts that Rhys would return from this journey. Lawrence had just bid Rhys a final farewell.

Rhys donned his heavy pack and joined Seimon, Sol, Matthew, and Robert as they waited by the northern rim of the glade whilst Arlas spoke privately with Lawrence.

"The two of them go way back," Seimon passed comment, noticing Rhys observe the men.

"He was the first of us that Arlas recruited—after the Purge that is," Matthew added.

Rhys looked to Matthew, eager to draw from many rising questions, but before he could do so, Arlas hugged Lawrence and began to make his way towards them.

The archon gathered up his own belongings, and threw a hefty pack across his broad shoulders, before picking up his dark wood staff. There was one final item the man retrieved: a bundle measuring just under six feet in length, bound in linen so as to conceal its contents. As he approached the five men, he passed it to Rhys.

"It is important this remains tightly wrapped. Do not let it contact your skin, or anyone else's for that matter. It must remain pure —untainted until the time of the ritual," Arlas explained releasing it into Rhys's hands.

"What is it?" Rhys asked, though he suspected he knew the answer.

"Currently it is a length of virginal elder oak, untouched and uninfluenced by any. It is what we call: unbound. The binding ritual shall see it altered as it fuses to your soul. Should the ritual prove a success, the secrets in your blood shall be kindled into flame that in turn will forge from the oak a staff, reflective of all that is arcane within you."

Rhys nodded with a nervous grin as he tried not to ponder the careful phrasing Arlas had used: *'Should the ritual prove a success.'* Deciding he had no further questions, Rhys strapped the bundled length of wood to the side of his pack as the others had done so with their staves, and stood in silence awaiting Arlas's next words.

"The Northern Circle lies one hundred leagues dead north of here. Three days' hard pace will see us to the village of Northcrest, a settlement straddling the verge of Alder's Pass, our route through the White Range. Heading through the mountain passage will see off the better part of a day, delivering us to the open plains of the Carparth Tundra. From there forth, it shall be a further six-day voyage over the frozen wastes, until we reach the henge on the eve of the solstice, in time for Rhys's binding." He paused to look over the group of them. "You four have made the journey before, and so you know what lies ahead of us. But Rhys, you know little of the road to come. Is there anything you wish to ask before we set off?"

Rhys shook his head silently.

"Very well. Seimon lead on."

With that, Seimon turned to head deep into the forest and the rest of them followed. Matthew and Robert were close behind Seimon, whilst Rhys took up position between Sol and Arlas at the rear. There was little of a path to follow, merely the remnants of a trail overgrown from lack of use that appeared intermittently and offered little ease in terrain from the rest of the forest floor. The light powdering of snow that covered the wood had thawed within an hour of them setting off, however the temperature rose little throughout the day. Yet Rhys was easily kept warm by the pace they held and the cloak tucked around his torso.

The pines drew closer together as they ventured further and further into the depths of Highwood. In the absence of a path, they wove their own, around the towering trees, over large moss-covered rocks, and beneath the occasional suspended trunk. Onwards they trekked, until the trees hugged so close together it became an effort to pass between them. Feathered curtains of needles meshed together to barricade the way ahead, and branches snagged on their packs like woody talons attempting to snare the sylvan trespassers. The wood succeeded in its attempts to stifle their pace, yet on they pushed, parting the vast labyrinth of emerald boughs. But of all the difficulties of the route they fought along, the overbearing shadows cast from the surrounding pines were what irked Rhys the most; even as midday approached the wood seemed dim and murky.

When eventually they pierced through the surrounding emerald veil to a gushing runlet, Rhys felt he could finally catch his breath in open air. Filling their waterskins from the creek, they rested for a moment as the afternoon sun cut down along the channel of the watercourse. Glancing to the woods that bordered the far side of the rivulet, Rhys sighed with relief at the sight of thinning forestry.

"The wood is less dense ahead," Sol remarked as he sat beside Rhys, uttering the first words spoken by the party for several hours. "From here on, the continent grows more barren with each passing mile, and you will notice the temperature drops quite rapidly. It is important you remain in high spirits!"

"How bad is it? Really?" Rhys asked. "You have made the journey before, for *your* joining. Was it really as terrible as everyone has implied?"

"Yes. And no," he answered cryptically. "It is certainly no trivial task to reach the Northern Circle. The worst part is the cold; it is as terrible as anyone has told you, and worse still. It seeps into your bones, wears you down. If you let it, it will suffocate all hope within you. There is little that can be done to escape it, for there is scarcely refuge to be found north of the White Mountains.

"That said, the journey is by no means impossible. There is beauty to be found in the Carparth Tundra; sights beheld nowhere else in this world. There are those who make their lives upon the ice, living on the frozen wastes year-round: The Carparthians. Before the Cambrian expansion, the Carparthians were the indigenous people of the northern realms. With the spread of the empire, much of their culture was wiped from the continent, but the empire seldom ventured north of the range, and thus to this day the descendants of those that lived beyond the White Mountains still roam the frozen wastes.

"Though the Carparthians are more primal in their culture, and tales of their kind speak of men that are bestial in nature, they are as human as you or I. That they have endured the brutal elements for millennia, making their lives upon the tundra, shows that such a place might not be as unforgiving as one first believes. With caution, and knowledge of the land, it can be withstood for great lengths. You are with five members of the Circle of Magi, all of whom have made this journey once before, and some several times more. Though we do not understand the ways of the wastes as well as its native inhabitants, we know more than enough to see you weather it. But—you must not only survive the journey to the Northern Circle, but arrive there in time for the coming solstice. That is the true challenge that lies ahead."

"Thank you," said Rhys, feeling now less anxious for what was to come.

Setting off again, they crossed over the stream and marched into the sparser woodland that stretch from its northern bank. Without rest, they trekked through the dimness of dusk and into the oncoming night to make up what time they had lost that morning. Still they spoke little whilst they walked, though Matthew and Seimon chuckled to themselves as they made continual reference to a particular tavern wench in Northcrest they both seemed eager to see. Stars twinkled against the flawless night, gleaming in full glory without an early moon to outshine them. Yet for all the heavens' magnificence, the eventual waxing half-moon's rise was well greeted, for the silver light it cast dispelled the gloom that obscured their way.

At a late hour, they finally made camp. Rhys and Sol pitched the tents by the light of their wands whilst Seimon and Matthew gathered up kindling and Robert foraged through the dark for the evening meal. During this time, Arlas stood in silence, gazing vacantly across the treeline, out to the star speckled horizon, never uttering a word nor straying from the spot.

Seimon and Matthew could be heard upon their return several moments before they appeared through the trees. The two of them laughed and jested at one another, and Rhys could only suspect their conversation topic had returned once more to the woman in Northcrest.

"I am telling you, Seimon, she is not interested in you. You have only met her twice anyway. I have seen her four times. She has a thing for me, you see. She wants herself a *real* man!" Matthew spoke loudly as they entered the clearing.

"And a real man is exactly what she gets with me. A good looking one at that. Last thing she wants is an ugly bastard like you!" Seimon boasted.

"A real man, huh? I may not be the prettiest, but I've seen you pissing and I am twice '*the man*' you are!" Matthew jibed.

"Well, I have never had any complaints about my manhood. It does the job just fine!"

"Boys, you realise that girl is probably married by now," Sol involved himself in the conversation.

"Wouldn't stop me though!" Matthew responded quickly.

Sol retorted with an expression of disgust.

"I'm kidding, Sol! Even I have rules about another man's wife."

"I'd be tempted though... if it were her," Seimon put in, not alluding to whether he was joking or not.

"Who is this girl then?" The apparent importance of the discussion had piqued Rhys's interest.

"Her name is Charlotte. She works in the White Hart in Northcrest," Seimon began.

"With looks that will melt the heart of any man!" Matthew interrupted. "Silky raven hair, pale flawless skin and..." Matthew cupped his hands and held them in front of his chest.

"I see," Rhys smiled.

"Don't listen to them. She is a good-looking girl, yes. But she isn't the goddess these boys describe her as," Sol insisted.

"Come on Sol, she is pretty high up there! Just because you are hung up on that Helena girl!"

Sol remained silent, acting for a time as if Seimon's comment had gone by completely unregistered, yet against his efforts a smile slowly rose across his cheeks.

"What's this? I haven't heard of this girl, Sol!" Rhys jibed. "Come on, who is she?"

"She was just some girl from back home," Sol uttered dismissively.

"That Sol wants to—"

"That I was friends with!" Sol interjected, preventing Seimon from continuing. "I always thought I'd end up with her..." he confessed. "But then I joined the circle, and I haven't seen her since."

With that, Matthew made a snoring noise. "Why do you have to make it sound so boring, Sol?"

Sol punched Matthew in the arm before the two of them proceeded to wrestle. It was not long before Matthew had Sol pinned and the smaller of the mages was calling for mercy. Matthew released him and the two climbed to their feet grinning.

"Tell you what Sol, when we get back I am taking you to the brothel in Highshire. I promise you, you'll forget all about Henrietta!"

"Helena!" Sol corrected him.

"You have an obsession with that place, Matt!" Seimon sniggered.

"What can I say? They serve great ale."

"I'm sure that's what it is," Rhys remarked sarcastically in faux whispers.

"I bet you have seen your fair share of action, North!" Seimon turned his indiscriminate attention to Rhys. "A lad as beautiful as you must be fending off women left, right, and centre."

Rhys hesitated in response.

"I don't know, he's too young and innocent, I reckon," Matthew argued

"Leave him alone lads. That is his business," Sol spoke.

"Come on, Sol, we are all friends here. So North, have you ever...?" Seimon asked.

"Honestly, I can't say I have," Rhys said

truthfully.

"Fair enough," Matthew returned. "Seimon here hasn't either!"

"You know I have, Matt! You have even walked in on me!"

"Doesn't count if it was by yourself!"

"I wasn't by... Shut up Matt! Don't listen to him, Rhys!"

The four of them laughed loudly.

"Right, shall we get the fire going then?" Sol questioned.

With that, the four of them quickly arranged some of the wood they had collected into a pile and surrounded it with rocks. Rhys drew his wand and ignited the wood before they gathered around the flames to absorb the warmth emitted.

"Robert!" Seimon called out after a time as he spied the southerner emerging from the trees with what appeared to be a couple of parsnips and a handful of mushrooms.

"Good man!" Matthew cried as he saw the food he was holding.

"This was all I could find," he explained. "Everything else was either poisonous or spoilt."

"Nah, this is great!" Sol assured him as he took the parsnips from Robert.

Skewering them upon two sharpened sticks, the men roasted the parsnips over the fire whilst they fried the mushrooms in a pan. During this whole time, Arlas had not once moved or made an utterance of any kind. Still, he peered off at the horizon, as if petrified by the starlight. The other four seemingly took no notice of this strange behaviour, though Rhys thought it queer. Instead, the other magi merely left a portion of food in the pan, before turning in for the night.

The next day, Rhys awoke to find Sol and Robert still resting. He exited the tent quietly to avoid disturbing them. The woodlands had been utterly transformed overnight, turned monochrome by the descent of heavy snowfall. The white blanket laid thick across the forest floor and heaped in balancing clumps over the evergreen branches, that with the glow of dawn, glinted and sparkled with a wintery brilliance.

Matthew and Seimon had not yet emerged from the second tent, but Arlas stood amidst the ice in very much the same position he had been the previous night. The mage was dusted across his head and shoulders with a powdering of snow. For a moment Rhys wondered if he had even moved since last he saw him, but footprints through the snow and the empty, clean cooking pan revealed that he had at some stage retired for the evening.

"Good morning Rhys," Arlas greeted him without turning.

"How did you know it was me?" Rhys asked in astonishment.

"It is hard to explain to one who has not felt the sensation, but magi and creatures of arcane nature emit an aura of energy that can be sensed by others of their kind. Your aura differs, for you are not yet a mage." Arlas still did not turn to face Rhys.

"Interesting." Rhys walked to stand beside him.

"You wish to ask if something is troubling me?"

Rhys was astounded for a second time now. "Err... yes. Is there? You seem somewhat vacant." Rhys knew Arlas little, but his behaviour since they had made camp did seem unusual.

"I fear something is troubling me indeed," Arlas spoke very calmly. "Alas, I cannot tell you what it is."

"I see," Rhys replied, now confused as to why Arlas had even instigated the conversation.

"You misinterpret me, Rhys. I cannot tell you, for I am uncertain myself as to what it is."

"I am not sure I understand," Rhys returned, struggling to follow the riddles in which Arlas spoke.

"I am filled with unease. It is a feeling that I cannot attribute to anything in particular. Perhaps it is the Grey that stirs this sense of unrest in me, but I am not certain as to why now, for I know little more than I did months earlier. Perhaps *that* is what troubles me: the fact that despite the efforts I have made to learn more, I am still in the dark. The future of Cambria is uncertain... as is my part in it."

Rhys stepped in front of the man to face him, but Arlas still stared vacantly towards the horizon. Rhys studied him, unsure whether or not the mage's words were intended to convey a deeper meaning.

"I appreciate the discussions we share, Rhys —and I appreciate your discretion," with those words, Arlas looked Rhys in the eyes solemnly.

Rhys issued a silent nod as he understood what was being asked of him. Arlas then turned to look behind them to see the others now emerging from the tents.

Rhys trudged through the crunching snow on wearisome legs when first they set out, barely recovered from the extended march of the previous day. His bag sunk heavily upon aching shoulders and his head fell to gaze at his trundling feet. But with the passing miles, the pains that ailed him seemed to fade. His pace quickened and he stepped lighter, now lifting his head to glance about the shimmering woods, as slowly but surely, the way began to incline. The pines spread further from one another whilst their heights gradually diminished and their limbs became more and more scantly needled, until by noon's approach, the trunks seemed almost naked and malnourished.

The woodland thinned enough now, that ahead of them, the jagged peaks of the White Mountains grazed upwards from behind the horizon. The range rose steadily with each mile, ascending higher and higher as it reached up to the sky until its domineering presence formed a single immense ridge of rock and ice that walled off all that laid beyond. The mountains seemed not far away now, yet still they grew larger and larger, and Rhys could scarcely believe it when Sol informed him they would not reach the foot of the range until the following evening.

Through the afternoon, the party became more talkative, and Rhys shared a number of conversations with Sol, Seimon, and Matthew. After a time, Matthew and Seimon spoke of a venture to a village bordering the West Band earlier in the year.

"The village had suffered several raids by goblins," Matthew explained. "Goblins are more animals than sapient beings. Their intelligence is generally limited beyond their capacity for theft and murder. They live in packs and rarely approach human settlements. But some of them have learnt to wield weapons they find, and others even make use of armour."

"Some of the really smart ones even learn to craft their own weapons, such as the ones that were raiding this village," Seimon added.

"Yes. This particular clan was abnormally large. Your typical tribe of forest goblins normally consists of around a dozen or so. There were closer to thirty of these," Matthew continued.

"How did you deal with them?" Rhys asked.

"Well, they were attacking the village under the cover of dark every month or so, stealing from the farmers' stores and slaughtering their livestock. We decided it would be best for us to wait for their next attack and spring our own ambush, as opposed to trying to track them down in the forest," Matthew answered.

"As it turned out, they were *really* smart, striking on the full moon when they had the best visibility. We sprung a trap, figuring if we killed a couple of them the rest would flee and wouldn't trouble the village any further. But the little buggers wouldn't give up—they fought us until every single one of them was dead!" Seimon exclaimed with his own disbelief.

"Unusual, considering how rarely goblins come into contact with man," Sol remarked, baffled by the story.

"Exactly what we thought," Matthew agreed. "It was as if they were driven to desperation by something. We decided to check the forest afterwards to investigate, but we scoured that wood for days and found no trace of their camp."

"I reckon they must have been travelling several leagues to reach the village, which makes the whole story all the more peculiar," Seimon added, equally confused by the matter.

"It would seem as if this, like many other strange happenings, may too be connected to the Grey," Sol suggested. "Speaking of which," he continued, "what did you find in your travels to Longford and Glenontauch?"

"Not a great deal," Matthew confessed. "At

Longford, the curse is still there for all who venture near enough to see. The land is soaked with a sickly grey and the air chills as you approach, but from my understanding, it was far worse on the day it struck. Glenontauch is much the same, though the isle has recovered more in the greater time that has passed since its fall. Every soul on the island perished that day, and still nothing lives there now."

"We tried everything we could think of to learn more," Seimon explained. "We cast several rituals in order to try and discover something from the residual magic that lingers there. But as Arlas said, it is unlike anything we have seen before. If it is truly ancient in nature, then it predates even our order."

"I believe one would have to find themselves in a village as the curse was striking to learn anything of use. Alas, we cannot know when or where it will next strike. It is a shame that Arlas was not able to take advantage of the time he was in Longford." Matthew lamented.

"Have you yet heard Rhys's account of the events that day?" Sol asked them.

"Not in any great detail, I must say," Matthew responded, clearly interested in hearing the story from Rhys's perspective.

"I am not sure what more you can learn from my account," Rhys confessed. "Surely you have already heard everything from Arlas?"

"But Arlas was not there when the curse

first struck," Seimon reasoned.

"A fair point," Rhys agreed, proceeding thence to tell his account of what happened that day. The story by now had lost its emotional ties from the sheer amount of times Rhys had replayed the memories in his head.

"Fascinating!" Matthew exclaimed when he had finished. "It must have been traumatic to endure. I am not sure if this helps, but what I now know may yet prove useful when we return to our investigations."

"You just reminded me!" Sol interjected. "Robert," he called out to the southerner who was walking some way ahead of them in silence. The man halted at the call of his name. Turning, he waited for the others to catch him up.

"What did you discover in Orthios? Did the merchant have the writings he claimed to?"

"No," the man responded abruptly.

"Then what was it?"

"It was nothing of significance… an occultist scroll several centuries old. I found a man to translate the text, but it referred to nothing that might help us."

"A shame," Sol sighed. "I truly believed it might have been useful in our search."

They journeyed on in silence for a time, walking past nightfall once again, yet they were forced to stop earlier than they had done so the previous evening, for in the evening sky had arisen swathes of cloud that in a matter of hours concealed all above. Thus, the night lacked any illumination by way of star or moonlight, and they found themselves wandering in near enough total darkness, alleviated only by light conjured from their wands.

When making camp, Rhys took it upon himself to set several snares around their campsite, as those set by Robert on the previous evening had failed on all accounts. It was difficult to see, even in the magical glow he had cast from his wand, but Rhys was sure he had set them in passages likely to be used by rabbits and hares. They ate modestly and huddled closely round the fire as snowflakes floated weightlessly in the breeze. Arlas was still particularly quiet, but he was far less vacant than he had been the previous night. A few jokes were cracked, and a story or two told, yet the cold and tired men saw fit to retire early that night.

Come dawn the snow had deepened, and the sky still loomed beneath a ubiquitous layering of cloud. Checking his snares, Rhys's spirits were raised. A rabbit sat quivering in the deep snow, snagged around the hind leg by one of Rhys's cunningly placed traps. Breaking its neck with a well-practised action, he returned to the camp to a series of congratulations. What followed of course was the persistent light-hearted ribbing of Robert for his failings the previous night. The decision was made to save the meat for when they were north of Alder's pass, and by the time of their departure from the temporary camp, the flesh had already frozen solid to preserve the meat from spoilage.

The day's journey saw what remained of Highwood thin to nothing, and the land rise upwards into foothills steeped in snow and ice. The White Mountains loomed ever grander, their summits now vanishing amidst the cloud. Alder's Pass became distinguishable: a passage furrowed deep and narrow over the saddle of two gargantuan stone sentinels that shouldered the convergence of the eastern and western ridges.

Finally, with the impending dusk, Rhys made out the distant details of the village of Northcrest, nestled within a crease where the feet of both mountains crumpled together. When eventually they drew closer, the small hamlet appeared even clearer. The quaint and remote settlement consisted entirely of cabins constructed of wood and stone, few rising higher than a single storey tall. Wisps of smoke rose steadily from chimneys, conjuring in Rhys's mind the vision of log fires roaring hot in stone hearths. Over a month had passed since last he had slept indoors, and now he grew excited at the prospect of a night spent in the warmth of a tavern.

Night descended quickly, bringing with it snow that spiralled and swirled about in the air, neither rising nor falling throughout the hamlet as they approached. Barely a soul stirred through the frozen streets, all tucked warm away, not daring to brave the outdoors. Those that did wander the snows did so in the direction of the hamlet's singular tavern

'*The White Hart*' was the smallest Inn Rhys had ever set eyes on. Undoubtedly, they would be sharing rooms. Seimon and Matthew were now giddy with the hope of seeing Charlotte, and the two men forced each other aside to be the first through the door. Matthew proved the victor, shoving Seimon clean away before quickly composing himself as he stepped into the inn.

Rhys followed in behind Robert and Sol, greeted by a most welcomed blast of warm air. The alehouse was especially quiet, with just three strangers sat at the bar, each of them drinking quietly alone. Matthew and Seimon rushed straight to the counter, yet the woman they were in search off was nowhere to be seen.

Rhys and Sol went to take seats at the nearest table, whilst Robert dragged a couple extra chairs over to allow the six of them to sit. Arlas was the last to enter the quaint tavern, stomping his snow-covered boots on the mat as he did so. The man glanced over at Matthew and Seimon as they pestered a tavern girl as to the whereabouts of Charlotte. Shaking his head with a subtle grin, he too made his way to the bar and spoke with the innkeeper stood behind it.

Only as Rhys removed his pack and placed it alongside his chair did he notice the ache in his neck and back. It had been three days' hard walking, the entire time shouldering a pack of far greater weight than he was accustomed to. He collapsed into one of the pine chairs to find it disappointingly uncomfortable, and let out a disgruntled sigh. Sol and Robert sat opposite him, but the three men did not speak. Instead, they simply took solace in the warmth for a time. Rhys struggled not to close his eyes and snooze right there; before he could do so, Arlas approached with three heavy brass keys in hand.

"You two are in a room together," he directed to Rhys and Sol. "And Robert, you will share with me."

"Thank you," he replied as he peered past Arlas at Seimon and Matthew who somehow already had tankards in hand, swigging the contents as quickly as they could.

"I figured it best to put those two together. I somehow doubt they plan to retire early this evening," Arlas chuckled as he again turned his gaze to Seimon and Matthew.

The two slammed their tankards back down upon the bar at the same time, having tied with one another in their drinking contest. They wasted no time, ordering another pint each before they had even wiped their mouths.

"Then again..." Sol said, "maybe they'll be out cold sooner than we thought."

"I plan on having a few drinks myself before retiring tonight, if the three of you would care to join me?" Arlas offered, pulling out a chair.

"I am game as always!" Sol smiled, winking at Rhys.

"Not for me, thanks," Robert refused as he picked up the key to his and Arlas's room from the table. "I will see you all in the morning." With that the man took his bag and left their company.

Rhys was exhausted, but he did not want to pass up the first opportunity to share a drink with the rest of the company, though in truth he longed nothing more than for the comfort of a bed.

"I'll have *one*," he agreed, as Sol and Arlas's eyes fell upon him.

Six pints of strong Ale later, Rhys found himself in drunken song with Sol, Seimon, and Matthew. Arlas did not join the ensemble, but simply observed from his seat with a grin from ear to ear, all the while the other patrons stared at the four men with disapproving looks.

Arlas appeared to have an unnatural constitution, as he was unmistakably sober. When their song ended, Rhys slumped back into his chair once again, struggling through his muddled thoughts to determine how he had gotten to this point in the evening. Last orders had come and gone, and the five of them put away the remainder of their beer. The thought of the next day's travel dawned on them all at that moment, and the group decision was made to turn in.

THIRTEEN

The next morning, Rhys awoke to a parched mouth and spinning head. He forced down a breakfast of bland porridge, throughout which he remained uncertain if he needed to vomit; an excess of water eventually returned him to a better state. The others, it seemed, showed no ill effects of the previous night's affairs. They made no mention of Rhys's all too apparent grogginess, but instead simply chuckled quietly to themselves, occasionally shooting him a sympathetic grin.

It was before dawn that they set forth. A thick freezing fog gripped the air, smothering both the land and sky. Ice crystals glistened in the hanging murk, and the village was very quick to disappear behind them. A shivering spasm clawed its way up Rhys's spine when a gust of chilling air swept down from the mountain pass, forcing him to clench tightly the fur about his shoulders.

They climbed the steepening saddle blindly towards Alder's pass, the mountains' presence ever felt, yet their rough and snowy faces loomed beyond the curtain of gloom around them. When dawn arrived, the first beams of sunlight cleft through the mists, dispelling their freezing swells and lifting the gloom from the range. Within moments, the clouds sailed apart and the towering peak scraping against the highest wisps of atmosphere were revealed to the golden sunrise.

The snow had formed an icy crust overnight, and now crunched and shattered underfoot like glass. The refrozen slush had been smoothed by weathering, and to Rhys's dismay, his boots could find little purchase on the treacherously slippery terrain. On numerous occasions, his legs slid out from under him, leaving him to slam hard and top-heavy against the alpine slopes. With every fall, he slipped and skidded back down the path, halted on each instance by the magi behind him, who with planted staffs and widespread balance, grabbed hold of him by the strappings of his pack, heaving Rhys back to his feet to repeat the trial of ascent once more.

On they clambered, up into the range, until the foothills domed several furlongs below them, and walls of rude black rock exposed themselves from beneath the ice on either side of the path. The incline fell to a more forgiving angle as they neared the lip of the saddle, and the bare stone walls that formed the mountain pass narrowed and grew taller, until they were trekking through a choking gorge that pressed imposingly on their flanks. The cleft only deepened the further they marched, and before long, all view of the White Range was obscured by the parallel curtains of stone that channelled twistingly northwards, leaving naught but a thin trail of grey sky above them.

When the track levelled, the canyon walls rose to a height of forty fathoms or more above their heads, yet beyond them, the peaks stood thousands higher. Snow sprinkled down in sporadic bursts, and torrents of wind occasionally buffeted their way into the rocky gulf, but Alder's path proved an easy and safe enough route to cross the jagged range. By late day, the gorge parted, opening to the cloud-streaked skies above. The pressing stone walls sloped gradually into sweeping banks steeped in fresh snows, and with one final meander, gave out to a view of the Carparthian horizon. In that instant, all shelter the pass offered subsided, and shrieking gales slammed hard into the party of men.

Rhys squinted his gaze against the freezing wind and peered through tearing eyes in awe at a land so alien and bleak, that his heart sank heavily with dread. League after league of blank and featureless wasteland stretched out in an endless expanse of snow and ice that reached to every horizon and curved further beyond.

With the dying light, they began their descent across a treacherous glacial slope that ground down from the western peaks, carving into the hills below. Rhys looked back in sorrow to view the northern faces of the range. The sun-facing slopes were bathed in a scarlet blaze, whilst to the east, immense shadows were cast down from the daunting ridge that grew fast as the sun's orb sank behind the mountains.

They fought down the glacier against the fists of the howling winds until the amber dusk faded to sapphire blue. As they clambered over a ledge of ice, a vast cave emerged into view below. Arlas gestured for them to wait outside the entrance whilst he inspected further.

The ice cavern did not stretch far, reaching only twenty yards or so from the mouth to the far wall. The floor was smooth, bare ice that sloped upwards, flattening towards its far end enough for them to make camp upon it. Arlas moved along the wall of the cave, examining it and the roof above for any cracks or flaws in the ice that might betray them to a glacial shift during the night. Satisfied in his inspection, he signalled the rest of them to follow.

They pitched camp against the far wall, sheltered from the ripping winds. The downward slope of the floor allowed cold air to flow out whilst trapping the warm air in a pocket of the cave where the two tents were erected. They melted snow for water using tinder gathered from Highwood and dined sparingly on the rabbit they had saved from the previous day. The tents managed to retain some heat whilst they slept, though it was still one of the coldest nights Rhys had ever experienced.

Morning dawned long before the sun finally rose beyond the southerly peaks, and without delay, they continued on down the immense river of ice. They tethered themselves to one another round the waist for the descent, Arlas explaining to Rhys that concealed beneath the layers of thin snow sank deep pits that tunnelled into the churning belly of the glacier.

"Crevasses," the mage named them. "Few men ever notice their presence until a single wrong step sends them plummeting to their death, or far worse a fate. To fall down beneath the mighty sheets of ice is to be imprisoned with no hope of escape, to either starve, or be crushed when next the frozen giant crawls onward."

"Sounds unpleasant," Rhys grimaced, quadruple checking his lifeline was secure. "Note to self: try not to fall into a crevasse."

"Tread carefully," Matthew smirked as he forcefully patted Rhys across the back, unnerving him further.

"Just keep your footing to bare ice as much as possible and you shall be fine," Sol assured him.

"If you fall into a crevasse, we will pull you back out," Robert added, though his tone did little to bring comfort to Rhys.

They navigated the crinkled glacier with tentative steps, tediously negotiating ridges and dips to steer clear of snow. The occasional hums of shifting ice deep below reverberated across the glacial expanse, yet Rhys found it difficult to believe the vast body of frozen water migrated in the way the others described. The slow downward progression saw the weather shift from flawless skies and still air currents to swirling clouds that rode in on sweeping bitter winds. The gales arrived fierce and howling, yet blew over in the space of minutes, returning once more to fickle clear conditions.

By the inward drawing of dusk, they had reached the sheer edge of the glacier that dropped jaggedly to solid ground below. They scaled the ice cliff by jutting steps and pitted handholds in the frozen wall, and to Rhys's relief, finally reached the foot of the glacier as the last light of day dissolved. Hundreds of gallons of meltwater spewed in white torrents from the ice face, pooling into swells that gushed forth in streams across the gravel, converging in winding gullies to form a single molten river that carved eastward over the tundra.

They made camp beside the black waters, filling their skins from the biting flow. Their small fire quickly burned away, and that night Rhys shivered furiously whilst battering winds unrelentingly rippled the canvas of the tent. The tent-poles quivered violently, and Rhys was certain the shelter would be torn from over them, yet the guy-ropes endured, and eventually he succumbed to exhaustion.

Come sunrise, they embarked out into the

open plains. The air turned vile, burning exposed skin with its fierce chill. Rhys pulled his scarf up over his nose and drew the hood of his cloak down as low over his brow as it would stretch. His waterskin was inside his coat, for without his body heat it would surely freeze in minutes.

The snow deepened with every mile, turning loose and dry like dust that swept up from the ground when winds rose from still air in mere seconds. The temperature plummeted further, sapping all warmth from Rhys's body; even his thick fur cloak offered little protection from the vicious temperature. His nose ran and the air made his eyes water, only for his tears to freeze solid on his cheeks. The blanketing of snow continued to grow thicker until it rose well above knee height, and the party waded awkwardly on into the tundra.

Rhys's energy reserves were waning; he could feel every joint in his body beginning to seize up. He stumbled on, fighting the elements with every breath, until suddenly, he faltered. Collapsing with exhaustion to hands and knees, he slumped into a snowdrift, in that moment unable to take even one more step forwards. Sol rushed over to him, heaving Rhys out of the snow, cradling him as he began to fade. The mage rummaged for something close to his chest.

"Drink this," he urged, uncapping a pewter flask and lifting it to his lips. Rhys sipped; sweet and syrupy fluid trickled hotly across his tongue and down his throat. The amrita coursed warmly through his innards, dispersing outwards with fiery fingers that massaged his muscles, rekindling vigour throughout his body. Energy he thought lost surged, and in a matter of seconds Rhys rose back to his feet feeling totally revitalised.

"Better?" Matthew asked him, with a genuine look of concern.

Rhys nodded

"Good," smiled Seimon with a sense of relief, before, after a short moment spent regathering themselves, they pressed on, further into the snowy abyss.

For leagues further they continued that day, on and on through the endless snow plains. The magi accompanying Rhys seemed especially resilient to the elements and stood fast against all the tundra threw at them. Their hardiness inspired in Rhys his own sense of determination, and through the bitterness he strove. The gruelling day dredged on akin to the sprawling desolate landscape, and as the sun finally diminished in the sky, the stark winds once more rose to ferocious speeds, serving as harbinger to an immense blizzard that sprung out of the wastes. The snow flurry raged about them, and now even the five magi needed to muster all their resolve against the storm.

Snow plastered the men and smothered the wastes in a roaring veil of blinding white. Each step onwards was its own battle into the resisting winds, and Rhys leant forwards with most of his weight to prevent himself keeling over. His arms and legs numbed, and after a time he realised that neither he nor the others had made any headway for quite some time. Through the whiteout, Sol emerged before Rhys, stabilising himself with his staff against the air torrents.

"We cannot continue!" the mage shouted, barely audible over the screaming weather. "There is no shelter, so we must make our own!"

"How?" Rhys dismayed, his voice lost to the gales.

"We are to dig an ice cave," he explained. "Arlas will hold back the storm. Be ready!"

Rhys nodded miserably, though he was unsure what Sol had meant. He wished nothing more than to escape the blizzard, yet he feared he lacked all will necessary to do so.

Arlas forced his way ahead of them, soldiering into the prevailing wind with his staff in hand. The mage erected himself, raising his weapon high above him, and thrust against the storm with a mighty effort. A low-pitched boom rushed suddenly outwards, and a bubble of force exploded from the mage's staff. The gales and snow ceased, and the shrieking winds muffled to almost silence. Surrounding the party, projected outwards from Arlas, was a barrier of glowing energy that shielded against the blizzard raging on the far side of the protective magical dome.

Rhys stood agape, bewildered by the display

of power.

"Rhys!" Robert called out, drawing his attention away from the force-field.

Rhys turned to see the other four were frantically burrowing into the side of a snowdrift with their hands and staves. He rushed over to join them. They dug fast, shovelling aside the powdery snow with benumbed hands. Within minutes, they had carved out a cave large enough for the six of them to lie in side by side. Matthew channelled a gutter down which cold air could escape the hollow, whilst the rest of them forced their packs to the rear of the dugout and laid out all their blankets and furs. With the shelter completed, the five of them then wriggled into their hastily excavated refuge.

"Arlas!" Sol called out, signalling the mage they were done.

The force-field collapsed inwards, and suddenly the blizzard raged loudly once more. Arlas staggered around to the entrance and slid into the burrow between Seimon and Rhys. The six of them then proceeded to pile chunks of the snow they had excavated to block the entrance of the shelter, leaving only a small opening for air.

Their shelter proved effective, the winds now merely whistling overhead. The six of them heated the dugout quickly with their bodies, and though closely packed, they were comfortable enough to wait out the storm. They did not eat that evening, but simply sipped a few mouthfuls of amrita each before slipping into a light sleep.

Emerging from the bank of the snow drift the following morning, they were greeted by a dazzling sunrise. The temperature had risen, and for now at least, the winds were at bay. The party of men set off without breakfast, hurrying to make progress whilst the weather held clear. Rhys soon noticed the land begin to give way, falling now to slopes, revealing that the snowy planes they had traversed the previous day were an extended highland shelf. Before them, the snow became shallower, and after a time, the endless expanse of white ahead fractured, as the snow cover became only patches that broke open more and more frequently with the passing miles.

Brown grass bristled up ruggedly through the permafrost, interspersed with sedges, crimson moss, and weathered rocks rusted with lichen. The new terrain urged Rhys on, and throughout the morning, they descended the gradual slope of the land to the tundra lowlands, where snow coverage was sparse amidst the stark and tawny wilderness.

By noon, hunger boiled in Rhys's gut, for neither he nor the others had eaten since breakfast the previous day. Their rations were far from depleted, but they resisted the urge to delve into them, saving their supplies for later in the voyage. Instead, the magi scoured the tundra with their keen eyes for any source of nourishment. Finally, Seimon called out to the others.

"Look, over there," he said, pointing several

furlongs ahead of them.

Rhys strained his gaze, but try as he might, could not see what the mage had pointed to. The others all seemed to have sighted whatever drew Seimon's attention, for without any discussion, they all veered from their course towards it.

"Oten plants," Seimon stated, pointing to a tall weed the same bronze hue as the grass. He pulled several from the ground and handed one to each of the others.

Unsure what to do with the plant, Rhys watched as the others cleaned away the dirt from the bulging root before peeling back the woody outer surface of the plant, eating the softer interior. Rhys mimicked the others, biting into the root to find it was pleasantly sweet despite the coarse texture. Glad to have any food inside him, he ate several of the oten before they carried on. Rhys's hunger only subsided a short while, and not long later, he plodded miserably along staring at his feet, struggling his best to ignore the pangs of his gut. Not looking where he was going, he walked straight into the back of Matthew who had halted in front of him.

"Sorry," Rhys apologised, but he was hushed by Arlas, the archon pointing to something in the distance. Rhys strained his eyes to see what looked like an ibex several furlongs ahead.

Arlas extended his hand, palm parallel with the floor, and slowly lowered it. The six of them crouched low to the ground in response.

"This kill is important," Arlas spoke in hushed whispers. "We may not see a chance such as this again for days. We must succeed, or risk depleting our rations entirely before we return to Northcrest."

The rest of them nodded in agreement.

"We need as much of the meat undamaged as possible—I want you to take the shot, Seimon. Matthew, Robert: the two of you and I will creep up on its flanks and flush it toward Seimon. The wind is in our favour, but we cannot be seen. Sol, you and Rhys wait back here. I want you ready, Sol, to make the kill should our ambush go awry."

All nodded accepting their roles.

With a swift gesture of his hand, Arlas signalled the magi to draw their staffs and move out. Rhys and Sol lay prone and watched from afar as the other four men crept forwards. Seimon hugged the ground as he moved up several hundred yards and lay in wait for the animal. Meanwhile, Arlas and Matthew arced left and right, keeping low in the cover of the rugged grass, maintaining their distance from the ibex. Robert snuck his way between the tussocks, darting quietly from cover to cover, ducking in behind stones, moving only when the creature stooped his head to graze. The men edged slowly and patiently to their designated positions, all the while the ibex remained unaware of their presence.

Nearly a quarter of an hour passed before the magi found themselves set up for the ambush, yet now they all lay in wait, perfectly poised, ready to strike. Robert, who had long been hidden to Rhys, rose up from the grass and began to charge towards the animal, roaring fiercely as he did so. The prey startled and bounded away across the tundra. It was then Arlas and Matthew leapt up from their hiding spots, each swinging their weapons in sweeping arcs. From Arlas's staff licked a line of purple flames, and from Matthew's fired a ray of scorching light, both magic setting the tundra alight to form two walls of flame that channelled the creature in Seimon's direction. Fearing the fire more than its pursuer, the ibex twisted to dart back Robert's way, yet it swivelled away as a cascade of black lightning now crackled from Roberts stave, singeing the grass with fearsome thunderous claps.

Committed now to the single route towards safety, the ibex sped between the burning walls of arcane fire, straight in the direction of the final mage. The creature cleared the flaming channel the instant Seimon sprang from his position. A swing of his staff ended it all faster than Rhys's eyes could make out. The ibex fell limp mid-bound, slumping suddenly from the air to hit the ground dead but a few yards from Seimon. Rhys had seen no flames, nor electricity, or magic of any kind. It was as if an invisible arrow loosed from Seimon's stave had slain the animal clean in its stride.

A whistle cut through the air, beckoning them to re-join the other three. Sol and Rhys clambered to their feet and jogged to meet the others. As they approached the carcass of the animal, Rhys realised what attack Seimon's staff had produced. A jagged shard of steel protruded from the skull of the ibex, lodged perfectly between its two orange eyes.

"Great kill, boys!" Matthew exclaimed as he approached. "Rhys, do you have a strong stomach?"

"Stronger than most," Rhys returned warily.

"Excellent. You will need it!" the mage smirked. "I think you should drink the blood from this animal."

Rhys grinned briefly before realising the mage was not joking. "I'm sorry?" he stammered, certain he had misheard.

"It is nothing sinister, I assure you. No vampirism or blood magic, I promise!"

"Then would you care to explain why?" Rhys inquired, still somewhat sceptical.

In these conditions, we cannot afford to waste any part of the animal, and the blood is both warm and very nutritious. It is exactly what your body needs right now."

"Okay…" Rhys uttered apprehensively. After a long moment of all eyes on him, he tentatively knelt beside the animal, still uncertain whether or not he was being fooled.

"Be ready," Arlas warned as he drew a knife and pressed it to the animal's throat.

Rhys prepared himself and nodded at the

mage. Arlas nicked the animal's jugular and scarlet blood spouted suddenly from the neck. Rhys pursed his lips against the wound, grimacing as he did so. He sucked down the hot, metallic fluid with his eyes squeezed tightly closed. The flow lasted for a dozen seconds or so before it reduced to a trickle. Rhys pulled away and wiped his mouth before quickly uncapping his flask and gulping down water to alleviate the taste. The other five chuckled amongst themselves and even Robert was smiling, which was a rare sight to behold.

"Don't worry," Sol reassured. "It isn't meant to taste good. But it will keep you going for some time."

They skinned and butchered the animal quickly, dividing it amongst their packs before the meat had a chance to freeze in the wintery air. They then marched on across the rude steppe as the temperatures dropped with the impending nightfall, but as dusk arrived, they sighted a small copse that offered shelter for the evening. They made camp and gathered enough timber from the trees for a substantial fire, upon which they roasted one of the ibex legs. They dined comfortably and set up the tents in the quiet grove. They did not retire immediately, but sat around the fire in conversation for a time. The night was clear, and the stars pierced brightly through the darkness, yet they went completely unnoticed by Rhys, for his attention was drawn entirely to another spectacle that was taking place across the heavens.

Ribbons of green, blue, and red light danced in the atmosphere overhead. They rippled and melded together in a myriad of colours, seething and swaying in ethereal beauty.

"The Aurora Norteius," Sol revealed, reclining beside Rhys to share the vista of the supernatural light show taking place across the heavens. "Also known as the Northern Lights. They can only be seen past the White Mountains on the clearest of evenings."

"What are they?" Rhys asked in fascination.

"There are some things in this world even magic cannot explain. Some say they are the cold winds being set afire by the stars; some that they are the pagan god of air: Awyr who resides in the north. Others believe that it is the source of all magic in Cambria. I doubt all these stories, yet one thing remains forever true: they are of unworldly beauty!"

"They are," Rhys agreed as he gazed on in wonder.

During the next day's travel, the terrain changed once more. A vast expanse of porous black rock matted the ground for miles upon miles. The cracked and rippled surface resembled sheet ice formed across a flowing river, giving the appearance that the rock had once been molten before spilling out across the open plains where thereafter it cooled and solidified. The rock was carpeted heavily with moss and formed a jagged and pitted shelf. The surface both looked and proved treacherous to traverse, for every step risked a foot slipping into a pothole, down which one could very easily twist an ankle or snap a shin.

The shelf took the majority of the day to cross, but eventually, they made their way down from the immense rocky tableland, and the ground turned back to snow and ice, as once more it began to climb steadily to higher altitudes. In the evening, they ate their second meal of ibex, along with some snow berries they had foraged that morning. The northern lights were faintly blurred through the thin cloud layer, and Rhys spent more time gazing up at them in amazement before he slept.

He awoke the following morning to realise it was their penultimate day of travel. The snow became deep once again as the remaining miles finally began to dwindle. They came to a frozen river obstructing their route. The ice was snow covered, but the loud sound of rushing water indicated that it was too thin to walk over. They navigated across by way of a set of natural steppingstones and camped that evening aside the ice-crusted lake into which the river drained. The frozen loch stretched ahead of them for several miles, perfectly flat, an eerily peaceful.

"You okay?" Sol asked as he sat beside Rhys by the fire, sensing that he felt uneasy.

Nerves had set in over the ritual that was

to come. Thinking that he had nearly made it, that he had survived the journey this far, had only reminded Rhys that the greatest risk was still to come. The solstice was the day after next, and Rhys now was haunted by the idea it might be his last. Until this point in the journey, Rhys had thought little of the binding, but it now preyed heavily on his mind.

"Yeah," Rhys lied.

"If you want to talk, just let me know," Sol offered, putting his hand on Rhys's shoulder. "Remember, I too have been through it. I know how you feel right now!" Sol remained sat with Rhys for a few moments longer before beginning to stand.

Rhys reached out and put his hand upon Sol's. "How many people don't...?" Rhys did not utter the words.

"What do you mean?" Sol asked Rhys suspiciously.

Rhys looked at the others who were stood by the lakeside out of earshot.

"How many people don't survive the ritual?" he asked in a hushed whisper.

"What makes you think that people do not survive?"

"Does it matter how I know?" Rhys pressed, not releasing Sol's hand.

Sol sighed heavily. "Rhys... I would have told you—but it is forbidden."

"I know," Rhys nodded. "I understand. But I

must know what chance I stand!"

"Know this," Sol replied after a time of consideration, "as many survive as those who don't. Try not to dwell on the numbers, for they do not matter. It is clear to us all, that you stand a better chance than any against what is to come!"

The final day's travel began across the ice lake. The surface was thick and bore their weight with ease. Once they reached the far bank, a white expanse lay before them. The snow was deep and the day of trudging through it proved long and tiresome. As night approached, a lonely hill became visible up ahead. The singular brow stood stark and solitary against the otherwise blank canvas of the landscape.

When it drew closer, a structure atop its ridge could be distinguished standing grey against the snow. Eventually Rhys could make out huge pillars of sarsen organised into a vast circular henge. Similar stones lay flat as lintels across the tops of the pillars. Though somewhat distant, Rhys could tell that the monument was massive in scale, and up close, it would surely be an incredible sight to behold. Eventually, they reached the foot of the hill, where they came to a stop.

"This is it, Rhys: The Northern circle!" Arlas declared as he too looked upon the standing stones in awe.

"What happens now?" Rhys asked.

"The ritual takes place just before dawn, but it will need several hours to prepare. Until then, I suggest you make camp and attempt to sleep for a few hours."

Rhys nodded.

"There is one more thing, Rhys," Arlas continued, "I gave you an item to carry at the beginning of your journey. I need ask for it."

Rhys unstrapped the length of elder oak still bound tightly in its linen wrap, from the side of his pack and presented it to Arlas. The archon thanked him with a bow of the head. Sol, Matthew, Robert, and Seimon unpacked the portions of the tent they had each been carrying. Sol shook Rhys's hand and embraced him.

"As is tradition, you are to be left alone during your final night as a free man. The others will help me prepare, whilst you remain here. When the time comes, make your way up the hill to meet us," Arlas instructed.

"See you at dawn," Sol smiled meekly, taking one final look at Rhys before the five mages turned and ventured up the hillside and out of sight.

FOURTEEN

R hys struggled to sleep. His body was exhausted, but his mind restless. The tent had taken some time to erect by himself, and the lack of other bodies inside it meant the air within remained too cool for comfort. But he must have finally drifted off, for he found himself suddenly awoken. Something had stirred him. A voice? A whisper? Something so subtle and quiet that he doubted his senses. Was it merely his imagination? A dream that still lingered in his mind? No, something was beckoning him.

Looking around, he could see it was still dark out. He had no clue as to the time. Stepping out of the tent he stared up to the night sky. The full moon shone with an intensity he had never seen before, casting the world below in an ethereal silver light that glistened across the shimmering snow, whilst all around the atmosphere quivered with fiery auroras. The voice, still indistinguishable, called once more to him, across the icy breeze that washed through the air.

Rhys turned to face the hill. The henge of stone that was the Northern Circle sat as a silhouette at its peak against the raging colours of the Northern Lights. It summoned him. Rhys slowly edged forward, his bare feet crunching softly in the snow. Climbing the slope step by step, the circle drew gradually nearer. His heart pumped so powerfully in his chest that his pulse throbbed through every fibre in his being. His breathing was exaggerated and slow, the crisp air swirling in and out of his lungs in long puffs. Never before had death been so near. Never before had he felt so alive.

The brow of the hill passed beneath his feet, and Rhys found himself stood before the henge in all its magnitude. The stones towered thirty feet high; single blocks of sarsen chiselled into massive menhirs. Together, the gargantuan pillars formed a perfect circle of eleven standing stones, atop which were lain equally vast lintels carved of the same rock. The sarsen pillars and lintels were covered head to foot in elaborate carvings of runes from a language lost to time.

The floor of the circle was smooth stone, its surface marked with the same runes, centred in which was an expansive, round altar. Perfectly straight lines were carved into the floor, stretching from each of the surrounding pillars and converging on an altar. The altar itself was engraved with various magical glyphs that seemed to direct all the other lines etched throughout the henge in towards a central focal point at the heart of the monument, up from which, a length of elder oak stood erect. The ancient wood, protruding from a slot within the stone, reflected white in the moonlight; perfectly smooth, completely lacking any blemishes in the grain.

Ahead of Rhys, within the circle, forming an arc around the altar, stood five colossal triliths that towered taller than all the other stones of the henge. Beneath each of the trilithons stood the hooded figure of a mage. The magi were adorned in the same vestments they had worn the night of the conclave; their faces obscured in shadow. Each man held in front of them their staff, gripped tightly in both hands. The dark robes and staff of Arlas distinguished the archon stood beneath the central great trilithon.

"Rhys North," Arlas's voice boomed, echoing deeply with an arcane essence. "Cast off your garments."

Rhys hesitantly stripped naked and discarded his clothes in a pile. He did not feel the cold; adrenaline coursed thickly through his veins, boiling his blood with every pulse of his heart.

"Step forward into the circle!" Arlas commanded.

Rhys placed a foot forwards, slowly lowering his bare sole onto the icy stone of the henge. Nervously edging onwards, he passed between the massive sarsen pillars, setting foot within the Northern Circle. As he passed through the threshold, he felt his senses suddenly awaken to a potent magical energy that seemed to permeate existence itself. The runes beneath his feet grew hot, and as he looked down, the carvings in the stone began to glow a searing white.

"Repeat these words as you hear them, Rhys North," Arlas boomed. "Here dies the man I was, and from his ashes shall be forged an instrument of valour, justice, and virtue!"

Taking a deep breath, Rhys repeated the words, "Here dies the man I was, and from his ashes shall be forged an instrument of valour, justice, and virtue!"

"I accept my duty to serve and protect, and am willing to make any sacrifice in doing so," Arlas's voice echoed once more.

"I accept my duty to serve and protect," Rhys declared, his own voice seeming disembodied as it carried throughout the henge, "and am willing to make any sacrifice in doing so."

"I hereby give myself: mind, body, and soul, to serve the Circle of Magi, now and forevermore."

"I hereby give myself:" Rhys swore, knowing these could be his final words, "mind, body and soul, to serve the Circle of Magi, now and forevermore!"

"Approach the altar!" Arlas commanded.

Rhys trapsed forwards across the stone as the runes continued to illuminate beneath his feet. Reaching the altar, he paused at the base of the steps which led up to its surface.

"Ascend!" Arlas commanded.

Climbing the three stone steps, Rhys halted atop the altar, now within reach of the length of elder oak.

"Turn to face the dawn."

Stepping around the circumference of the stone, Rhys faced away from the five magi, the elder oak still in front of him as he now looked between the two pillars ahead at the amber sky that pressed against the horizon.

Whispers began to echo within his mind. At first the voices sang too quiet to hear, but as they grew in volume, Rhys could tell they were chanting in an ancient tongue. The chanting grew ever louder; the language unlike anything he had ever heard, and yet it was eerily familiar. As the chorus continued to rise within his mind, Rhys felt as if he could almost understand the words. Rhys gazed ahead to the east where the sky boiled scarlet and pink, the sunrise drawing ever nearer.

The illuminated runes across the floor began to channel their energy along the eleven lines focussed towards the altar. The carvings etched into the stone pillars likewise started to glow, the searing hot light floating upwards through the sarsen, and then across the lintels above them. The glow of dawn was but moments from erupting above the horizon. All the standing stones were ablaze. The concentrated energy started to trickle inwards towards the altar. The carvings under Rhys's feet began to shine, the magic creeping ever closer to the elder oak at its centre. The chanting in Rhys's mind was now deafening, drowning out the entire world.

The power channelled throughout the henge finally converged upon the length of elder oak at its heart. Within seconds, the length of wood began to absorb all the magical energy that charged the Northern Circle. The searing brightness swept down from the lintels, draining through the stone pillars, across the sarsen floor, racing up the altar and into the elder oak. Rhys could feel the magic radiating from it as now the length of wood shone blindingly hot.

Straining his eyes, Rhys glimpsed passed the oak, between the pillars ahead of him. The horizon exploded with crimson. Dawn was upon him. The aurora above quivered and pulsed in raging flames of green. It was then Rhys noticed the storm clouds that were brewing overhead. Billowing and swelling out from nothingness above, they were spawned by the sky itself beneath the fiery emerald aurora, blackening the heavens. The clouds swirled and crackled loudly, audible even over the deafening chant that rang through Rhys's mind.

Lightning struck the ground surrounding the circle. First one bolt, then another, then another. The top of the sun's disc peaked above the horizon, at which instant, its rays cut between the alignment of stones ahead. The golden beams struck the elder oak length, overloading it with power, its surface glaring impossibly bright. The tumultuous chorus raging across Rhys's mindscape began its final crescendo.

"The time is now!" Arlas's voice boomed through all other noise. "Bind!"

Rhys outreached both hands, and without hesitation, clasped the blazing elder oak. Vast quantities of energy and magic surged through his body. His grip painfully tightened like a vice, his hands no longer under his own control. Excruciating agony exploded through all of his nerves. His muscles seized up. His skin singed. His bones throbbed. His blood boiled. His lungs suffocated shut. His heart convulsed uncontrollably. Every fibre of Rhys's being screamed for mercy. He felt himself praying for death. The light from the sun burned his retinas and Rhys's vision began to fade. The roaring chant grew so intense that he was deafened.

Rhys was dying. He could feel it. Everything in his life up to this point had been a waste. This was it: the end.

No! He had to fight it. With every ounce of strength he had left, he had to resist. The pain was unbearable. He forced his mind to resist: to struggle against the powers sapping his life. Darkness spiralled around him and he began to suffocate. Rhys let out a final terrible cry as lightning descended from the storm clouds above, striking the staff in his grip. The stave exploded in

Rhys's hands, and blackness swallowed him whole.

FIFTEEN

The world was dark and silent. Rhys inhaled. A soft heartbeat whispered in his ears and pulsed in his hands. He was alive. Reborn. Slowly, he opened his eyes. The darkness parted and the sunlight glared through his eyelids, blinding him before his irises finally adjusted. The sun had risen above the horizon, casting magnificent rays of gold across the frozen landscape. The intense amber shimmered off of the snow and shone through the stones of the Northern Circle.

Rhys was kneeling upon the icy sarsen altar of the henge; the runes and markings in the stone cold, no longer ablaze with energy. In his hands, the length of elder oak had come free from the altar. As Rhys's sight finally came into focus, he gazed down at the staff he was holding: the most beautiful thing he had ever seen.

The length of once white wood was now as clear as glass, its surface perfectly smooth and polished. Within the stave, veins of green energy pulsed in rhythm with his heart: a complex network of branching emerald capillaries that stretched through the core of the stave, running its entire length, twisting and fragmenting as they did so. The staff bulged towards the top of its length into a rounded wedge, whilst at the other end, the shaft swelled in diameter before tapering to a curved butt. With every beat of Rhys's heart, the emerald energy throbbed with a greater intensity at the tip of the stave, flowing down its length through the intricate web of arcane veins.

Weakly, Rhys rose to his feet, his entire body trembling as he did so. Turning slowly, he looked down at the five magi still stood beneath the triliths. In unison, they each lowered their hoods to look upon him.

"Welcome, brother," Arlas greeted him anew.

Rhys stepped down from the altar, and Sol quickly retrieved him his clothes from where he had undressed, handing them to him. A frosty breeze blustered gently through the air, flowing around his bare skin, but he did not shiver.

Rhys passed his newly forged staff to Sol to hold so he could redress; as he did so, the veins of green light quickly faded as it left his grip. The five surrounding magi admired the weapon as Sol turned it over slowly in his hands, Rhys hastily throwing his clothes back on as they did so. When he took the staff back into his possession, the energy within it pulsed with vitality again, rhythmically swelling with the thrum of his chest.

"Pay up!" Matthew said as he elbowed Seimon.

"I left my coin in my clothes," the mage replied with a sigh.

"What did you bet on?" Sol asked.

"I said Rhys's staff would have a blade."

"And you were wrong! So you owe me ten shillings," Matthew smirked.

"I don't think any of us would have imagined Rhys's staff would have an appearance like *this*!" Robert commented as he continued to stare at the pulsating weapon.

"Indeed," Arlas agreed, scratching his beard. "It is most unique."

"What does that mean?" Rhys asked, speaking for the first time.

"I cannot say," Arlas answered. "A mage's staff is believed to be bound to his soul. The elder oak takes on characteristics of its owner. It is both an expression of his personality and his most primal arcane essence."

"Look at Sol's staff," Seimon elaborated. "It appears as if it is forged from copper and it occasionally crackles with an electric aura. One only needs to observe Sol in combat to see that it is reflective on his over-reliance on using lightning as a form of attack!"

"I am not *over-reliant* on using lightning!" Sol protested.

"Come on, Sol! Every other spell you cast is some form of electricity!" Matthew laughed.

"It's quick to cast and has a far greater accuracy than just about any other element!" Sol argued.

"But you *are* over-reliant on it," Seimon repeated.

"I can see this is an argument I am not going to win," Sol sighed.

"But then what does this staff reflect in me?" Rhys asked, twisting it gently in his fingers, feeling the weapon's perfect weight distribution as he did so.

"Try it out!" Arlas suggested. "Maybe then we shall see."

"Wait!" Matthew interjected. "If we are going to do this, then let us do it properly!"

"Oh!" Seimon exclaimed with barely contained excitement. "I know what you have in mind!"

"Rhys, wait here!" Matthew insisted. "Sol and Robert—come with us."

"Okay," Sol agreed with slight apprehension, glancing at Robert who shared his trepidation.

The four men quickly disappeared through the standing stones and descended down the slope of the hill out of sight.

"How do you feel?" Arlas asked, as he and Rhys were left alone.

Rhys stretched as each of his muscles

seemed to twitch with a newfound energy. "Different!" he replied finally.

Only now was he beginning to realise the changes to his body. His eyes were growing sharper by the minute as he started to notice details in the world that he had never even realised existed. As he looked upon the mage ahead of him, he could see every aspect of the man. Every hair, every pore in his skin, the individual threads within Arlas's clothing, now seemed all in focus at once. Rhys averted his gaze from the man and looked off to the horizon which appeared as crisp and precise as if it were but meters away. An eagle swooped down from the air upon a rabbit camouflaged perfectly in the snow. Its razor-like talons pierced through the white fur into the flesh beneath in, and the animal's scarlet blood spilled across the snow. All this took place miles in the distance, and yet Rhys watched it unfold with incredible acuity and definition.

Feeling almost overwhelmed by all he could see, he shut his eyes. But sight was not his only sense to have improved. Sound seemed now somehow richer, deeper, sharper, as if until now the world had been muffled and distorted. His ears prickled with sound carried through the air. He could hear footsteps groaning in the snow as the other four raced around at the foot of the hill. The wind carried with it noises from the far distance; the screech of a second eagle that circled high above the first, looking to steal its kill; the beating of his own heart as the valves within the ever-throbbing muscle slammed shut against the backward flow of blood.

Every sensation seemed heightened. Rhys's body was now perfectly attuned to the world around him, calibrated sharply to impeccable precision and awareness. His muscles tingled with energy as he continued to stretch them out, tensing each in turn as he did so. Was he stronger now? Faster even?

"It may seem overwhelming at first," Arlas explained, observing Rhys. "But you will quickly grow used to your heightened senses. Your body's full potential has finally been unlocked; the magic in your blood activated. You will find what previous limitations you held are now shattered. You are stronger, faster, more agile, and nimbler than ever you were. You can heal faster, react quicker, and push yourself beyond what you ever thought possible!"

"Wow," Rhys exhaled, feeling more invigorated than ever before.

"But I must advise caution and restraint," Arlas warned solemnly. "At least to begin with. You must be patient and take the time to discover the limits of your newfound powers. You must be careful to not overexert yourself to begin with. Be clever, and do not push yourself too hard. In time, you will achieve an understanding of what you are truly capable of, but until then, you must be patient."

"I will," Rhys promised.

"Then I believe it is time we see what the others have prepared for you!" Arlas smiled, leading Rhys out of the stone circle.

When they descended the slope of the hill, Rhys could not help but grin as he looked down at what the others had prepared. Three snowmen now stood in a row thirty yards or so from the tent, to which the four mages were now adding the finishing touches: some sticks for arms and charcoal for the eyes. One even had a parsnip for a nose.

"Rhys!" Seimon called out as the magi noticed him and Arlas approach. "What do you think?"

"Target practice!" Matthew explained.

"Not bad, eh?" Sol asked.

"Thanks guys," Rhys beamed.

"Oh, I think this is going to be worth it!" Matthew assured, stepping away from the snowmen.

"Come!" Sol beckoned, rushing back towards the camp. "Stand here!"

Rhys walked over to Sol and the others, who all took up position behind him as the new mage turned to face the three snowmen.

"What am I supposed to do?" Rhys asked, looking down at the staff in his hands.

"Swing your staff," Arlas explained. "Provided you do so with some force, your weapon will generate energy throughout the swing, which will launch from the tip of the weapon at the end of the arc. It should come naturally. You do not need to concentrate or focus your mind. Instead, simply allow the magic to flow through you."

"Alright," Rhys nodded determinedly, tightening his grip.

He readied himself. The others all warily took several paces back. Coiling up his body, Rhys drew back his weapon. Tensing every muscle, he unfurled, twisting his staff in a powerful arc. As he did so, the blood within his veins fizzled, channelling waves of energy from his chest, down his arms. The surge continued through his hands, leaving his body through his fingertips, flowing rapidly into the staff.

The weapon seemed almost to vibrate in Rhys's grip as it became imbued with magical energy, and as the stave cut through the air, the weapon charged in his hands. At the end of the mighty swing, an explosion of force ruptured the atmosphere and tore from the end of the weapon. The air rippled and twisted as a bolt of silver energy hurtled towards the nearest snowman. The blast of magic careened outwards impossibly fast, and in the blink of an eye, an immense cloud of snow and ice erupted from where a snowman had stood less than a second earlier.

"Whoa!" several of the men stood behind Rhys cried out.

"Shit!" Seimon yelled as chunks of snow began to rain down from a dozen fathoms up in the air. When the cloud of ice parted in the breeze, the six men stood in silence staring at where the first snowman had stood. Nothing remained, not even a small pile of snow, for it had been decimated by the force of Rhys's attack.

"What is that?" Robert asked as Rhys turned to look back at the five magi.

Gradually, they all turned to Arlas for answers.

"That my friends, is pure force energy!" the archon remarked with a smirk.

"Force energy?" Sol questioned. "I have never seen it before."

"You have," Arlas assured him. "I use it in its pure form from time to time. But it is normally a component in other spells," he explained.

"What do you mean?" Sol questioned further.

"When you cast a bolt of lightning, Sol, you can create various accompanying effects to the electricity. A pure bolt of lightning can only electrocute a foe, yet your lightning spells can often launch your enemies backwards when they strike. In such instances, you have generated a force energy component to your spell. Each of you do this with the various elements you wield as weapons in your magic."

"But what of pure force energy?" Seimon asked.

"Each of you is capable of wielding it in its pure form," Arlas explained. "I imagine the reason why none of you do so, is simply because you did not consider it as an option available to you."

"And it is Rhys's primal element?" Robert asked.

"It is," Arlas confirmed. "Just as fire is to me, lightning is to Sol, and iron is to Seimon."

"Is that unusual?" Rhys asked, confused as to why the others seemed so surprised by the spell he had cast.

"In the Circle today it is," Arlas replied. "You are the only one of the thirteen magi currently in existence to wield kinetic energy as your primal element. But that is by mere chance. Among the magi that came before us, there were many that wielded force energy in the way you do.

"Fire is one of the most prevalent primal elements used by the magi of the circle today, though admittedly there are key differences to the types of flame we produce. You will likely have noticed that the fire I frequently cast from my staff burns with a purple flame, whilst Matthew's fire burns in intense beams that almost appear as white jets of light. Indus however conjures flame as it is seen in nature: crackling red and amber.

"Today there are three mages of the Circle that wield flame as their primal element, but when I was first inducted to the Order; fire as a mage's primal element was a rarity. Force energy is not necessarily unusual, but within the Order of Magi as it currently stands, it is rare."

"And what of other elements?" Rhys asked.

"Am I capable of wielding them?"

"Yes," Arlas answered. "Force energy is your primal element; by which we mean it comes most naturally to you. You can cast it with little thought, and it will likely prove the most flexible in your usage of it, compared to any other element. But with practice and experimentation, you will learn and discover how to wield any element as a weapon. It is a similar process as to how you learn enchantments with a wand. Certain thought patterns and somatic components will allow you to alter what type of attacks you cast."

"Makes sense," Rhys nodded as he finally began to understand the principles behind it.

"If I were you, I'd stick to your primal element to begin with," Robert advised. "Move on to other elements only when you have mastered the basics of force energy."

"That way you will find it easier in coming to grips with other elements when you move on to them," Matthew added.

"Thanks for the advice," Rhys expressed gratefully.

"This lesson is all fascinating stuff!" Seimon put in impatiently. "But there are still two snowmen left standing over there! And I don't know about the rest of you, but I really want to see Rhys blow them up too!"

"All right!" Rhys chuckled as he turned to look back at the remaining targets.

Readying himself once again, Rhys pulled

back his staff as he prepared for another spell. Arcing his staff forwards, he felt the build-up of energy flow through him and into his staff once more, before an explosive bolt of kinetic energy shot out the end of the staff, smashing into the second snowman, leaving nothing but a shower of ice.

"Again!" Sol cried as the snow rained down.

Following through from the first swing, Rhys twisted around and launched another missile of silver energy that decimated the third and final snowman to smithereens.

"Awesome!" Seimon breathed in satisfaction of the destruction.

All of a sudden, Rhys felt out of breath, weary from energy he had just exerted. The exhaustion began to slowly subside as he turned to face the others again.

"When you project magic into this world, you draw from your energy reserves in a similar way to when you physically exert yourself," Arlas explained, seeing the fatigue that had come over Rhys. "There is a limit to how much magic you can cast, just as there is a limit to how far you can run before tiring, or how much weight you can lift before your muscles grow weak.

"With practice, you will be able to draw from larger reserves, in such the same way that one becomes fitter the more they run or becomes stronger from harder labour. You have never cast this kind of magic before, therefore your body and mind have little tolerance for it. Pace yourself. Train frequently without overexertion, and you shall find your capacity to cast spells will rapidly increase."

"Will do," Rhys remarked as he finally recovered fully, feeling charged with energy again.

"Right," Arlas said changing the subject. "I believe we should not wait before beginning our return journey. We shall pack up and leave within the hour, but before anything else, let us eat!"

The other five men changed out of their robes and back into their travelling gear before beginning to cook the last of the ibex. Whilst the mages began to pack away the rest of the camp, Sol approached Rhys holding in his hand a small mirror.

"Take a look," he offered as he handed Rhys the reflective piece of highly burnished metal.

Perplexed for a moment, Rhys peered down to see a set of eyes staring up at him that were not his own. The gaze of a mage peered back with a mesmerising intensity. Rhys's eyes now glowed with torrents of emerald and green that plumed and sparked with a magical aura, flickering with whispers of the power now awakened inside him.

SIXTEEN

They set off within the hour, tracing their route from the previous day, back the way they had come. For the most part, their footprints had remained undisturbed, though late in the afternoon the weather took a turn for the worse and a heavy snow began to fall, smothering their previous tracks in a fresh blanket of white.

The air was savagely cold; perhaps the coldest it had been over the course of their entire journey, though Rhys did not suffer like he had done so before the binding. His body stood fast against the ever-plummeting temperatures, never faltering in the frigid weather. The six men walked a harder pace than ever they had on their journey northward; now Rhys could keep pace with the others, and so, by the time they reached the site where they had camped previously, it was only mid-afternoon. Thus, they pressed on, covering several more miles before eventually they stopped to rest for the evening. The following day they continued south, across the snowy plains and over the frozen river, rarely straying from the path they had taken north.

The day after led them once again over the black, moss-covered shelf of rock. Its crossing was easier this time, as Rhys's heightened sense of balance prevented him ever slipping across the stones. Instead, he skipped light-footed over the uneven rock, alongside his fellow magi, joyed by his nimble feet. The afternoon saw Rhys set the pace, as he strode out ahead of the others across the potholed stone. The black plateau was porous and irregular, pitted with caves and toothed with jagged obelisks. No longer burdened by precarious footing, Rhys relished in the landscape around him in a way he had not been able to the first time he had crossed the expansive shelf.

Rhys stepped up onto a ridge, and all of a sudden, to his shock, the rock groaned underfoot. Perplexed by the deep rumbling, he turned to glance at the others behind him. They appeared as mystified as Rhys, halting and exchanging looks with one another. Cautiously, Seimon stepped up onto the same ridge, whilst Rhys crept forward several paces. The rock beneath them shuddered and groaned once more, preceding a deafening crack that fractured through the plateau. The ground underfoot lifted sharply. Rhys stumbled before regaining his balance, realising that the section of the shelf on which he was stood was now several feet higher than it had been seconds before.

"Shit!" Rhys cursed under his breath.

"Rhys, Seimon, get back here!" Arlas called out to them. "I know what—"

Before the archon could finish his sentence, the rupturing resumed, this time even louder, as the entire face of rock on which Rhys was stood cracked and split, surging upwards higher and higher. The ascending ground tilted, sloping rapidly away under Rhys and Seimon, throwing both magi off their feet as the craggy face lurched out from under them. Falling painfully on his side, Rhys tumbled down the rising bluff. The gnarled and jagged stone grazed his skin as he careened downwards, thumping into a patch of exposed earth beside Seimon as the mass of rock rose to its feet above them.

"Troll!" Matthew exclaimed over the thunder of shattering of stone.

Rhys leapt to his feet and span around to gawk at what was taking form out of the craggy steppe before him. A creature hewn from the rock itself now stood thirty-foot-tall in front of them; moss, stone and sand still cascading down from its lithic form.

Its arms and torso were disproportionately engorged when compared to its short and stumpy legs. A massive, bouldery head sat upon its uneven shoulders without an adjoining neck. Two large crystalline eyes glowed red within craggy sockets, asymmetrically pitted in its rocky skull. The hulking stone goliath stood motionless as its fierce gaze bore down upon the six magi.

Staves drawn, they remained perfectly still.

"Hold," Arlas commanded as quietly as he could, but so all could hear. "It is not yet hostile. We cannot afford to provoke it into attacking!"

The creature twisted its rough, stony pate as it continued to examine the magi, all the while emitting a low tremorous growl. Slowly it leant towards them, opening the rocky seem that formed its immense jaws, and let bellow a thunderous roar. The stone quaked beneath their boots as the creature howled. For a second, all fell silent, before the creature lifted its two gargantuan stone fists high above its head, and smashed them downwards into the ground, shattering the rock beneath it.

"Attack!" Arlas cried, swinging forth his staff to launch a flurry of fiery projectiles at the raging beast. The purple flames from Arlas's staff licked against the stone flesh of the monstrosity, but the magic merely glanced off of the creature's rocky skin. Further enraged, the gargantuan troll wildly swung its boulder-like fist at its nearest foe: Rhys. Reacting faster than he would have thought humanly possible, Rhys leapt aside, narrowly avoiding the mass of rock as it slammed hard into the ground, reducing the patch where he had been stood an instant earlier to mere shingle.

The other mages unleashed a torrent of attacks. Lightning and flames struck the troll but did little other than blast away the moss and mud from its black, stone skin. The troll began to advance slowly towards them, the rock shelf shuddering with each heavy step it took. It violently lashed out, swinging its two fists in huge arcs.

Matthew cried out as he was caught by the end of one such blow, the impact launching him off his feet and sending him sprawling across the ground. Rhys emitted a horrified gasp as he watched the mage struck down, breathing a sigh of relief seconds later as Matthew then leapt back to his feet uninjured.

Seimon drew the elemental's attention, flourishing his stave in a series of swings, but the shards of metal launched by the mage merely whistled and clanged as they ricocheted harmlessly off the troll. Undeterred, the mage continued his fusillade of iron fragments until a carefully placed shot caught the creature in its left eye. The red glowing crystal shattered in the troll's pitted socket, and the beast let out a bone-shattering holler, clasping a giant palm over its face in anguish.

With its eyes covered, the troll proceeded to thrash blindly with its other arm. Sol and Arlas ducked under a flailing punch, backing away from the humungous creature before resuming their salvo of arcane attacks. In the meantime, Matthew had shaken off the blow he'd been dealt, and re-joining the fray, he launched a jet of light which struck the creature's side. Rock crumbled from the troll's chest, though the thrashing monstrosity seemed oblivious to the wound, continuing to pummel the area surrounding it with wild blind strikes.

Watching the fracas continue to unfold, Rhys crept around to the beast's flank. He took aim and span his staff in a powerful arc. A bolt of pure force energy formed in the air and collided with the creature at tremendous speed. In the impact, the troll was battered sideways, staggered by the kinetic blow. But to Rhys's dismay, the attack had left no visible damage. Stunned for only a brief moment, the troll regained its heavy footing and continued to swing furiously at the mages darting around it.

Rhys knew he had to find a weakness somehow; he needed some way to penetrate the elemental's stony outer skin. Exhaling in apprehension, he decided to act boldly. Sprinting off the mark, he dashed up to the creature and arced his staff to strike at the troll's leg with a melee blow. In the short instant of drawn-out time that followed, Rhys saw the unexpected unfold before his eyes.

Before his staff made contact, a shrill chime rang out. Rhys watched through the dilation of a splintered second as the staff inched closer to the creature's leg. From the leading end of Rhys's staff, a translucent blade of green energy unfurled out of nothingness. The magical edge followed the curvature of the wedged end of the staff; suspended and inch or so above its surface. The glowing blade of energy resembled a glaive or guisarme in nature: tapering to a long point as it extended from the stave's tip. On the reverse edge of the arcane blade, the ethereal weapon was armed with a backward pointing fluke, and below that, a sharp hook curved back down toward the shaft of the staff.

Rhys landed the blow, and the magical blade struck the creature's leg, sinking deep into the troll's stone skin. The beast roared monstrously in pain and brought the hand protecting its face crashing down at Rhys. Wrenching his weapon free, he leapt backwards, narrowly avoiding the giant fist of stone as it cascaded into the rock where he had stood but a second earlier.

Regaining his footing, Rhys lanced forward at the fist driven into the newly formed crater in front of him, spearing the emerald arcane blade hovering from the end of his staff through the troll's rocky flesh once again. The hulking elemental let out another bellowing cry. Its face was now unprotected, providing the opportunity that Seimon needed. The mage fired another shard of jagged iron at the beast, striking and shattering its second eye with deadly precision. The red crystal exploded within the pitted socket. The troll howled deafeningly again, now entirely blinded.

Blood ran from both eye sockets and the wounds to its leg and hand, but the injured monstrosity, fuelled by rage and desperation, fought on. The troll charged, trampling the solid rock into gravel beneath its feet. Seimon and Arlas dove aside as the stone giant stormed passed them in its blind fury. Turning clumsily on the spot, the elemental twisted to face the six mages once more. It sucked air in loudly through two porous nostrils, sniffing out its foes. Rearing its rude and ugly head, the troll locked on to Sol's scent. In a berserking rage, it began to windmill its fists fiercely and stomp towards its target.

Sol edged away, continuing his salvo of lightning whilst on the backfoot, but the thunderous onslaught proved utterly ineffectual against the stampeding stone titan. Rhys darted to the creature's flank again, ducking under a flailing boulder-like fist whilst on the run, the magical blade still extended from his staff. Sol continued to backpedal, but focussed on the mountain of rock bull-rushing towards him, he snagged his ankle in a pothole and toppled backwards off his feet. He looked up in horror as the troll bore down on him. The mage vanished beneath a stone fist as the elementals craggy knuckles crunched into the ground with tremendous force. Only as the monstrosity reared back again did Rhys see that Sol had managed to roll clear of the strike, narrowly avoiding being flattened.

Stone crumbled from the creature's face as another powerful blast of light seared from Matthew's stave, catching the troll across the temple. The blow was enough to distract the beast from Sol. Rearing upwards, the monster growled in Matthew's direction and began to trudge cumbersomely towards its new quarry.

Rhys seized the opportunity and leapt towards the beast, rotating his staff as he did so. The hooked spike on the reverse of the magical blade dug clean into the rock of the troll's lower back. It bellowed deafeningly. Clasping a crack in the stone giant's armour with his free hand, Rhys hung suspended in the air from the troll's back. He then pulled loose the blade and drove the hook higher, heaving himself upwards in the process. Hollering another time, the troll tried to swat at Rhys as the mage dug his fingers into another crimp on the beast's anatomy, climbing upwards as he steadily pulled himself higher. Alas, the troll's broad hunched shoulders and hulking structure rendered it incapable of reaching the mage clung precariously to the small of its back.

The stone titan began twisting violently, thrashing its goliath form left and right in an attempt to try and shrug the mage free, yet Rhys gripped tightly, refusing to be thrown clear. The other mages had now ceased fire to ensure they did not strike Rhys. He scaled higher, replanting the hook of his blade as he did so, until eventually, he reached the beast's shoulders nearly thirty feet up from the ground.

Raising his staff high, Rhys drove the point of his blade down with all his might, spearing between the troll's shoulders and head. The giant's cry of pain was deafening. It crumpled to its knees, quaking the rock beneath it. Gripping the staff with both hands now, Rhys felt a surge of energy flow from his chest, down his arms, and into his staff. Channelled through the ethereal blade, a shockwave of force drove deep beneath the troll's stone skin, shattering it as it did so. The elemental fell silent, its life rapidly snuffed out by the finishing blow. Its hulking mass began to topple, with Rhys still upon its shoulders. The mage braced for impact as the troll's massive body keeled over and collided hard with the ground. The shelf trembled deafeningly; and then, all fell still.

Rhys slowly clambered to his feet atop the vanquished giant. With a quick chime, the blade from his staff spun back into nothingness as it sheathed within the air. Rhys leapt down to the ground and turned to face his comrades. The five of them gaped in awe, their countenances a mixture of disbelief and pride. Sol began to clap his hands together slowly before the others joined in applauding.

"Rhys... that was awesome!" Seimon exclaimed as he patted him firmly across the back. "How did you... with the magic blade... and the climbing...!?"

"You literally climbed on top of that bastard to kill it!" Matthew chuckled.

"Yeah, I'm not really sure if what I just saw actually happened!" Sol laughed as Rhys stood before them equally dumbstruck by what he had just done.

"Colour me impressed, Rhys," Arlas told him. "Something not easily achieved."

Rhys shook his head as if everything that had just happened was a blur. "I just... acted on impulse," he breathed as he looked upon the massive stone corpse.

"What *was* that?" Sol asked Arlas. "The blade that appeared from the end of Rhys's staff?"

"An ethereal blade," Arlas explained. "I haven't seen one in many, many years. Now they *are* rare. I know only of one other mage to have ever wielded such a weapon.

"They stem from a form of magic that is sparsely seen and poorly understood. The capacity to wield such weapons is believed to come naturally to a select few; such as Rhys, it would seem. I have heard tales of magi of old learning how to summon forth such magical weapons, though I am afraid I know so little of them, that I would not know where to begin in doing so."

"I have never heard of them before," Seimon stated as he examined Rhys's stave. "It seems pretty useful. I'd like to see it again."

"Err..." Rhys responded in puzzlement. He had not summoned the blade consciously, nor had he actively dismissed it after the fight. The blade had simply appeared when needed, and once it was no longer required, it had vanished. Focussing for a moment, Rhys tried to call the blade into existence once more, but to no effect. He attempted to imagine the troll in front of him again, hoping to recreate the moment of the weapon's summoning, but still it did not appear.

"If I am not mistaken," Arlas continued, "I believe it will only appear in combat. That is one of the reasons why so little is known of them, for how can you study something when the only opportunity to do so is in the heat of battle?

"My understanding is that they are conjured from a magic not controlled by a mage's conscious mind, and thus they cannot be summoned willingly into existence. Instead, the latent parts of the mind control their expression, calling them forth when their wielder believes themselves in danger.

"I am pleased to see such magic again in my lifetime. I did not think I would have another opportunity. I have little doubt that you will have the chance to see it again, Seimon."

"Hmm... Makes sense, I suppose," Seimon responded slightly disappointed.

"How are they more useful than a traditional staff blade?" Robert asked.

"Once again, I know little of their nature," Arlas reiterated. "But I believe they have the potential to cleave through substances too hard or strong for a traditional blade to cut. You witnessed how easily Rhys's blade passed through the stone hide of the troll!"

"I could definitely get used to having it!"

Rhys remarked with a smile.

All of a sudden Seimon forced a loud, fake cough as he elbowed Matthew in the ribs. "Ahem!"

"What?" Matthew asked.

"Pay up!" Seimon replied with a broad grin.

"What…? No! That doesn't count!" Matthew refused.

"The bet was that Rhys's staff would have a blade. You sir, owe me ten shillings… *and* the ten shillings that I already paid you!"

"No!" Matthew refused. "I said his staff wouldn't have a blade. I didn't say anything about any ethereal or magical blades!"

"Was there a blade on his staff or not?"

"Technically no. It was hovering an inch or so off of it!" Matthew argued stubbornly.

"Just pay him already, Matt!" Sol laughed.

SEVENTEEN

The magi continued the day's journey in jubilation of Rhys's triumph over the troll. Trekking a fast pace, they made camp on the brown grassy tundra that evening, where only a few days earlier they had hunted the ibex. The weather held clear, unveiling the flowing ribbons of light that made up the Aurora Norteius in the star speckled skies above. The following day, they marched an even greater distance, covering a leg that had taken them a day and a half when travelling northbound. Their increase in pace meant that, come evening the day after, they had already crossed the glacier, making camp at the precipice of Alder's pass. During the night, a light snowfall descended in the still air as the six men chatted around the campfire. The following dawn, they rose early and made a clean push through the pass, straight to Northcrest. Excited by the prospect of a warm bed and a roof over their heads, the magi made haste, arriving at the small hamlet shortly before sundown.

Upon their approach, Rhys noticed the stave across his back diminish in aura, transmogrifying to a more inconspicuous and subtle aesthetic; the crystal clouded from its natural transparency, the glowing emerald veins fading until they appeared little more than mineral seams embedded within quartz. 'Just as well,' Rhys thought to himself, for in its intrinsic form, the weapon would draw much unwanted attention, revealing him quickly to be a sorcerer. This intuitive obfuscation his staff had self-performed negated the need for him to conceal the weapon from onlookers; Sol and several of the other magi whereas, were obliged to bundle their staves in linen wraps on their final approach of Northcrest to avoid arousing too much attention.

"Do you reckon she'll be here this time?" Seimon asked Matthew as the two of them began to rush ahead.

"I hope so!" Matthew chirped optimistically, the two men now a good dozen yards in front of the others as they made their way through the snowy streets. When Rhys, Sol, Robert, and Arlas entered the White Hart, they saw his question answered. Seimon and Matthew, though having only entered the inn several moments before, were already seated at the bar, staring wide-eyed as they chatted to a raven-haired tavern girl. The woman was undeniably beautiful, though Matthew and Seimon's description might have been slightly exaggerated. The other four mages could not help but chuckle to themselves as they watched the two men grinning stupidly from ear to ear as the girl began to pour them both a pint.

Rhys and Sol sat at the same table as before, a little wearier and worse for wear than on their last visit.

"Will you be joining us for a drink this time, Robert?" Arlas asked the man.

Robert seemed troubled by the question.

"You all right, Rob?" Sol asked, offering the man a reassuring smile. "It's not like we'll pin you down and funnel ale into your mouth if you refuse!"

"Very well," the stoic southerner finally replied, returning an all too rare and fleeting smirk. "I will have a drink with you," he agreed as he took a seat across the table from Sol and Rhys.

"Excellent!" Arlas remarked with a clap of his hands, rubbing his palms eagerly together, somewhat surprised by Robert's willingness. "Four ales, coming right up," he added cheerily as he made his way over to the bar.

"That's if he can get through those two to the barmaid!" Sol remarked as he glanced back over at Seimon and Matthew.

Robert cracked a loud chuckle, before quickly falling silent again as if he had intentionally restrained himself.

"What do you think then, Rhys?" Sol asked, turning his attention to the Order's newest acolyte. "Was it as tough as everyone said it would be?"

"It wasn't far off, that's for sure!"

"Well, you made it... and not a single finger lost to frostbite!"

"Yeah, I guess that is something," Rhys conceded, smiling as he leant back in the chair, enjoying the warmth of the tavern as it washed over him.

The six men drank heavily that night. They had crossed Alder's pass and had left the frozen wastes behind. Back in the populated regions of Cambria, with food and comforts once more to hand, they relished the evening. Seimon and Matthew came to sit with them intermittently as the two men took breaks from harassing the young barmaid. They told stories and jokes of past adventures, and recounted events from the journey just made. And to everyone's surprise, even Robert laughed along and told a few stories of his own.

It was during his seventh tankard of ale Rhys found he was sat alone at the table, the effects of the beer beginning to haze his perceptions. Sol and Arlas had left momentarily to relieve themselves, Robert was getting some much-needed air outside, whilst Seimon and Matthew sat in conversation with the innkeeper by the bar. Rhys took a long sip of his pint, savouring the luxury of being indoors and out of the blistering elements, something that had become a rarity in recent months, when suddenly, the raven-haired barmaid sat down in the seat next to him.

"Ugh!" she sighed heavily. "I have been on my feet all day," she said rubbing her slender ankles. "It feels so good to just sit down."

"I know what you mean," Rhys remarked empathetically as he too stretched out his aching legs under the table.

"Yeah, your friends say you have been travelling beyond the White Mountains. It must have been pretty tough up there—especially this time of year?"

"I am definitely glad to be back this side of the range," Rhys smiled, glancing for a moment at Seimon and Matthew who had taken note of whom he was sitting with. "My friends seem quite... interested in you."

"Interested?" she smiled. "I would have used the word infatuated!" She giggled, and as she did so, Rhys could now see the allure of the girl. As stunning as she was, it was her smile and gaze that melted hearts.

"I can see why though," Rhys spoke with alcohol induced confidence. "I am sure you are used to it. You probably get far worse from most who travel through here."

"You are too kind. But I can't say that is true."

"Really?" Rhys questioned. "I find that hard to believe!"

"Well for a start, there are very few who

do actually travel through this way; Northcrest isn't exactly situated on the Northern Highway— so I am definitely not used to it! Secondly, those who do journey here are nowhere near as, um... forward as your two friends over there."

Rhys looked past the girl to the bar where Seimon and Matthew were still watching, curious as to the conversation Rhys was having.

"They are staring, aren't they?" she asked having read Rhys's face.

"Err... a little, yes," Rhys confirmed.

The girl leant in close to Rhys who found himself doing the same. "Forgive me for this," she smiled.

"For what—?" Before Rhys had barely finished his sentence, she had pressed her lips against his.

Dumbstruck, Rhys hardly knew what was happening. He did not pull away as the beautiful woman kissed him for what felt like the briefest of moments. When she gently withdrew, the girl winked at the mage and smiled.

"Are they still looking?"

Still confounded, Rhys stared blankly at her for a moment, before realising what she had asked him. He finally glanced back over to Seimon and Matthew, struggling desperately to keep a straight face as their jaws hung open. "You could say that," he smirked.

Her grin widened as she pictured the sight. "My name is Charlotte," she issued softly.

"Rhys," he replied.

"It was nice to meet you, Rhys."

With that, she rose to her feet and walked straight past Seimon and Matthew without uttering a word to them, into the kitchens and out of sight. Moments later, Sol, Arlas, and Robert returned, retaking the seats around the table.

"What did we miss?" Sol asked.

"Not much," Rhys smiled, still watching Seimon and Matthew as they gawked dumbfounded at him.

The four of them each took a long swig of their ales before chatting once more. A short while later, Seimon and Matthew finally re-joined them, shaking Rhys's hand each as they did so, without speaking a word of what had happened. Rhys could not resist winking smugly at the two men. They beamed back at him as they shook their heads in jealousy, the other three barely noticing the exchange.

It was at this stage in the night that Rhys realised how happy he was. The men that sat around the table with him were his friends, and though he had known them but a short time, it seemed as if they had gone through so much together. The world had opened up to Rhys. He was now a part of something much bigger than himself. For the first time in his life, he truly felt like he belonged.

EIGHTEEN

The next morning Rhys awoke feeling surprisingly fresh. He attributed his new-found constitution as one of the many perks the binding ritual had imbued him with. The party of magi rose later than usual, and so it was not until after ten o'clock that they left Northcrest behind. Their southward journey led them back into Highwood, which steadily grew denser with each passing mile. They made camp in a small clearing that night and set off promptly the following morning. A long day's travel saw them cover ten leagues, before setting camp for the final time of their pilgrimage, only a dozen miles north of the clearing in Highwood from where they had set out just over a fortnight ago.

"The remainder of the Order should hopefully be awaiting our arrival," Arlas explained as they began the final day's trek.

The sky above was grey and overcast, shrouding the forest in a sullen light. The six men strolled leisurely through the thick woods as they covered the final miles of their long and gruelling journey. By mid-morning, snow was descending once more, falling thick and fast in feathery flakes. The morning was growing late as they neared their rendezvous point.

"It should be this clearing just ahead," Arlas stated. "Though I'd have thought we'd be able to hear them by now." His expression turned to one of perplexity as they trudged the final few yards.

They pushed into the clearing and Arlas halted dead in his tracks. The party fell eerily silent. Unable to see, Rhys shimmied out from behind the archon, finally laying eyes on what had stopped the others and reduced them all to silence. His stomach flipped as a sickening sense of horror grasped him. Centred in the glade, a mage's staff was driven into the icy ground. Trails of crimson blood had frozen down the shaft. Piked atop the staff was skewered the head of Lawrence Swail.

"What...?" Seimon stammered in despair, unable to utter anything else.

Arlas still stood paralysed in disbelief, gaping in dismay at the severed head of his friend spiked upon his own staff. Rot had set in. The man's eyes had been devoured from the sockets by crows or the like, but since the initial mutilation, the flesh had frozen in the frigid winter air, slowing the decay. It was hard to tell how long he had been dead. The body was nowhere in sight.

Minutes passed without anyone so much as

moving. Rhys could not quite fathom the muddied turmoil of emotions churning through his body. Anger burned hot, despair raged powerfully, and grief clawed throughout his being; but above all, he felt cold. A fierce chill gripped him tight, fiercer than the biting winds of the Carparth Tundra, fiercer than the sapping taint of the Grey. The bereaving cold numbed the surrounding world to a frigid and hopeless abyss, as the mage stood, unable to move or speak, gawking at the decapitated head of his mentor.

Eventually Arlas regained his composure. "We must find the others," he pronounced solemnly as he trudged over to Lawrence's head and covered it with the blanket from his pack. "We don't know who or what is responsible for this. It may still be close at hand." Arlas sighed heavily, not turning to face the others. "We should split up. That way we can search a greater area. Sol, Robert, and Rhys, cover the ground east of here. Seimon and Matthew, take the south. I will search to the west."

"Arlas!" Matthew argued. "It's too dangerous for you to go alone!"

"No!" Arlas refused. "I know the risks. I am more than capable of handling myself should something go awry."

"Not like this you aren't!" Seimon objected. "We just found out that Lawrence is dead! None of us are level-headed right now. Not even you! You should take Robert with you."

"I do not have the luxury of letting grief cloud my judgment—nor do any of you!" he returned, sharply raising his voice. "Rhys is too inexperienced. Should he and Sol encounter trouble, they will need Robert!"

"I agree," Robert put in. "Arlas is more than capable of watching his own back. We should not question him on this."

"No! It is too dangerous," Seimon refused. "We shouldn't split up. It will take more time to search the area, but it will be safer!"

"My mind is made up!" Arlas declared. "Be wary of anything out of the ordinary. Trust no one you come across; and be mindful that whoever or whatever did this, is capable of slaying a magister of the Order—they may be lying in wait for the rest of us. Regardless of whether you discover anything or not, return here within the hour."

The five of them nodded silently.

"Don't let each other out of your sight!" he stressed.

With those words, he strode off through the trees, disappearing to the west. The remaining five stared at one another for a long moment before departing along their allocated routes. As Sol, Robert, and Rhys left the glade, they turned for a final look at the head of Lawrence, now concealed beneath the blanket.

Sol, Robert, and Rhys zigzagged silently through the trees, looking and listening for any sign that might help them piece together what had happened. They found nothing. No blood stained the snow or soil, no branches were broken to suggest a struggle, nor were there footprints of any kind.

"Who could have done this?" Rhys finally asked.

Sol did not answer.

"There are few creatures or men of this world that could best Lawrence in a fight," Robert returned.

Still, Sol remained silent.

It was clear to Rhys he best be quiet. Rhys felt strangely distant, as if neither what had happened, nor the gravity of the situation had yet sunk in. They continued to search as they crept through the trees, but still they found nothing.

"We need a vantage point," Robert suggested. "I know of one not far from here. From there we can better survey the area. We stand little chance of spotting anything from ground level."

"You are right," Rhys agreed, looking to Sol for his input. "Sol?"

But the mage did not seem to have heard.

"Sol?" Rhys repeated as he moved over to his friend and placed a hand on his shoulder.

"Sorry!?" he asked, shaken from a moment of reverie, his eyes filled with grief and confusion.

"We are going to head to a vantage point— to see if we can get a better view of the forest," Rhys explained.

"Okay," Sol nodded passively in response.

"It is this way," Robert declared, leading them along a northeast bearing.

They came to the foot of a ridge that rose steeply on either side and began to climb up its sloping length. The top of the rise was mostly devoid of trees and quickly ascended above the tops of the surrounding conifers. At its end, the ridge extended to form a narrow rocky shelf, dropping sharply on either side to the woods a hundred feet below them. A single pine stood sentinel upon the ledge, overlooking the surrounding woodlands. Miles upon miles of coniferous trees stretched to the horizon in every direction. The snow began to fall even heavier, buffeted about in the biting winds.

"I'm not sure if we'll be able to see anything," Rhys despaired as he peered downwards. The woodland was so dense, and visibility deteriorating so rapidly, that they stood little chance of sighting anything that did not rise above the treetops.

"Sol, see if you can spot anything towards the east," Robert instructed, pointing towards the precipice of the cliff as he leant against the solitary pine tree.

Sol nodded feebly in response, obediently trudging towards the southern ledge of the rise.

Rhys followed close behind in the hope of spotting something amidst the snowy pines of the east, though before he could reach the ledge, Robert called out to him.

"Rhys," he said beckoning him over.

"What is it?" Rhys asked solemnly as he approached the man.

At that moment, Sol let out a terrible cry.

"Sol!" Rhys screamed as he spun to look back at his friend.

Electricity rippled across the man's skin, leaping upwards from the ground. Sol spasmed violently before collapsing in a heap on the floor. Rhys sprinted towards the downed mage, but Robert shouted after him.

"Rhys, wait!"

Rhys skidded to a stop at his friend's side. He went to grab Sol, only to be jolted with a crackle of lightning that leapt up from his body. Every muscle in Rhys's anatomy seized up as pain twinged through him. It was over in an instant. Rhys was flung backwards off of his feet, thumping hard into the snow as he reeled dazedly from the shock. His whole body benumbed and tingled as he heaved himself up from the ice. Shaking off his disorientation, he stumbled back towards Sol. Kneeling beside the mage for a second time, he noticed curved lines of light beneath the man, cutting upwards through the snow.

"Don't touch him again!" Robert warned from behind.

"It's a trap!" Rhys breathed in realisation as he recognised what he was looking at. Beneath the snow, a magical glyph was carved into the ground. When Sol had stepped upon it, it had been triggered. "Sol!" he gasped, identifying the arcane boobytrap to be one of the very same Lawrence had taught him a month earlier. "I can disarm this!" he declared, drawing his wand, recounting an enchantment to dispel such magical snares. Removing his pack, Rhys dug out his codex, and began flicking through dozens of pages as he tried to find the spell he needed.

"He is still alive," Robert uttered indifferently. "For the moment, at least."

Rhys glanced down at Sol, seeing to his relief that his friend's chest continued to rise and fall with his breathing. Looking back to his codex, he found the page he sought and skimmed his scribblings as fast as he could. Pointing his wand to the glyph, he focussed hard, pushing his mind through the thought sequence required to disarm it. To Rhys's dismay, the glyph resisted his efforts and continued to glow through the snow that covered it.

"It's no use," Robert uttered coldly. "The glyph is blood linked."

"Blood linked?" What do you mean?" Rhys faltered, as he continued to try and crack open the arcane snare before him.

"It is tied to the blood of the caster. In order for it to be dispelled, the caster must deactivate it themselves... or be killed."

"How do you know this?" Rhys questioned suspiciously as he reached for his staff. His heart sank as his fingers clutched at nothing; his weapon was no longer strapped to his pack.

"I'm sorry it had to happen this way, Rhys," Robert sighed with an icy tone.

Rhys turned to face the man, his fears fully realised as he saw Robert holding his staff. "What are you doing?" the mage demanded, watching in horror as Robert proceeded to dangle the weapon out over the ledge. "Don't do it!"

But Robert had already released his grip, and Rhys's staff tumbled out of sight, falling a hundred feet into the forest below.

Rhys's eyes darted to the solitary pine tree. In the trunk was carved a glyph: a scaled down version of the one beneath Sol. The arcane marking was smeared with fresh blood. Rhys turned his gaze back toward Robert and now saw the crimson fluid dripping from his fingers, tainting the white snow beneath him.

"It is over for the others," Robert spoke solemnly. "I did not want it this way, but Indus will not allow them to live. They are too loyal to Arlas. They cannot be trusted. But it is not too late for *you*, Rhys!"

"Why are you doing this?" Rhys screamed, unable to fathom the betrayal taking place.

"You don't yet see Arlas for what he truly is! He is a coward, forcing the Order to live in exile, never revealing ourselves to the world. How possibly can we protect Cambria if it does not even know we exist?"

"Robert... please!" Rhys begged.

"Don't you see, Rhys!? This is the chance the Order needs to survive! We must rise from the ashes of the old circle and form it anew. I have seen your potential! What you have already achieved—it is enough to impress Indus. There is a place for you in the world we are forging! It is not your destiny to die today! You can join us. Pledge yourself to our new order and we can accept you with open arms!"

"I don't understand why you are doing this!?" Rhys shook his head.

"Cambria is dying! Only we can save it. But we cannot do it under Arlas's rule. It is Indus that will lead us to Cambria's salvation. You *must* understand. You must see our plight: our cause is just and true! Rhys, you *must* join Indus!"

"Indus killed Lawrence!" Rhys breathed in harrowing realisation. "And *you*!?" he stammered, looking at Robert now with a bitter resentment. "You were culpable!"

"He could never have survived! He was blind. Loyal only to Arlas, never realising that he had betrayed the oath he took when joining the Order. Indus did what he had to."

"It is you that has betrayed your oath!" Rhys scorned.

"I am offering you a chance here, Rhys! Do not be a fool! You do not need to meet the same fate as the others. Please Rhys, see reason. Join us!" Robert took a step towards Rhys, offering him his open hand.

All fell silent as Rhys stared down at the man's palm. He breathed deeply as the winds picked up and snow swirled quickly through the air. "I'd rather die!" he hissed.

"If that is your choice," Robert pronounced disappointedly as he raised his staff and pointed it at Rhys's chest. "I am sorry, Rhys!"

Rhys jabbed his wand quickly at Robert and a jet of blinding light erupted. The southerner cried out as the flare struck his face. Robert staggered backwards, clasping his hand over his eyes, swinging his staff blindly, loosing a dark projectile in Rhys's direction. Anticipating the blind strike, Rhys leapt aside, dodging a black bolt of energy as it crackled through the air. Robert lowered his hand, squinting his reddened eyes as his sight began to return. Rhys threw himself at the man, tackling him into the pine tree. They slammed hard into the trunk and Robert's staff was flung out of his hands, landing several feet away in the snow.

Rhys threw a punch into his foe's side, only to receive a powerful knee to his gut. Knocked back, Rhys fell to the ground. Robert darted towards his staff. Scrambling through the snow, Rhys snagged the man's ankle. Robert tripped. The moment his foe struck the ground, Rhys was already on top of him, swinging wildly with his fists at the traitor.

His knuckles smashed repeatedly into Robert's face, but after only a few swings, the southerner managed to grapple both of his wrists. Robert threw his brow upwards, cracking Rhys in the cheek with a powerful head-but. Rhys recoiled from the impact, and before he could regather himself, Robert had thrown his weight off of him. A quick scuffle sent the two men rolling over one another down the slope in a brawl of kicks and punches, until thumping to a halt, Rhys found himself pinned helplessly beneath Robert. Pressing downward, the southerner knelt across Rhys's arms, freeing up his own hands as he restrained the mage beneath him.

"I am sorry!" Robert uttered with a twisted grin of bloodied teeth.

He slowly curled his fingers around Rhys's throat and began to squeeze with all his strength. The mage distraughtly tried to gasp for air as his windpipe began to shut. He struggled against the southerner on top of him with all his might, but could not wriggle free. Thrashing frantically in suffocation, Rhys attempted desperately to free an arm, but Robert's weight pressed down upon him too heavily.

He was growing weak, his lungs screaming for air. Robert glared down at him with his intense, swirling copper eyes, continuing to choke the life from Rhys, his fingers clamping ever tighter around his throat. Rhys's eyes flicked around in desperation. He began to grow faint. His chest burnt in agony. Robert's staff of wrought iron lay only a few feet away. He stretched his fingers towards the weapon, straining his arm to full length, but it laid just beyond his reach. His vision began to grow dark as the last vestiges of hope seemed to fade away. Groping for his belt, he clawed at the snow to try and pull his hand towards his waist. His fingertips were tingling as they fumbled at the hilt of his father's dagger. He tried in anguish to clasp hold of the knife, wriggling his arm beneath Robert's weight as he struggled for the blade, all the while, the villain on top of him continued to strangle the mage with grim indifference.

Rhys's eyesight blurred and darkness pressed in on him. The resistance on his arm gave a little, and suddenly, he felt his fingers lock around the haft of his knife. Wrenching the weapon free of its sheath, Rhys stabbed the blade into Robert's leg. The southerner screamed as the dagger sank into the muscle of his thigh. For a second, his clasp around Rhys's throat loosened, allowing the mage a singular gasp of air.

Robert squeezed hard once more, pressing close Rhys's throat a second time. Rhys tore the blade out of the man's thigh and stabbed Robert's leg once more, this time twisting the dagger. The weight lifted from his limb, and freeing his arm, Rhys ripped out the knife again.

Without hesitation, Rhys lurched upwards with the blade, driving the point of the dagger with all his might into the side of Robert's neck. Blood spurted from the wound, and Robert finally relinquished his grip around Rhys's throat, his hands clasping now at his own in a frenetic attempt to stem the flow of blood around the knife stuck deep into his neck.

Rhys wheezed. Frigid air rinsed through his screaming lungs as he gasped and sputtered. His senses refocussing, his strength returning, adrenaline plunged him straight back into the heat of the fray. Knowing he was fighting for his life, Rhys wrenched free the blade from beneath his foe's jawline, tearing the flesh and releasing a spout of blood as the knife came free. Without pause, he thrust once more into Robert's collar, pulling the blade back out and stabbing again and again. Each jab gored deeper, brutalising the flesh as the blade plunged in and out between crimson spurts. Robert's gurgled screams drowned swiftly as blood spilled hot and thick from the puncture holes down Rhys's face. Flipping the southerner off of him, Rhys now pinned Robert beneath his own weight, still repeatedly sinking the dagger mercilessly into him time after time as the mage thrashed beneath him. The snow stain dark incarnadine. Tears burned down Rhys's cheeks. His arms ached and grew weak.

Heaving the knife free one final time, Rhys realised the mage was long since dead. He scrambled backward away from the corpse. His hands quivered uncontrollably. The dagger slipped from his fingers. He glanced back at Robert Kwesi as blood seeped wider across the ice. The mage's vacant gaze looked back at him, dull and lifeless, devoid of the magic that once crackle through it. Rhys wept in horror, coughing and retching through his bruised and swollen throat. Curling his knees into his chest, he shivered, sobbing in the snow.

"Rhys?" Sol's voice called out to him.

Rhys had no idea how much time had passed.

"Rhys?"

Slowly Rhys turned to look at Sol. "Sol?" he breathed in a daze.

"Rhys? What happened?" Sol asked as the mage turned back to look at Robert's body.

"He tried to kill me!" Rhys whimpered. "He tried to kill *you!*"

"He set the trap?" Sol asked.

Rhys nodded silently.

"Why?"

"Indus!" Rhys hissed, his eyes widening. "Indus betrayed us all! It was he who killed Lawrence. He means to kill the rest of us too! We have to go now!" Rhys urged, his senses now returning to him.

"Go where?" Sol asked.

"We need to warn the others—before Indus finds them! We may already be too late!"

Rhys leapt to his feet and grabbed his pack before darting down the slope, back into the woods, with Sol in close pursuit. Realising he was without his staff, he skirted the wall of the ridge to try and find where his weapon had landed. As he neared the place he thought it had fallen, he could feel the stave whispering to him through the trees. Following its call, Rhys quickly spied it caught in the lower branches of a giant fir. When he pulled it from the boughs, the weapon pulsed to life in his grip.

"Quickly!" Rhys exclaimed. "Back to the clearing!"

The two men raced back the way Robert had led them. The trees rushed past as they sped onwards through the wood. They rapidly approached the clearing once more and Rhys prepared himself to face whoever might be awaiting them.

Sol pushed into the glade ahead of Rhys and dropped to his knees, clasping his head in his hands. The snow throughout the clearing was streaked crimson. Three men lay dead.

Matthew was face down, his innards spilling through a gaping wound to his side. Seimon lay beside him, staring upwards into the sky with two glazed over eyes, his temple crumpled inward. The final body that lay in the clearing belonged to Ethan Hall. The mage was centred in a frozen pool of his own blood, his throat slit.

"No..." Rhys gasped. He did not believe it. He would not believe it! "No!" Rhys roared as a hot fury burned within him.

"Where is Arlas?" Sol croaked. "Where is Arlas!?" he demanded again in desperation. He turned to look at Rhys with raw eyes.

Rhys shook himself free of his grief's paralysing hold and tried to focus his scattered thoughts. "I don't know," he stammered, looking frantically around whilst trying to avert his eyes from his fallen friends. His mind burned, unable to compose itself. They had to find Arlas, and fast; otherwise, a similar fate awaited the three of them. The snow was disturbed by multiple sets of footprints, several of which led off west in the direction Arlas had ventured.

"There!" Rhys pointed.

He lifted Sol to his feet and the two of them both drew their staves. They rushed into the forest, following the tracks. Trees sped by in a blur. Wiping the tears from his face, Rhys charged on, his body fuelled only by adrenaline and rage. Erupting through the edge of the forest, they halted. Gaining their bearings, they scanned the environment. Ahead, moorland rose sharply on two sides, forming a gorge walled by naked rock, roughly ten fathoms deep. The footprints continued forwards, leading straight into its throat.

"There!" Sol yelled, pointing to a distant figure several furlongs ahead.

Rhys focused his eyes. The figure was unmistakably Arlas, stood alone atop the far wall of the narrow gulch. Sol broke into a sprint and

Rhys chased close behind. The snow crunched loudly underfoot as the two mages stormed across it towards the gorge. Arlas was now clearly visible, but something was awry. The man appeared to have his hands bound behind him, and his mouth gagged. They drew nearer. Rhys could make out Arlas's eyes. They were opened wide, struck with terror as he looked down at the two of them racing towards him. At that instant, Rhys realised too late what was already happening.

Suddenly Arlas dropped from the precipice above. The mage plummeted for several seconds before the rope around his neck snapped taught. Halting suddenly in mid-air, Arlas's neck broke, killing him immediately.

Rhys skidded to a stop in the snow. He watched Arlas's body swing lifelessly above. Falteringly, Rhys peered back up to the ledge. Indus stood where Arlas had been seconds before, now gazing down at Rhys and Sol with a twisted grin.

"No!" Sol screamed in utter despair as he collapsed to the floor.

Rhys slowly scanned the ledges of the gorge. Atop the surrounding bluffs, the menacing figures of Byron Lance, Marus Stone, Jack Ironwood, and Stanton Grey steadily emerged. It was an ambush.

The ground in-front of Rhys exploded in flame. Rhys glanced back at Indus to see him launch another blast of fire straight towards him. Ducking, the conflagration seared overhead.

Sol was thrown from his feet as a bolt of

lightning struck the snow beside him. The gorge around Rhys began to disintegrate. Dust and ice erupted into the air as the very ground detonated underfoot. Thrown upwards, Rhys tumbled through the air, slumping hard amidst the clouds of snow and ice raining down throughout the gulch. A sharp ringing pierced his ears. Everything else seemed muffled as he tried desperately to clamber back to his feet.

Scorching flames licked inches past, striking the trench wall and cracking the rock. Scrambling clear of the next explosion, Rhys threw himself into Sol, saving his friend from an immolating ray carving down from the clifftops. Fighting back to his feet, Rhys dragged the mage behind the cover of some fallen rocks, the deafening bombardment of the gorge continuing to rage around them.

"Sol!" Rhys screamed in his face.

The man's eyes rolled in their sockets. Debris rained down as the bluffs crumbled around them.

"Sol!" Rhys shouted a second time.

Sol's eyes focussed as he snapped out of his stupor. Shaking his head, he looked into Rhys's gaze.

"We need to get out of here!" Rhys yelled, barely audible over the explosions surging throughout the gulch.

"Arlas?" Rhys could only read Sol's lips.

"He's dead! We need to go!" Rhys shook him

violently and Sol began to come around. "Now!" Rhys cried out.

Rhys leapt out from behind the cover and fired a bolt of silver force at Indus. The energy soared clean above his enemy's head. Indus retaliated, sending down a meteor of flames on target straight for Rhys. Without hesitation, Rhys fired a second bolt of force. The kinetic energy struck the fireball in mid-air, deflecting it back towards its sender.

Seizing the opening, Rhys grappled Sol's arm and pulled him up, as Indus leapt clear of the redirected projectile. The two magi fled back down the valley, sprinting with all their might. An elemental fusillade hurtled past, raining destruction and chaos down around them. Clearing the pass, the two magi sped onwards out across the expanse of snow. They raced towards the woods, daring not slow down, daring not look back.

NINETEEN

"**D**on't let each other out of your sight!" Arlas stressed. He turned and walked through the trees, out of the clearing. Obscured in the shadows of the foliage, he looked back to watch the other four. They stared at each other, not fully comprehending what had happened. Eventually, they too turned and headed in their own directions, off into the woods.

Inhaling deeply, Arlas strode back the way he had come, stepping again into the empty glade. He looked once more at the impaled head of his friend, now hidden beneath a blanket.

"What have you done Indus?" Arlas spoke out to seemingly no one.

But with those words, Indus emerged from the shadows on the far side of the clearing. He appeared tormented, as if part of his humanity had left him since the last time they had spoken. A moment later, the remaining five mages of the Order appeared, looming out of the trees on all sides of the glade to surround Arlas.

"I will make this easy for you." Arlas's voice was as calm as ever. He drew his staff and cast it on the ground at his feet. "Know that there is no way back from this—for any of you!" he spoke once more, in one last attempt to make his old allies see reason.

The clearing remained quiet. Byron Lance moved slowly behind Arlas, staff drawn. Indus silently nodded to him, and the hulking man struck Arlas across the back of the skull with the shaft of his weapon. Arlas dropped to his hands and knees, gritting his teeth, refusing to cry out in pain.

Indus strode slowly over to him and crouched to face his old mentor. "It didn't have to come to this old man!" he hissed in Arlas's ear. "We cannot hide in the shadows of this world any longer. It is our sacred duty to rule over the world!"

"We are Cambria's protectors, not its rulers!" Arlas refused as he looked into Indus's fiery eyes. "Do not betray the creed of our order!"

"I have learnt the secrets you keep from us: the lies you spin about our order to justify your actions. I know who and what you are. And I know all you have done! You forced the Order into exile. It is *you* that betrayed our creed long ago. Ruling is the only way we can truly offer Cambria our protection! How can we save Cambria when it does not even know we exist?"

"If you truly knew all you claimed to—if

you had seen what I have witnessed, you would condone the actions I have taken to protect this world! Abandon this pursuit of power, Indus." Arlas pleaded. "This road you are on does not lead where you believe it does!"

"I know the actions I must take. You are merely too cowardly to do what is required," Indus sniped. "The power we possess... we are gods among men! And it will take nothing less than the power of gods to save mankind from what is to come!"

"If you pursue this, the world will burn!" Arlas warned.

"No, Arlas," Indus shook his head. "This is the only way to prevent just that!" Indus rose back to his feet, and with the butt of his staff, he struck Arlas across the face. "Tie him up!" he ordered his followers.

Byron wrenched Arlas's arms back and coiled them in rope. Marus Stone then forced a rag into his mouth and gagged him.

Arlas was hoisted to his feet, and suddenly Seimon and Matthew burst through the trees into the clearing, their weapons drawn. A frenetic skirmish broke out as the two magi sprung their ambuscade, the glade rapidly dissolving into chaos. Matthew cast a bolt of white flame at Indus as he charged towards the leader of the coup, but the rebel mage deflected the blast of fire with a sweep of his stave. Capitalising on the element of surprise, Seimon rushed Ethan Hall. Before Ethan could so much as raise his own weapon in defence, Seimon had sliced clean through his throat. Ethan Hall fell dead, blood spewing from the gash across his neck.

Locked in a duel with Indus, Matthew launched another crackle of flames. But as he leapt clean aside of a bout of fire launched back his way, Marus Stone intervened, sending forth a shrieking scythe of purple energy towards Matthew's exposed flank. The howling arcane projectile blindsided the mage, ripping clean through his abdomen.

"Matt!" Seimon screamed as his friend dropped to the snow, trying to hold in his guts, stopping them from pouring out the massive wound to his flank.

Seimon leapt aside, evading an eruption of flames from Indus's staff, stepping straight into the path of Jack Ironwood as he dodged clear. Jack brought down the weight of his shield with all his might. The edge of the bulwarked crunched as it struck hard against Seimon's skull, staving inward the man's temple.

Arlas winced as he helplessly watched Matthew; in his final moments of life, the mage desperately was trying to shovel his innards back into his torso. After a few excruciating seconds, the mage went completely limp, dying there in the snow.

"Fucking bastards killed Ethan!" Byron scowled as he looked at the three dead men.

Marus strode over towards Seimon and spat upon the man's corpse.

Indus knelt in front of Arlas once more, grasping the man's face tightly. "Where is your pet, Thomas?"

Arlas made no sound as he averted his gaze from the bodies.

"No matter," he chortled. "Robert has his orders. I am confident he will bring me Solomon's head." Indus released his clasp of Arlas, and with a quick gesture, he signalled Byron. The goliath of a man began to drag Arlas across the icy ground, into the trees. The others followed.

The five of them walked with their prisoner for several minutes, leaving the wood behind them. They entered a narrow valley with steep rocky walls on either side. At the far end of the gorge, a natural stone staircase led them up to the top of the escarpments. Byron forced Arlas towards the ledge, Indus taking the archon's staff and driving it powerfully into the ground behind the mage.

Attaching a rope to Arlas's staff, Indus fashioned a noose at the other end and passed it over the Archon's head. Byron released his grip of Arlas as Indus took hold of him.

The mage pressed his lips up close and whispered in his ear. "You die a traitor's death!" he hissed. "Goodbye, old friend," he added coldly.

Indus forced Arlas closer to the precipice. The archon looked to the distance ahead. His eyes widened in horror at the sight of Sol and Rhys sprinting towards him. Indus's foot slammed hard into his back. His stomach lurched as he was thrown from the ledge. The air rushed past. He plummeted towards the bottom of the gorge. The rope snapped taught. All went black.

Rhys bolted upright. Icy air plunged frantically in and out of his lungs whilst crystals of frozen sweat clung to his brow. The dream still wove itself through his mind. The terror hung heavily from him as he twisted his head in desperation. He scanned the frosted moorland, gathering his thoughts, yet the niggling fear and the sensation of wrongness whittled at his mind.

He looked to Sol curled beneath his cloak in the ditch beside him. Not an hour had passed since they'd taken refuge, collapsing in the dyke for the solace of brief rest. Two days' flight. Barely a moment of recovery. His mind was hazy, yet still jittering through adrenaline racing in his throbbing blood vessels. Then the sudden realisation cut through his grogginess. They were near!

"Sol," Rhys hissed, violently shaking the mage awake.

Wide-eyed, the man shocked into consciousness. He gasped in terror as he too understood the impending danger: the aura of magi drawing rapidly closer. They gathered up their packs, and without hesitation, raced down the hillside, leaping between snow-capped tussocks in the bleakness of dusk.

Rhys's ears caught sound of the commotion behind them.

"They are near!" the booming voice of Byron Lance roared some way away.

"They know we are coming!" added Jack Ironwood.

"Do not let them escape!" threatened Indus.

The two magi spurted on, traversing the rugged terrain in leaps and bounds, sprinting as fast as their legs could carry them.

"How did they find us?" Rhys cried out.

"They're tracking us—hunting us!" Sol replied.

"Will they chase us to the ends of this world?" Rhys despaired.

"We must lose them!"

"There!" Rhys pointed across the desolate moor to a copse that sprawled through the valley ahead. "We'll lose them in the wood!" he insisted through short sharp breaths, veering now in its direction.

"They will still find us!" Sol argued.

"Trust me!"

Rhys glimpsed back across his shoulder and his heart spasmed in dread. The silhouettes of their stalkers emerged from above the hill's brow, and the pursuing mages cried out in sighting their prey.

"Kill them!" the voice of Indus roared.

A piercing shriek hurtled towards them, and a blur of purple magic twisted clean past Rhys, spinning into the ground, churning up soil and grass as it ripped apart. Thunder bellowed, and without delay, a bolt of crimson lightning forked mere feet in front of the fleeing magi. The ground detonated behind with the collision of a flying boulder. Frosted rays beamed across the grass to their flank, and a ball of crackling flame seared narrowly overhead, impacting the icy moor, setting the sedges instantly ablaze.

The bombardment continued to assault them as Rhys and Sol surged on, dodging and weaving as the very moor disintegrated around them. The treeline drew near when the arcane salvo briefly subsided. Rhys glanced back. Their pursuers were giving chase, looking to narrow the distance between them and their prey.

The trees rushed past as Sol and Rhys burst into the copse. Rhys panted against the screaming stitch in his gut. On they raced, deeper into the wood, darting with desperation between trees to break their followers' line of sight.

"What's our way out?" Sol gasped desperately, looking to Rhys for a plan of escape.

"There!" Rhys screamed, his vision zooming to a precipice a furlong through the woodlands where the forest fell away to a cliff.

"We won't survive!" Sol dismayed.

"Then we die either way!" Rhys argued, not relenting in his race towards the ledge.

Another peek back over his shoulder revealed the chasing magi had now followed into the woodland. They too had spied the precipice up ahead toward which Rhys and Sol sped. They halted their pursuit to form a firing-line, and all at once continued their assault. Rays of fire and frost scorched through the woods. Crackling electricity fizzed red in arcs between the trees. Trunks and earth exploded in clouds of dust and wood, and the howls of purple blades ripped towards Rhys and Sol.

Coursing adrenaline splintered the passing seconds into dilated moments as both mages watched the unparalleled destruction unfold around them. Soil and stone fountained out of the ground ahead of Rhys. He veered aside, swerving narrowly clear of the detonation. Sol vaulted over a fallen trunk as a twisting razor of magic from Marus's stave whizzed close to his chest, cutting through the fabric of his coat, marginally missing flesh. A fiery mist raged suddenly about them and Rhys ducked to avoid the scathing heat. Another leaping stride from Sol saw him escape a scarlet branch of lightning as it traced beneath his feet. The bark of the encompassing pines shattered away as another meteor of rock pummelled and bored through trunk after trunk. The barrage of hurtling stone travelled faster than eyes could see, decimating the wood to showers of splinters. Rhys raised his hands to protect his eyes and face as all elements whistled and boomed in a maelstrom of death.

The chaos ensued, growing louder and more powerful with every second the two men spurred on. Each step, they defied mortality. Shredding debris and scathing heat scratched and scorched their skin, yet the onslaught of magic continued to tear past without slaying them. The seconds fractured further, and for a fleeting moment that seemed to stretch endlessly, the ear-shattering booms fell silent. The lull then ended when suddenly the soil beneath their feet blasted away with a swelling of fire and force.

Rhys and Sol were flung from the ground, thrown high upwards by the powerful eruption. Tumbling and flipping in the air, Rhys gasped as the ground punched the air clean from his lungs. Ringing hammered through his ears and the canopies blurred and swirled above him. He clawed at the snow and earth and his spinning vision focussed once more. Fighting to his feet, he spied Sol lulling around dazedly upon the forest floor beside him. The cliff ledge was but a dozen yards ahead. He stumbled closer to his friend and gazed back over his shoulder. The magi were in pursuit once again, charging directly for the two of them. Regaining his wits from the shock that had stunned him, Rhys grabbed Sol by the scruff of his collar and heaved him to his feet.

"Come on!" he urged in desperation, stumbling back into a sprint.

Sol followed, running with all the energy

he had left. The lip rushed up to meet them. Rhys threw himself from the ledge. Flailing arms and legs, he and Sol dropped over the precipice and plunged from the clifftop. Far beneath, the tops of fir trees rushed rapidly upwards. Clawing through the air the two men reached for the sylvan limbs to break their fall. Down they plummeted, disappearing into the emerald fir feathering below.

TWENTY

"You die a traitor's death!" Indus snarled in Arlas's ear. "Goodbye old friend," he uttered with an icy tongue.

Grasping the back of his robes, Indus thrust the Archon towards the jagged cliff-edge. The mage anguished as he gazed down from the ledge at the fall that awaited, despairing as he sighted Sol and Rhys, racing out across the snowy plains, into the trap that was set for them. With a twisted grin, Indus drove his boot into his mentor's back and watched in spite as the man toppled from the precipice. The rope snapped taught, and the lifeless corpse swung heavily from the ledge.

Indus then leered down at Rhys and Sol despairing in the canyon below. "Kill them," he hissed.

Rhys roused with a quickened pulse. Panting down bitter lungfuls of frigid air, he clawed at his sweating face, squinting against the haunting images of the nightmare that plagued him even now he had awoken. Only as he glanced around, assuring himself the dream was over, did it seep out of his thoughts. He shuddered beneath his frost-covered blanket, hunched uncomfortably between the knotted roots of a grand elm. Rhys spied Sol looking to him once again with an expression of concern.

"Sorry," Rhys breathed, "I did not mean to wake you."

"No matter," Sol uttered as he rose from beside the mage, rubbing his palms vigorously in the biting chill. "It is time we made haste once more!"

Rhys arose, still shaking, keeping his frosty quilt cloaked tightly around himself, and stomped out the remaining embers of their pitiful fire. The tiny flames had kept them alive through the worst of the night, though barely, it seemed. Sol scooped a few handfuls of snow over the cinders, burying the ash until it was utterly concealed. The two men donned their luggage, and off they sped again, into the gnawing fog and wind.

They stepped lightly, planting their feet on roots and stones, daring not to leave any trace of their passing. Dawn swept in from the east, bathing the gloomy mist that smoked through Brenwood in amber haze. They did not halt or even rest but a moment for several hours as their weary legs carried them hard and fast through the old woodland. When finally the amber light streaked to golden rays, cutting swift like a blade through the smothering fog, did the two mages eventually pause to gather their breath.

"It was that dream again... wasn't it?" Sol wheezed, sucking in what remained of the thin veil of frozen mist.

"Yes," Rhys nodded as he leant against the bark of a beech.

A fortnight had passed since the deaths of the others, and each night had been wrought with the same nightmare that still ailed Rhys even now, several hours after waking.

"What do you think it means?" he asked after a time.

"I think it is merely the reconstruction your mind has made of the events that took place," Sol explained.

"Yet it is so vivid and fluid in my thoughts!" Rhys argued. "I cannot help but feel there is more to it! What if I were witnessing what really happened?"

"I have never heard of such a thing before Rhys. And even if such were the case, what meaning would there be to it? We know already what happened that day. If the images of your dream proved true in their happening, then very little if anything is changed."

"You are right," agreed Rhys as he shook off once more the prying thoughts.

"Come," Sol said, "we can afford to rest no longer."

"Surely, they aren't still pursuing us!?" Rhys proclaimed. "We've not sighted them since our escape across the moor eleven days ago. Since then, we've left little evidence of our coming and goings. We have pressed hard, rested little, and made sure to change our bearing. We have fled nearly three hundred leagues—a distance I thought impossible for any man to cover in such a length of time, be he mage or not! Do you even think it possible they still follow?"

"I do not know," Sol confessed. "But if they do, and we ease up, then I doubt we will survive another encounter. When this day is done, perhaps then we can rest a while longer—but for now I wish to press on."

"And then what?"

"And then we try to find somewhere to take shelter for a time. Somewhere out of this sapping cold, where there is food, and if we are lucky, maybe even drink."

"But what then?" Rhys demanded in frustration.

Sol stared back at Rhys with cold eyes. "We kill Indus!"

"Just like that?" Rhys scowled.

"We will find a way," Sol insisted. "Whether it is in a month, or ten years from now, we will hunt them down and execute them one by one. We will avenge our brothers. Justice must be done!"

Rhys nodded solemnly as hatred for their enemies burned deep in his gut.

"Until that time comes, we must flee and bide out time. We two are no match for the five of them. We must wait until chances better favour us. The day will come Rhys—I promise you. But it isn't now."

So onward they raced, over frozen creeks and under snowy canopies, until afternoon turned to evening, and evening to night. Come midnight they took refuge from the gnashing winds under a craggy overhang. They lit themselves again another meagre fire, dining on the very last crumbs from their packs. Huddling together, they struggled to sleep against the fearsome chill of the January night.

Upon wakening the next morning, Rhys had never felt quite so miserable. Howling gales had made slumber near impossible, and had their blankets not been enchanted to repel the cold, Rhys suspected they might have frozen to death during the night.

"I think it safe now for us to lessen our haste," Sol said as he roused.

"Let us hope they abandoned their pursuit, for we gave them good reason to!"

"I doubt we could continue at the pace we have fled so far, even if we needed to," Sol confessed. "I am battered and beaten by the elements, and I fear my legs are not far from failing. I think it best if we try to reach the nearest village. There can find an inn—I can't bear another night out in the cold. Moreover, we are both in dire need of a proper meal!"

Rhys nodded silently.

"Come," Sol beckoned, "the village of Wythe lies to the east, and but a league south of here we should find a road that walks to it."

Swinging packs over shoulders and forgoing yet another meal, the two men embarked on a southward bearing on aching legs and blistered feet. Even now, they avoided leaving a trail in the snow as best they could, though they doubted their foes still hunted them. Within the hour, the dawn transitioned to early morning, and the deciduous oaks and elms to coniferous pines and spruces whose boughs bristled against their adjacent brethren sentinels. The forest became so dense that they did not realise the road's approach until they were nearly upon its banks.

The gentle crunch of boots in fresh snow placed the magi on their guard, and hunching in shadows, they crept towards the highway's border. Pushing hesitantly through the thicket, both men perched atop the ditch that ran aside the thoroughfare. Still swathed in shadows, they peered intently up and down the bridleway, spying the source of the footfalls as they grew steadily louder.

A single wayfarer walked the route: a tall man of fair complexion wrapped warmly. Concealed loosely across his back was a longsword sheathed in a scabbard. He strode purposefully along his westerly route, passing Sol and Rhys mere feet away without ever noticing their presence.

The magi sat in silence as the traveller passed them by, patiently waiting for him to pass out of sight before they would step out into the open. But the lone man never made it so far, for not many yards west along the path from where the two mages observed him, out stepped another man with intent clear, who too had been lurking in the trees off to the wayside.

The footpad clasped a gnarled dagger of rusting iron that appeared never to have been cleaned nor sharpened, and with a depraved grin, he directed it in an outstretched arm at the wayfarer. He used no words to threaten his victim, merely uncurling a dirtied palm missing multiple fingers, expecting a purse to be fearfully placed in it. The traveller did not bow to the threat. Instead, he stared down the brigand with a stern gaze, the villain having failed to spot the sword across his back.

"Should we do something?" Rhys asked in a hushed whisper.

"Not yet," Sol replied quietly as his keen eyes surveyed the trees that bordered the road's far side. "I am willing to bet this thug has allies that have yet to reveal themselves. This location wreaks of an ambush, the scale of which is unbeknownst to us!"

Deftly unshouldering the scabbarded sword, the man unsheathed the blade, twirling it in a flourish so rapid it seemed a trick of the eye. The weapon glistened in the frosty air, the blade forged from high-grade steel and burnished to an almost mirror like finish.

"Be on your way scoundrel!" the traveller barked. "You shall get no coin from me!"

The bandit licked his lips, issuing a toothless smile as he realised the value of the sword alone far exceeded any coin he had intended on robbing from the plush traveller. All of a sudden, over the ditches and out of the woods, leapt the rest of the highway gang, swiftly emerging from out of their many hiding spots. The disparate band swarmed around the swordsman, encircling him quickly, brandishing a mismatch of makeshift and stolen weapons.

Nearly a dozen highwaymen in total, each shadier than the last; clubs, axes, daggers, and billhooks all drawn and raised as they cackled and roared at their trapped prey. A lone bowman was the last to emerge from the wood, a hunting arrow nocked in his half-drawn longbow.

Neither Rhys nor Sol could have expected what came next. Instead of dropping his sword and surrendering his coin, as any other man so grossly outnumbered would have done, he darted forwards blindingly fast, driving the point of his bastard sword clean through the gut of the toothless ringleader.

Utterly stupefied, the surrounding brigands merely stood watch in horror as the swordsman ran their leader through. The ambushed traveller rent free his blade and the footpad dropped to his knees, clutching the gaping wound to his stomach, before seconds later, slumping dead in the snow at the swordman's feet. Before the crew of bandits had sense to react, the traveller swung for the next of the thieves, his blade cleaving into the man's neck, carving open his jugular, slaying him in an instant. Two dead, but far more left standing, the swordsman readied to strike again. By now, however, the element of surprise from his brazen retaliation was beginning to wear off. First to react was the bowman, his weapon already drawn and ready to fire. Releasing the bowstring, the archer loosed his arrow.

The arrow blurred through the air, burrowing deep as the head pierced clean through the traveller's shoulder. The swordsman staggered back from the force of the impact, yet managed to remain on his feet. Refusing defeat, he dived through the gap in the circle where he had cut down the first two men, rolling quickly back to his feet to face the highwaymen, now no longer surrounded.

As taken back by what they were seeing as the highway gang themselves, the two mages merely looked on in bafflement, failing to act as they stayed concealed within the brush. The brigands finally regained themselves, those still left standing managing to free themselves of their bewildered stupor, and all at once, the gang charged the wayfarer, lunging and flailing their weapons in a torrent of wild attacks. Skating backwards through the snow with nothing short of prodigious footwork, the swordsman retreated away, fending off the overwhelming sally launched by the bandits. Twirling his sword in a direct succession of flourishes, he parried a series of cleaving axes and lancing billhooks, backpedalling as he deflected each blow aimed for him. Using the rearward momentum of the charge, the traveller managed to snag his crossguard beneath the hook of a thrusting bill; with a sharp yank, the swordsman nearly rent the brigand clean off his feet, sending the villain stumbling forwards off balance. Stepping swiftly in behind his staggering foe, the traveller spun in a pirouette, parrying an incoming axe blow before carving a slash clean up the billman's back. The footpad sprawled forwards, slumping into the snow, staining the road beneath him crimson.

With another of the crew of outlaws cut down, and the odds now somehow seemingly favouring the lone swordsman, the melee momentarily ceased. Terrified by the masterful swordsmanship of what they had hope to be an easy victim, the highwayman backed hesitantly away from the traveller as he raised his sword into a high guard and stared the gang down, daring them to engage him once more. For a short time, it looked as if the bandits would not. Three of them lay dead, slain hard and fast by a single man in nothing more than the space of a few seconds, those still alive all fearing they might be next. But in that moment, the traveller faltered, his guard lowering for a split second as a fleeting daze seemed to suddenly spill over him.

The swordsman shrugged off his momentary weariness, but it had been enough to dispel his foes' dismay. They threw themselves at him a second time, roaring and snarling as they assailed in a whirlwind of wild slashes and jabs. The swordsman backpedalled once again, fending away the fervent assault, yet the precision of his counters and parries had lost their edge; as the fight wore on, what moments earlier had been a chain of deft blocks and deflections, were now deteriorating into unruly and uncoordinated swings.

"The arrow!" Rhys gasped. "It was poisoned."

At the end of his strength, his constitution failing, the wayfarer dropped to his knees. A fell swoop of an axe sent the sword tumbling from the traveller's grip. The man's defiant defence had seemingly come to an ill-fated end, but before Rhys realised it, he and Sol were already out in the open, charging toward the gang, who until now were completely oblivious to the magi's presence.

A salvo of lightning forked from Sol's staff, striking first the bowman, then next two more thugs at his side, each crumpling dead as the electricity rippled through their bodies. Rhys let fly an explosive bolt of force that cascaded at blistering speed into an unsuspecting bandit. Thrown clean from his feet, the villain whirled upwards, his body breaking as it thumped into a slanting tree trunk overhanging the road. Lightning flashed once more as Sol dispatched another pair of brigands, whilst Rhys closed the remaining distance to the last man standing. The shrill cry of an ethereal blade rang out through the frozen wood, and the final bandit crumpled dead at the mage's feet. Their ambuscade had been so fast and swift that Rhys had slain the last of the gang before he had even turn to see who had launched the ambush.

The gang lay dead, soaking the white snow-carpeted bridleway incarnadine. Among them was the swordsman, face down on the ice. If he weren't yet dead, he was close. Sol did not hesitate. Rushing to the traveller's aid, the mage knelt at his side, flipping the man, checking to see if he was still breathing.

Rhys however, stood paralysed in the centre of the road. He stood gaping in horror at his surroundings. Near a dozen bandits were sprawled out, butchered in the snow, but Rhys failed to see them; instead, wherever he looked, all he could see was the bloodied body of Robert Kwesi.

"Rhys!" Sol cried out.

Rhys heard nothing but the distant muffle of Sol's voice. Haunting images continued to ghost across his mind. He watched himself plunge his dagger into the mage's throat, wrenching it free, only to sink it back into the southerner's flesh again and again without mercy. He was on top of Robert, stabbing unrelentingly into the long dead body, savagely butchering what little remained of the man's throat. There was blood on his hands. It soaked into the snow. It stained his clothes. It dripped from the tip of his knife. And now, it also tainted his staff. What had he done? He was no killer, but he tallied two more to the lives he had taken. What had he become!?

"Rhys!" Sol yelled louder than before.

Rhys suddenly regained himself, finally hearing his friend's cries.

"We need to act fast!" Sol stressed as he clutched the now convulsing stranger in his arms.

Sol, ripping the arrow from the man's shoulder, revealed an arrowhead congealed with blood and a sticky black residue. The spasming traveller fell suddenly limp. The mage examined the substance closely before bringing it close to his nostrils to take a cautious sniff.

"Mortoc flower!" he thought aloud. Sol dove straight into his pack and pulled out a bound leather book, similar to Rhys's codex. He flicked rapidly through the pages of notes until he found one upon which was sketched the detailed image of a spiny, black-leafed weed. Atop the drawing, penned in Sol's hand read 'Mortoc,' and all about the page were scribblings that Rhys could not fully make out.

"Lie him on his side," Sol instructed Rhys as he leapt to his feet. "And off of the snow, else he may freeze to death before the poison can kill him!"

Rhys nodded. He produced his bedroll, unravelling it out beside the traveller before dragging the unconscious swordsman over onto it.

"I will be back in a minute!" Sol called back to Rhys as he was already vanishing between two spruces.

Sol was absent for what seemed a long while, though in reality it was a mere ten minutes before the mage made his return to the road. Rhys draped his blanket over the stranger and gathered enough kindling from the roadside dykes to hastily construct a small fire beside the man.

The traveller's breathing was shallow and irregular, his skin cold and clammy. Occasionally, the stranger's eyes rolled open as he momentarily regained consciousness in his fight against the venom coursing thickly through his blood, but each time he did so, he quickly plunged back into deep stupefaction.

Finally, Sol emerged back through the trees. He strode hastily towards the comatose swordsman, carrying with him a selection of herbs and two scarlet toadstools. Quickly peeling the crimson fungi, Sol hastily chopped the gathered herbs, and using the flat of his blade, mashed the white interiors of the toadstools. Mixing the contents in a wooden bowl, the mage then tore open the traveller's shirt, revealing the weeping arrow wound, the flesh tinged blue round its borders. Swollen veins fractured all across the man's shoulder as the taint continued to flow from the wound back towards his heart.

"There is not long left for him!" Sol warned as hastily he smeared the salve he had prepared thickly over the injury. "Let us hope it is not too late. I have done all I can for him. It is up to him to fight for his life now!"

But Rhys's thoughts were far from the traveller's wellbeing. Once more, he was gaping at the bodies of the men he had slain, haunted by their blood, and by that of Robert's that seemed still to cling to his hands.

Sol looked to his friend, reading clear what thoughts plagued the mage's mind. "You have only done what is necessary of you, Rhys. The deaths of others by your own hand should never be taken lightly—but you must not let your actions haunt you. We do not have the luxury at this time for you to become consumed by these thoughts—So pull yourself together!"

Snapped out of his trance, Rhys turned to Sol, slightly vexed by his friend's lack of sympathy. Though before the moment had passed, Rhys realised this had been Sol's intention, for now his mind had been averted from the otherwise all-consuming dark thoughts that had afflicted him.

"Many more will likely have to die by your hand before this ordeal is over, Rhys. When the time comes, you must be ready to spill blood again. If ever you hesitate, it will be your life that is taken instead!"

"I know," Rhys returned coldly, turning away. "You need not worry yourself of it."

TWENTY-ONE

In the next hour that passed, the two magi remained by the swordsman's side, as gradually his pulse strengthened, and his breathing became deep and rhythmic once more. When his condition had significantly bettered, the two men carried the stranger off the road, into the cover of the woods, to avoid the attention of any passers-by.

"We cannot leave the road like this," worried Sol, gazing out at the scattered remains of the bandits. "Particularly with wounds inflicted by our magic. Any who see such injuries will think them queer and speak word of what they saw. Such rumours will spread far, quickly—rumours that all mages are trained to listen for."

"Indus will know we're here," Rhys nodded as he understood Sol's reasoning. "We must dispose of them and fast."

"He should be all right for the time being," Sol asserted, glancing back at the unconscious swordman through the thicket.

Turning their attention to the matter at hand, they dropped down from the wayside, back onto the highway. They moved quickly, dragging the bodies one by one off the thoroughfare, up the roadside bank, through the trees, into a clearing several yards from the bridleway, piling the cadavers at its centre.

"The wind blows southward—away from the road," Sol explained as he pointed his staff at the heap of dead highwaymen. A vortex of flame spiralled from the mage's weapon, quickly swallowing the corpses in an inferno of sparks and smoke. Sol sustained the jet of heat for a long moment, ensuring the carcasses had fully set alight. As the tongue of fire from Sol's stave petered out, the hastily erected pyre continued to blaze self-sustainingly. The sweet stench of burning flesh and hair wafted sickeningly up from the conflagration. Black smoke billowed through the trees, drifting southward above the canopies as it was swept up in the winds, neither detectable by scent nor visible from the road.

"This isn't the first time you've had to do this, is it?" questioned Rhys.

"Sadly, no," returned Sol gravely.

The two magi returned to the highway, looking now to the blood-soaked ice that paved the route.

"Is there anything we can do to conceal the blood?" Rhys asked.

"Besides burying it," Sol sighed. "I do not believe so. There may well be a spell that could perform such a task—alas I do not know it."

"There is much to cover..." Rhys said looking at the wide scarlet stains.

"Then we had better make haste. We have been fortunate so far—anyone could have stumbled upon us before we could hide the bodies. Were it a more hospitable season for travelling, I imagine we would already have been discovered."

"What if we were to melt the snow?" Rhys asked.

Sol stroked his stubbled chin as he considered the idea. "Patches of bare road amongst the otherwise thick snow would be a peculiar sight to any who come across it—but I doubt it would raise too much suspicion; far less than bloodstains, in any case."

The two men set about hastily melting any and all the red-tinged snow. Sol quickly cleared great swathes of the road surface, casting a broad pillar of fizzling heat from his stave that he swept back and forth across the bridleway. Rhys, having not yet learnt the art of conjuring fire from his staff, instead set himself the task of masking any patches Sol missed, melting the flecks of blood that had splattered further afield from the main site of the fray, using a thin ray of heat cast from his wand to thaw the speckled snow. Not long had passed before all evidence of the skirmish had melted away, leaving only a short track of the muddy road laid bare.

"Come," Sol said, "let us see how fares the traveller."

Rhys followed his friend through the trees on the northern bank, back to where they had left the swordsman a short while earlier. When they pushed through the spruces into the small glade, they were surprised to see the man sat upright, inspecting the wound to his shoulder caked in the dried salve. As the two magi entered the clearing, he leapt to his feet in terror, fumbling for a dagger strapped to his thigh. Drawing the short blade, he held it outstretched toward the two men before him.

The magi looked at one another with subtle grins.

"This is the thanks we get after saving his life, huh?" Sol chuckled.

"Be at ease, friend," Rhys reassured, raising his hand in a non-threatening manner. "If we wished you harm, it would have been far easier to kill you whilst you laid dying in the road."

"I was poisoned?" he deduced in a deep voice.

"Yes," Sol nodded. "By the arrow that struck you."

"You saved me!" the Swordsman asserted, sheathing the dagger.

"Sol had a much greater hand in it than I— but yes, we did," Rhys smiled.

Sol nodded.

"I am in your debt!" he thanked the two of them. "My name is Alkis Mason. Might I know the names of the men to whom I owe my life?"

"I am Rhys North, and this is Solomon Thomas."

"But you owe us nothing, Alkis Mason," Sol assured him.

"It would seem we are at a disagreement there, Solomon Thomas. I do not intend to leave my debt unpaid," he insisted. "To where do you two travel?"

"To Wythe," Sol replied.

"To what ends if you mind my asking?"

"We are just passing through," explained Rhys.

"You do not wish to divulge your true intentions to a stranger," he smiled with comprehension. "I understand. I will not pry—nor will I disclose your *nature* to others," he added furtively, eyeing the staves across their backs. "You have my word."

"Then you know what we are?" Rhys asked the man.

"I know enough of the legends of Cambria to make sense of what I saw before the poison rendered me unconscious."

"We appreciate your discretion," Sol thanked him warily.

"I myself am also travelling to Wythe— I would be grateful if you would allow me to accompany the two of you?"

Sol looked to Rhys for an answer.

"Your company is welcome, Alkis Mason," Rhys nodded amiably.

Alkis beamed and the three of them stood in silence for a short while.

"The poison in your system may be for the most part neutralised by the salve I applied," Sol explained, "but the wound itself requires some attention before we head out. I *was* intending to stitch it closed so as not to reveal our magic—but as it would seem that the cat is already out of the bag..."

Without finishing his sentence, Sol gestured for Alkis to sit back down upon the bed roll. Using the back of his blade, the mage scraped away the herb and fungus salve from around the wound, before then drawing his wand.

"Will it sting?" the swordsman smiled grimly.

"No more than when the arrow went in— and that seemed hardly to bother you."

"Back then I had the energy of the fight coursing through me to dull the pain," Alkis chuckled.

"I could fight you whilst he does it—if you think that would help?" Rhys teased.

Sol held his walnut wand close to the open wound as blood steadily wept from it. "Be still," he instructed.

The swordsman grimaced as the flesh began to weave itself back together. The trickling blood flow ceased, scabbing quickly over, before seconds later, peeling away to leave a prominent pink scar across the man's shoulder. When Sol lowered his wand, Alkis sat in stunned silence. The swordsman looked down in awe as he gently ran his fingers over the newly formed skin and scar-tissue.

"Thank you," he issued finally. "Though such words cannot possibly express my gratitude for all you have done for me."

Rhys gathered up his blankets and bedroll whilst Alkis redonned his clothes. Once fully dressed, the traveller retrieved his glistening longsword, wiping the blood from the steel, before sheathing the weapon back in his scabbard, shouldering it gently around his back and covering the pommel and hilt beneath his cloak.

"What business do *you* have in Wythe, Alkis?" Sol asked as the three began to make their way in the direction of the road.

"I am just passing through," the man smiled.

"I see," Rhys returned, raising an eyebrow.

"I have no business with the village of Wythe. I travel there because it is far enough away from the Iarbhaile."

"You are from Iarbhaile?" Sol asked as they cautiously stepped out on to the road, heading eastward down the bridleway.

"I am; though it is my home no longer."

"I can say the same of my village," Rhys

empathised, before quickly changing the subject. "You are something of a swordsman, Alkis. You held out against near a dozen attackers—and for a moment there, it looked as if you might have won, had the poison not set in! Wherever did you learn to fight the way you do?"

The man hesitated before answering, "My father taught me how to wield a sword from a young age—though I have learnt much from many others since then. But, if I recall correctly, it was not my swordsmanship that slew the remaining seven highwaymen; my admiration of your own skills far exceeds any esteem that you hold for me."

Sol and Rhys shared an anxious look with one another.

"As I have already assured," he continued seeing their concern, "I do not have a loose tongue. I swear never to tell any of what happened along this road today for as long as I live—should it please you?"

"Well," Rhys smiled, "it does make a pretty good tale. Two *very handsome* sorcerers emerge from the woods, *heroically* rushing to the aid of a lone traveller who found himself grossly outnumbered by a fierce gang of highwaymen. They arrive just in time, saving him from the clutches of death against all odds!—Maybe it wouldn't be a tragedy if such a tale were told years from now."

Sol cleared his throat loudly, suppressing as best he could the smirk that curled his lips.

"Or not," Rhys sighed. "Perhaps just leave out the magic from the story. Don't feel as if you have to play down how handsome or daring we were, though!" Rhys jested.

"So it will be told," Alkis grinned.

"And here I thought we were trying to be discrete," Sol mumbled under his breath.

The three men strolled along the path in silence for a time, soon leaving Brenwood behind them. The forest presently yielded to farmland that rolled on either side of the highway. Hunger groaned in Rhys's gut; he tried desperately to sate it with water from his flask, but never in all his life had he been so famished. He did not let it dishearten him however, instead allowing his hunger to spur him onwards, towards Wythe, where lay the promise of a hot meal and maybe even a warm bed.

"The two of you seem close friends," Alkis remarked after a time. "How long have you known each other?"

"A few weeks," Rhys replied nonchalantly.

"A few weeks!?"

"Rhys and I met a little over two months ago," Sol reiterated.

Alkis paused. "Then I imagine you must have endured much together in a short time to form the bond I see between you."

"That is certainly one way of putting it," Rhys said to no one in particular.

Sol nodded silently.

"Another interesting tale I am sure—though one, it would seem, I doubt either of you wish to discuss."

They all fell silent once more after that.

The sun faded early in the January sky, and night was closing in, when finally, they reached the village of Wythe, a small and unassuming hamlet, forested on its southern and western borders, consisting mostly of thatched stone houses.

They made straight for the inn, '*The Fat Pheasant,*' stood centre in the snowy village. The local residents had tucked away indoors as darkness set in, taking refuge from the bleak midwinter chill. As they stepped inside, through the tavern door, a blanket of warmth swelled around them. Neither Rhys nor Sol had escaped the gnawing cold of wintertime since they were last in Northcrest. The crackling warmth of a hearth and the flavoursome smells of food melting through the air had never seemed so appealing before.

The three men sat themselves around the nearest table and made no delay in ordering a plethora of dishes. Though Alkis had not been starved like Sol and Rhys, his brush with death had clearly roused a fierce hunger within the man, for between the three of them, they gorged nearly an entire joint of ham and enough bread to feed a whole family for the day.

When their stomachs were filled, Sol and Rhys spoke to the innkeeper and paid for a room between them with their dwindling coin. Ditching their knapsacks in the room, they returned downstairs to the bar for an ale.

"I'll get them," Rhys declared, patting his friend on the back as he descried that Sol's coin purse was faring even lighter than his own.

"Thanks," Sol beamed wearily as the two men glanced over to the table where Alkis still sat, nursing a pint by himself. "I will be with our new friend."

Rhys nodded before turning to the bar.

"What can I get you?" a young tavern wench immediately asked.

"Can I have two... in fact, make that three, pints of the house ale," Rhys asked, glancing back at Alkis, who seemed pleasantly surprised when Sol took a seat beside him.

"The cask up here hasn't had enough time to settle," the girl behind the bar apologised kindly. "I will need to head down to the cellar to get you those drinks."

"No problem," Rhys smiled warmly. "I am in no rush."

"I'll just be a minute."

Unhooking three tankards from above the bar, the wench stepped through a doorway and disappeared down a flight of stairs. Rhys leant against the spruce countertop as he loitered, shifting his weight between ankles to ease the burn of nearly a month's hard travel. Whilst waiting patiently for the serving girl to return, a

Entonces

young man of pale complexion and wavy sandy locks strode into the tavern and made his way to the bar. He was a young fellow, little older than Rhys, cleanly shaven and well kempt. His frame was slender, and he stood shorter than most, though he held himself purposefully, with confidence, irrespective of his diminutive stature. He walked hastily towards the tavernkeep who stood polishing tankards at the far end of the bar, seating himself on a stool opposite him.

Rhys studied the man, realising the stranger's countenance was wrought with distress. The innkeeper clearly knew him well, for before he had even taken a seat, the tavern owner had ready a cup of brandy for his patron. Nodding sternly at the innkeeper, the man tipped back his head, swallowing the fortified wine in one swift gulp. He tapped the bar impatiently, gesturing for a refill. Ewer in hand, the innkeeper quickly obliged, though almost before he had finished pouring, the patron had necked the second drink and was once more signalling for a refill.

This time the barman hesitated. "What's wrong, Cade?"

"The search party hasn't returned," the man murmured in frustration.

"I heard," the bartender sighed.

"Joshua was with them."

"They're probably just late returning, Cade."

"They planned to be back before nightfall!"

"They must just be searching a little

while longer. They'll return, soon enough." the bartender assured him.

"No, they wouldn't do that! It makes no sense. They wouldn't be able to continue the search after dark. They should have returned hours ago!"

"They'll be back before morning—You'll see! In the meantime, take it easy on the drink—and don't do anything rash!"

"I am heading out to find them tomorrow. I'll gather what hunters we have left and lead a second search party to find them."

"Cade—"

"No, Ed, you can't change my mind!"

With that, the bartender sighed and left the man to drink.

Moments later, the tavern wench returned with three full tankards of the house ale. Issuing a polite thank you, Rhys paid the girl and carried the drinks over to the table where Sol and Alkis laughed quietly.

When next Rhys went to the bar, sometime later in the evening, it was the barman who stood ready to serve him.

"Should be ready to go now," the man remarked, heavily patting the side of the enormous cask that held the house ale.

"Excellent," Rhys returned, glad he needn't wait for the man to head down into the cellar to fetch his order. "I'll take three pints."

"Coming right up!" the bartender said

merrily, taking the three empty tankards off Rhys and refilling them from the spigot of the gargantuan barrel.

"I couldn't help overhearing earlier," Rhys nodded to the man sat wallowing in his brandy down the far end of the bar. "You say a search party has gone missing?"

"Yeah," the barman nodded solemnly, placing the first frothy tankard in front of Rhys. "A few hunters and other folk went out this morning and haven't come back yet."

"You said they were a search party. Might I ask for what, or whom they were searching?"

"The other hunters," the man answered unhelpfully.

"They were searching for other missing hunters?"

Finally, it clicked for the man as he realised that Rhys genuinely knew nothing of the situation. "Well err... you see, over the last few weeks, a couple of the village huntsmen have been disappearing in Southwood forest. At first it didn't seem all that strange—folk go missing from time to time—maybe falling prey to bandits, or perhaps wolves or a bear or something; it's pretty wild territory!

"But recently, the numbers have begun to add up: we lost six folk—locals, all of 'em, in a fortnight! It became clear that something weren't right. This morning, a group of six or so went out in search of them lost souls—see if they could find out what's been happening.

"Thing is: they was supposed to be back hours ago, and no one's had word." The barman had now altogether forgotten about pouring the final pint.

"How many people have gone missing?" Rhys pressed.

"Including the six today... it must be a dozen or so. But travellers also head through them woods— can't say there's any way of knowing if any of them have gone missing!" The bartender seemed to become more concerned as he recited the facts himself.

"And you have no clue as to what has happened to them?" Rhys resumed.

"No... none at all."

Rhys nodded to himself as the bartender remembered the final tankard needed filling. Rhys paid without asking any further questions and returned to the table.

"It could be bandits," Sol suggested, his keen ears having heard Rhys's whole conversation with the barman. "But I doubt it. I don't see why they would target hunters; they normally keep to the roads and would have little business with local huntsmen. And a simple wolf pack or bear would be no match for six men."

Rhys nodded in agreement.

"Either way, if the search party still has not returned by morning, I think we best investigate these missing persons ourselves."

"Agreed," Rhys nodded, looking to Alkis who seemed utterly perplexed.

"I feel I may have missed something, friends," he grinned. "Would either of you care to explain what you were just talking about?"

Rhys and Sol exchanged a look, silently debating whether or not to enlighten the swordsman. Reaching consensus, they explained what they both had heard, but had been beyond the range of Alkis's hearing.

"I should come with the two of you," Alkis suggested when they were finished.

Sol and Rhys looked upon him with uncertainty.

"Half a dozen hunters have disappeared. There is obvious peril awaiting you in those woods. I am skilled and perceptive enough to be no hindrance to you, and as I am sure you would agree, three sets of eyes are far better than two."

"I don't mind if he wishes to join us," Rhys shrugged, looking to Sol. "He already knows what we are—and his skills speak for themselves."

Sol paused. "You are right," he agreed finally. "A third man would make the expedition somewhat safer, if nothing else."

TWENTY-TWO

R hys awoke at the sound of the latch on the bedroom door clicking softly shut. He sat up as the cold winter's sun gleamed through the cracks in the shutters. The crisp air of dawn hung within the room as Rhys glanced around. Sol stood at the entrance, already fully dressed.

"How are you?" he asked.

Rhys rubbed his eyes before opening them widely. He swung his legs out from under the sheets and sat on the edge of his bed. "Rested!" he replied finally, rising to his feet.

Rubbing his arms in the frigid air, Rhys trudged across the cold floorboards towards the window, pulling open the shutters. A blinding spell of sunshine poured into the room as the amber dawn glowed bright across the white hilltops to the east. Rhys squinted against the glare, his drowsy eyes taking a longer time than usual to adjust to the twilight. Exhaling deeply in the still air, he gathered up his clothes, and hastily dressed in his travelling gear.

"I have spoken with the innkeeper and a few of the townsfolk," Sol informed him as Rhys forced his feet into his boots. "The search party for the hunters never returned last night."

Rhys stood to face his friend, issuing a solemn look before turning slowly away to gaze through the window once more. This time, Rhys peered south, where over the rooftops of Wythe, Southwood forest was visible, wending off towards the mountains that lay beyond.

"Then we have no time to waste," Rhys declared finally. "Have you seen Alkis?"

"Yes, he accompanied me this morning."

"What do you suggest we do?" Rhys asked as he notched his belt around his waist.

"What do *you* suggest?" the mage threw back at him.

"The woods look fairly expansive," Rhys stated as he continued to survey them through the window. "The forest is too vast to explore in its entirety; we need to narrow down the search parameters. There will still be hunters in the village that have not yet fallen victim to these disappearances. I think we should make finding one our first priority; or in failing that, someone who knows the hunting grounds that they most frequent.

"As for the expedition: we should travel light—leave our packs here and take only what provisions we need for the day—that way we can move quickly and cover a larger area before nightfall."

"A well-thought-out plan," Sol praised. "Lawrence didn't waste any time in your training."

"No, he didn't," Rhys returned sombrely as a fleeting image of his mentor's head on a pike haunted his memory.

"My thoughts were very much in the same vein as yours. I've already started making enquiries—I figure I've got a half decent lead on where to begin." Sol strode across the room and retrieved his staff propped in the corner.

Donning his furs, Rhys gathered what he needed for the day before finally he too retrieved his staff leant up behind the door. The weapon instantly fizzled to life in his hand, pulsing green for a brief moment, before fading into its less conspicuous guise. Both men exited their room to find Alkis awaiting them. The swordsman was cloaked in navy, garbed beneath in travelling raiment of very fine tailoring, his collar trimmed in fur to ward off the bitter winter gales. His longsword was now belted around his waist, the man doing his best to ensure it remained concealed beneath his cloak.

"Good morning," he smiled at Rhys.

Rhys greeted the man and explained their plan to him as they made their way downstairs. Paying the innkeeper for another night, and eating a quick and light breakfast, they made ready for the day. Stepping out into the frozen village, the three men found the sunlight offered little warmth. Wythe was ghostly silent, very few of the inhabitants wandering through the streets amidst the biting chill. Sol led them briskly past the widely spread rows of cottages, towards a dull clinking of hammer on steel that rang out from the blacksmiths. As they rounded the corner the smithy came into view. A tall and stocky man of bulging muscles was working the forge, his bald head and whiskery beard already black with soot from the morning's labour.

He paid them no notice as they stepped under the shelter of the forge, the three men taking a moment to appreciate the warmth radiating from the hearth. The burly smith pulled what appeared to be a partially worked scythe head from the blazing coals. Resting the glowing blade upon a massive anvil, he lifted high his hammer, clanging it down hard on the red-hot metal. Sparks sputtered from the steel as he repeatedly worked the blade beneath his hammer.

"Hello," Rhys greeted the man in hopes he would pay them some attention.

The smith struck steel once more with a final deafening clank. Setting down his hammer, the smith tossed the glowing scythe head into a barrel brimming with slush-topped water. Steam hissed and spattered as the blazing metal sank into the icy fluid.

"Ho there, friend," Rhys greeted him once

more as the smith finally raised his head to acknowledge them.

"I don't recognise the three of you," he uttered in a gruff voice, eyeing them suspiciously. "You traders? Pilgrims?"

"Not exactly," Rhys returned.

"What can I do for you? Horseshoeing? Tools?" he paused for a moment before narrowing his eyes and adding, "Weapons?"

"Information," Rhys interposed.

The smith nodded silently as he continued to eye them perceptively. "That looks like some fine steel you are carrying." he gestured to the hilt of Alkis's sword as it poked barely visible from beneath his cloak.

Alkis immediately tucked it back away furtively.

"My guess from the craftsmanship—that came out of a lord's forge. A master smith made that, by my reckoning. How is it a man carrying such a weapon finds himself in Wythe?"

Alkis remained silent.

The smith cocked his head as he further scrutinised Alkis, before subsequently turning his attention to Rhys and Sol, studying the two mages with no lesser intensity. "The three of you want information about the forest, I take it?"

Rhys nodded, stunned by the man's insight.

"Yes," Sol confirmed.

"We have lost eleven men to the southern woodlands. I suggest you travel elsewhere!" the smith warned as he turned his attention back to the forge.

"We wish to aid in the search for those lost!" Rhys spoke out.

"I know your intentions. The three of you are fools. The men we lost were no simple travellers or peasants; they were the village's finest huntsmen. Each of them was a skilled tracker who knew Southwood better than most do their own homes. The search party sent out after them yesterday have now also gone missing. You are a bunch of arrogant halfwits if you believe you'll have any luck where better men have failed!" the smith growled. "Your attempt to help will see you dead."

"Sir, your town is in desperate need of help!" Rhys reprimanded with an authority he did not know he could portray. "Help that may not come from elsewhere. Do not be so quick to judge our chances, for they are better than you know. We know of the risk, and we are willing to take it!"

The smith grumbled, somewhat taken back by his scolding. Studying them once more, he remained silent for a time. His eyes were drawn to the stave across Rhys's back, and then to the bundle of linen that concealed Sol's.

"I didn't see it at first," the smith said finally ending his silence, "but his sword is by far the least curious of the weapons you three carry. I have seen a stave like that before." He paused. "A man by the name of Arlas travels through these parts every few years. He's… queer—keeps mostly to himself, though on occasion he has sought my services. His staff gives the same odd feeling that I get when I look at yours. I know how to forge steel and how to shape wood—I say with confidence: his weapon was not forged by any smith, and neither are yours!"

Neither Rhys nor Sol spoke.

"Many folk are suspicious of the man. Some even think him a warlock," the smith shrugged. "My dealings with him have always been courteous. And after each time he visits, the roads to and from this village always seem safer for a time." The smith fell quiet once more, examining them a final time with his stern brown eyes.

"I'll tell you what I know about the woods," he offered finally.

"Thank you," replied Rhys.

"Do you have a map of the area?"

"No," Sol answered.

"Very well. I've got one here somewhere."

The smith turned to his workbench behind him. He opened a drawer and rummaged around in its muddled depths. Nails and rivets chimed as the man moved them aside, before finally, his sooty hand emerged once more from the drawer clasping a tattered roll of parchment. He beckoned the three of them over, clearing space atop the workbench before sprawling out the map upon its surface.

In the northeast corner of the map, marked

in ink was the village of Wythe, through which ran the River Afon that wended southeast, before meandering due south several leagues upstream. The river cut clean through Southwood forest, flowing down from the eastern ridge of the Virminter mountain range.

"Do you have any means of copying this out?" the smith asked. "I'd rather not part with it."

"Err… yes" Rhys confirmed as he drew his codex from the pouch in his belt.

"I have quill and ink." The smith pointed to the edge of his work bench.

Dipping the heavily-worn quill into the bottle, Rhys hastily sketched the map on a blank page in his codex, taking care to stay true to the scale whilst also including as much detail he could manage. Whilst he drew, the smith began to explain the route they should take.

"Following the Afon is your best chance," the smith began as he traced the winding river with his blackened finger. "A path runs along its eastern bank that is well-trodden. Roughly two leagues upstream from here, you'll come to a natural rock tower—aside it, there's a fallen pine laying across the river. From there, you can go three ways: first option for you would be to cross the river by the steppingstones that lie just shy of a mile upstream." The blacksmith tapped the map, indicating a point a way upstream. "Some of the hunters stalk deer west of the river. It's a wide hunting ground and would take you the better part of a day to merely scout it.

"The next option is to head east of the stone tower. There's not much of a path to follow, but if you head on a straight bearing, you should come to this here clearing," the smith said pointing to a small glade marked on the map. "There are more deer and even a few boar to be hunted anywhere as far out as three miles from this point. Also, the wood's not as dense—it would be a bit easier to search.

"Your best bet though, I reckon," the blacksmith continued, "would be to continue south, along the Afon, through the heart of the wood. Last few weeks, a lot of them hunters that've gone missing—they were all talking ptarmigan."

"Ptarmigan?" Rhys repeated.

"You know—rock grouse? Game birds."

"I know what they are," the mage returned. "I'm just not sure what you're getting at?"

"Lot of the hunters were saying this part of Southwood is plush with ptarmigan at the moment—reckon they've migrated down from Mount Arthest for some reason. Easy pickings if you know how to trap them!"

"And you reckon that's where folk have been going missing?" pressed Sol.

"I do," the smith nodded. "Just about everyone that's gone missing—all of them were looking to make a quick bit of coin off the ptarmigan. You want a place to start, it's right here," he finished, emphatically tapping the point on the map, leaving a sooty fingerprint on the southern fringes of the woodland where the forest edged across the foothills of Mount Arthest.

Once the smith had finished speaking, Rhys continued scribbling a while longer, marking the last few details they needed to navigate the wood.

"This will not be in vain!" Alkis promised as the blacksmith rolled the map away, placing it back in the drawer of his workbench before returning to his forge.

"For your sake, I hope you are right!" The smith turned his back to the three men, drawing the unfinished scythe from the drum of water, grasping it firmly in a set of tongues before setting it back in the heat of the forge.

"Thanks once again," Rhys insisted, replacing the quill in the inkpot, and blowing the page dry. Stepping out from under the shelter, the trio set off south, out of Wythe toward the forest boundary, following the path alongside the Afon. The murky waters swept against their bearing, flowing steadily down the broad river, the opposite banks stretching two dozen yards apart. Clumps of snow floated northward in the rippling current, whilst the slowest moving water, closest to the banks, had crusted over with thin sheets of warped ice.

When they reached the fringes of the wood, a man called out, "Hold." The voice was somewhat distant, though clearly directed at them. Rhys turned to see three figures trudging through the deep snow towards them. On the right strode a woman, tall and broad with knotted brown hair and strong heavyset features. Her muscular frame was clad in hide. An ash longbow was strung across her back, whilst a quiver brimming with arrows hung at her waist. To the left of the group, a tall dark huntsman marched, like his female companion aside him, he was garbed in hide and fur, armed with a longbow and quiver of his own.

Between them walked a much smaller man, seemingly dwarfed by the other two, slender and nimble in build, his face concealed beneath an umber cowl. This third hunter was too a bowman, yet instead of an ash longbow, the archer was armed with a yew recurve bow, laminated with horn and sinew. As they drew closer, the central figure drew back his cowl, revealing him to be the man Rhys had seen in the tavern the previous night.

"I'm Cade Williams," he introduced himself, coming to a halt before them. "This is Howell Barats and Jade Marcel." He gestured to his companions.

"Rhys North," the mage responded.

Sol and Alkis introduced themselves likewise.

"I heard the three of you intend to search the forest for the missing villagers?"

Rhys looked to Alkis and Sol before answering, "You heard correctly."

"We too are in search of them," Cade returned. "We should work together."

Rhys stayed silent. He contemplated the idea of the three hunters accompanying them, though quickly decided against it. Their assistance would mean he and Sol would be faced with either revealing their nature to three strangers, or avoid using any means of magic, putting themselves at considerable risk from an unknown enemy. Neither was an option.

"I am sorry, but we prefer to keep to ourselves," Rhys finally replied.

"Sir, my husband is one of the men who did not return yesterday," Cade argued. "I'll be heading into the forest today, regardless of whether it is with you or by ourselves! I would much prefer it if we could combine our parties. We three know these woods well. The land is familiar to us and we are skilled in tracking. Needless to say, there is safety in numbers! You would be truly foolish to refuse our help—we are likely of far more value to you than you would be to us!"

Rhys sighed heavily and looked once more to Sol, though he already knew there was little choice in this decision. "Very well," Rhys conceded. "I assume you can handle yourselves?"

"Howell and I are a good shot—Cade is the real marksman though," Jade replied, speaking for the first time.

"You say you are keen trackers?" Alkis questioned.

"Better than you" Howell bragged confidently.

"Forsooth," Sol returned indignantly. "Regardless, keep your eyes peeled. We don't know what we're looking for, so if anyone notices *anything* out of the ordinary, inform the rest of us," he insisted.

"Understood!" Cade replied.

"Very well," Rhys nodded. "Then let us begin our search."

TWENTY-THREE

Snow squeaked under the boots of the party of six as they walked the path that carved along the river's winding banks. Their breath plumed in the frigid air, though the skies held clear for the first few hours of their journey. Verglas beaded leafless branches and armoured the trunks of the wood's deciduous trees whilst the intermingled emerald spruces and pines were dusted white with powdery snow. A league upstream from Wythe, the Afon began to narrow and twist between high-rising rocky banks. Several miles further on, the water flow hastened, breaking periodically into foaming rapids and churning plunge pools; the watercourse grew ever more turbulent the further upriver they hiked, until after a time, the thundering of successive cascades roared deafeningly through the otherwise still wood.

The sun climbed its low winter arc, but by mid-morning dark clouds had begun to roll across the sky, casting a gloom about the world. When they finally sighted the natural stone tower rising nearly ten fathoms from the Afon banks, flakes of snow were drifting in the air. Following the path around the meander, the fallen pine was revealed, lying flat across the river, its longest boughs trailing through the icy waters that raced beneath.

"The village smith suggested we follow the river southward from here and search the southern fringes," Alkis explained to the three hunters.

Cade looked to his followers before taking a knee in the snow, examining the dense blanket of white that smothered the bridleway. "A fresh snowfall descended during the night," he began, "but I can still make out the remnants of footprints." The hunter paused for a long moment of silence as he lowered himself as close to the ground as he could. "There are a large number of tracks heading east into the forest from here," he stated.

Rhys too stared at the snow looking for the imprints that the hunter claimed to see, yet his untrained eye saw little disturbance in the snow covering.

"It appears the tracks double back on themselves however—but a fresher set of footprints *do* seem to follow the river south," Cade finished, standing once more.

"Impressive," Sol praised as he too looked upon the shallow ripples where men had trodden the day before. "I concur with Cade... though I feel it would have taken me far longer to reach his conclusion by myself."

"This is only the trail of the search party," the huntsman explained. "There are no signs of those they were searching for."

"South it is then," Rhys declared, before adding jokingly, "I can tell you've hunted men before, Cade Williams!"

"Err... no," Cade returned rather taken back.

"He was pulling your leg," Sol explained.

"Oh, I see," the hunter chuckled half-heartedly.

"Come," Rhys beckoned them. "Our prey awaits!"

The sky grew darker, thick clouds condensing and swirling overhead. The trees closed tighter together, birches and hawthorns superseded by larches and firs that pressed ever nearer to the steep and icy banks. Over the treetops, Mount Arthest drew nearer; its lone white peak standing away from the rest of the Eastern Virminter Ridge that cut along the southwestern horizon.

The Afon narrowed further until its gushing waters reduced to a white and darting torrent that turned to meander east. Looking far upstream, along the snaking banks of the waterway, Rhys spied a distant shadow cast upon the path. Taking lead of the party, the mage raised a fist, signalling those behind him to halt. Lifting a finger to his lips, he prompted silence amongst the group, before slowly and stealthily they crept up the path towards the figure slumped in the snow.

When they neared the dark form sprawled motionless across the path, they could each see it for what it truly was: neither man nor animal, but something harrowingly in between. The beast was dead. Its body was layered thick with a mangy brown fur, though it seemed also to be clad partially in tattered hide. The creature was canine, resembling a dog or a wolf in form, though its pelvis seemed oddly canted for such a beast, its hind legs outstretched in such a way that hinted the creature stood erect; if such were the case, it would likely rise seven foot tall.

Realising the fiend had been slain, Rhys approached the bestial corpse, standing over it to examine the bizarre humanoid abomination. The head was wolfish in appearance; along jaw hung agape to reveal a large set of pointed yellow teeth. Two glassy white eyes stared blankly without pupils or irises of any kind. A set of pointed ears sat tattered atop the creature's head, one of which bore two iron ring piercings. The beast's arms ended with a pair of paw-like hands, padded and clawed yet equipped with opposable thumbs. A crude flint axe was gripped in one such fur-covered fist.

From the creature's neck stuck a hunting arrow. Streaking from the wound were crimson lines of blood, frozen and clumped in the beast's matted fur and soaked into the snow beneath its body.

"What is this?" Rhys asked, looking to Sol. "A lycanthrope?"

"No. This beast is not, nor ever was, human. They are known by different names across the continent: cynocephali, gnoll, amarok, werejakals —*We* refer to them as adlet." Sol directed at Rhys.

"I have never seen a creature such as this!" Howell spoke with terror in his voice.

Cade knelt, once more studying the ground. "A skirmish took place here," he announced. "I can make out the footprints of several of these beasts muddled amongst those of the hunters we have tracked." Cade paused as if what he read in the snow confused him. "These paw prints... it's almost as if the...adlet, walk around on two feet!?"

"They do indeed," Sol confirmed.

"This creature was not the only thing to be killed here," Cade continued, his voice growing suddenly more panicked. "There's more blood," he uttered, pointing to three faint crimson stains buried beneath the fresh snow covering. "There are footprints that continue along the river: two sets are human; the rest belong to the beasts. But, by the looks of it, a number of bodies were dragged through the snow behind them." Cade's voice quivered with those final words.

"They were ambushed, no doubt," Sol surmised. "Adlet seldom attack in any other way. These creatures live in tribes, occasionally taking humans as their prey—though those who usually fall victim to such attacks are most often lone travellers. It is peculiar for them to ambush a group so large!"

"Is there a chance any of them are still alive?" Rhys asked, seeing Cade's obvious distress.

"It is possible they took them as prisoners... though for what purpose, I would not hazard a guess."

"Then we best make haste!" Rhys commanded.

Following the tracks, they marched hurriedly along the trail, continuing to trace the Afon banks upstream. The river veered southeast, and the woods grew even thicker along the sides of the gully until the forest formed a dense bulwark of green. The distant sound of a snapping twig carried by the wind pricked at Rhys's ears. Glancing around to see nothing, the mage chose to ignore his senses, but moments later, he heard another disturbance in the trees beside the road. Raising his fist, Rhys signalled the others to halt behind him. Locking eyes with Sol, he realised his fellow mage likewise sensed something moving out of sight.

The pines beside the road began to rustle, and with little forewarning, an ambush of adlet burst from the thicket. Before Rhys could comprehend what was happening, the huntress Jade let out a gurgled scream. Rhys span on the spot just in time to see the woman run through with a flint spear. The surrounding ambuscade of snarling beasts darted quickly to and fro, blurred in the shadows as they circled their prey. Alkis, Cade, and Howell scrambled to draw their weapons.

A bowstring twanged as Cade notched, drew, and loosed an arrow in a singular swift motion, the missile whistling through the air, driving cleanly through the throat of a bestial spearman charging his way. Rhys curled his fingers around the shaft of his stave, feeling the arcane energy of his weapon humming in his grip, but loath to reveal himself, he hesitated, forcing the stave to maintain its guise as a nondescript quarterstaff as he tentatively drew it in the heat of the fray.

Another creature lurched from the shadows, straight for Howell, the panicked hunter frenetically trying to nock an arrow as the fiend bore down on him. Realising he no longer had a choice, Rhys acted. His stave thrummed with energy, casting off its façade, revealing its true crystalline form, the interwoven luminous veins throbbing from within as the mage swung it in a wide arc. A silver dart of force pulsed from the weapon's end, taking flight in a translucent haze, intercepting the beast pouncing for Howell an instant before it could drive its spear into the stupefied huntsman. The adlet reeled back, its body crumpling in the collision as it was slung from the bank, sent plunging into the rapids below.

Thunder suddenly peeled from behind, and Rhys twirled to catch sight of a crackle of lightning forking between canine figures. With their anonymity now shattered, Sol too had produced his arcane weapon, revealing himself to the others as he unleashed his magic upon their surrounding foes. A chaotic skirmish broke out as Rhys and Sol rained force and lightning down on their ambushers, whilst terrified by the supernatural display unfolding before him, Howell fumbled at his quiver, spilling arrows clumsily across the ground as he froze helplessly in fear.

A second wave of adlet suddenly sprung from out of the trees, cackling and snarling with howls that resembled laughter. Longsword drawn, Alkis parried a spear thrust for his chest, countering with a drive of his own that gored the attacking adlet with the point of his blade. Another arrow was let fly from Cade's recurve bow, plunging into the chest of the next nearest beast.

A final fiend remained, its resolve unbroken by the slaying of its brethren; it snapped its foaming jaws and sprung forwards on its muscular hind legs for Rhys. The beast descended through the air and was met by the emerald shriek of an ethereal blade. Cutting down the final varmint mid-flight, Rhys watch the thrashing canine snarl and whimper before slumping lifelessly in the snow. With the heat of battle at an end, the ethereal blade of Rhys's staff chimed, folding back into nothingness as it faded from existence.

All of a sudden, Rhys became aware of the eyes upon him. Both Cade and Howell stood staring at Rhys and Sol, their expressions wrought with fearful astonishment. Silence fell, leaving nothing but the churning of the Afon.

Finally, Cade shook himself free of the shock, turning now to the body of Jade. The huntress lay slain by the wound to her side. Gently, Cade drew shut her eyes before crossing her arms over her chest and straightening her legs, whilst Howell continued to glower at Rhys and Sol in dumbstruck countenance.

Rhys approached Cade and knelt beside him. "What would you have us do?" he asked.

"She knew the risks of coming into this forest. She would want us to continue," Cade answered calmly. "We can retrieve her body on the journey back. For now, we need to head onward!"

"Very well."

The bleak noon came and passed as they ventured further and further upstream. The woodlands thinned as they climbed into the Virminter foothills, until after a time, the forestry dissipated altogether. In the wood's wake was left a barren, snow-patched regolith that ascended the slopes of Mount Arthest to its rude and icy summit. To the southwest rose the rest of the Eastern Virminter Ridge, the cordillera curving westwards across the continent in a rugged unbroken chain that carved Cambria near in twain. Yet set away from the remainder of the spine, Arthest stood alone and solitary, its apex scraping through the dense blankets of gloom that smothered the heavens above, the world below sulking amidst hushed snowfall.

A tense silence had sunk across the group; none had spoken since the fight. Howell continued to leer fearfully at Sol and Rhys, keeping his distance at the rear of the party. Cade, on the other hand, appeared somewhat less troubled by the revelation that his search companions had revealed themselves as sorcerers; instead, his attention remained squarely fixed on their task, the diminutive huntsman striding at the head of the party beside Rhys, as they pressed further up the rolling mountainside, following the Afon as it snaked mile after mile up the slopes towards its source at the snowy peak ahead.

"The trail heads east from here," Cade announced, calling the party to a halt. "It's becoming harder to make out—the snow is coming down too fast; it's smothering the prints. But as far as I can tell, the tracks are heading around to the southern face of Arthest."

"We've come a long way," Sol remarked as he gazed up into the dimming sky. "Dusk isn't far off—let's pray there's not much further to go."

"How wide is the usual territory of adlet?" Rhys asked.

"Far smaller than the distance we've already covered," Sol replied gravely. "Something is truly awry."

Rhys nodded. "Lead on Cade—or these tracks may vanish altogether before we see where they lead us."

They turned east, pursuing the rapidly vanishing tracks as they wove across the southern foothills. The prevailing winds swelled as they emerged out beyond the shelter of Arthest's western reaches, conjuring currents of biting air that swept up ice and dust across the exposed tableland. All the while, the light continued to fail, the veiled sun rapidly plunging towards the mountain ridge at their backs. Yet just as dusk was breaking, the pall of clouds tore open, bathing the slopes of Arthest in an ominous scarlet hue.

"There is smoke rising from behind that rock formation." Sol pointed to a craggy tor perched atop a hill some distance away.

"I cannot see anything," Cade uttered sceptically as he strained his eyes.

Rhys turned his own gaze to the rocky outcrop, and sure enough, twisting faintly upwards in the dying light, were several ribbons of smoke.

"I can't make anything out either," Alkis added, the swordsman squinting against the twilit horizon.

"I can," Rhys assured. "I think we may have found what we've been searching for."

"I pray you are right," Cade murmured.

"Perhaps this time, we can spring an ambush of our own," Rhys suggested as they hastily made for the tor.

"Agreed," Sol returned. "But we don't yet know what lies over that hill. We need a vantage point—to survey the area, see what we're up against."

When they finally reached the tor, the sun had vanished behind the Virminter Range, the gloom drawing closed once more. In the last vestiges of half-light, the party swiftly crept across the snowy hillside, taking up position in amongst the stone stacks of the outcrop, to survey the lands below. Peering down into the vale beneath them, they immediately sighted the crude adlet encampment nestled in the crux of the dell. Lacking any form of tents or shelter, the rudimentary camp comprised mainly of beds of fur and straw haphazardly positioned around a raging bonfire. The conflagration churned out thick billows of black smoke that floated the grim scent of burning flesh and hair up the mountainside. Butchered meat charred on spits around the flames as a score of adlet lazed and skulked at the fringes of the fire. Many of the abominations sprawled out on the snow around the fireside, already gorged from feeding, chewing bones and picking their teeth, whilst others were squabbling in shrill cackling exchanges over the cuts of flesh still cooking above the flames.

"Look!" Sol whispered in dismay, directing the others' attention to the far side of the bowl.

A series of wooden posts were erected on the distant limits of the camp; to two of then were bound a pair of motionless silhouettes, arms drawn upwards, heads bowed lifelessly into their chests as they hung from the stakes. Rhys struggled to descry many details of the individuals in the waning light, but one thing he could make out for almost certain: neither rope nor chains fettered the two prisoners, instead, iron spikes had been driven through their palms into the posts in a crude and brutal method of restraining the pair.

"They have nailed them straight to the posts!" Rhys gasped under his breath.

"Who!?" despaired Cade. "Where are you looking? I can't see!"

Realising the scene was beyond the limits of normal human vision, Rhys turned to the pair of huntsman at his side to explain the situation. "There are two men bound to a post on the far side of the camp—It's too dark to determine from this distance if they are still alive."

"We need to rescue them!" Cade stressed.

"We will try," Rhys assured him.

"These creatures must be dealt with," uttered Sol grimly. "Ere they claim their next victims!"

"Indeed," Alkis nodded sombrely. "Do you have a plan of attack?" he asked, looking now to Rhys.

Rhys peered back down to the gathering of adlet, quickly denoting their numbers and arrangement as he considered their options. "A few have weapons on them, but as far as I can tell, many of the creatures are unarmed."

"Their weapons won't be far from hand," warned Sol.

"Even still, if we can strike quick enough, we can maybe overwhelm them before they have a chance to arm.

"That may just work," Sol approved.

"Cade and Howell," Rhys addressed the hunters. "Stay high. Skirt around the rim of the valley and find a good position. Stay hidden until the rest of us strike, then let fly everything you have in your quivers. Sol, Alkis—the three of us will sneak down into the basin; when we're in range, we'll ambush them. With Cade and Howell flanking from above, and with a little luck, we might just slay all of them before they can retaliate!"

"We can't forsake the prisoners," Sol put in. "Adlet would usually lack the intelligence to use their hostages as leverage; but as we have already determined, these creatures are anything but usual for their ilk."

"You are right," Rhys nodded in agreement as he took one final glance down at the camp. "If it looks like they are making a move towards the prisoners, we'll rush to intercept them."

"Let's hope it doesn't come to that,"

returned Sol gravely.

"Everyone ready?" Rhys asked, glancing around.

The other five nodded silently.

Issuing a long and tentative exhale, Rhys felt a cold rush of trepidation wash through his body as he prepared himself for the imminent fight. As ready as he would ever be, he rose out from their hiding spot, beckoning the others to follow. "Let's go!"

Rhys's feet carried him nimbly down the rugged slopes through the descending darkness, as he and the others hastened stealthily in a wide arc towards the north end of the basin. Howell and Cade split off, maintaining their elevation as they circled further around, whilst the two magi and the accompanying swordsman continued to delve towards the crux of the vale. The snow and gravel sank loosely underfoot, spilling down the slope ahead of them as they scurried in furtive descent. Glancing ahead, Rhys checked the scene lying in wait; the adlet were still unaware of their presence. Drawing up to the perimeter of the camp, they passed several mounds of foul-smelling spoil, stacked with rags, gnawed bones, and putrid carrion, discarded at the fringes of the encampment.

The glow of the fire began to illuminate their silhouettes as they pressed closer, but before they could push forwards any further, Rhys saw numerous canid heads perk up ahead of them. Ears pricked and noses reared as the wind at the magi's back and the sound of their footfalls betrayed them to the adlet. Freezing in their tracks, the trio of men hunkered down, hoping the alarm would not be raised, but seconds later, a cacophony of yapping howls sounded throughout the camp, the bestial tribe leaping to their feet as they warned one another of encroaching intruders.

With their hopes of springing an ambush rapidly fading, they drew their weapons and charged. Storming into open ground, Rhys flourished his staff, the impetus building energy within the weapon; skidding to a halt across the icy regolith, he unleashed the momentum, lancing forwards in a mighty thrust, renting apart the air in front of him with an explosion of silver energy. The missile of kinesis took flight, hurtling in a blur of speed towards a set of luminous eyes snarling in the darkness ahead. Smashing powerfully into the monstrous canine, the blast of energy smote the beast off its feet, launching it with a whimpering cry into the raging inferno of the bonfire. Thunder peeled across the mountainside as a fork of lightning carved out of the darkness, illuminating a bestial pair of fiends as the bolt electrocuted them both. Hinging on a point, Rhys fired another volley of force ahead of him, crunching a second adlet beneath a driving fist of shimmering energy. Lightning flashed again, as out of the skies, the black streaks of whistling arrows began to rain down, loosed from the hillside above, Cade and

Howell's bowstrings thrumming out of sight. The hail of arrows riddled the ground, several of the shots skewering into fur and flesh as the pack of adlet panicked and flocked around the bonfire in disarray.

Rhys and Sol continue to bombard the swarming canids ahead with lightning and force to the horrible discord of bloody squeals and howls. In mere moments, the pack had been thinned to near half their original strength, but the initial chaos of the ambuscade was rapidly wearing thin, and swiftly, the adlet scattered, bolting off into the darkness as they stalked through the shadows to launch a counterattack against their assailants.

A dozen glowing eyes reflected the amber glare of the bonfire as the adlet darted towards the magi and the swordsman in the cold night. Rapidly closing the distance, the canine tribesmen charged their ambushers, sniping from the fringes, as one by one, they darted in to harry Rhys, Sol, and Alkis. A shrill chime cut through the monstrous cackles of the adlet, and suddenly the gloom was awash with an emerald glow, Rhys's ethereal blade shining through the dark as it cut down a pouncing fiend.

A second beast lunged from the shadows, run through by a defensive thrust from Sol's copper blade. Alkis roared fiercely, raising high his glinting longsword, and reversing the momentum of the fray, he stormed forwards across the ice and snow, cleaving through fur and flesh as he slashed at a retreating adlet before it could skulk away. The swordsman continued his advance, turning away several spear thrusts driven towards him with a series of parries, deflecting the last with a twirling counter that decapitated a beast in a single blow.

Rhys unfurled another missile of energy, smiting a rabid fiend stalking on the fringes of the fray, before instinctively ducking as a stone axe whirled narrowly overhead, launched from the clawed hand of another adlet bounding his way. The berserking canine sprung off its haunches, pouncing for Rhys with a second axe raised above its head. Clashing weapons with the creature, Rhys twisted the staff in his grip, dealing a rapid riposte, the fluke of his ethereal blade carving the aberration from nave to chin.

Lightning and steel continued to flash, arrows thumping into the surrounding ground, as one by one, the sets of floating eyes blinked steadily out. Breaking rank, Rhys charged a final figure looming in the black as the canine beast backed towards the fire, snarling menacingly, and baring its teeth as it raised its spear. Cutting upwards with his staff, Rhys's blade cleft straight through the shaft of the spear, slashing across the monster's gaping jaws. The fiend reeled back as the blow sliced across its face, toppling off its feet as it tripped over into the roaring fire at its back. Howls and whimpers roared from within the blazing inferno, the beast's mangey form writhing in a smoking tangle of limbs in its death throes, before finally, the fiend fell silent, its body consumed in flame.

For a brief moment, all was still.

Footsteps suddenly rattled across the gravel, as from down the hillside, towards the direction of the row of stakes erected on the far side of the camp, raced Cade. "Joshua!" he despaired, tears glinting in the light of the fire as he recognised one of the prisoners fettered to the posts. Skidding to a halt, he dropped to his knees in horror.

TWENTY-FOUR

Rhys trudged slowly over to Cade. The hunter was knelt weeping in front of one of the prisoners. The man was black with dirt and grime. His flesh was battered and bruised, his nose broken, his eyes puffy and swollen. Dried blood streaked his face and scabbed across his bare torso, the skin all down his back and sides grazed away from where he had been dragged across the snow and gravel for several miles. The man was alive, barely, but a deep wound in his side dripped blood and pus, wreaking heavily of corruption. The second prisoner, hammer to the stake beside Cade's husband, appeared to have died many hours earlier, his skin ghostly pale, his vacant eyes glazed over.

The sound of Cade's cries roused the dying man. His eyes opened and he drifted into consciousness. He looked up at the hunter with a glassy gaze and smiled painfully to reveal a jaw of bloodied teeth.

"Cade..." he gasped weakly. "I knew you would come."

"Joshua," Cade croaked. "Everything is going to be all right."

"Sol..." Rhys turned to his friend beside him, speaking in a hushed tone. "Is there anything you can do for him?"

Sol shook his head woefully. "He is too far gone; even magic cannot save him now."

"I held out..." the man struggled, "...to say goodbye."

"No!" Cade refused. "Josh, you are going to be fine! I am here now. We can take you back to Wythe. We can heal you!"

"No, Cade..." the man winced, "it is too late." The agony in his voice was growing as he fought to speak. "I should have died with the others... but the Creator... he gave me enough time. I love you Cade!"

"I love you too!" Cade wept as he caressed his husband's face.

Joshua smiled weakly once more as the light faded from his eyes and his head sank into his chest.

They stood in silence in the moments that followed. Eventually Cade rose to his feet, and with all his might, pulled free the iron rivet that had been driven through both of Joshua's palms, pinning him to the wooden post. As his husband's body slumped limp in the snow, Cade clutched him tightly and sobbed uncontrollably.

Rhys turned away, unable to bear Cade's despair. Retreating back up the slope of the dell, he felt a slight tingling in the air. A cold breeze whispered past with an eerie presence. Rhys looked to Sol; the mage had clearly sensed the same phenomenon.

A cry of terror tore out through the gloom. Howell stood paralyzed with fear at the foot of the mountain. He outstretched a finger, pointing in horror to a nightmarish figure lurking between the crags in the bluffs above. The mangled form of a crone ghosted slowly downwards out of the shadows. The woman's body was deformed and skeletal: a frame of twisted bones wrapped tightly by leathery flesh. Her face was hideous beyond belief, grey skin pocked in lesions and warts, eye sockets cavernous and hollow. Dark and knotted hair floated in the air, her entire form defying gravity as if she were adrift underwater.

Grim rags bound her monstrous form, swirling around her, unbeholden to the effects of the wind. A pair of shrivelled bare feet dangled limply from her crippled legs, trailing across the regolith as she glided over the ground, swiftly descending the slopes of Mount Arthest towards Howell, outstretching a monstrous taloned hand towards the terror-stricken huntsman.

An evil aura of black magic emanated from the infernal being, chilling the air beyond its already bitter temperature and thickening the darkness of the night to pitch. Suddenly, a tendril of black flames cascaded from her fingers, susurrating through the air toward Howell. The dark fire ensnared around the hunter, and in a matter of mere seconds, Rhys watched the man's flesh desiccate and decay, the poor huntsman emitting a harrowing scream as his entire body seemed to decompose whilst he was still alive. A rotting husk slumped to the ground where Howell had stood moments earlier, any and all life sapped from the carcass. Stood frozen in awe, Rhys and Sol watched on in terror as slowly, and menacingly, the demonic crone turned its attention towards them.

Rhys readied his stave, rapidly firing off a bolt of force at the fiend, but as the missile of energy raced towards her, the vile demoness raised her clawed hand in defence, effortlessly brushing aside the blast of silver magic as it struck, the fist of kinesis petering out as it was dispelled. A crackle of electricity leapt from Sol's staff, successfully striking the mangled phantasm, but as the snaking tendrils of lightning conducted across her spectral body, the malevolent crone seemed utterly unfazed. Her floating robes smouldered slightly as the final sparks died away, before slowly she turned her hollow gaze on Sol.

Alkis unsheathed his longsword as he gawked in terror at the ghostly crone.

"Stay back!" Sol cried out to the swordsman, warning Alkis to keep his distance.

Curling her talon, the wretch conjured

another ripple of necrotic magic, the frond of dark fire weaving through the night in Sol's direction. The mage raised his staff to intercept the bolt, but as the spell dissipated across the arcane weapon, Sol was hurled backwards.

Unable to tell how badly Sol and been struck, Rhys sent another blast of force toward the hag, but to his dismay, the energy merely ricocheted off her skeletal body, showering gravel and snow into the air as it deflected into the ground. The vile fiend let out a harrowing wail as she locked her malefic gaze now on Rhys. Her spectral form suddenly exploded, disintegrating into a hundred trickles of shadowy vapour that serpentined through the air towards Rhys. Streaming through the wind in a blur of speed, the black fluid immediately congealed, reforming back into the hag's gnarled and disfigured frame, all within a fraction of a second. She had darted nearly thirty feet closer to the mage in the blink of an eye, and now, only a dozen yards away, she once more took aim with her knotted fingers, this time at Rhys.

Another ray of necrotic energy conflagrated from her talon. Hurling himself aside, Rhys narrowly dove clear of the rotting beam. Rolling across the gravel, he bounded back upright, twirling around and retaliating with a fizzling blast of his own magic. But before his spell could meet its target, the crone's body shattered for a second time into a mesh of dark ribbons, the tattered smoky threads spiralling towards Rhys with unfathomable speed. The crone resolidified, now mere feet ahead of Rhys, gliding ever closer still.

The strident chime of Rhys's ethereal blade rang out. He lanced forwards at the phantasm. The green glaive of energy speared into her wicked carcass. The dark crone let out a piercing shriek, baring her blackened teeth. She clasped the shaft of the staff impaling her, wrenching the ethereal blade deeper into her abdomen, pulling herself painfully closer to Rhys.

With death inching steadily closer, terror surged through the mage. A hot energy burned in his chest, singeing rapidly down his arms as the fiery power poured into his staff. The green veins of energy within the weapon flashed crimson, the ethereal blade plunged deep into the crone's heart glowing suddenly red. The stave began to spark and smoke, warped vapours of heat radiating outwards from the blade. All of a sudden, a tongue of flame licked outwards in a blazing whoosh of torrid air, engulfing the monstrous hag in a jet of fire that lit up the night. Swallowed by the scarlet inferno, the crone emitted a final chilling shriek as her dark form was immolated in the blaze.

As the flames died away, the veins of magic in Rhys's stave and the glowing blade extended from its tip returned to their emerald hue. In the hag's wake was left nothing but a few smouldering rags that dispersed in the wind, dissolving as they were carried away on the air currents.

With the phantasmal crone vanquished, Rhys rapidly span to look back at Sol, seeing to his relief that his friend was clambering painfully back to his feet, somewhat dazed from the blow he'd been dealt. Rhys hurried to ease Sol back upright, the mage emitting a low groan as he rubbed the back of his head.

"What was that?" Rhys panted as a wave of crushing fatigue washed over him.

"A hag," Sol grumbled in return, still rubbing his pate. "One of the most vile and powerful creatures in Cambria."

"No big deal then," Rhys uttered wryly.

"Their powers rival even our own—and are infinitely more sinister! They are resistant to magic of almost any kind," he explained half stumbling as he stood on shaky feet. "I cannot believe you just killed one!"

"Nor I," Rhys puffed in return as he finally began to catch his breath. "Fire seemed to do the trick though."

A dull burn throbbed across Rhys's right hand, and as he examined it, the flesh appeared inflamed, the upper layer of skin already peeling like a rash.

"This is what a brush with necrotic magic will do," Sol remarked, denoting Rhys's irritation before tenderly touching his own reddened skin across his cheeks and brow. "Be thankful neither of us took a direct hit or—"

"Or we might have ended up like Howell," Rhys replied gravely as he glanced over to the rotten corpse face down on the mountainside a short distance away.

"Yes," Sol confirmed, shuddering as he averted his gaze from the decaying cadaver. "I'll help you with that hand," he continued. "But I think I came away from that fight far worse." The mage continued to gently probe his puffy face, the aggravated skin growing angrier as the moments wore on.

"Of course. Tend your own wounds first. My hand merely stings."

Rhys collapsed in the snow and closed his eyes to rest a short while. He had exerted himself harder than ever before and it had taken a toll on both his body and mind. He was on the verge of falling asleep then and there, shivering in the frigid night, spent of what little energy he had left, when after a time, an arcane susurrus carried on the wind down the mountainside. Stirred from reverie, he opened his eyes, glancing around. Sol was stood a way away healing his wounds, Cade was still in the heart of the Adlet camp cradling the body of his spouse, Alkis at his side consoling him, whilst Howell's body lay dead in the snow; all was still and silent in the forlorn night, but from somewhere above, Rhys felt a call. The whispers spoke to something within, so imperceptibly faint they felt inaudible, but the allure was there, the same allure that had roused him on the night of his binding, beckoning him up the hillside towards the Northern Circle. He was being summoned; but for what?

Climbing to his feet, he scanned the slopes above; a verge rose upwards from the bluffs out of which the hag had emerge, and as the mage traced his eyes across the shelf, he felt the draw grow stronger. His feet moved without instruction. The essence carried him forward.

"Rhys?" Sol called from behind, but he did not answer.

He strode up the slope as the snow and shingle trickled away beneath his footing. Up he climbed, out of the sunken dell, the whispering growing louder and yet somewhat more distant with every step he ascended. Several minutes later, time for which Rhys felt he could not account, the mage was heaving his weight up the last step of the bluffs, onto the rocky shelf at their apex. As he rose to stand, he stopped dead in his tracks.

Eleven sarsen stones, each six feet or so in height, were arranged in a perfect circle, carved with familiar runes. The monument was far smaller in scale than the Northern Circle, the standing stones lacking the horizontal lintels that spanned across the larger henge's pillars. Likewise absent, were the great triliths from the heart of the megalith, but centred in the ring, akin to the monument's larger relative, was an altar carved with runes and glyphs identical to those Rhys had born witness to in the far northern reaches of the continent. Atop the altar were placed several human skulls, and the stone from which it was hewn was drenched in blood.

"The hag was using the circle to cast rituals," Sol's voice spoke out.

Startled, Rhys revolved in surprise to see his friend had followed him up the mountainside. Sol could not have been far behind him, yet Rhys had been oblivious to the mage tailing him throughout his ascent.

"It is likely this circle amplified her powers," he continued. "My guess: she used this henge to enthral the adlet through blood magic—it is possible she dominated their minds, bending them to her will, turning an otherwise savage and bestial tribe into a pack of obedient slaves to carry out her bidding."

"That's horrible," Rhys breathed.

"Hags seek nothing but power; they are witches that have fallen victim to the perils of their own dark arts—magical practitioners corrupted by their use of blood magic. If a witch practising blood magic pushes too far beyond her limits, it can prove fatal; those who are killed in such accidents return as creatures akin to what you just saw. They are twisted embodiments of what they were in life—hungry for power, always seeking to grow in strength.

"Blood magic grants the ability to control weak-minded creatures," Sol explained. "With this henge serving to focus her dark rituals, the adlet never stood a chance."

"Why were the adlet preying on Wythe's hunters if they were under the hag's influence?"

"I imagine they were acting in accordance with the hag's commands—she no doubt sent them in search of individuals for sacrifice for the vile rituals she was carrying out here."

Rhys stepped through the stones and approached the altar. Producing his flask, he emptied it over the stone, rinsing away a congealed layer of fresh blood from its surface. As the crimson fluid dripped from the sarsen, a carved glyph was revealed beneath it.

Ten lines converged to a central axis in the altar. The longest two lines aligned dead north and south respectively, bisecting the rest, which otherwise branched out at various symmetrical angles. Each line was tipped with a small circle etched into the stone, with an additional ring positioned halfway down the southerly stretching line, and a twelfth situated at the confluence of the mysterious sigil. The circle that tipped the northernmost line gleamed with a faint white energy.

Rhys looked to Sol for answers, but the mage merely shrugged his shoulders, clearly knowing as little as Rhys did. Extending his hand, Rhys brushed his fingertips across the weathered grooves in the stone and watched to his amazement as a second circle, the ring carved a tip the easternmost pointing line of the sigil, illuminated with a soft, white glow. The light slowly trickled from the halo along the groove until halting when it reached the point of convergence. Both Rhys and Sol stared wide-eyed, mesmerised by whatever magic laid within the stones.

"What is this?" Rhys asked

"The stone somehow activated to your touch!" the mage replied. "But what this circle is or what that sigil represents—I cannot say."

Picking up a piece of charcoal that sat atop the altar, Rhys sketched the sigil onto a blank page in his codex.

"What of the rest of the runes carved into the stones?" Rhys questioned as he gazed around the small henge. "They are almost identical to those of the Northern Circle. Do you know of their significance?"

"I do not," Sol confessed. "It is not believed that the Order of Magi built the Northern Circle. If they did so, the records of its construction and the secrets to its power have been lost to time. It was believed by Arlas that these runes were the script of a long dead race of people, though there have been many other theories as to their origin. Some mages say that they are an ancient form of the dwarven script, whilst others think they are the lost language of dragons!"

"Then we have no way of knowing what they represent, or who laid these stones?" Rhys asked.

"Not to my knowledge. It is possible that *this* circle may have been constructed by magi in the image of the Northern Circle, for the purpose of carrying out rituals in this region of Cambria. But whenever I have seen sarsen circles constructed by mages before, they were all far smaller in scale than this one—and never did any of them have etched in their stones the same runes as found at the Northern Circle.

"This site must be capable of channelling vast quantities of energy, else the hag would never have been able to enthral such a large number of adlet, irrespective of the blood magic she used! My guess would be that: the carvings in these stones serve as enchantments that focus magic within this henge."

"So, if ever we find ourselves in need of a site to perform a powerful blood magic ritual of unspeakable evil—we know where to come!" Rhys quipped.

"Sounds about right," Sol nodded without smiling, his eyes still drawn to the arrangement of skulls and the dried blood caked across the altar.

A short while later, the two men returned down the mountainside to the dell below. Alkis and Cade were laying the final stones across the graves of the fallen at the foot of the mountain. The body of Howell, and the hunter who had passed before they had arrived to slay the adlet, both now lay at rest, buried beneath two cairns at the foot of mount Arthest. A third grave, destined to be the final resting place of Joshua, still lay incomplete. The man's pallid, lifeless face was still uncovered, Cade stood mournfully over him, seemingly incapable of placing the final stones.

"He looks so peaceful... as if he were only sleeping," Cade sobbed as Rhys placed a gentle hand upon his shoulder. "He did not believe in the pagan gods, but the single Creator that the men of the south worship. It is forbidden to burn the bodies of those of his faith. Instead, they must be buried so their flesh and soul can return to the stone."

The hunter chuckled with tears in his eyes. "We would always argue about our faiths. I would tell him that should he pass before me, I would cremate him and scatter his ashes as is custom to the old ways... I never meant it of course, and he knew that," he smiled weakly wiping away the tears from his cheeks.

"It all seems so trivial now. I do not know why we ever argued over such foolish things, like what happens after death. No man can truly know if there is an afterlife, or if our soul is reborn to the elements. I care not what lies beyond this life; I merely wish that Joshua and I had been given more time together in *this* world!"

The hunter stood silently for a long while as the final light of the distant bonfire slowly burnt to embers. Eventually, he knelt and placed the last few stones across his husband's body to complete the cairn, before bowing his head and issuing a silent prayer to both the pagan gods and to his partner's creator.

"Irrespective of faith," Rhys began in an attempt to console the grieving man, "he was granted his dying wish: to see you one last time. Whatever becomes of his soul, he is likely at peace."

"Thank you," the hunter said, "for all you have done!"

The four men did not arrive back at Wythe until long past the witching hour. The moon and stars where hidden behind a dense veil of clouds, snow continuing to fall thick and heavy throughout their bitter and bleak return. They marched by light conjured from Sol's wand, retracing their tracks through the Virminter foothills, following the flow of the Afon through the woods, towards the cold and remote village to the north. Stopping along the way, they retrieved the body of Jade, sparing an hour to erect a small pyre on the water's edge, before giving the huntress a brief but respectful send-off not far from the site she had fallen.

When finally they entered the village, Cade issued the company a silent farewell, making his way back to his home alone. Upon returning to the inn, they discovered to little surprise that they were locked out. A loud bang on the door, however, was enough to rouse the innkeeper, and within a few moments, a heavy bolt was drawn back, and the wooden door creaked open.

They were greeted with a strange look of surprise from the tavernkeep. "Come in, come in!" he beckoned hurriedly as the cold winds rushed through the open door.

The three men stepped briskly out of the chilling gales and into the cosy warmth of the inn. The door slammed shut and was hastily bolted once more before the innkeeper turned to them with a look of bewilderment.

"Bron, the smith, said you three ventured into the woods in search of the hunters!" he explained. "I thought for certain you had met their same fate when you did not return."

"Southwood is safe once more," Rhys assured, rubbing his arms by the warmth of the fire.

"Then you discovered the cause of the disappearances? What of the missing hunters?" he questioned, eyes wide with anticipation.

Rhys shot him a solemn look.

"I see," the innkeeper sighed. "You three must be famished. Come; I will prepare you each a supper and give you hot mead to warm your blood; and then I will listen to your tale."

TWENTY-FIVE

Gulping down hot stew and mead, Rhys, Sol, and Alkis took turns explaining the day's events to the innkeeper. Beginning with the ambush in the woods, they then recounted the journey south spent tracking the adlet to their camp, and the fight that followed thereafter, climaxing with Rhys and Sol's faceoff against the hag on the slopes of Arthest. No mention was made by any of the three of Rhys and Sol's magic, their success instead inferred to be the result of careful planning and substantial luck; to Rhys's judgement, the tavernkeeper seemed none the wiser, instead, hanging off every word as he listened intently.

"A dark day!" he remarked when the tale had ended. "We lost some good folk—but, no doubt, you save many more who otherwise would've fallen prey to those wretched monsters!"

The stranger's words were surprisingly comforting to Rhys, lightening the weight his heart had borne so heavily in recent weeks. The innkeeper retired for a second time that night shortly thereafter, leaving the three men alone, with a brimming flagon of mead to finish between them, in the quietude of the small hours. As they took solace in the warmth of the tavern, drinking silently, Rhys found himself gazing at Alkis with a sense of deep admiration. The traveller had rallied to Wythe's plight, placing himself in peril without a second's thought, joining Rhys and Sol to aid a village to which he had no connexion, graciously accepting only a simple thanks and a complementary flagon of honey wine as recompense.

"Half a year ago," Rhys began, breaking the long silence that had endured, "I awoke to find my entire village had perished during the night—I was the sole survivor." Rhys looked up from his tankard, now speaking directly to Alkis. "A curse had taken the lives of everyone I had ever known. As I wandered lost amongst the ruin, I met a man by the name of Arlas; a man unlike any other I had met before.

"Arlas aided my escape from the village when wraiths descended upon the wreckage, remaining behind so that I could flee. Were it not for his timely arrival, I would too have died that day.

"Several months later, Sol sought me out on Arlas's instruction. He explained to me what I was—what I am, and how he and I were different from ordinary men. We are magi: members of a legendary order who wield magic with unparalleled mastery, casting forth the very elements and bending them into weapons of our will.

"I was introduced to the rest of the Order, and began an intensive period of training in the basics of combat and spellcraft, before setting off on a pilgrimage with Sol, Arlas, and three others to the Northern Circle, an ancient henge situated in the remote reaches of the Carparth Tundra, where, on the winter solstice, I underwent a binding ritual, and became a mage. The ritual was a success, granting me the power that I now possess. But upon our return from beyond the White Mountains, we were met with betrayal!

"Indus Mark, and six other magi, murdered Arlas and three more of our friends. Of the seven traitors, only two were slain during the mutiny. Outnumbered, and outmatched, the two of us fled for our lives!

"Those who betrayed us did so with the intention of pursuing a conquest of Cambria, and I fear they will do so by any means necessary! Of the seven magi left in existence, we two are the youngest and least experienced. Yet to save Cambria from their tyranny, we must kill the other five of our kin, each of whom are more powerful than either of us."

Rhys fell silent again, lowering his gaze back to the tankard he was nursing. Alkis had listened quietly during Rhys's brief account of the last six months, his piercing stare giving nothing away. As the room plunged back into stillness, the traveller likewise gazed down into his cup as he swilled it about in the low light, before finally, after a time, he began to speak himself.

"From a young age, I always wanted to help people—we all grow up hearing tales of gallant knights, fighting for chivalry and honour. Every young boy dreams of becoming that hero—a protector of the realm, a defender of the people; but very few ever see their dreams fulfilled. My father, a Westverness veteran, began teaching me the basics of swordsmanship from the moment I could hold a stick; I spent my entire childhood honing my skills.

"At sixteen I was accepted into the city guard, and several years later, my dream came true; I was on duty at night in Iarbhaile Castle, normally a fairly mundane watch, when, through mostly sheer luck, I apprehended an assassin outside Lord Wargrave's chambers, the Earl of Westverness.

"I was awarded a knighthood for the feat, by Lord Wargrave himself, and served as a knight of Iarbhaile, a protector in the Earl's Guard, for six years. Wargrave was a just ruler, a man I admired. He treated those who served him with respect and compassion—the same compassion with which he governed the realm. We spoke often. He was very generous to me, especially at the time of my father's passing. I considered him a friend.

"But, several months ago, the man I knew and respected died, leaving in his place a figure of corruption and hatred. Something in Victor Wargrave changed, almost overnight. It wasn't clear to see at first, but looking back, statements and actions which seemed out of character, now sit in place.

"Wargrave is building an army—but to what ends I do not know! At first, he took small steps, merely raising taxes, sending out recruitment officers—but not long had passed before grain reserves were being requisitioned and conscientious objectors beaten in the streets.

"Taxes continued to rise, until soon, they became impossible for even much of the gentry to pay. Wargrave's advisors, and those who had thought themselves his friends, sought to reason with him; yet the mad ruler would no longer listen. He sent companies of soldiers instead of tax collectors to extort his subjects of every last farthing they had to their name. By Autumn, when the people had nothing else left, the soldiers were pillaging entire towns of their harvests. With winter now fully upon us, many have begun to starve. But the tyranny does not end there.

"Wargrave has begun conscripting every able-bodied man old enough to hold a sword to join his military. With the army well-fed off the realm's plundered grain, many have joined with little resistance—but as I am sure you can imagine, there are plenty who still refuse.

"Having openly decried Wargrave for his brutality, hoping, like many before me, to break through to the sensibilities of the man I had once known, I found myself stripped of my knighthood, demoted to nothing more than a captain in Iarbhaile's amassing army. I was soon dispatched with a company of soldiers to a small village in the north, to perform the foul task of conscripting the unwilling townsfolk. The orders sickened me, yet to my regret I carried them out, forcing men both young and old to join our ranks against their will!

"Little time had passed when we came to the first objector. He was a farmer—husband, and father of six. He stood his ground, refusing to be enslaved to an army without a cause. I reported to my superior—a man I also once respected. He told me..." Alkis swallowed, issuing an uneasy sigh. "He said we had orders for any objectors—to bar them inside their homes and... and to raze them to the ground.
He ordered me to set alight that man's house with his wife and children inside. I refused.

"My mutiny was as well received as you might expect. I was beaten and bound—dragged back towards the farmers house and forced to watch in horror—I had to listen to those children's screams coming from that burning cottage. It was not over quickly.

"I can scarcely remember how it came about, but somehow, I managed to break free of my bindings... I tried to unbar the door. Yet the other soldiers were there to stop me. I drew my sword —I killed several of them before I was eventually disarmed!

"So many lost their lives that day; burnt alive in their homes. I was imprisoned for my treachery, and awaited execution for treason. But I still had friends within the city guard who had not forsaken their oaths to protect the innocent. They helped me escape, and I fled the city, running for my life. A month later, I found myself on the road to Wythe. Like the two of you, I too flee from those I once believed allies to a common cause; and should my past catch up with me, what awaits me is a hangman's noose."

Rhys and Sol sat in silence, moved by his story.

"What do you intend to do next?" Rhys finally asked.

"The three of us did more good today than ever I have done in all my years of service to Iarbhaile, not for want of trying. The two of you are not from this village, and the plight of its people was not of your concern; yet you risked your lives with hope of no reward. I have heard the legends surrounding your kin. Knighthood was a false promise—in the end, my years of dedication only paid dividends to the wicked and the corrupt, whereas you—your order and what it stands for... I understand you have suffered similar betrayal, yet in spite of this, you still sought to save this village from the evils it was facing. I trust yesterday was not a one-off affair; I don't pretend to know the two of you, but I do not believe you are capable of turning a blind eye to those in need."

"We do what must be done," returned Sol matter-of-factly.

"Then I want to join you... I want to help you in your fight, and in any causes you undertake —if you will have me?"

The two magi turned their gaze on one another, wordlessly understanding that they both were in agreement.

"Your company would be most welcome," Rhys assured him.

Toasting their newly forged comradeship, the three men finished their drink, before overwhelmed with tiredness, they retired to their rooms to rest.

When next Rhys opened his eyes, he was far away. The sky above glistened with the light of billions of stars, stretching around to a jagged horizon of snow-capped peaks that swung in all directions. Rhys peered downward to see a vast expanse of stone underfoot, the sheet of sarsen spanning nearly a hundred feet across. Encircling the wide disc were heaps of fractured rubble, collapsed around the periphery of the great henge he found himself stood within.

Rising before Rhys stood a giant bluestone monolith; towering ten fathoms high, the roughly hewn surface was engraved with runes Rhys had now seen twice before. Across the floor ran an intersection of carved lines coalescing to form the mysterious sigil the mage had seen etched atop the altar of the stone circle on Mount Arthest. Here, in this bizarre dreamscape, the symbol stretched nearly the entire diameter of the henge underfoot, the sculpted halos terminating each line at the henge's border. The halo directly ahead glowed white within the floor beneath the shadow of the menhir, but as Rhys turned his gaze eastward, he could see a second shimmering from the stone. Though faint at first, the light rapidly brightened, the energy emanating from it growing in radiance.

Rhys felt the ground subtly began to tremor. The sound of a pebble skipping across rock rattled and Rhys watched in wonder as a singular stone defied gravity, steadily bounding up the cairn ahead of him, ascending to the top of the pile. Seconds later, a second piece of shingle leapt from the ground, rapidly climbing the heap of rock, swiftly followed by another, and then another, until an entire cascade of gravel was flowing up from the cairn, pillaring skywards as it rose into the air where it fused together. Larger and larger chunks of stone flew upwards, each shard of rubble crunching into place, as slowly but surely, Rhys watched a second monolith piece itself back together. Finally, the last few grains of dust sifted into the cracks, sealing them shut, and the completed structure loomed dark against the night sky.

The halo glowing beneath the second standing stone pulsed upon the menhir's resurrection, immediately after which the light began to spill into the line extending towards it, flowing down the etched groove, in towards the heart of the henge where Rhys was stood, halting just as it touched the central halo carved at the sigil's core.

Moments later, a bright golden light blazed through Rhys's eyelids. The mage sat bolt upright in bed. Covering his face with his hands, he waited for his eyes to adjust to the sunlight. Squinting, Rhys made out Sol stood by the window. The mage had pulled open the shutters and now the midmorning sun streamed into their room in wide beams, bathing Rhys in a warming radiance.

"You know..." Rhys groaned, pulling the bedsheets up around him, "there are more considerate ways to wake a man."

"Good morning to you too," Sol chuckled. "Though it won't be morning for much longer. It is half eleven!"

"It was a late night," Rhys smirked as finally his eyes became accustomed to the sunshine.

Sol issued Rhys a gentle smile before his expression quickly faded to a solemn one. "I think it would be best if we left Wythe as soon as possible," he declared.

"Why?" Rhys returned in confusion, still shaking free the images of his dream.

"Yesterday's deeds have already become the

talk of the town."

"And this is a problem, I assume?" Rhys surmised as he rose from the cosiness of his bed and proceeded to dress.

"They do not yet seem to know of the magic we wielded in slaying the adlet, but it is only a matter of time before they realise what you and I are."

"I am still not sure why it is so important for us to hide ourselves?"

"There are many different opinions of magic in this world, Rhys. Some, much as you did, do not believe it really exists, thinking it merely the stuff of tales and legends. And few who do believe in it actually understand the arcane in any meaningful way. Many throughout Cambria regard magic with the utmost suspicion and fear —it is man's instinctive response to that which he does not understand. Witchcraft and sorcery are seen as dark and evil, and those who practise it are persecuted. Many a witch and warlock has been put to death for its use.

"Those who do not condemn magic see it as divine in nature. They worship those who wield it, regarding them as gods and prophets, following their will unquestioningly. It is for these reasons that, under Arlas's leadership, the Order remained hidden in the shadows, kept secret from the rest of Cambria. Indus seeks power—he'll exploit mankind's perceptions of magic to achieve it, wielding both fear and reverence as tools to obtain rulership."

"Okay," Rhys uttered sombrely, agreeing with Sol's sentiment, at least in principle if not entirely. Figuring a swift departure was more than likely in their best interest, he pulled on his boots and quickly packed his belongings into his bag. Exiting their room, they made for Alkis's, informing the knight of their intentions. When he too was ready to depart, they sought out the innkeeper to return their keys, before setting out into the cool afternoon air.

A tranquil aura had descended upon the village. Golden sunshine reflected brilliantly off the unblemished blanket of snow that had fallen throughout the night, and a crisp breeze wove between the icicles dangling from thatched eaves. Few of the villagers stirred as they made their way west out of the settlement, back along the road that had led them there. Just as the sleepy village of Wythe was fading in the distance at their backs, Rhys turned to the sound of racing footfalls charging towards them from the rear.

Cade slowed to a jog as he neared them. Across his back was strapped his unstrung bow and a full quiver; beside it was a traveller's pack.

"You are leaving," he said, though it was not a question.

Rhys nodded silently as he noted the man's knapsack.

"Let me come with you."

"I am not sure..." Rhys began. "You don't

know who or what we are, or where we are going! Why would you wish to join us?"

"The two of you are mages, are you not?" Cade asserted.

"We are," Sol confirmed.

"I have heard the legends; I know what you do. You protect everyone from... from what we saw yesterday."

Rhys and Sol offered no response.

"There is nothing for me here now!" Cade argued. "Without Joshua, Wythe is no home to me. I know the path you tread is fraught with danger. You fight monsters and demons, and uphold all that is right. You stand vigilant, against the darker aspects of this world—ready for whenever you are needed. I understand the perils ahead; I'm not afraid to face them with you."

"It is not as simple as that," Rhys returned.

"I am skilled with a bow, and without me yesterday you might not have found what you were looking for!"

"I wasn't questioning your abilities—"

"Will you turn away help when it's offered? Your other companion suggests not," he insisted wryly, looking at Alkis stood beside them.

Rhys examined Cade closely. "We *are* in need of skilled help," he sighed after a long while. "But the road ahead of us will likely be far more dangerous than what we faced yesterday."

"I suspected as much. I will not falter—I promise you!"

Rhys exhaled deeply. "Very well. Welcome Cade Williams—There are several things you should know."

TWENTY-SIX

"The village of Llanmyd lies ten leagues north of Brenwood," Sol declared as he examined their map by the light of the fire. "We should arrive by mid-morning the day after next, provided we keep straight along our bearing."

"What lies in wait for us in this village?" Cade asked, stirring the peas pottage hung above the flames.

"Nothing," Rhys asserted. "At least we hope."

"Then why are we journeying there?"

"It is as inconspicuous as any village can be in this region of Gwent," Sol explained. "It's not located along any of the realms main highways, hence it is seldom travelled through; however, it lies not too far from the capital, and thus is not so remote as to escape news and rumours of happenings beyond its borders. We will unlikely attract the attention of our enemy by residing in

Llanmyd, yet should Indus and the others in their actions cause ripples across Gwent, we should in due course hear of it. We can spend what time we need there to plot our first move against them with sufficient information on any developments, but without risk of being discovered."

"If you'd prefer, we could bide our time out in the freezing wilderness till we have a plan of action," Rhys joked. "However, I for one prefer the prospects of figuring out our strategy from the warmth of a tavern, with food, and more importantly, ale close at hand!"

"I'm not yearning for a life as a hermit," Cade smiled. "I merely was curious as to why we were travelling to such a seemingly random village. Your plan is sound."

"It isn't much of a plan yet," Rhys confessed. "We are mostly just making it up as we go along at the moment."

"You will think of something!" Alkis directed at Sol and Rhys.

"Your confidence is reassuring," Rhys chuckled, lacking the certainty that the swordsman held.

"Let us hope it is not misplaced," remarked Sol with a somewhat more sombre tone.

"If all else fails, a flagon of ale always helps to inspire ideas!" Rhys added light-heartedly.

The four men ate in relative silence as they huddled close around the fire. The frigid night closed tight around them, though the sheltered woodland did well to stave off the bitter winds. At daybreak, they rose and rekindled the embers of their fire, cooking a small pot of porridge from the last of their oats, before setting on their way north to Llanmyd. With the passing of noon, they left Brenwood behind, journeying across rolling hills and sweeping plains of snow. When night fell once more, they sheltered in a hilltop grove, poaching a rabbit for their evening's supper.

The next day's travel saw the wilderness yield to tilled fields and snowy paddocks. The icy track they followed steadily widened to a well-trodden road as it wound its way through the steepening valleys. Eventually, the main highway veered west towards the City of Ultair, setting the company of men north along a twisting bridleway that climbed swiftly up out of the vale, towards a saddle hanging between two peaks on the distant ridge.

When Rhys summited the brow, he was granted a view that stretched north to the horizon, but as he gazed down from the ridge, he halted dead in his tracks. Horror knotted inside the mage's gut, rooting him to the spot as he peered onwards to the grim landscape below, nestled in the heart of which was the village of Llanmyd. A sickening shade of grey smothered the countryside, all colour vanquished, leaving in its wake nothing but a dire reflection of the land. The world was dead. The Grey had come to Llanmyd. The same curse that had robbed Rhys of his home so many months ago raged ahead, rebirthed, summoned again, haunting Rhys with a dizzying whirlwind of flickering memories that raced through his mind.

"Shit!" Sol cursed under his breath as he realised what stared back at them.

"By the gods!" Cade exclaimed in shock. "I..." he stammered. "It is more terrible than I could ever have imagined!"

"I am at a loss for words!" Alkis breathed as he gazed-wide eyed at the aftermath of the foul magic.

They stood unmoving, unspeaking, unbreathing, never averting their gaze. The world ahead seemed by first appearances grim and lifeless, but as Rhys stood frozen in despair, he began to unpick the scene before him. Colour was absent, a toxic aura radiating up from the bleak valleys below, yet the skies above were clear, devoid of the venomous clouds that had descended into fog to drown Longford. Though they were too far away to make out any villagers, Rhys descried a few thin yarns of smoke rising from the settlement's chimney stacks.

"The curse has only just taken hold!" Rhys declared in realisation. "This is our chance!" he breathed.

"What do you mean, Rhys?" Sol uttered timidly.

"Arlas never had this opportunity: to observe the Grey as it manifests!"

"Rhys, we cannot possibly go down there!" Sol refused. "If we did, we would imminently fall victim to the curse. I don't know how to cast the wards necessary to protect us against it! That level of aegis magic is beyond me."

"You don't need to!" Rhys declared. "I can go."

"What!?" Sol cried in alarm, realising what Rhys was hinting. "No, you can't!"

"I can do it," Rhys assured him. "I survived this curse before, back when I held no magic of any kind!"

"Rhys, we don't even know how you survived last time!" Sol argued. "We don't know what will happen if you go down there!"

"We won't have this opportunity again, Sol. I know the risks. This is something I must do!"

Sol stared silently at his friend. "Be careful. And do not linger too long!"

Rhys nodded solemnly to the mage, before turning to face the grim fate before him. Sucking in a final lungful of fresh air, he issued a long exhale and sprinted off down the hillside.

Rhys's feet carried him swiftly along the steep track as he hurtled down into the valley. In a matter of moments, he had reached the foot of the ridge, and the grey gloom swelled immediately around him, its stench of dismay all too familiar. The winter air grew even colder, its biting chill fiercening with each step he took, gnashing viciously at Rhys's face and hands as he sped on. Sure enough, clouds were congealing out of the air above, sinking as they formed, settling as corrupted vapour over the rooftops ahead. Steadying his breath, Rhys hurtled across the ice, watching as the last vestiges of colour vanished, the border of the village rushing up to meet him.

Wooden houses rose out of the murk on either side. Rhys's boots clopped heavily against cobbles as he flew through the empty streets. The town seemed abandoned, the streets vacant of inhabitants, both living and dead, but as he rounded the corner, he skidded to a halt, stopped in his tracks by the sight before him. Stood in the avenue were half a dozen villagers, alive and conscious, distraught, despairing at the curse that was rapidly consuming all. Though the Grey's apocalyptic climax was approaching fast, it had yet to reap the villagers of their lives. There was still time to save them.

"Get out of here!" Rhys roared, flailing his hands in panic.

The villagers looked back at him blankly, their distress stupefying them.

"Leave the village immediately. Your lives are in danger! Head south atop the ridge!"

The peasants gawked silently back at him, but Rhys did not have time to properly explain what was happening. He could only hope they heeded his words.

Praying his warning had gotten through, he took off, breaking into a sprint once more, racing towards the heart of the settlement. If those few had survived, then there would likely be more that had not yet been claimed by the dark magic. He tore on through the vacant thoroughfares, towards the sound of a distant hubbub of people that continued to grow in volume as he drew closer. Turning another corner, Rhys found himself running down a long boulevard to a large village-square ahead. Crowded into the marketplace were hundreds upon hundreds of villagers, all gathered together as a distant voice boomed over the rabble. Rhys sped on towards the vast gathering, his keen hearing picking out the shouting voice as it cut through the roar of the mob.

"This is your last chance, witch! Lift the curse or your fate is sealed!"

Boos and hisses bellowed loudly.

"You have chosen this for yourself. Do not try to poison us with your lies!" the voiced yelled louder.

Bursting into the square, Rhys gazed across a sea of heads to a wooden scaffold around which the entire town had gathered. Atop the platform, raised high above the crowd, dressed in furs and finery, a man vehemently addressed the mob. Clutched in his hand burned a torch of dull white flame. Stacked high upon the scaffold beside him was a mountain of tinder and firewood, summiting from which rose a massive wooden stake. Fettered to the post by lashings of heavy rope, a young woman wept in terror.

"Thia Smith, you have been found guilty of practising witchcraft, blood magic, and the dark arts; the punishment for which is burning at the stake! I hereby rid this village of your dark curse and sentence you to death!" With those words, he callously tossed the torch onto the mound of kindling.

The flames licked outwards, spreading swiftly across the dry timber. The woman let out a terrified shriek as the wood rapidly combusted, fire and smoke curling upwards to meet her.

Without hesitating, Rhys ploughed into the crowd. The villagers cried out as many were knocked off their feet, but Rhys paid them no heed. Forcing through the dense mob, Rhys drew the wand from his belt and pointed it high into the air. A thundering crackle of amber sparks exploded upwards against the grey skies and the villagers suddenly parted in panic. Peasants screamed and leapt aside, yielding in every direction as they dismayed at Rhys's brandishing of magic. The way ahead cleared, a path opening before Rhys to the scaffold in front.

The man atop the platform glanced frantically around, looking for the source of the spell, quickly sighting Rhys as the throng around him dispersed. Barking a series of feverish orders at the guardsmen stood watch around the scaffold, he lanced a finger in the mage's direction. As Rhys emerged out of the scattering mob, two village militiamen nervously drew swords, and moved to intercept the mage.

Rhys's fingers locked around his staff, pulling it from across his back as he charged towards the guardsmen. The shriek of an ethereal blade rang out over the roar of the mob, and a blur of green clashed against steel. Sustaining his momentum, Rhys delivered a rapid circular parry, driving past the militiamen's guard, smashing his knee up into the man's gut. The watchman's hauberk jingled as he reeled back, staggering off balance, granting his ally an opening to engage.

Rhys's emerald weapon twirled in a rapid flourish as it clinked against the second incoming steel edge, the blades binding as Rhys twisted his stave. Using the hook on the reverse of his weapon, he locked out the guardsman's sword. A sharp jerk rent the weapon clean from his opponent's grip, sending it clattering off across the cobbles. Spinning his staff back around, he lunged, spearing the butt powerfully into the man's chest, knocking him backwards with a magically charged blow that slammed his foe into the scaffold behind.

Riposting the first militiaman's attempt to reengage, Rhys feinted, skipping past the next incoming counter, sweeping out the guard's legs with a low swing. Flailing his sword from the ground, the guardsman made a last-ditch attempt to strike at Rhys, but his blade clattered against stone as the mage darted clear, dashing up the steps of the scaffold in a series of bounds.

Drawing his wand back out from under his belt, Rhys took aim at the blazing bonfire. Black smoke and white flames conflagrated across the wood, licking around the woman bound to the stake as she screamed inside a shroud of smoke. An abrupt gesture was all that was needed, Rhys snuffing out the flames like a candle in the wind, leaving nothing but a few smouldering embers and a cloud of cinder.

As the lingering smoke began to evaporate, Rhys clambered quickly up the charred pyre, the scorched tinder crumbling underfoot. Within moments, he had reached the top of the bonfire, where from out of the thinning fumes, a pair of sapphire eyes glistening with tears met his. A slash of his blade severed her bindings, and the woman, black with ash and smoke, collapsed into his arms.

As Rhys steadied her, she embraced him, coughing and sputtering violently as her lungs dispelled the choking ashes she'd inhaled in the conflagration. With the heat of the flames surrendering to the icy chill of the Grey, the woman began to quiver, her body in shock after a narrow escape from gruesome immolation.

Ensuring she was on stable footing, Rhys leapt back down to the scaffold, helping the woman shakily ease her way down from the smouldering pyre thereafter. Rhys turned back to face the executioner, just as a half dozen guards rushed up onto the platform, swords drawn in trembling hands as they half-heartedly rallied to the village reeve's defence. Stepping in front of the ash-covered woman, Rhys drew his stave once more and stared down the watchmen.

"Guards!" the man in finery roared as he glared loathingly at Rhys. "Seize the warlock!"

No one moved. The swordsmen dared not engage.

Rhys tightened the grip of his staff. A shrill chime reprised as the mage's ethereal blade unfurled a second time. He took a step forwards, cocking his head tauntingly as he flourished his weapon in challenge. A tumult of clanging steel sounded, as one by one, the guards threw down their swords in surrender.

"Cowards!" the reeve scorned. "Can't you see!? He is the one that has summoned this curse! Kill him!"

"I am not responsible for what is happening to this village! Nor is this woman!" Rhys protested, realising he was addressing not only the men gathered atop the scaffold, but the entire village as a whole. The sense of panic in the throng below had abated, and as onlookers drew closer, all fell silent, listening as the mage prepared to speak once more.

Taking a deep breath, Rhys turned to address the crowd. "I don't know who or what weaves the dark magic that fuels this curse... but I have seen first-hand the devastation that it inflicts! Everyone here is in grave peril. We need to evacuate the village immediately if you are to have any chance of survival!"

Gasps and cries of shock erupted from the crowd as many began to dismay at Rhys's warning.

"Do not listen to him!" the reeve screamed. "Can you not see that it is *he* who has brought this foul magic down upon us!? His words are poison! He seeks to enthral you all with his dark enchantments. If he is not to blame, then how else would he know of this curse?"

The rabble grew loud once again with whispers of suspicion and shrieks of terror.

"Because," Rhys yelled recapturing the crowd's attention, "the same curse that dwells here today brought death and destruction down upon my own village. And now, every man, woman, and child of Longford is dead!"

Murmurs stirred amongst the villagers as they began to heed his words.

"Every moment we stay here, the curse thickens. Before long, it will reap the life of everyone it touches. We must leave now—or none will survive!"

"Do not listen to him!" the persecutor spat, sensing the crowd was turning against him. "His lies will see you all slaughtered!"

"Don't be a fool!" Rhys pleaded with the man. "You are in perilous danger!"

"Your trickery will not deceive me, warlock!" he snarled, drawing a glinting dagger from under his robes. He lunged rapidly for Rhys, but the mage moved faster.

Stepping deftly aside, Rhys swung around his staff, thumping the reeve across his back as he thrust into open air. The man slipped on the icy scaffold boards, tumbling off balance as he careened over the ledge. The crowd cleared below as the man slammed hard onto the cobblestones. When he rolled over, a jewelled dagger hilt was protruding from his abdomen; the reeve had skewered himself in the fall. Black blood steamed as it trickled between the cobbles. He rasped painfully with his last lungful of air before his body drooped limp, his eyes upturned vacantly to the churning clouds overhead.

TWENTY-SEVEN

"We must make haste!" Rhys urged, shouting over the screams of the crowd. "If there is any hope, you must flee now!" A heavy aura of pervasive death was thickly descending upon the village. Rhys could feel it all around.

He turned to look at the woman beside him as her slender frame swayed wearily, barely able to stand. She gazed back at him, azure eyes sparkling through tears, reddened by the smoke and ash that had cindered her fair skin and platinum tresses. Despite the inferno that seconds earlier had almost engulfed her, the flames had done little more than singe the hem of her dress and blacken the fabric with ash. A split in her lip was crusted with maroon blood, whilst purple welts marked her cheeks and brow. The fingers of her right hand were blue and crooked, whilst up the lengths of her bare arms, the skin was flushed with pink contusions.

She had been beaten to within an inch of her life, that much was readily apparent, but as Rhys continued to study her, his pity over the extent of her injuries became less and less the centre of his focus. Azure eyes. Maroon blood. Purple bruises.

Steadily, Rhys lowered his gaze to examine himself. The faint thrum of emerald light pulsed from within the shaft of his stave, yet aside from the dim residue of colour holding out inside the arcane weapon, every shade had otherwise been utterly bleached from his body and clothes. His skin had greyed to a pallid and ashen complexion, his clothes faded to murky shades of black and white.

Suddenly wrought with suspicion, the mage traced his gaze back over the colourful bruising that marred the woman's otherwise fair complexion, finally meeting a pair of sapphire eyes peering back at him. His countenance narrowed, mistrust, apprehension, and regret battling across his mind as the realisation dawned, that the woman before him was radiating arcane energy. Was she responsible for the malevolent curse descending around them?

Transported back through memory to the moment he had been discovered by Arlas amidst the ruin of Longford, he recounted the suspicion the Archon had beheld him with. With perhaps good reason, Arlas had leapt to the conclusion that Rhys was in some way responsible for the Grey, subjecting him to something close to an interrogation. Stupefied by the horror that had engulfed the village around him, Rhys had been distraught at the accusations fired his way. Grieving for the incomprehensible loss he had suffered, he was forced to withstand Arlas's scalding, whilst still oblivious to the true foul nature of the encompassing curse.

Looking now at the battered woman standing shakily before him, Rhys decided he would not make the same mistake Arlas had erred. Though the villagers of Llanmyd yet lived, this woman was every much a victim of the Grey as Rhys. Pushing his suspicions to the back of his mind, he offered her a reassuring look.

"Where are we to go?" a voice cried from within the din of the throng.

"We will seek refuge at Ultair!" Rhys replied, turning back to address his audience. "But first we must escape the village! I have friends awaiting my return, atop the ridge to the south." He pointed over the rooftops in the direction he had come. "It is a mile from here—beyond the reaches of this foul curse. There is no time to gather your possessions, nor supplies! The magic grows darker with every passing moment. Come! Let us not waste a moment longer!"

After several seconds of deliberation, the discord of mutterings seemed to draw a consensus, and with little delay, a mass exodus from the market square swiftly followed, the villagers filtering into the streets as they hastily, but with relative calm, began the evacuation.

"Can you walk?" Rhys asked, turning back to the woman beside him.

"I think so," she exhaled softly, stumbling slightly as she edged forwards on trembling ankles.

"Here," Rhys offered, catching her as she swayed, putting his arm around her for support as he helped her down the steps of the scaffold.

Following in the wake of the flight, Rhys led the girl through the darkling streets, following the thousand refugees ahead as they made for the edge of the village. Along the way, they pass those left behind. Some rushed into their houses, bolting shut doors behind them in refusal to abandon their homes; others hurried to gather valued possessions and supplies in panic, in spite of Rhys's warning. There was nothing that could be done for them. The Grey had come to Llanmyd. Soon, they would be dead.

With each step, the air grew denser, the gloom swirling overhead sinking in choking swathes that flooded the streets. Despite his innate resilience to the malefic sorcery, Rhys could feel the life being sapped from him, the Grey's draining affliction taking its toll on both he and the woman limping in his arms.

"Who are you?" the woman asked weakly, clinging to Rhys ever tighter as together they sensed death closing upon them.

"My name is Rhys North."

"I am Thia," she offered in return. "Thia Smith."

"Nice to meet you, Thia Smith," the mage smiled gravely, his strength beginning to fail against the devouring darkness swelling around them.

"Thank you, Rhys North…" Thia panted as they struggled on, "…for saving me!"

"Don't thank me yet," the mage returned. "We're not safe until we are out of here—until we make it atop that ridge!"

"I know," she wheezed. "I just wanted to say it… in case we don't make it!"

"We'll make it," Rhys promised, though for the first time, he began to doubt it himself as they hobbled onwards through the deathly streets. "We'll make it," he repeated, more for himself than for Thia's sake.

They fought on, escaping the limits of Llanmyd as the murk swallowed the village whole behind. Continuing to flee, Rhys helped the woman up the winding road as they began the steep ascend to the ridge ahead. Steadily, the taint of the Grey began to diminish as they drew beyond its reach. Highlights of colour shone through the haze, the fogs thinning, life returning, the evil dissipating. Finally, battling up the last furlong of the slope, they sighted the rest of the village: a thousand refugees amassed atop the ridge, gazing back in horror at the decimation of their home.

"Rhys!" Sol cried out in relief as the mage sighted his friend emerging from the gloom with Thia clutched in his arms.

Peering ahead, Rhys saw Sol, Alkis, and Cade push through the crowd towards him.

"What happened!?" Sol pressed.

"I don't know," Rhys returned. "I got there just in time—something slowed the curse down. The villagers were all still alive, but had we arrived even a few minutes later..." he peered back over his shoulder at the impenetrable haze engulfing the valley below.

Helping Thia up the last few yards, Rhys gently set her down, leaning her against a stone trail marker on the roadside. She squeezed his hand, issuing him a look of gratitude with her dazzling eyes. Rhys returned a half smile her way; now that the imminent danger had past, the suspicion first aroused down in the heart of the village was steadily returning to the forefront of his mind.

"I'll be back in a moment," the mage promised, turning aside to speak with Sol, Alkis, and Cade.

"What happened down there?" Sol questioned.

"The entire village was gathered in the market square," Rhys explained, peering back over his shoulder at Thia Smith as the woman sat cradling her broken fingers, the surrounding villagers paying her no heed as they made sure to give the woman a wide birth. "They were going to burn her at the stake—for witchcraft."

"They reckoned her responsible?" Sol deduced.

Rhys nodded in confirmation.

"Is she?" Cade asked in a hushed voice, peaking furtively past Rhys at the woman.

"I don't know," the mage confessed, before shaking his head and adding with greater confidence, "No. I don't think so."

"How can you be sure?"

"I can't," the mage returned. "I've not questioned her—I figured it wasn't the best time."

"Fair enough," Sol conceded.

"She has power—a control over magic that warded her from the Grey. But, as we well know, that does not confer any kind of guilt."

The woman looked back their way, realising that she was the topic of discussion.

"We can't take any chances," Sol countered, eyeing Thia suspiciously. "She was there in the midst of it—protected, whilst no one else was. We have to assume she is at least connected. She could be responsible."

"Just as Arlas thought *I* was responsible?" Rhys rebuked. "I can't vouch for her—I'll admit, it looks suspicious, but I'll be damned if I go throwing any kind of accusation her way when we still know so little about this bloody curse!"

"There is one thing we can say with certainty," Alkis put in, "that girl is alive because of you!"

"As is everyone else from the village,"
Sol added, as they looked across the gathering
amassed atop the ridge.

"I was lucky," Rhys returned dismissively.
"I just wish I could have discovered something
useful whilst I was down there—something that
might have helped us figure out what is causing
the Grey!"

"Fret not," Sol assured. "The girl may know
something—even if the curse is not of her doing."

"All right," Rhys agreed. "But let *me* question
her. She has been through an ordeal—I understand
something of what she must be feeling right now."

"As you wish," Sol consented.

"We'll hang back," offered Alkis. "Just
listen."

Rhys nodded, "I think it best."

Rhys turned, making his way back over to
the witch. She sat quivering in the bitter winter
air, goosebumps prickling across her bare arms as
she apprehensively awaited his return. Removing
his cloak, Rhys draped it across her shoulders and
took a knee in front of her, his gaze immediately
meeting her own. Drawing the warm mantle
tightly around herself, she sighed heavily, Rhys
once again catching sight of the black and swollen
digits of her broken hand as she clutched his fur
across her chest.

Tentatively, he reached for her injured
hand, slowly making his intent clear as he gently

cradled it in his own palm to examine the extent of the damage. Thia winced, cringing as Rhys cautiously ran his fingertips over the swollen, broken skin. Three knuckles were shattered beneath the flesh.

"What did they do to you?" Rhys uttered disdainfully under his breath. "My friend Sol can help you," he offered, raising his voice for her to hear.

He glanced over his shoulder, towards his fellow mage, beckoning Sol to come closer, but as he turned back, Thia was reaching with her good hand for the wand tucked in his belt. Rhys's blood suddenly chilled. He released his hold of her and recoiled away, his wand retracting beyond her reach.

Realising the distress she had caused, she withdrew her hand and raised her palm in a gesture of goodwill, tucking it back beneath the warmth of the cloak as she continued to shudder in the cold. Put at ease by the woman's calm and unthreatening demeanour, Rhys lowered his gaze to the magical implement tucked at his waist; slowly drawing it from his belt, he offered it handle first towards the witch.

"Rhys!?" Sol protested anxiously, his hand moving to the staff on his back as he waited to see what move the woman would make.

Leaning tentatively forwards, she gently took the wand from Rhys, directing it immediately to her swollen and discoloured fingers. She gasped, gritting her teeth and grimacing as she did so. Rhys watched in both horror and amazement as the crooked digits of her hand crunched, one by one, back into place. In the seconds that followed, the black and puffy flesh shrank and faded, turning mauve, then jaundiced, before finally taking on a healthier pigment.

With her hand repaired, Thia drew back the mantled draped across her shoulders, focussing on the array of cuts and contusions streaked across her arms and face. Flesh knitted rapidly back together, lumps and bruises smoothing over and fading in an instant, fresh skin weaving over the various gashes and nicks that riddled her body. Finally, lifting the hem of her dress, she unveiled a bulging ankle red with inflammation. With the wand focussed over the joint, a loud crack followed by a sharp yelp from Thia signalled the fractured bone fusing back together, before the flesh calmed and the swelling abated, leaving the witch seemingly returned to full health. Drained by the experience, Thia feebly handed the wand back to Rhys.

Returning the arcane implement to a notch in his belt, Rhys uncorked his waterskin, offering it to the woman. "Here," he offered, watching as she greedily took the skin from him and swallowed several large gulps.

"Thank you," she exhaled, wiping her mouth in refreshment.

"Where did you learn to cast healing spells

like that?" Rhys asked as both he and Sol beheld her in wonder.

"My mother," she returned, rubbing away some of the soot from her face. "She was a cleric— second to the High Priestess."

"The Occult?" Sol questioned.

Thia nodded. "She left the order when she fell pregnant with me."

"That certainly explains a few things," Rhys returned. "Whilst also raising a number of other questions."

"Chief among them being: did I conjure the curse that lies before us?" she asserted.

"I am not accusing you of anything," Rhys insisted. "But irrespective of what your village's reeve had condemned you of, I saw first-hand how the curse waned in your presence. It held little effect over you. Some might see that as suspicious."

"But you do not think me responsible?"

"Conjuring dark magic, and knowing how to ward against it, are two very different things," Rhys assured. "But even still, I must ask you: what do you know about this curse? Why is it that your village was so quick to accuse you?"

"The curse was conjured before first light this morning," she began. "I woke up, sensing something awry—I'm not entirely sure how I could tell, but I just felt..."

"A sense of dread," put in Rhys, recalling the same evil presence that had awoken him all those months ago. "The menace... the pain... a feeling of hopelessness, like the air turning steadily to poison."

"Yes," she nodded, realising that Rhys understood perfectly. "I knew it was a curse of some sort—through intuition, I imagine. but I did not know what it was nor whence it was invoked. I sought to find out, though.

"Knowing I was at risk of succumbing to the curse, my first action was to cast a series of wards upon myself. The arcane protection shielded me from the dark magic, allowing me time to begin a ritual taught to me by my mother. Its effects are to lend protection to a wide area, and shield against dark energies. Never had I cast such a ritual before, but I had read accounts of its uses. It is capable of producing a zone of protection large enough to safeguard a village or small town for a short time from black magic and ill effects.

"I completed the ritual just before dawn, but to seemingly no effect; the curse continued to descend despite my attempts to abate it. The sun rose to a colourless sky, dark shadows lurking around the fringes of Llanmyd."

"No," challenged Rhys. "Your protection ritual did more than you know. Without it, everyone in Llanmyd would have perished before sunrise!"

"That is what happened to your village?" she asked timidly. "To Longford?"

"Yes," the mage confirmed.

"Then... thank goodness. I can't imagine such a horror!"

"Before today, none but me have survived the Grey. Each time it has struck before, it has devoured the lives of everyone within."

"Each time...?" Thia murmured. "This curse has struck multiple times?"

"Numerous," Rhys nodded solemnly. "When I ventured into Llanmyd, I expected only to find death and ruin! And yet, I found that the entire village still lived! Even now, the curse seems to be progressing slower than when I watched it ensnare Longford. I believe you may just have saved the lives of everyone here!"

"Then this curse is powerful magic indeed!" she exclaimed. "To persist still when the aura of protection was summoned against it. Only blood magic could produce such potent effects!"

"It is blood magic," Rhys affirmed. "But aside from this, my allies and I know little else of its nature. That is why I entered the village—to see what I could discover about its origins."

"I might know of a way!" Thia proposed. "My knowledge of blood magic is not extensive," she explained, "but if I am to assume this curse follows its basic principles, it could not be summoned with the mere casting of a spell. Its conjuring would require a prepared ritual of channelled energy. Such rituals must be sustained by the will of the caster until their completion, else the curse would collapse in on itself."

"Therefore, whoever or whatever is responsible may still be performing the ritual now!" Sol exclaimed in realisation.

"Yes," the witch confirmed. "Thus, with the proper ritual of our own—"

"We could theoretically trace the curse back to its caster?"

"What do you mean?" Rhys pressed.

"The curse itself is linked to its caster's will—their mind and their consciousness!" Thia explained. "Should you follow the magic back to its source, you can potentially glimpse the mind of whoever is casting the ritual. It may be possible to discover their location, or even their identity."

"So we could actually find out who is responsible?" Rhys questioned.

"No," Sol answered sombrely. "If there is such a ritual that can trace back this curse to its source, I do not know it. And even if I did, we would need to cast it from the heart of the village."

"I know of such a ritual," Thia proclaimed.

"You do?" Sol asked somewhat sceptically.

"Yes," she returned emphatically. "I don't have it memorised, but in one of my mother's tomes, I am certain there is such a ritual described! But yes, you are right," she directed at Sol, "it would need to be cast from the heart of the curse."

"Where there are now likely to be dozens of wraiths lurking," Rhys remarked.

"Wraiths?" Thia repeated with alarm.

"Such was the case with Longford. They

are drawn to the curse's effects, thriving off the death and ruin. If they are down there, they won't hesitate to attack any who enter the village... that is, assuming anyone could make it into the village anyway, without falling prey to the curse itself beforehand!"

"There is a spell of which I know that might conceal our presence from the wraiths..." Sol mentioned, clearly conflicted as to whether even entertaining this plan was wise. "Wraiths are undead creatures: the remnants of tortured souls that fought too hard to cling to this world when their bodies died. They do not perceive the world with sight or sound—they sense their surroundings through the essence of life."

"So what does this spell do?" Rhys asked.

"It will camouflage us, in a veil of undeath, making us appear to them the same as their kin."

"They will think us wraiths as well?"

"Yes," Sol confirmed.

"Yet as soon as I begin casting the ritual, will it not dissolve the concealment—give ourselves away?" Thia questioned.

"I fear it may," Sol confessed. "But, it would allow us to make it as far as the village—to the heart of the curse... provided you can cast the same wards against the Grey on us as you have done for yourself?"

"I can do that," she nodded. "But when I begin the ritual, the wraiths will surely be drawn straight to us. What then?"

"We make a stand!" Rhys asserted. "How long will it take you to cast the ritual?"

The witch's eyes flickered back and forth as she tried to produce an answer. "Without ever having cast it I cannot say," she replied. "My assumption would be, that due to the scale of this curse, there may be quite a pronounced trail leading back to the caster's mind. But still—it would take several minutes to perform at the very least!"

Rhys nodded, looking to Sol. "Then we had better make sure we are prepared to hold out for that long!"

Sol shifted uneasily. "Rhys, I don't know about this. Adlet and hags are one thing, but wraiths are another! They are the embodiment of death itself! I have never even seen one before. Arlas himself had trouble repelling those you encountered in Longford. I don't know if we would stand any hope against them!"

"You may be right," Rhys confessed, "but we won't have an opportunity like this again—it could be our only option if we ever want to discover the cause of the Grey! If you believe the peril is too great, then we will end this discussion here and now, and forget we ever suggested this plan. But I have to discover why Longford fell victim to this curse! I am willing to take the risk."

"You realise we may not discover *why* Longford fell," Sol stated, "even if we discover who is responsible!?"

"Regardless," Rhys persisted, "this is the first step in doing so."

Sol stared long and hard at Rhys, and then gazed silently at the billowing vortex of fog and dark clouds that swallowed Llanmyd. "Okay," he uttered finally. "I am willing to do this; so long as she is," he directed at Thia.

"You believe you can keep the wraiths at bay whilst I carry out the ritual?"

"They will come at us thick and fast," Rhys began, "but with both Sol and myself... we may just stand a chance!"

"And I!" Alkis insisted.

"And me!" Cade added.

"No!" Sol refused. "Alkis, you are an exceptional swordsman! And Cade, you are the best shot with a bow I have ever seen. But a bow and a sword are useless against foes of this kind. Wraiths are effectively ghosts—you would have no defence against them."

"Not necessarily," Thia interrupted. "A simple enchantment upon their weapons would be enough to render them effective against these undead creatures."

"Then it is settled!" Alkis asserted before Sol could protest any further. "Cade and I will assist you, bettering your chances at staving off these wraiths!"

"Okay," Rhys agreed, bringing the matter to a close as he began to feel a sense of urgency. The Grey was climaxing, and with no more lives to reap, the conjurer would no doubt soon end the ritual. With little option other than to trust the witch's promises would hold true, Rhys knew the time to act was nigh. "We had better ready ourselves—and quick. Time is of the essence!"

"Alkis, Cade," Thia said addressing the two men for the first time, "hand me your sword and your arrows so that I can cast some enchantments upon them."

The two men nodded in compliance. Alkis drew his longsword from across his back and held it horizontally before the witch. Realising Thia had nothing with which to cast her magic, Rhys returned her his wand. Taking the arcane implement, she pointed it to the well-burnished blade and began uttering an enchantment under her breath.

Rhys stepped away from the others and looked around at the gathering of villagers, the despairing crowd still wrought with anguish over the loss of their home. Rhys spied several members of the village militia assembled not far from him. Parting the crowd, he wandered over towards the guardsmen, who upon noticing his approach turned his way.

"Sir?" one of the men delivered nervously.

Rhys studied the guards, quickly realising that they were the same men who had drawn their weapons on him in the village, the man addressing him even being one of the two that had clashed blades with the mage.

"Be at ease," Rhys reassured in an attempt to calm them.

The group continued to gawk back at him in awe.

"Is it true?" one man asked. "Are you planning on heading back down there?"

"It is," Rhys confirmed.

"We did not mean to eavesdrop!" another of the men vowed apologetically. "We merely overheard!"

"Hmm, I won't turn you into a toad then—" Rhys chuckled, "—since you apologised."

"Erm... Thank you... Sir Warlock," the guardsman stammered, bowing his head, clearly having not grasped that Rhys had been joking.

"What are we to do?" the first guard asked. "If we cannot return to the village, then where should we go?"

"The City of Ultair may be able to offer refuge to you and the villagers," Rhys suggested. "It is little over a day's journey east of here, but many of these people will need help in making it so far without food, water, or blankets. You men must take charge!" Rhys urged them. "Now that the village's Reeve is dead, you must see that these men, women, and children make it to Ultair safely.

"Petition the city's rulers to offer you aid. If you can dispatch the fastest of your men to march ahead of the villagers, they can send word of your coming, and the city guard might ride out to meet you with supplies. Can I count on you?"

"You can Sir," the first man nodded.

"Might we know the name of the man who led us to safety in Llanmyd's darkest hour?" another asked.

"My name is Rhys North."

"We will see that these people make it to Ultair safely, Rhys North!"

Rhys nodded as the men issued him a salute. Turning to the crowd, they called out, drawing the attention of the surrounding villagers. With the focus of the throng held, the group of guardsmen began their address, declaring their intent, readying the multitude of refugees to travel east to Ultair.

When Rhys returned to the others, Thia was revolving the wand in her hand as she placed a magical ward over Sol. Alkis was examining his longsword in his hands; the blade seemed to glimmer with a purple iridescence that flickered up and down the burnished steel blade. Cade leant heavily upon his recurve bow, bending its limbs so that he could string it.

"Are you ready Rhys?" Thia asked, turning now to face him. "You are the only one left."

"Do it," he nodded, stepping closer to her.

She pointed the wand towards him and began motioning its tip in a curving pattern. A calming energy began to wash over Rhys. Though from atop the ridge the Grey's effects were negligible, he felt a sense of unease lift from his mind as the protective magic began to shield him.

"Finished," she breathed, lowering her wand as their eyes met again.

"This concealment I am to cast," Sol spoke, "should it work in disguising us from the wraiths, I can hopefully re-conjure it once Thia finishes her ritual. But whilst the ritual is being performed, they will all flock towards us!"

"We will be ready!" Rhys assured him. "Cast it," he nodded to Sol.

Sol drew his own wand, and concentrating intensely, he focussed upon a small pocket of air before him. Steadily, a bubble of rippling translucent energy spawned out of nothing. The sphere expanded to the size of a fist, before, with the guidance of his wand, Sol directed it to the tip of his stave. The bubble of magic hovered above the copper staff for a brief moment before Sol raised his weapon and tapped it to the ground. Suddenly, the sphere of energy erupted outwards, expanding in an instant to surround the five of them, quickly fading in the seconds that followed until it vanished entirely.

"Is everyone ready?" Rhys asked, looking to the others, his heart now racing in his chest.

They nodded silently.

Rhys sucked in a cold lungful of air. "Then let's do this!"

TWENTY-EIGHT

The streets of Llanmyd suffocated under an opaque, freezing fog. An eerie silence penetrated the air, as anxiously, they edged through the dense mist. Dozens of bodies, those too stubborn or too late to heed Rhys's warning, littered the way. A shadow blurred through the gloom ahead. Rhys's heart leapt out of his chest, but in the blink of an eye, the shade was gone.

"They are definitely here," Rhys whispered.

"Then we know that Sol's spell is working," Thia replied.

"How much further?" Sol asked anxiously.

"My house lies at the end of the next street over," Thia explained in a hushed voice.

A black silhouette suddenly whirred past them and they all recoiled in shock. Halting for a moment, fearing the wraith had detected them, they waited on bated breath. Moments later, the dark spirit rippled away, fading into the haze once more, skulking out of sight.

"I don't like this," Cade fretted.

"I think that is an understatement," Alkis shuddered as his eyes darted around.

It took the party several minutes to creep the last furlong to Thia's home. Every movement in the shadows put them further on edge. By the end of it, they had grown so paranoid that Rhys feared he might well have been imagining half of the shrouded figures sweeping through the fog.

"Here it is," Thia announced quietly when they arrived at the end of the street. She beckoned them toward the entrance of the small corner house, the door hanging slightly ajar. The unoiled hinges creaked softly as she pushed against the peeling paint and edged slowly into the dark room.

Checking over his shoulder, Rhys followed the witch into her home, gesturing for the others to keep watch outside. Sol nodded and took guard in front of the small property with Alkis and Cade stood by his side, ready for whatever might emerge from the murk around them.

The small dim sitting room was lined with bookcases whose shelves bowed beneath the weight of dozens of scrolls and dusty tomes. Strewn across the floor and across various tables were more books and writings, cast open upon pages that depicted glyphs and verses; from many of which the ink had faded in the age that had passed since their penning.

Half melted candles, jars and pots of herbs, and various other arcane ingredients stocked shelves mounted along the walls, along with pestles, mortars, athames, incense, balances, ichors, phials, poultices, salves, balms, crystals, inkpots, and quills. Though the myriad of items, both natural and supernatural, cluttered the room in an almost random manner, there seemed still to be order amongst the chaos. The witch went about the place filling a small pack, finding what she needed quick and without fuss.

"When the village awoke to the sight of the curse, their first reaction was to blame me," she explained. "The reeve sent his guardsmen to arrest me in my home. They broke open the door to find me having recently completed the ritual that warded the village."

"And not understanding what you were doing, they assumed you were invoking the curse!" Rhys discerned.

The witch nodded silently as she gathered the last few supplies, finally making her way over to the largest of all her bookcases where she began scanning the shelves.

"I think it's in this one," she remarked under her breath, as she caressed the spine of an old and weathered tome.

Drawing it carefully from the shelf, she cleared the surface of the nearest table and splayed open the discoloured pages, turning through them for several moments before finally she loudly tapped the leaf in front of her.

"Is that it?" Rhys asked, leaning over

her shoulder to glimpse a complex glyph scribed across the page with paragraphs of text surrounding it.

"Yes," she said as her eyes scanned quickly over the flowing ink. "I have the supplies," she added after a time. "There are few components required. And the casting should not take too long; but before I can begin the ritual, I must lay down this glyph."

"How long will that take?"

"Only a few minutes," she replied. "But that is a few minutes longer than I would have liked to spend in this place!"

"But will we be vulnerable whilst you are laying it?"

"I shouldn't think so. The glyph will hold no power until it is activated. Only then will it disrupt Sol's concealment spell."

"Good to hear," Rhys nodded. "Where should we perform the ritual? Here?"

"I am not sure if that would be wise. If all I have heard of wraiths from myths and legends proves true, they are not restricted by physical barriers in this world the same way we are—they can supposedly pass through walls as if they are thin air."

"Then we had better perform the ritual in an open area," Rhys suggested. "Somewhere we can best see them approach; but with the fog, I'm not sure there is such a place."

"The market square may offer the best

visibility," Thia proposed. "Even in this unnatural gloom, you can still see clearly for a short distance."

"You are right," Rhys concurred. "That's where we need to make our stand!"

Thia carefully tore the page from the book, and folding the paper, she inserted it between the pages of a smaller journal which she slid into her pack. Adorning a warm cloak, she handed Rhys back his own.

"I'm almost ready," she assured, glancing around the floor, turning over a number of scattered loose pages and scrolls as she searched for something else. "I just need my..." she sighed heavily as she found what she was looking for, "wand," Thia finished defeatedly, clasping the two halves of an ornately carved beech wand. "This must have happened when they seized me!" she explained in frustration, casting the broken implement aside.

"You'll have to use mine," Rhys offered, returning his wand to the witch.

"Thank you," she sighed, carefully taking the arcane instrument and tucking it under her cloak. "I have everything I need," she added, making her way towards the door.

Rhys nodded, following her back out into the street.

Once Rhys had explained their plan to cast the ritual from the square, the group tentatively crept the rest of the way through the village, towards the open marketplace. The black shadows prowled the plaza in greater numbers, swooping in and out of sight as they searched for bodies of the fallen.

"I can cast from here," Thia whispered.

Rhys's heart was thrumming fast in his chest. He looked to the others as they readied themselves. Cade nocked an arrow. Alkis unsheathed his longsword.

"When you are ready," Rhys nodded to the witch.

Thia knelt down on the icy cobbles, drawing Rhys's wand from under her cloak. Opening the messenger bag hung at her side, she drew the page from her mother's tome with the ritual instructions. Reaching back into the bag, she produced a candle, and what appeared to be a variety of phials filled with brightly coloured metallic salts. Wedging the candle between the cobblestones, the witch sprawled the torn page upon the ground and spent several moments studying its markings.

"You might want to give me a wide berth," she explained, gesturing for the others to step back. "This glyph is rather large."

Rhys shuffled away and watched as the woman began to trace a line of gleaming blue energy in a wide arc across the cobblestones with his wand. Thia worked quickly, carving a near perfect circle, before marking several intersecting lines that wove in and around the ring of light. When she had completed the basic shape of the glyph, she proceeded to inscribe a series of intricate runes and symbols at various points inside the shape. After several minutes, the glyph matched that of the diagram, stretching a dozen feet in diameter with the unlit candle positioned at its centre.

"It's ready," she announced nervously as she uncorked all of her phials in preparation.

"Are you?" Rhys asked sympathetically as he observed a quiver in her hand.

She nodded silently.

Rhys clenched his fingers tightly around his staff as cold blood infused his muscles and mind. "Do it."

Thia pointed to the wick of the candle and in an instant, it was alight with a cyan glow. Pouring the contents of the first phial into her palm, Thia cast the handful of saline crystals into the flame. The burning wick crackled and popped, suddenly blazing now with a crimson tint. The markings of the glyph caught alight and scarlet flames leapt several inches upwards from the lines, forming a burning ring of fire. The invisible veil of concealment that surrounded them collapsed inwards, shrinking back to a translucent orb atop Sol's stave.

In that moment, an all-encompassing choir of ear-splitting howls suddenly crescendoed throughout Llanmyd, as all at once, each and every wraith prowling the gloomy ruins of the village, sensed their immediate presence. The wails steadily ebbed, fading to an eerie silence, and for an uncomfortably long moment, everything grew ghostly still.

"Steady," Rhys ordered as the four men stood with their backs against the flames. His eyes darted around as he glimpsed the shadow of several spectres swooping about the haze before him. The apparitions continued to blur on the edge of Rhys's perception, vanishing each time he directed his attention upon them. Then, with little forewarning, they disappeared altogether. The four warriors held fast, waiting in silence as Thia began the ritual in earnest, muttering under her breath as she focussed on trying to discern the source of the Grey.

Waiting for the inevitable, Rhys clenched his hand ever tighter, until the knuckles bound around his staff turned white. Then, out of the mist, a rank of dark spectres ominously materialised, skulking through the fog as they prowled towards their prey: the very same phantoms that had haunted Rhys the day of Longford's demise.

Dark skeletal talons webbed with translucent flesh clutched blades of black iron. Their cloaks blurred and twisted into the mist itself as the malevolent spirits crawled towards them, hissing and shrieking beneath the shadow of their hoods.

"Now!" Rhys cried.

Driving his staff into a forward lunge, Rhys let fly a fist of silver magic. The arcane battering ram churned through the mist as it took flight, pummelling into the nearest shadow as a wraith darted out of the haze. A tormented wail carved through the air as the creature vanished in a twisting flail of smoke and shadow, driven back into the seething fogs at its rear.

At that same instant, a flash of lightning lit up the gloom, thunder echoing across the market square as a bolt of electricity arced from Sol's stave, connecting with the next phantom scudding through the murk.

Immediately afterwards, Rhys heard a bowstring twang at his rear, Cade finally loosing the tension he had held so long in anticipation, the arrow streaking out of sight, disappearing through a wall of gloom before a third shrill howl cut the atmosphere like a knife.

Rhys unleashed another blast of force energy, the torrent of kinetic magic punching another of the foul beings back through the surrounding pall of fog. He fired another silver missile, striking true a third time, then another, and another, as quicker and quicker the wraiths shot out of the gloom, darting and weaving in harrying charges, each advance drawing nearer to the group.

Soon they began to surge out of the haze in greater numbers, repelled only by the steady cannonade delivered by Rhys and Sol, and the rapid volley of arrows from Cade's strumming bowstring. But as the phantoms continued their assault, the elusive spirits blurring left and right, many of the shots delivered their way sailed clean wide, and before they knew it, Rhys and his allies were being overwhelmed, several of the wraiths having slipped past their defence to close in on them.

An ethereal blade unfurled atop Rhys's stave, clashing with a descending edge of wrought iron clutched in a skeletal grip. A twirling counter parried the thrust wide, the emerald blade slicing through the ghostly wrist that clutched the dagger, severing the limb, carving down into the spectre's shadowy form. The phantom evaporated, banished from the material world with a final haunting scream that reverberated through the plaza.

Blocking another stab launched from out of the mist, Rhys drove the next wraith back, spearing the apparition clean through, annihilating it in another dark puff of shadow. Peering back over his shoulder, Rhys watched Alkis dodge clean aside as a similar lunge was driven his way, bringing his sword around as he stepped clear, cleaving through the back of the wraith assailing him, dispelling the spirit from existence with his enchanted longsword, before clashing blades with the next spectre hurtling his way.

Cade continued to loose arrow after arrow, but as his once brimming quiver drew near empty, he retreated, seeking protection behind Sol, choosing his shots carefully to make the last of his arrows count. Sol advanced, maintaining his guard as he shielded the archer at his rear, carving through any phantom that darted his way.

The incoming tide of spirits continued to wash out of the gloom, flooding across the plaza as they swarmed towards a beacon in the mist: the unfolding ritual. But as they stormed out of the haze, they were met by a stalwart defence of twirling copper, steel, and malachite. Undeterred by the chaos raging around her, Thia never so much as glanced up from the page in front of her, continuing to recite the lengthy incantation, her concentration never breaking.

Rhys swivelled away, dodging back as a trio of spectres scudded towards him all at once. Flourishing his stave in a wide arc, the emerald veins within his weapon flashed crimson, the ethereal blade suspended from its tip igniting as a lash of flames leapt out from the edge, flailing across the shadowy forms of the wraiths blurring his way. Struck by the infernal whip, the three spectres were immolated, combusting into a cloud of embers and dark smoke that lingered in the murk thereafter.

A hot line sliced across the mage's forearm as a glancing blade cut through Rhys's sleeve. Riposting the attack with a funnel of flames, Rhys incinerated the spirit that had dealt the blow, seizing a brief moment of respite that followed to inspect the wound. The gash was shallow, but even still, the flesh stung with the taint of sinister necrosis induced by the undead blade that had dispensed the cut.

Peering back up at the growing numbers of inbound spectres, Rhys knew it would not be long before they were overwhelmed entirely. If the wraith continued to advance in these numbers, they would barely survive the next wave. The subsequent charge closed in, a half dozen phantasmal shadows streaking out of the murk straight for Rhys.

Without time for thought, the mage struck the cobblestones with his ethereal blade. Searing energy gushed through his stave, the crimson glowing weapon flashing as it sliced across the ground, igniting the cobbles underfoot in a wall of fire. Retreating behind the flaming bulwark, Rhys peered through the churning smoke and warping air as several of the spectres through themselves into the burning barricade. The shadows were immolated on contact, catching alight as their dark forms smouldered away into toxic fumes.

Unable to sustain the spell through concentration, Rhys yielded, allowing the wall of fire to peter out. But through the residual smoke rising from the ground, Rhys descried the next wave swooping his way, the tormented wails carving through the air as they drew in.

Scratching his blade across the cobbles for a second time, Rhys resummoned his flaming bulwark, extending the length of the incendiary barricade to better protect his and his allies' flanks. The party closed inward, backing toward the ritual circle at their rears as the assault continued, wraith after wraith plunging heedlessly into the fiery barrier in front of Rhys as he strained his mind to keep the flames alive.

"How much longer, Thia?" Rhys groaned through exertion.

"I can't—he's resisting the ritual!" the witch cried out, focussing intensely. "He knows what I am trying to do! He is resisting me—preventing me from glimpsing his thoughts!"

"Who? Who's blocking you?"

"I'm trying..." she struggled.

Rhys glanced over his shoulder to see that Cade, arrows depleted, and Alkis, were on the verge of being overrun. The burden of keeping his wall of flame alight was rapidly sapping Rhys of all energy. His mind ached and his muscles began to shudder from the strain. Fighting with sheer will, he trudged across the cobblestones, circumnavigating the glyph towards Cade and Alkis, the flaming bulwark still raging at his rear.

Rhys sliced into the ground again with his flickering amber staff. Sparks leapt out from the cobbles, and through a defiant act of might, Rhys summoned another blazing screen into existence, merging the new wall of flames with the first, creating a curving barrier that burned two thirds of the way around the ritual glyph, shielding himself and now also Alkis and Cade from the unrelenting onslaught.

Rhys collapsed to one knee as the burden of sustaining the vast barrier of flames depleted him. The feat of magic draining every ounce of his strength, every fibre of his being began to scream in exhaustion.

"Thia?" he gasped as his body was wrought with pain.

"Almost..." she cried, screwing up her face as she forced her mind upon the caster of the ritual. "I can't locate him!" the witch shouted in frustration. "But I think I have a name!"

"What is it?" he puffed, his vision beginning to blur.

"Indus!" she called out. "Indus Mark!"

"No!?" Sol stammered in confusion.

The flaming glyph was snuffed out as Thia ended the ritual.

Cutting down a final wraith with his charged blade, Sol slammed his stave into the ground and the sphere of shrouding energy expanded around them once more.

The flaming barriers erected by Rhys were instantly quenched as his strength failed. His legs buckled. The ground rushed up to meet him. His teary eyes caught blurred and unfocused glimpses of figures rushing about him. What remained of his vision quickly faded. As he slipped into unconsciousness, his hearing was the last sense to go.

"Rhys?" Alkis cried out.

"What happened to him?" Thia gasped.

"I can't see any wounds!" Cade panted.

"He overexerted himself," Sol's muffled voice echoed. "He is lucky to be alive."

"If he hadn't, we'd all be dead!" Thia insisted.

"It's still not safe here! We must get him out of the village," Sol urged. "He is fading fast!"

TWENTY-NINE

A hazy light filtered in through Rhys's eyelids as they slowly peeled open. The sky above loomed grey, dusk tinging the horizon a crimson hue. White feathers of snow blurred around, levitating in the dying light. Rhys's eyes strained to focus. A dull pounding ground inside his head. His mouth was parched, his brow clammy and cold. He was bound tightly in several layers of blanket. As he tried to move, ripples of pain twinged through his muscles. He grunted against the soreness.

"Easy," the soothing voice of Thia whispered. "Take it slow."

"Help him up," Sol urged, as the mage knelt beside Rhys and eased him to a sitting position.

Rhys raised a heavy, aching hand to his face and rubbed his eyes. Cade lifted a waterskin to his lips and he sipped slowly. Looking around, he realised they were atop the ridge once more; Llanmyd lying to the south still drowned in grey gloom.

"How are you feeling?" Sol asked.

"So-so," Rhys grinned wryly.

"Well, you look terrible!" he smiled back.

"I find that hard to believe!" Rhys chuckled, wincing as he did so. "What happened?"

Sol glanced to the others and then back to Rhys. "You pushed yourself too hard in sustaining the fire barrier—it nearly killed you!"

"But you may well have saved all our lives in doing so!" Alkis added as he too knelt beside Rhys.

"Here," Thia offered, drawing a small phial of amber fluid from her messenger bag, and handing it to Rhys, "drink this."

Turning the tiny bottle in his fingers, Rhys watched the viscous fluid coat the sides of the phial. Uncorking it with his teeth, he poured the silky contents into his mouth. Warm, and tasting strongly of honey and spices, the elixir was unmistakably amrita, and a potent draught at that. His head buzzed and a hot flame burned in his chest, its invigorating warmth quickly flowing throughout his body in rejuvenating waves. Yet even such a powerful concoction was not enough to alleviate the debilitating fatigue gripping him.

The fog that clouded his thoughts began to lift, the memories of his final moments before succumbing to lassitude started to play out in his mind.

"Indus!" he breathed in disbelief. "No..." he refused, "it's not possible!"

Sol issued him as grave a look as ever he had portrayed.

"No!" Rhys shook his head, clambering to his feet in spite of his languidness. "No!" he repeated louder now as he looked into the abyss of the curse. "But then...?" His thoughts raced. "Indus killed everyone I ever knew," he said in cold realisation. "He razed Longford... my home—and who knows how many other settlements!"

"His crimes are beyond absolution!" Sol hissed through gritted teeth.

"But why?" Rhys questioned desperately. "For what reason!? He's slaughtered so many innocent people! Its genocide!"

"I believe I may have an inkling," Thia interjected.

Rhys and Sol swivelled to look at her.

"I suspect the desolation you see before you is by no means the full extent of this curse," she posited.

"What are you suggesting?" Rhys questioned.

"What if the purpose of this curse, the Grey, is not to quench life, but to harvest it?"

"Harvest?" Sol repeated in alarm.

"So it can be used to power something else—life force utilised as fuel for some greater purpose?"

Sol's eyes widened. "Like what?"

"I cannot possibly fathom," she conceded. "I have never heard of anything that would require so much power. But any magic demanding the life-force of hundreds in order to cast, is bound to be devastating!"

Silence gripped them until Sol finally spoke, "Then what does this mean?"

"It means our mission is far more momentous than we thought!" Rhys declared.

"Where do we go from here?" Sol asked, looking to Rhys now for answers.

"To Ultair!" the mage replied. "This goes far beyond our vendetta. Indus is a threat to all of Cambria! Llanmyd was not the first to fall to his wrath, nor will it be the last! We can no longer afford to keep our presence in Cambria a secret. All must know of Indus and his crimes, and of our fight to stop him—we cannot hope to stand against him alone! We must petition the Earl of Ultair for his aid."

Sol remained silent for a long while as he gazed at the devastation wrought by Indus's magic. "It goes against the tenets Arlas fought so hard to uphold within the Order," the mage mused.

"Too much has changed," insisted Rhys. "The Circle is broken—the Order in ruins. If we do not reveal ourselves now, it is only a matter of time before Indus does so himself, and then it will be on his own terms. Better we act now and deny him the opportunity!"

"Damn it," the mage sighed defeatedly. "You are right. Okay," he agreed finally. "I trust your judgement. If you think this is how we must proceed, then I will follow your lead."

"I will come with you!" Thia insisted.

Sol and Rhys exchanged a look with one another, knowing they were both already in agreement.

"There is nothing left of my life here… and I believe I have more than demonstrated my worth to you today. Let me join you. I want to see the man who summoned this evil upon my home brought to justice!"

Rhys beamed at her, issuing a nod of approval.

"You know we've already pledged ourselves to you," put in Alkis, speaking for both himself and Cade.

"Looks like we're building something of a team," Sol remarked.

"The more the merrier," returned Rhys.

"Then what now?"

"We set forth to Ultair at dawn, and take our first step towards stopping Indus!"

That evening they made camp on the southern slope of the ridge, taking refuge from the bitter northern wind as snow flurries bore down on them constantly throughout the night.

"The villagers are out in this," Rhys worried, as they huddled around their small fire taking refuge beneath a rocky outcrop.

"The weather is harsh, but it is not as cold as it has been in recent nights," Alkis consoled.

"They have no shelter, no supplies—nothing but the clothes on their backs," Cade lamented. "I fear that many will not survive the night!"

"They will have to keep moving," Sol returned. "There is shelter to be found in the refuge of the valleys, and enough water sources between here and Ultair to sustain them. If they keep pushing forth, and ensure they light campfires for when they *do* need to rest, they may yet make it to the capital without suffering any casualties," Sol assured them.

"Then let us hope for the best," Rhys nodded as he rubbed his chest beneath his cloak.

Sol, Alkis, and Cade drifted off in the hour that followed, sheltering beneath thick layers of blankets and furs. Despite his weariness, Rhys struggled to fall into slumber. Every fibre of his body ached, and no matter how he positioned himself, he could not get comfortable.

He turned over on his bedroll to see Thia beside him was likewise still awake.

"Are you okay?" she whispered, noticing his discomfort.

"I've had more relaxing evenings," he smirked. "But all things considered, I guess I can't really complain."

Thia smiled gently as she pulled her blanket tighter around herself.

"Are *you* alright?" Rhys asked solemnly. "You went through something of an ordeal."

"I would be lying if I said it was not keeping me awake," she confessed. "I keep replaying what happened over and over in my mind."

"Why did they blame you for what happened? How is it they knew of your magic?"

"For years I offered healing to the village of Llanmyd, and my mother before me."

"You were open about your practices!?" Rhys questioned in confusion.

"Yes. Naturally. It never bodes well— keeping secrets like that."

"But why!?" the mage puzzled. "Did they not persecute you?"

"There were some that looked upon me with suspicion because of the stigma that practising magic carries, but most of Llanmyd welcomed the aid I offered them, just as they did with my mother. I healed their wounds, provided medicine, offered blessings, cured their sick children. I was valued by a great many people within the village—several were my close friends."

"And yet when the curse arose, they still turned on you?" Rhys uttered gravely. "Held you accountable in spite of what you had done for them?"

"Such is human nature," she returned sorrowfully. "Our minds naturally fear what we do not understand. Those who know little of magic fear it; and when it carries a malevolence like the curse, they are right to do so. But magic is neither inherently good or evil; only its users and uses can be labelled as such.

"When the curse descended, many were struck with terror. Some chose to blame me because they did not know what else they could do. They needed more than anything to hold someone accountable—then, they could believe it was within their power to prevent the curse!

"I do not believe that the entire village turned on me. I choose to think that it was but a few that called for my death. Everyone else was merely swept up in the mob, listening out of fear to those who claimed to have answers."

"But do you not feel betrayed?" Rhys pressed, perplexed by the witch's objective demeanour.

"That is all I feel," she grieved, momentarily allowing the pain of her wronging to slip through her stoic mask. "Irrespective of whether everyone condoned the injustice that I was dealt or not—they all stood by and watched as I was dragged from my home and tied to a stake!" tears glinted in the corners of her eyes as they caught the light of the campfire. "I was sentenced to death by burning! Without a trial, despite my pleas for mercy! None came to my aid... None except you."

Rhys was at a loss for words. "I just... I knew they were wrong. I could see you needed help. I didn't really give it any thought—I just acted... did what I knew was the right thing."

"I can see why these men follow you," she remarked.

"They don't follow *me*," Rhys refused with alight chuckle. "If we follow anyone it is Sol."

"That is not what I saw earlier," she smiled.

They chatted quietly for a while longer before Thia eventually nodded off. Rhys lay awake for some time longer, tossing and turning in stiffness, but eventually sleep came to him too. When morning arose, the mage finally felt reinvigorated. His aches and pains had faded, and a new energy flowed through him. The cool winter sun glazed over the fresh snow as the party set off northeast towards Ultair.

Together, they strode along the broad highway cleaving through the winding and frozen vales, the bridleway carrying them eastward towards the fortified city. As night descended once more, they set camp in Crannwood just off the roadside. The trees provided a break in the sweeping northern winds, and to the party's relief, the clear skies above held out against the clouds and snow. Constellations twinkled in the blackness whilst they slept, fading with the break of dawn.

"Ultair is but a few leagues west of here," Sol informed them as they packed away their bed rolls and dined sparingly on what little rations they had left in their knapsacks.

They continued along the highway in the frigid morning air, passing through the woodland for nearly a league before they reached the eastern limits of the forest. When they exited

Crannwood, passing through the treeline out on to open plains, the City of Ultair rose into view beyond the dazzling amber horizon. Stood against the dawn sun, a lonely hill curved in silhouette above the rolling pastures of the surrounding farmlands. Atop its ramparted slopes, a defensive wall crowned the snowy hilltop, inside of which rose the parapets of the city keep, Fort Ultair.

"There it is," Rhys remarked as the entire company stopped to squint onwards at the city's silhouette against the glare of the sun.

"It is still nearly two leagues from here," Sol observed as they resumed the journey towards the city once more. "We should arrive at the capital's gates by mid-morning."

With the passing miles, the sun rose higher and the shadows lifted from the metropolis, casting the stone walls and the castle within in a golden light. Drawing nearer, Rhys's keen eyes made out a camp erected amongst the ramparts of the hill. Wisps of smoke dithered in the still winter air as men and women gathered around fires before the western barbican.

When the highway finally arrived at the foot of the hill, continuing upwards towards the city gates, Rhys and the others had their suspicions confirmed; the camp erected before the barbican belonged to the refugees from Llanmyd.

"They have been refused entry to the city," Alkis concluded, pointing ahead of them to the lowered portcullis of the gatehouse, a dozen guardsmen stationed outside to keep watch.

"There are but a couple hundred of the villagers—mostly men," Sol puzzled as he glanced at the gathering of asylum seekers huddled around various fires crackling throughout the encampment. "We passed no dead along the road during our journey here."

"You reckon the others were allowed through?"

"It seems likely," the mage returned. "Perhaps the woman, children, and the elderly were given immediate refuge. It would be difficult to find accommodation within the city walls for the entire village—at least on such a time scale; they no doubt only arrived outside the gates last night at the very earliest."

"How can there not be enough room inside the city?" Thia contested. "It's the capital of Gwent!"

"And Llanmyd was hardly a small village —I'd reckon it a town were it any larger," Sol explained. "Ultair may be Gwent's main city, but compare it to the likes of the other capitals: Orthios, Iarbhaile, Dinas Môrllyn— heck, Ultair is barely larger than Westport. Nearly a thousand refugees suddenly arriving at this city gates... well, that's more than a twentieth of the population inside the walls!"

"But surely there is enough room, even still?" Cade queried. "I could see how many houses there were inside the walls from a way back!"

"Imagine trying to house fifty people who suddenly arrived in Wythe without warning," returned Sol. "Where would you put them? The inn could hold about half of them at a push, but then what?"

"They'd have to stay in people's houses," replied the hunter.

"Exactly," agreed the mage. "People are pretty trusting in Wythe, but I can't imagine every household would be happy to put up a stranger at short notice—especially when they might not leave for some time. And people in cities are far less trusting of strangers!"

"I see your point," the archer conceded.

"Fact of the matter is, many places might have sealed the gates to everyone," Sol concluded.

"Not to mention all these tents erected outside the walls," added Alkis. "We know full well the refugees didn't bring them with them from Llanmyd. The Earl must have provided them!"

"It seems the situation is somewhat fortunate, given the circumstances," appraised Rhys as they began their ascent towards the gates.

"It's a bloody miracle by my account," returned Sol.

As they climbed the hillside, passing the encampment more closely, Rhys descried that the refugees were well stocked and provisioned against the elements. There appeared ample kindling to fuel the fires, supplies of food and water were stacked at the heart of the site, and many of the refugees sat cloaked in woollen blankets with steaming bowls of broth clutched in their hands.

Arriving at the barbican, they were greeted by the most authoritative of the guardsmen stood sentinel before the portcullis lowered across the gateway. "Ho there, travellers!" he welcomed them. "We sighted your coming from the west. I trust you too arrive from Llanmyd?"

"We do," Rhys began, though before he could continue, the guardsman spoke again.

"I am sorry, but there is not space for you within the city. The public houses are filled, and the fortress is brimming with refugees. We are trying to find citizens willing to offer shelter to those without, but as of yet, there is not room enough to house you.

"You five appear young and fit. We have asked that those better suited to brave the elements remain outside the city walls until we are able to accommodate you. You should be able to find room in the tents we have erected; and there is plenty of hot food for you out here, though, you may find better shelter in the nearby villages."

"Many thanks," Rhys began once more, "but we are not refugees. We do not come to the city seeking shelter," he explained.

"No?" the guardsman responded raising an eyebrow. "Then pray tell, why have you ventured here from Llanmyd?"

"We seek an audience with the city's Earl.

My friends and I bring important knowledge of the curse that befell the village."

The guard chuckled heartily, "Alas, I cannot let you into the city. All who have travelled here from the forsaken village claim to bring important word of Llanmyd's fate. I have heard the tale a hundred times over by now, and every different variation of it!

"You bring word of a witch who dwelt within your very midst, posing as a benevolent healer for years, only to turn on you, conjuring a sinister black magic that reaped the village of all colour and life?

"Or perhaps the version you tell blames the warlock who appeared after the curse descended, who murdered the village reeve before everyone's eyes?

"I have heard every account there is—some from more reliable sources than others, and I do not believe any truly know what befell Llanmyd. Thus, I trust you will forgive me if I do not take you at your word when you claim to bring knowledge of the curse."

"I assure you," Rhys insisted, "you have not yet heard this account!"

"Regardless, my orders are to not let any pass into the city. Now, I ask again that you turn away and stop hassling the guard, else I will have you removed."

Rhys issued the man a disgruntled look.

"Come, Rhys," Sol beckoned him away. "I do

not believe we can change his mind."

Rhys sighed heavily, unsure what else to say.

"That's him!" a voice suddenly called out from behind the mage.

Rhys span to see one of the militiamen from Llanmyd pointing his way.

"Rhys North!" he cried, bowing his head respectfully to Rhys before turning to address the city guards. "It is him! Rhys North, the warlock of Llanmyd! And with him Thia Smith, the witch he freed!"

Rhys swivelled around to look at the men guarding the gate. He backed away furtively as the rank of guardsmen eyed both him and Thia with suspicion.

"He is the one!" the man insisted, drawing the attention of several nearby refugees who soon gathered closer to investigate the commotion.

Rhys retreated further. His pulse quickened as many of the surrounding villagers started to recognise him.

"It *is* them!" a woman cried, pointing to Rhys and then Thia, drawing an even larger crowd.

The guard chief met eyes with Rhys as he examined him. "Wait!" he commanded over the growing rabble of the amassing crowd; raising his palm, signalling Rhys and the others to halt.

THIRTY

"That's him!" the village militiaman repeated. "The saviour of Llanmyd!"

Rhys glanced around, realising they were now surrounded by refugees, any route of quick escape blocked.

"Is it true?" the guard captain asked him, stepping closer. "Are you the warlock of whom all have spoken?"

"Well…" Rhys began still looking around. "I guess that depends on what you have heard about me!" he chuckled nervously.

"I have heard a great many things," he returned stoically, advancing even closer now, with several of his men at his back. "Many blame you for what happened to Llanmyd."

"Then they would be wrong!" Sol protested. "Rhys saved the lives of all who made it here!"

"Many have also claimed *that*," he added. "They call you the 'Saviour of Llanmyd.'"

"It does have a rather nice ring to it," Rhys

jested anxiously.

The guardsman continued to examine him sternly.

"And what do you think?" Sol asked, his fingers twitching for the staff across his back.

"I do not believe the man responsible for the devastation of Llanmyd would be foolish enough to show his face here," the guard captain finally replied. "Not when so many suspect him."

"I am relieved to hear you say that," Rhys exhaled, relaxing for a moment.

"And you?" the man turned now to Thia, who up until this point had been furtively attempting to fade into the background. "You are the witch of the village? The one this man saved; condemned to burn at the stake without trial, for the crime of cursing the village?"

Abandoning her attempt to shy away, Thia stepped forwards, drawing down the hood of her cloak. "I am."

"I have heard the ordeal you suffered at the hands of Reeve Gregor. You have my greatest sympathies for the injustice done to you. It is fortunate that this man arrived when he did."

"Very fortunate," she agreed, glancing Rhys's way.

"I assure you, miss, had Reeve Gregor survived, he would have been reprimanded and punished accordingly for his actions," the guard captain vowed apologetically. "But as I have heard it, he met his end in a curious twist of fate after drawing his blade on you, Rhys North."

Rhys remained silent.

The guard captain looked up to the surrounding crowd ogling at Rhys and his companions. Leaning closer to one of his men, he muttered a few commands under his breath. With that, the guards began to herd away the surrounding throng, ushering the villagers back into their camp.

"Nothing more to see here folks," one remarked as the crowd dispersed, leaving Rhys and his companions alone with the guard captain.

"I am Captain Joseph Dunlain of the Ultair city-watch," he introduced himself.

"It would seem you already know Thia and myself," Rhys replied. "These are my companions: Solomon Thomas, Alkis Mason, and Cade Williams."

"It is a pleasure," he nodded to them. "You have news then? Knowledge of the curse beyond what these villagers have shared?"

"We do," Rhys confirmed.

"Then I will see to it that you receive your audience with Lord Brandis," he declared. "Come," he beckoned, striding now towards the portcullis. He banged his heavy gauntlet against the iron grill, and from the shadows of the gateway stepped another city guardsman.

"Captain," the man greeted him through the lattice.

"Nathaniel," the captain returned. "Raise

the portcullis. We are coming through."

"At once, sir," the guard replied, slipping back into the shadows and disappearing into the gatehouse.

The groaning of iron and chains rang out, and slowly, the heavy grating began to lift before them. As the lattice bulwark inched upwards, downward spikes lifted from their receiving pits in the stone, rising slowly until the iron barricade had been winched above their heads. "Hold it there!" the captain shouted over the rattling of the portcullis mechanism. Ducking slightly, Captain Dunlain briskly strode into the vast archway of the barbican, gesturing the others to follow. With everyone inside, he called out once more. "Let it back down."

Suddenly the clattering of iron resumed, the clanking winch accelerating as the gateway guillotined closed, slamming into the receiving pits, sealing the way shut behind. With the last ringing echoes fading throughout the tunnel of the barbican, all fell silent. Stood in the shadows of the archway, before the inner gates, Rhys discerned the muffled hubbub of the city beyond, the streets of Ultair lying just beyond the vast wooden doors.

As the other city watchman re-emerged from out of the gate house, the captain introduced them, "This here is Guardsman Nathaniel Rossiter."

Rhys and the others nodded his way in

greeting.

"Nathaniel, this is Rhys North, the man whom the Llanmyd villagers are heralding as their 'saviour'," he explained. "He and his companions have knowledge of what really happened there, and they are seeking an audience with Lord Brandis. Would you take them to see His Lordship so that he can meet with them?"

"Right away sir," the guard obeyed unquestioningly.

"See that their audience takes priority. And be sure to mention that it was *I* who sent you."

"Of course, sir."

Stepping past the others, Captain Dunlain rapped his armoured knuckles against the gates sealing the way ahead. After a brief moment of delay, Rhys heard the bulwarks being unbarred from the far side, before presently, the vast doors groaned as they began to part. Golden rays spilled suddenly through the widening aperture, steadily unveiling the sunlit bustle of the city beyond. As the gates pulled fully apart, Rhys gawped in wonder at the busy streets of Ultair; never before had the mage seen so many people in one place. The flowing masses swept up and down the black cobbled streets, chattering, shouting, singing, and whistling as they went about their business.

"Thank you, Captain," Rhys expressed, turning back to the man.

"I believe it is you that is owed thanks," he replied. "And by a great many," he added, bidding them a farewell.

Following Guardsman Rossiter, they emerged through the gateway, into the streets of the capital, and began navigating a sea of people. The watchman led them up the main thoroughfare, towards the peak of the hill, where lied the city keep. Buildings rose high on either side, leaning wonkily inward, tapering the street upwards to snowy, overhanging thatched eaves several stories above, leaving little more than a narrow strip of morning sky visible overhead. Mules drew carts of winter vegetables, and vendors stocked all manner of goods in their stalls. The smells of sweets, spices, and roasting chestnuts wove through the breeze, and the near deafening din of chatter roared all around.

Sol nudged Rhys to get his attention and issued him a teasing smile. Rhys realised how ridiculous he must have appeared, gawking at everything they passed, yet a subtle point from Sol revealed that both Cade and Thia were likewise just as awestruck by the city.

"First time in the city, I take it?" the guard leading them assumed.

"For some of us," Alkis replied as he and Sol continued to grin at the others.

"It's a little overwhelming at first," Guardsman Rossiter chuckled. "But you'll get used to it."

Negotiating a labyrinth of twisting thoroughfares and narrow alleys, they climbed steadily uphill, until after a time, the streets widened, yielding a view of the citadel that loomed atop the hill's crest. The throngs thinned, the humming of the crowds diminishing, giving way to a steady traffic of carts and carriages rolling up and down birch-lined avenues. Grander brick and limestone manors replaced the half-timbered shops and houses of the lower ward, whilst landed gentry, and lower aristocracy, garbed in colourful velvet finery, replaced the woollen-clad peasantry flocking the streets below.

On the final approach to the castle, the buildings fell away entirely, the heart of the city surrendering to the citadel's vast encircling court. Fort Ultair towered high above the rest of the capital, rising as the highest peak across miles of surrounding countryside, standing sentinel over the eastern plains of Gwent. The keep's curtain walls climbed nearly fifty feet high, the limestone baileys stretching between square turrets that rose even higher still. At ground level, the buttressed foundations of the walls sloped away into a murky, ice-crusted moat that ringed the entire keep. Crossbowmen patrolled the battlements above, frequently halting to peer down through the crenels to the court below.

The castle's drawbridge was already lowered, extending across the moat from the fortress's main gatehouse, and without pause, Rossiter led them briskly across to the barbican. The doors hung agape, the portcullis raised, the way open to the inner bailey, guarded only by a stationing of four pikemen stood blocking the path. Recognising the approaching man of the city watch, the posted men parted as Rossiter neared, granting him and his escort passage to the courtyard beyond, issuing him a silent nod of greeting as they did so.

They passed through the gatehouse, emerging into a courtyard, the snow perturbed by thousands of footprints as the city watch drilled and trained various units of new recruits throughout the bailey. Men sparred with swords and polearms, whilst archers and crossbowmen practised against straw targets around the fringes of the court. Elsewhere, the castle servants and non-militants went about their everyday business, mucking out stables, loading and unloading goods and supplies from carts, running messages back and forth. The dull clang of hammer on anvil rang out from a forge, whilst bowyers and fletchers whiled away alongside the armourer and weaponsmith. The smell of baking bread and roasting meat emanated from the kitchens somewhere up ahead, whilst the warmth of several braziers burning throughout the yard issued brief respite from the frigid winter air. Everywhere Rhys turned his attention, dozens of people were hard at work, ensuring the castle remained stocked, supplied, catered for, and well defended. In many ways, the citadel seemed busier than the bustling streets outside.

The keep itself sat against the far curtainwall, rising above all the surrounding turrets and bastions of the bailey. A set of stone steps descended into the courtyard from the fort's grand doors, before which another post of pikemen stood sentinel.

"His Lordship has met with many of the villagers of Llanmyd this morning," Rossiter explained as he led them towards the entranceway.

"Nathaniel," one of the pikemen greeted Rossiter as they arrived. A thump on the doors from the gatekeeper signalled the men stationed inside, and with little delay, the way swung open.

With a brief moment of disbelief, Rhys stepped forwards onto the flagstone floor of a grand entrance hall. The arched ceilings vaulted impossibly high overhead, supported by rafters of dark mahogany and two rows of stone pillars that spanned the hall's length. Daylight streamed in thin rays through lofty arrowslit windows, whilst torches flickered in sconces below, mounted along the ranks of pillars, illuminating what would otherwise have been a dimly lit foyer in their amber glow. A timber mezzanine rose against the perimeter, and elaborate woven tapestries hung floor to ceiling between the columns. A run of carpet trailed down the centre of the immense chamber, upon which a queue was formed; the line of people, undoubtedly comprised almost entirely of Llanmyd refugees, stretched from but a few yards inside the doors, down the full length of the hall, culminating before an empty throne at the far end.

Despite the hundred odd people gathered inside the keep, the atmosphere was strangely still, a mere single voice echoing softly throughout the chamber. Guardsman Rossiter led on, jumping the queue as he guided Rhys and the others past the line of people, making straight for the throne. Whispers grew as they passed, first those of discontent, as many perceived the queue jump as a slight dealt against them, but soon replaced by excited mutterings, as the villagers began to recognise Rhys and Thia.

Drawing to within a few yards of the throne, Rhys sighted Earl Brandis for the first time. The lord was seated on the steps to the dais, beside him, sat on the same level as the earl, was one of the villagers, the nobleman and peasant conversing as informally as if they had been sat drinking in a tavern.

Earl Brandis was draped in velvet robes collared and lined with dark furs, yet despite the fine tailoring of his vestments, there was nothing overtly frilled or decorative about the garbs. His weathered face was hardened and aged, yet his stormy eyes beamed with vigour. A bald scalp was more than made up for by his hirsute jawline, a thick beard of silver whiskers groomed tidily across his chin.

The earl sat listening intently as the

Llanmyd refugee took his turn in the conversation, speaking of his family's plight, and all that they had lost, all the while Brandis nodded with quite respect, his countenance grieved with empathy.

"Lord Brandis," Guardsman Rossiter interrupted politely.

"Ah Nathaniel," the lord turned to gaze upon the man. His rich voice softly spoken yet holding within it a deep unquestionable authority. "How can I help you?" he asked, his eyes smiling as he did so.

"My Lord," Rossiter bowed his head. "Captain Dunlain requested I bring these people to see you. May I present Rhys North."

Lord Brandis's eyes widened as he looked to Rhys.

"The Captain insisted your meeting with him and his companions take priority."

"Of course," the earl agreed, still scrutinising Rhys. "Nathaniel, would you fetch Colin from his study."

"Yes, My Lord,"

"Tell him that I require his help in seeing to the villagers."

"At once," Rossiter obeyed, bowing, before swiftly making for a door in the far corner of the hall.

Lord Brandis turned once more to the man seated beside him, resting a palm firmly on the commoner's shoulder as he did so. "John—many have suffered greatly at the hand that dealt this fate upon your village. The plight of your people pains me greatly and does not fall on deaf ears. I will do all I can to help your family."

The villager returned a timid smile, nodding with lamenting eyes as he took the nobleman's words to heart.

With their exchange complete, Brandis rose to his feet and climbed the steps of the dais, turning to survey the remainder of the refugees. Raising his voice powerfully so that it carried throughout the entire length of his halls, the Earl addressed those still awaiting an audience with him. "A matter of urgency calls me away; one no less related to the fate of Llanmyd. Fear not, however, for each and every one of you shall be heard! My right hand and chief scholar will be along momentarily. He will hear your plight whilst my focus is elsewhere and offer what aid and counsel he can. My thoughts are with you all!"

Brandis stepped down from the dais and approached Rhys and the others. "We should speak in private," he uttered quietly. "If you could follow me."

The earl turned away and strode briskly towards a room tucked at the rear of the chamber. Opening the door, Lord Brandis led the five of them into a small study lined with bookcases and oak panelling, bathed in the soft glow of a dozen candles set in a chandelier. Positioned in the centre of the flagstone floor stood a grand desk of varnished walnut, cluttered with scrolls, maps, and inkpots.

Brandis seated himself behind the desk to face the others and gestured to the array of chairs arranged in front of them. "Take a seat," he uttered warmly. "Feel free to move over those chairs in the corner," he nodded to a pair of extra seat stacked behind the door.

Cade and Alkis repositioned two of the chairs, whilst Rhys, Sol, and Thia sat in those already there. A brief moment of silence descended as Brandis studied them each in turn. A gentle knock proceeded the opening of the door to the study, and Nathaniel Rossiter poked his head into the room.

"Lord Brandis. Scholar Edwards is on his way now."

"Thank you, Nathaniel," Brandis replied.

"Is there anything else, My Lord?"

"Yes, actually," Brandis confirmed. "Would you come in and shut the door please."

Nathaniel stepped into the study and the door's latch clicked shut behind him. "What is it, My Lord?" he asked.

"I wish for you to remain here and listen to what is said in this room."

"Yes, My Lord," the man nodded compliantly, positioning himself meekly in the corner, before adding, "Might I ask for what purpose?"

"I might want your opinion on what is said."

"Of course, My Lord," the guard replied falling silent for a brief moment with a confused expression. Stood there, shuffling awkwardly, unable to contain himself, he then asked, "Would you not prefer someone else for this role? Perhaps one of the scholars... or one of my superiors?"

"No, No. Your opinion is as good as any Nathaniel. I wish to hear what *you* think."

"If that is what you wish, My Lord," he bowed, finally falling still.

Another long moment of quietude passed as Brandis reclined in his chair and twiddled his thumbs, glancing over the five strangers before him. "Rhys North!" he exclaimed loudly, turning to Rhys. "A name, that until yesterday, I had never heard before. Yet nearly every villager from Llanmyd with whom I have spoken has uttered your name. I have heard a great many things about you!" he paused stroking his beard. "Mostly good. Though a few have painted you in a somewhat less favourable light," the Lord grinned. "You are not only the talk of the villagers of Llanmyd, but now of Ultair. Word of your exploits was spread quickly among the populace. They are calling you the 'Saviour of Llanmyd!' A rather lofty title, would you not say?"

"It does roll off the tongue rather nicely. But I cannot say it is what *I* would have chosen. It is a bit too grandiose for my liking," Rhys smiled. "My Lord," he added hastily, realising how unversed he was in the appropriate decorum when speaking to a member of the nobility.

Brandis chortled loudly. "It is, isn't it?" he agreed, issuing a broad smile. "Well, regardless, if half of what I have heard of you is true, then it would seem an appropriate title."

"I am not the hero I seem to have been made out as," Rhys assured the man. "My only doing is that I brought warning in time! And I was only able to do just that because the same curse struck my own village last summer."

"Yet you ventured into Llanmyd, despite knowing fully the peril that faced you, to bring warning. You saved nearly the entire village in doing so! It seems somewhat heroic to me."

"Fortuitous, perhaps," Rhys offered. "But not heroic, My Lord."

"You saved the witch, did you not? As I hear it, you fought through a dozen guards and leapt into the flames to do so!"

"Is that what they are saying?" Rhys chuckled aloud, directing a glance at Thia. "A gross exaggeration! The fire was already extinguished when I leapt into it—and there certainly were not a dozen guards in my way!"

"Well," Lord Brandis smirked, "every good tale needs some embellishment!" The earl turned to look at Thia. "I presume you are Thia Smith, then: the witch condemned by Reeve Gregor, before he met his untimely, yet perhaps deserved, end? I had heard that you remained with the warlock Rhys North."

"I... err, yes My Lord," Thia replied.

"I must say, I had not expected you to be quite so fair, my dear," he smirked. "The term 'witch' normally conjures images of a withered crone, with warts and putrid skin."

"That would be a hag, My Lord," corrected Sol. "Though with the way magic is often perceived, it is easy to see where the misconception arose."

"Then you are also a warlock?" he deduced, scrutinising Sol. "You seem far too informed and hold too strong of an opinion otherwise."

"I am," Sol confirmed. "Of a sort at least, My Lord," he added alluding to his true nature.

"Then are you five some sort of coven?" he asked.

"No, My Lord," Alkis put in. "Neither myself, nor Cade here, have any inkling for the arcane."

"Curious," the earl remarked, stroking his beard once more. "I have never met any who practised magic before; not openly at least. My father believed it a dark and malevolent force that should be feared."

"And what is your opinion?" Rhys asked.

"I do not believe I can pass judgement," the nobleman offered diplomatically. "I know so little of sorcery beyond the myths and legends woven throughout Cambria's history—other than a few epic poems and folklore sagas read in my youth, my knowledge of the arcane extends little beyond the tales recounted by my wetnurse. I am somewhat ignorant to the esoteric mysteries of this world—but I am not oblivious to their dangers! Nor, should I add, am I unaware to the potential force for good such powers could be, provided they are used selflessly.

"But do tell me: how is it, that two warlocks, merely happen upon the village of Llanmyd at such a critical moment, when an unprecedented dark curse is in the act of striking? Especially when, one of those two, has encountered the very same afflicting curse before? This preternatural phenomenon is not commonplace, but assuredly infrequent—were it not, I would have heard of it prior. The odds that you, Rhys North, arrived when you did by chance, seem nigh impossible!"

"I'll admit, the likelihood of such occurring does seem unlikely—unbelievably so, perhaps," Rhys confessed. "But I promise you, it was mere coincidence! Yet we do not claim to know nothing of this curse, for in truth it is quite the opposite. What we have learnt of the Grey... the knowledge we now possess—that is what brought us here to your court."

"Then perhaps you should start your story from the beginning," the lord suggested.

Rhys glanced at Sol who issued him a silent nod. "Very well," he agreed, beginning his tale of the day he awoke to find Longford in ruin, and all that had happened since. He spared no detail, explaining his meeting of Arlas, his introduction to the Circle, the Rite of Reckoning, the Binding, and Indus's betrayal. Finally, after Rhys had been speaking for what likely exceeded an hour, he reached the point in his account where they had performed the ritual in Llanmyd.

Brandis sat in silence, listening without interruption to all Rhys said, nodding every so often to signal the mage that he still held his full attention. Eventually, Rhys finished his account. Quietude fell, and all was still for a long while as Brandis rubbed his whiskered chin, considering everything he had heard. "Nathaniel?" he uttered, eventually breaking the silence. "What say you?"

Nathaniel, having forgotten that he might be called upon for his opinion, stood wide-eyed to attention. Nervously, he studied Rhys, slowly forming an opinion in the enduring silence. Finally, having arrived at his conclusion, he spoke. "I believe what they say to be true. I think that this fellow: Indus, he is a danger to us all—a threat that should not be ignored!"

"As do I!" Brandis announced, falling silent again as his grey eyes stared up at the ceiling. "You made the right decision in seeking my aid. Though, short of launching a realm-wide manhunt for this Indus Mark, I am not certain what help I can offer you.

"I will notify my military leaders, and the heads of every town and village within fifty leagues of here. I will send word of what you have told me to the other four capitals in Cambria. Should Indus rear his head within my borders, I will know, alas if he resides within another realm, or keeps a low profile, I fear we may not find him."

"I doubt Indus will remain hidden for long," Sol assured them.

"Thank you, My Lord," Rhys beamed gratefully.

"Beyond this, I am not sure what is within my power. I trust you will be heading off to seek this man for yourselves?"

"I imagine so," returned Rhys, realising he had not yet contemplated their next move.

"Very well," concluded Brandis. "Until you decide to leave the city, you are my guests here in the keep."

THIRTY-ONE

"It would seem that being the Saviour of Llanmyd has its perks!" Rhys grinned as he collapsed back into the four-poster bed, nuzzling against the soft quilt atop the feather mattress.

"It does seem too good to be true," Sol agreed as he gazed at a rich tapestry hanging from the chamber wall.

"I assume that you have laid claim to this room then, Rhys?" Alkis chuckled.

"Yep," returned the mage, sitting up to look at the others.

"Very well," Sol nodded. "I am contempt with any of these rooms."

"As am I," Alkis agreed as he and Sol stepped back into the lounge adjoining the six guest chambers. Cade and Thia followed, briskly making their way across the sitting room, hoping to claim steak to the rooms of their choice before the others. Rhys, meanwhile, relaxed back into the soft mattress once more, soaking in all of the decor and finery surrounding him.

The mage must have dozed off, for when next he opened his eyes, the light streaming through the windows was of a dim dusk. Emerging from the bed chamber, he found the others sprawled out across the upholstered chairs and cushions set about the lounge. A fire crackled in the enormous hearth, radiating warmth throughout the suite.

Sol greeted Rhys with a smile as he trudged into the lounge and took a seat with the others. They chatted for the next few hours until there came a knock on the door. Alkis rose to answer the call, and in strode a half dozen servants, their arms laden with platters of food and decanters of wine.

Laying out the small feast across a table before the party, the servants dramatically removed the cloches from the platters all at once, unveiling a miniature banquet. Plates steeped in cuts of meat ranging from rare beef to roast pheasant glistened in the firelight, whilst dishes of boiled vegetables issued clouds of steam. Loaves of bread, wheels of cheese, bowls of dried fruits, puddings, and pies stacked what little space remained atop the table. The serving men and women moved quickly about, setting out plates and cutlery, before filling goblets and tankards with more wine and ale than any of them could hope to drink.

The company thanked them graciously,

eyeing the food with mouth-watering hunger, before hastily loading their plates with all they could bear. They ate, drank, and laughed until they could no more, and as the night drew late, exhausted, they each retired to the comfort of their individual bedchambers.

When Rhys awoke, the morning sunlight was streaming through the window, across the sheets, bathing him in a gentle warmth. He lay still for a long while, not wishing to leave the cosiness of his bed. After what may have been an hour, Rhys finally sat up and drew back the covers.

The cool flagstones sent a shiver up his ankles as Rhys made his way about the room, dressing in his weathered travelling gear. Quietly, he pulled open the door of his bed chamber and stepped out into the lounge. All was still; none of the others had yet arisen. Rhys poured himself a mug of water from a ewer and slowly walked the room's perimeter, admiring the ornaments and artwork decorating the lounge. He glanced over tapestries, vases, and paintings of historic battles, each more magnificent than the last. Finally, his attention was drawn to a framed map that depicted a vast landmass of twisting coastlines, rugged mountain ranges, moors, marshes, rivers, lakes, forests, tundra, and desert; all interspersed with markings of villages, towns, and five great cities sitting within the borders of the five realms.

Never before had Rhys seen a map of Cambria in its entirety. He was taken back by the immensity of the world in which he lived. Though the map possessed no scale, from glancing at distances between places he knew, Rhys figured the continent stretched over a thousand leagues from north to south. He sighted Longford, nestled in the foothills of the White Range to the north. Ultair, marked with the city's emblem, the black head of a great bear against a yellow, heater-shield escutcheon, stood centre of Gwent, positioned at the confluence of the River Afon and the River Long. To the east, the jagged coast bordered the Ocean of Essentar, to the south Gwent was fringed by the Virminter Mountains, the range sweeping from the eastern shores into the heart of the continent; and to the west lay Westverness.

Rhys spent a long while studying the map, plotting the route he had taken since leaving Longford. He spotted Oakton and Highshire, above which extended Highwood, all the way to Alder's Path, with Northcrest resting at its gate.

The map beyond the White Mountains was mostly bare. No towns or villages were marked, and hardly any geological features were charted in the vastly unexplored Carparth Tundra, yet Rhys descried the rough location where he believed the Northern Circle to lie. It was then an inkling came to him.

Rhys trod quickly back across the empty lounge, making for the knapsack lazily strewn on the floor of his bedchamber. Rifling through it, he soon produced his codex, and strode back over to the map. Flicking through the pages, he came suddenly to the charcoal sketch of the sigil he had copied from the stone circle on Mount Arthest. Finding the mountain's location on the map, Rhys held the page up against the chart and his eyes widened in curiosity.

Placing his codex down on a writing desk in the corner, Rhys searched for a quill and ink. Finding both tucked inside a drawer in the desk, Rhys set to work sketching the outer coastline of Cambria over the top of the charcoal etching. Some time later, Rhys lowered the quill, ink splattering across the table as he held up his codex to stare at the page in revelation.

"Morning," Sol greeted him, rubbing his eyes as he stepped out of his bedchamber.

The mage barely acknowledged his friend, not so much as diverting his eyes from the page.

"What is it?" Sol asked, reading perplexity on his friend's face. He stepped closer, approaching Rhys, and glanced over at the page for himself.

The tracing of the map overlaid the symbol perfectly, every line and point sat within the coastlines of Cambria. The geographical location of the Northern Circle and the henge on Mount Arthest aligned exactly with two of the points on the sigil.

"That's a mighty big coincidence," Sol breathed, taking the book from Rhys and comparing it against the map on the wall.

"I don't know," Rhys argued, playing down

the discovery. "I can't have traced the map that accurately—and the charcoal etching... I was just playing around."

"Do you know what you've stumbled upon?" Sol asked. "What these lines are?"

Rhys shook his head dumbfoundedly, not certain exactly as to what Sol was getting at.

"Rhys—I think these are ley lines!"

"Ley lines?" Rhys repeated.

"Arlas explained them to me once," the mage began. "Magic isn't ubiquitous... that is, it's not evenly dispersed throughout the world. There are pathways—lines of focussed energy that crisscross Cambria, where magic is at its most intense."

"Yes!" Rhys exclaimed. "Arlas mentioned them to me too!" understanding now why the idea of overlaying the map on top of the sigil had come to him. "He was talking about elder oak —he explained that they could only grow along ley lines. It was when I underwent the Rite of Reckoning... where Arlas had built a—"

"A stone circle?" Sol questioned.

"Yeah—like the Northern Circle, or the one on Arthest, just scaled down."

"And it would have mapped along this ley line here," Sol indicated, running his finger across the line that carved straight north to south down the centre of Cambria. "Directly beneath the Northern Circle!"

Rhys shook his head incredulously. "This

has to be just a coincidence!"

"But if it is not merely a coincidence…" Sol proposed.

"Then the Northern Circle and the henge at Mount Arthest may be part of a larger network of monuments throughout Cambria!"

* * *

"It does seem somewhat of a stretch," scrutinised Thia after Rhys had finished explaining their theory to the others. "That you were able to plot two points over a map means little. You would likely be able to do such with many symbols and patterns."

"I thought as much at first," Rhys confessed. "But the more I consider it, the more compelling it seems. When I came across the sigil carved into the altar at Mount Arthest, the Northward point, the one which maps over the Northern Circle, was illuminated. Then, the moment I touched the altar, this circle," he jabbed the appropriate point on the page, "the one that overlays exactly where Mount Arthest lies on the map, lit up! After which, the entire ley line stretching back to the centre of the sigil illuminated."

"Okay," Thia conceded, "that lends greater credit to this theory of yours—but it still not much to go on."

"There are eleven points on this shape that converge upon a central one, just as there are eleven stones in both the Northern and Arthest circle that converge upon a central altar," Sol rationalised. "It would make sense if the circles themselves were arranged throughout Cambria in a similar manner. The henges could be set out across the continent in a vast formation that in itself channels and focusses magic."

"Then what lies in the centre of all of these circles?" Thia asked.

"Another henge?" Rhys supposed, as images of a half-remembered dream flickered through his mind. "Perhaps larger than the others—the epicentre of all the energy focussed together by the other eleven!"

"But this is all just conjecture, right?" Alkis asked as he and Cade followed what the other three were debating.

"Well, yes," Sol confessed. "We are just speculating."

"It could be easy enough to test," proposed Rhys. "All we would have to do is travel to one of these points on the map and see if we discover another circle."

"But you yourself admitted that the sigil you copied may be inaccurate," Sol reminded him. "Each point marked on the map could be off by hundreds of miles."

"True," Rhys conceded. "But I do not think that should stop us from trying to find one of these circles. The hag at the Arthest circle was using the henge to amplify her rituals. The blood magic she performed within that stone circle allowed her to enthral an entire pack of adlet. For Indus to have performed a blood magic ritual with the power we all witnessed in Llanmyd... perhaps he too utilised a stone circle!"

Silence descended amongst them as they came to the revelation Rhys and Sol had both already made, but until now kept to themselves. The henges could be the missing piece of the puzzle. Suddenly it became clearer as to how Indus might have accomplished such a powerful feat as conjuring the Grey.

"It does seem likely," Thia agreed. "I can think of no other way he could have performed such a powerful ritual."

"Then you think he knows of these circles?" Sol asked.

"Why wouldn't he?" Rhys replied. "He has been a mage of the Circle for over two decades. He has travelled the length and breadth of Cambria. In all his time journeying across the continent, surely it's not unreasonable to suggest he could have discovered one, or perhaps even several of these henges."

"True enough," Sol acknowledged.

"Besides," continued Rhys, "I reckon there is a good chance Arlas may well have known about them. The smith in Wythe knew Arlas. Do you not think it peculiar that the Order's Archon supposedly frequented a village that seemed otherwise insignificant?"

"He was travelling there for the henge,"

affirmed Sol.

"Exactly. And if Indus knows of a circle that lies at the heart of the others—the focal point for all the other henges across Cambria, then we can be sure he'll put it to use!"

"It's practically a weapon!" exclaimed Sol. "If it exists…"

"Then we can't let it fall into Indus's hands!" concluded Rhys.

"Rhys is right," Thia declared. "It is important we investigate whether this theory is valid, regardless of how likely or unlikely it seems!"

"Then what?" Sol asked. "We simply head to one of the locations on the map and see if we stumble upon a stone circle?"

"Yes," Rhys nodded. "But let's not head to just any—we make for the heart of it all: the epicentre!"

"And where is that, exactly?" questioned Alkis, craning his head to peer at the roughly sketched map on the table.

"If I've plotted it correctly, it should lie somewhere in the Cor valley, south of the Virminter Range—Cambria's heart!"

Sol nodded. "When do we leave?"

"Today," Rhys replied. "Ready your packs and we will speak with Lord Brandis."

They went about gathering up their possessions as they began to pack their bags, when a knock came at the door to the chamber.

"It is probably the servants," Alkis remarked as he approached the door to open it.

"Maybe with breakfast," added Cade wishfully.

Alkis pulled open the door, expecting to see a servant, yet to his surprise and everyone else's, Earl Brandis himself stood outside the chamber.

"I trust you are all well rested?" he beamed.

"Err… exceptionally, My Lord" Alkis stuttered, issuing a low bow and stepping aside to grant the earl entry.

"Excellent," he smiled, striding into the lounge, glancing around at the others as they bowed politely at his arrival. "It would seem as if you already have plans for departure. No delay, I see!" he chuckled.

"We have discovered something," Rhys explained. "A lead that requires our investigation. It may prove paramount in our fight against Indus."

"Good, good," he mused, sinking into one of the upholstered chairs and reclining. "I trust you will need supplies?"

"Well," Rhys began, such a thought having not crossed his mind, "if His Lordship is offering…" Rhys smirked, "who are we to refuse?"

"I will see to it that you are supplied with any provisions you need for your journey through the wilderness at this time of year."

"Thank you, My Lord," Sol said graciously.

"There is *further* aid I can offer you,"

Brandis added.

"Oh?" Sol questioned.

Lord Brandis remained silent, staring expectantly towards the open door to the chamber. Loitering just outside the doorway was Guardsman Nathaniel Rossiter, quietly listening to the conversation within.

"Come in Nathaniel," Brandis greeted him, before looking back to the others with a somewhat wry smile.

"You mean to say that *Guardsman Rossiter* is the additional aid you offer?" Rhys surmised, after a moment of silence.

"Yes," the earl replied, stroking his bearded chin bemusedly.

"Lord Brandis," Rhys began, "we appreciate the offer greatly, but it is not necessary—"

"Actually, Sir," Nathaniel spoke up, "I myself requested leave to accompany you—Lord Brandis merely granted my request. I was given no orders to go with you; this is something I have chosen... that is, if you'll have me? Your quest seems like a noble cause, and I figure you'll need all the help you can get. Please... feel no obligation to take me with you—but should you desire it, my shield is yours!"

Rhys nodded, somewhat taken back. "It would seem we've garnered quite a following," Rhys grinned at Sol. "Very well Nathaniel Rossiter. Should you be mad enough, you are welcome to join our company!"

THIRTY-TWO

Orange radiance flickered across the snow as a fire crackled and popped in the centre of the party's camp. The warmth of the flames emanated outwards, battling the frigid chill of the winter night as Rhys and his companions huddled closer, seeking refuge from the biting winds. Overhead, the sky glittered in full glory, millions of stars piercing through the blackness. All was still and calm, and the world seemed somewhat at peace with itself.

Thia sat before Rhys, her fair skin and golden hair glowing in the firelight. Once more, she demonstrated the spell for the mage, spiralling her wand gently until its tip illuminated. Suddenly, an orb of faint light burst outwards, swelling rapidly from the wand in a silent shockwave, that in the blink of an eye, expanded beyond the limits of the camp and faded into the darkness of the night. The world fell instantly mute. The fire flickered inaudibly. The whistling gales fell silent. Rhys felt his lips move as he tried to speak, but no sound issued from his mouth. He strained his chest, his throat burning, as he attempted to scream at the top of his lungs, yet still not so much as a distant murmur reached his ears. The only sound that managed to penetrate the supernatural deafness was the muffled throb of Rhys's heart inside his chest.

Thia directed a wry smile towards the mage, and with a flick of the wand, she dispelled the invocation. The dissonance of the surrounding world came rushing back in crescendo; what seconds earlier had been a tranquil night now seemed to thunder like a deafening cacophony. The fire roared, the wind howled, and distant owls shrieked. As Rhys shook his head in disorientation, the wool of his clothes rustled loudly, and the snow beneath him crunched and groaned under his subtly shifting weight. Within moments, his senses seemed to recalibrate, his ears no longer overcompensating, the volume of Rhys's surroundings diminishing back to a state of calm.

Thia carefully handed the wand back to Rhys, meeting his fingers for a brief moment in the exchange.

"Alright," Rhys uttered, readying for another attempt, "I've got it this time!"

"No, you don't," Sol goaded from beside the fire, stirring the pot of stew hung over the flames. "That's an advanced spell she is teaching you; I'd be surprised if you could manage it by the week's end, even if you practised every night!"

"I don't know," Rhys countered. "I've got a big incentive for mastering this spell in particular, Sol."

"Oh? And what is that?"

"If I can cast it, I won't have to put up with your snoring anymore!" Rhys chided.

"I don't snore!" Sol rebuked, glancing at the others for affirmation.

As if comedically rehearsed beforehand, everyone suddenly avoided Sol's eye contact, averting their gaze with barely contained grins.

"Do I?" he asked now in uncertainty.

"Not *all* the time," Alkis offered sympathetically.

"Yeah," agreed Cade. "Once in a blue moon you quieten down enough for the rest of us to get some sleep."

Rhys chuckled softly to himself as the others continued to amiably lambast Sol, turning his attention back to Thia's tuition and the incantation at hand.

"Clear your mind," the witch encouraged him softly. "You aren't trying to supress or drown out the sounds surrounding you. Imagine silence as a noise in and of itself. It is both equal and opposite to the reverberations of the world around.

"Visualise sound flowing through the air like ripples meeting across the surface of a pond. Each wave is in part both a crest and a furrow.

Where two crests meet across the surface, the wave is amplified, the ripple rising to a height of the two combined. Such is the same for two overlapping furrows. But where the crest of one wave meets the furrow of another, the pond's surface appears still. To produce silence, the resonance of your spell must act in exact opposition to the vibrations of the world around you."

Rhys nodded, attempting to visualise the analogy. "That makes sense," he remarked, having never previously thought to imagine sound in such a way. Clearing his mind, he closed his eyes and listened intently to the world around him. Wood popped and snapped in the whoosh of flames, the voices of Alkis and Sol chirping and rumbling in gentle conversation, whilst the mellow whistle of the nightly breeze flowed coolly passed his ears.

When Rhys opened his eyes, he smiled. The tip of his wand glimmered with subtle energy, a quivering bubble of magic faltering in the air as it attempted to inflate. Refocussing his thoughts, Rhys doubled down on his concentration, willing the orb of silence to grow. In a moment of lucidity, his mindscape fell still and quiet; the sphere of energy expanding from the wand rapidly swelled outwards, engulfing Rhys and the camp surrounding him in a muted serenity. The perfect silence Thia had been able to summon had escaped the mage, the fire still fizzling faintly in stifled resonance, Sol and Alkis's conversation reduced to a barely audible and utterly unintelligible hubbub, but despite the absence of absolute quietude, Rhys had succeeded far beyond his own expectations.

Thia issued a silent smile of appraisal as Rhys proudly gazed around in wonder, before, after a few short moments, his concentration wavered, and the encompassing sphere of calm collapsed inwards, ending the spell.

"Huh!" Sol remarked in surprise, peering Rhys's way with a look of admiration. "I stand corrected. Not bad, Rhys."

"Not bad at all," praised Thia.

"What can I say? I have an excellent teacher," he smiled at Thia, "…and an unrivalled aptitude for magic!" he added, raising his eyebrows smugly.

"All right," Sol sighed stirring the pot once again, "don't ruin the moment!"

"So, can anyone learn to wield magic?" Nathaniel asked after a time.

"To an extent, yes," Sol replied. "But most would struggle to grasp even the basics. Some, as Rhys rather boastfully pointed out, have a far greater aptitude for magic than others. If most strove to learn the arcane arts, they would likely toil for years and years to master even the simplest spells. To a select few, such as Thia, magic comes naturally."

"Okay," Nathaniel nodded, "I think I am beginning to understand."

"If you think you understand magic, you don't understand magic," Thia mused aloud.

"What does that even mean exactly?" Nathaniel asked with a puzzled look.

"It's something my mother use to say," the witch explained. "Upon first inspection, magic may seem to follow a set of rules—yet the more you learn of it, the more it seems to break those very same rules."

"You seem to understand it pretty well though!"

"And yet, I know full well that I have only the faintest level of comprehension. I know a wide array of the spells and enchantments commonly practised by the occult, but quiz me on the innate abilities of Magi, the primordial magic of the Carparthian tribes, or the ancient esoteric powers of the elves... and well, in those schools of the arcane, I am just as oblivious as you are, Nathaniel"

"Oh," the guardsman puzzled with a look of consternation.

"Never mind the laws of magic," Sol jibed, nudging Nathaniel with his elbow as he seasoned the stew bubbling in the cast iron pot. "You are supposed to be learning the esoteric nature of cooking! I hope you are paying attention."

"After that meal you served the other night, I have to agree with Sol!" Rhys chuckled. "You have a better grasp of magic than cooking!"

"It wasn't that bad," the guardsman crossed his arms.

"It was," Cade retorted. "How do you even burn a stew?"

"With great skill," Rhys returned. "Or lack thereof!"

The company continued to chat and joke light-heartedly throughout the remainder of the evening, supping bowlfuls of Sol's steaming stew, before turning in for the night under canvas in the tents Earl Brandis had gifted to them. They arose at first light, breaking their fast with the reheated leftovers from the night before, before dismantling camp and setting out further westward.

For nigh on a month, they had journeyed through the wilderness of Gwent, eventually passing beyond the realm's borders into the rough countryside of southern Westverness. The jagged peaks of the Virminter Mountains persistently jutted across the southern horizon like endless rows of teeth in an immense stone jaw, forming an impassable wall that stretched from the heart of the continent, all the way to the eastern coastline. Thus, their journey to Cor Valley took route skirting the Virminter foothills, following the range further and further inland towards the heart of Cambria, until finally, the chain meandered southward, culminating at the tripoint of Gwent, Westverness, and the Capital Realm, where the expansive ridge finally dwindled away into rolling hills. Only once they had circumnavigated the extensive mountain chain would they be able to head east into the Cor Valley.

For the larger portion of their journey, they followed the Pilgrim's Highway, a vast open road that crossed Cambria east to west, linking the capitals of Ultair and Orthios. Even in the depths of winter, the wide bridleway was well trafficked, the company regularly passing caravans and carts as traders transported goods back and forth between the realms. Wayfarers likewise frequented the path, setting out or returning from Orthios on pilgrimages to the array of temples and shrines the city was famous for.

Rhys and the others greeted most of whom they passed with friendly words, occasionally stopping to barter with traders for food and supplies. Each night they made camp a short distance from the road, foraging what they could, living off the land to the best of their abilities to stretch out the provisions they carried with them. Cade more often than not supplied the evening's meal; at dusk, the archer would lay in wait, arrow nocked on his bowstring, often for hours at a time, surveying the warrens and roosts around the fringes of their camp. With godly patience, the hunter watched, waiting for his chance, ready to impale any rabbit that dared rear its head from a burrow, or skewer clean out of the air any wood pigeon that took to the wind.

February drew steadily to a close. The snows thawed and the first hints of spring whispered across the land. Finally veering away from the Pilgrim's Highway, they ventured south, leaving the main road to pursue the dogleg of the Virminter Range, towards Cor Valley, nestled against the southern faces of the ridge. Eventually, on a murky day in early March, the tail end of the vast chain sank into the foothills, allowing them to double back eastward; after a month and a half on the road they had finally made it south of the Virminter Range.

"There it is," Rhys declared days later, folding away a map of the area Brandis had gifted him. "Cor Valley!"

Before them stretched an immense lowland basin, cradled by the southern faces of the western Virminter rim. The vale descended from the slopes ahead, sweeping downwards into dense ancient woodland that carpeted nearly the entire floor of Cor Valley.

"It is still a day's travel to the forest border from here," Sol announced.

"My best guess is that the henge lies somewhere within the forest," supposed Rhys. The mage glanced back over his shoulder to the sun sinking into the western horizon. "If we set camp here, we should be able to reach Heartwood Forest by nightfall tomorrow."

Pitching their tents for the night, they set off early again the following day, descending into Cor Valley as gloom swelled overhead. By midmorning, a persistent drizzle had sunk down from the summits above. The party continued their descent towards the forest border below, and come noon, the slopes of the vale eased down to the floor of the basin, bringing them to within a mile of the woodland ahead.

Finally stepping between the trees, Rhys immediately sensed the age of the woodland. The ancient sentinels stood massive and gnarled, the forest floor a twisting tangle of knotted mossy roots.

The bare canopies of oaks, chestnuts, and elms interwove overhead, their kinked limbs matted with liken and entwined with ivy. Traversing across the uneven ground proved just short of treacherous, each step thwarted by slick moss and upturned roots that forever threatened to trip or slip Rhys and the others up. By dusk, they'd barely made it more than a few miles into the dense forest, and in the waning twilight, the party struggled to find even the smallest patch of ground flat enough to make camp upon. Through providence, they came eventually to a small glade nestled in a hollow, that granted just enough space for them to erect their tents and light a modest campfire.

"Any plan as to how we might scour these woodlands for the henge?" Sol asked as he put a pot of water on to boil.

"If need be, we can divide into groups in the hope of covering more ground," he explained. "But I had hoped we might be led to the circle by its aura."

"Aura?" Sol questioned. "What do you mean?"

"The aura..." Rhys repeated, confused by Sol's own perplexity. "The field of magic given off by the henge—like that of the Arthest Circle."

"I sensed no aura at Arthest," Sol replied. "The stones were hidden to me until you came upon them. I couldn't detect any magical field being given off."

"But..." Rhys stuttered, baffled by what Sol was claiming. "...I could feel it." Rhys assured. "It called to me. That is what led me up there! I assumed you had felt the same as me!"

"No," Sol returned. "I was just following you! I thought you were investigating where the hag had come from!"

Rhys shook his head.

"You could sense the henge?" Sol asked again in disbelief. "Are you certain?"

"Unmistakably so. The whisperings of the stones' magic are what drew me up the mountainside."

"But..." Sol rubbed his brow. "*I* certainly felt no presence. I thought we'd just happened upon the circle!"

"That makes no sense..." Rhys uttered as now he doubted the accuracy of his memory. "Could there be a reason as to why I would sense an aura whilst you did not?"

Sol shook his head. "None that I would

know of."

"I suppose it is possible that I was mistaken," Rhys sighed.

"Perhaps—we shall find out soon enough," returned Sol.

THIRTY-THREE

"How long do we intend to continue this search?" Nathaniel pressed, peering around the gloomy forest.

"He has a point, Rhys," Sol issued defeatedly. "We've spent days endlessly trapsing back and forth without so much as a hint as to this henge's existence!"

"The woodland spans for hundreds of square miles; surely we cannot comb it in its entirety?" the Ultair guardsman posited.

Rhys issued a long and weary sigh. "You're right. I was sure we'd have discovered something by now—but this entire forest... it's untouched by man, lost to time. It's as if we're the first people to set foot here in years!"

"We might just be," Sol returned. "We're in the northern reaches of Mediussex—the region is fairly sparsely inhabited. Most of the realm's settlements are on the east coast and along the shores of the Halwyn."

"I'm not suggesting we abandon the search just yet," insisted Nathaniel. "But how much longer do you want to keep going if we still don't find anything?"

Rhys gazed around to see the others were all awaiting his response, everyone clearly plagued with the same doubts as the guardsman.

"Look, Rhys..." Sol spoke up. "It was a good theory—I was sold on it too. But maybe that's all it was. Maybe there is no henge here in Cor Valley—no central focal point of the ley lines of Cambria."

"Maybe," Rhys conceded, his own doubts creeping around the fringes of his mind. "Alright," the mage agreed, feeling as if he was admitting defeat. "For the time being, we continue as we have. But if by the week's end we've still not found anything, we'll abandon the search."

A series of nods confirmed they were all in agreement, though Rhys was still reluctant to give in. Regardless of the other's doubts, he was convinced there was a henge awaiting them out there, concealed somewhere within the depths of Heartwood, just beyond the limits of his perception, awaiting discovery.

With the tension among the group now eased, Rhys rose to his feet and pressed on, the others following his lead as they delved deeper still into the ever-thickening woodland. The ancient trees continued to push closer together, and after a time, several trunks and low hanging boughs developed a thin coat of what at first appeared to be a white lichen. As they pressed on, the milky gossamer thickened, matting up into the canopies in dense weaves that enveloped the treetops overhead. Sometime later, vaulting over a fallen trunk, Rhys steadied himself against an adjacent tree, only to find that, as he drew his palm away, claggy strands of a translucent substance had stuck to his skin, stretching in long gooey fibres between the tree bark and his hand.

"What is this?" Rhys pondered aloud as he examined the elastic fibres matted between his fingers.

"I don't know," Sol mused as he inspected the gunk closely. The mage pinched gently at the glutinous mesh coating the tree. The threads clung to his fingertips, recoiling back as he tore away. "I have not encountered anything like this before."

"It's spread to every tree," observed Thia.

"Let's hope is not poisonous," Rhys remarked, wiping his hand clean on his cloak.

They pressed forth, but the further they continued, the thicker and more tangled the sticky gossamer seemed to grow. Dew beaded in glinting droplets across strands of the web as the temperature dropped, and after a time, the gossamer became woven into sheets of netting stretched between the tree trunks. The walls of diaphanous gauze swiftly formed cocooning tunnels, transforming the dense woodland into an ominous labyrinth of webbed corridors. Overhead, the gossamer warren was domed in spiralled funnels of the same glutinous material, the webbed ceiling blocking the faint sunlight, eerily dimming the forest floor. Against their better judgement, they continued deeper into the woods.

"This is not right!" Rhys breathed, finally refusing to lead on any further.

"No," Alkis agreed uneasily, "It isn't!"

"I think we should head back," Cade proposed. "This place feels wrong!"

"I disagree," argued Sol as he inspected the webbing once more. "Whatever this is, it warrants further investigation."

"Sol is right," Rhys granted reluctantly. "I'll be the first to admit that this stuff unsettles me—but after nearly a whole week scouring Heartwood, this is the first sign of anything unusual that we have come across! Chances are, it has no connexion to the henge we're looking for, but I reckon we would be remiss if we didn't at the very least investigate further!"

"Very well," Cade agreed, shuddering as he did so.

"Everyone be on your guard," Sol warned. "We do not know what lurks in this place."

Together, they tentatively ventured deeper into the alien environment, creeping along the webbed passages as they continued to delve further. A short time later, the gossamer spread to the forest floor. Glutinous strands clung to the soles of their boots, steadily tangling up their legs as they pushed forwards. Soon, each step they took became a battle in and of itself, the thick webbing sticking their feet to the floor and clumping together in elastic strands as it began to ensnare them.

"If this gets any worse, we are going to get ourselves stuck!" Thia cautioned as she strained to free a foot glued to the ground.

Realising the witch was right, the party momentarily halted their advance. An uneasy discord of mutterings erupted throughout the group as they tried to decide what to do next. Resigning from the discussion, Rhys gazed about, studying their surroundings. Dozens of long translucent threads were strung across the cocooning passage, extending between the walls of webbing. Stretched across the tunnel like lyre strings, the nearest chord was drawn taught, anchored to a thick root at ground level, slanting up into the branches above them. Stepping tentatively closer, Rhys curiously plucked it gently, watching as it silently quivered. Raising his gaze, the mage watched in wonder as the vibrations seemed to carry across a vast network of cords, transmitting the tremor swiftly down the webbed passage into the shadows ahead. Cocking his head in bemusement, Rhys felt the steady chill of harrowing realisation dawn, but the dreaded revelation had come all too late.

A drop of cold fluid splattered across the back of Rhys's neck, scalding his skin. Wincing, the mage quickly wiped away the stinging fluid, frenetically swivelling his gaze about as he searched for the venom's origin, but before he had time to crane back his head, a writhing mass of armoured legs and spindly hair dropped from above, pinning him to the ground.

"Rhys!" Sol cried out in horror, the rest of the party likewise emitting a chorus of terrified screams.

Gnashing fangs bore down on the mage as Rhys struggled against the hulking creature on top of him. Rolling supine beneath the thrashing monstrosity, he drove upwards with the shaft of his staff, hooking his weapon beneath the curved venomous fangs stabbing down at him. Eight black orbicular eyes locked with his own, whilst an equal number of clawed legs twitched from an enormous, armoured abdomen. The colossal arachnid hissed and wined as it fought against Rhys's might, venom dripping from its glistening teeth as it continued to thrust towards the mage beneath it.

Feeling his strength begin to fail him, Rhys grimaced as the two enormous, dripping fangs inched closer to his neck. A blast of silver energy exploded from the tip of the mage's stave, but with Rhys pinned beneath the spider's hulking mass, the bolt shot clear, thumping uselessly into a nearby tree trunk. His arms burned as the giant cob bore down on him. His heart pounded. His breathing quickened. He gritted his teeth. An agonized scream grated through his throat. Tingling energy began to fizzle across Rhys's chest, building as it conducted through his searing shoulders, channelling down his nerves as electricity that surged through his arms. The emerald veins inside his stave flashed cyan and the air surrounding the weapon sparked with conductive charge. The power building within the staff suddenly surged, and from out of Rhys's weapon, forks of lightning zapped in snaking bolts through the spider's monstrous form.

The stench of charred hair and chitin filled Rhys's nostrils as the demonic arachnid atop the mage convulsed and shrieked in its death throes. Its eight-legged body reared back, unpinning Rhys from beneath it, before toppling supine, its armoured legs curling tightly into its underside.

No longer pinned down, Rhys swivelled his head left and right as the sound of fighting resonated throughout the nest. A blur of spindly legs scuttled through the shadows. Steel whirred in the air. Lightning flashed and thunder peeled. A bowstring twanged. Screams and grunts sounded all around. From the ground, Rhys caught glimpse of Thia sheltering behind Nathaniel as the guardsman wrestled against a second monstrous cob battering his heater shield with its forelimbs. Alkis was backpedalling, sweeping his bastards sword in defensive arcs, the blade severing chitinous legs as arachnids harried him on all sides. Sol stood back-to-back with Cade, the hunter loosing arrows from a rapidly emptying quiver, whilst the mage conjured another thunderbolt to vanquish a spider in a cloud of sparks.

Rhys's neck snapped front and centre, as another arachnid abseiled down from the ceiling in front of him, its beady eyes locking on to the grounded mage. He attempted to scramble back on hands and knees, but to his horror, Rhys quickly discovered he was ensnared by the webbing matted across the floor. The gossamer stretched and congealed around his hands and legs as he strove to fight free, but the more he struggled, the more tangled he became.

Rhys watched the wolfish arachnoid prowl closer. Its hulking exoskeleton twitched left and right as its dark beady eyes locked with his. It rocked back on its haunches, and suddenly pounced, taking flight in the blink of an eye as it sprung towards Rhys. The mage threw his head back, swinging his staff in desperate defence. The air rent with an emerald glare and a howl of energy whirled outwards. Rhys's ethereal blade carved through chitin as the spider bore down on him, lopping through legs and carving deep into the beast's thorax. The injured arachnid sprawled over Rhys, rolling off the mage in a crippled mass as stinking ichor sprayed everywhere. The cob flailed and twitched as it attempted to heave its broken body back upright.

Rhys's emerald weapon slashed through his web fetters, freeing him from the coagulated gossamer that had glued him to the ground.

Hoisting himself back to his feet, he turned the butt of his stave towards the maimed spider thrashing towards him and fired a bolt of force. The kinetic missile crunched clean through the fiend's exoskeleton and its squirming legs curled taught.

A hiss sounded to the mage's rear, and as Rhys twirled on the spot, he clocked a third arachnid preparing to leap at him. A silver fist of impetus collided with the spider mid-flight, punching the arachnoid out of the air, crushing the monstrosity as it was driven into the bough of a nearby tree.

With that, the tumult of battle fell quiet. Rhys panted, wiping away the black gore splattered across his face, and took stock of his surroundings. Several dead spiders scattered the vicinity, the remainder of the cobs having retreated back into the shadows. Rhys's companions all appeared shaken, but they had escaped the fray with their lives.

"In hindsight," Rhys breathed heavily, "maybe turning back wouldn't have been such a bad idea!" The mage continued to gawk at the slain monstrosities littering the ground. "Is everyone all right?"

"Define: all right!" Thia shivered as the legs of the closest spider to her continued to twitch.

"Alive. Uninjured," Rhys clarified. "No one been cocooned up and carried away to feed their spider queen?"

They all in turn morbidly shook their heads.

"Are *you* alright?" Sol asked him.

"Surprisingly yes," Rhys said, patting himself down, "though it was a bit touch-and-go for a few moments there."

"That's one way of putting it," Thia scoffed, denoting the inflammation across Rhys's neck caused by the venom that had dripped down on him. "I should take a look at that."

"I still have all my limbs," Rhys smiled, looking at the three-legged spider carcass beside him. "I consider that a victory!"

"Hold still," she scolded, examining the irritation. Drawing Rhys's wand, she pressed its tip against the raw skin.

Rhys winced as the flesh began to rapidly heal. "I'm sorry," he declared to the group. "I shouldn't have led us so carelessly into here."

"No," Sol refused. "We all should have been warier!"

"Do you think that is the last of them?" Cade asked, his head pivoting anxiously as he remained on guard.

"I should hope so!" Alkis prayed.

"Wishful thinking," Sol returned pessimistically.

Rhys nodded in agreement. "We can't take any chances. Everyone, remain vigilant until we are out of this lair!"

"Does anyone remember which way we

came from?" Alkis dismayed, looking at the array of bifurcating tunnels webbed between the surrounding trees.

"No," Sol sighed in frustration.

The group quickly began to debate which silken tunnel whence they had emerged from. Rhys gazed silently around, his own sense of direction likewise failing him. The noise of the others drifted away until their chatter became faint and distant. Closing his eyes, Rhys made out a muffled whispering. Voices inside his head beckoned him closer. Opening his eyes, he turned to face the direction from which he was being called: a narrow passage in the mesh of webbing woven between two matted oaks that stood shoulder to shoulder.

"Rhys!?" Sol spoke out to him.

"Yes?" the mage replied, realising that Sol had already called his name several times. The others were all looking to him, awaiting his response to a question he'd missed.

"What is your vote?" Sol pressed.

"Vote?"

"Which tunnel should we take?" the mage reiterated.

"That one!" Rhys answered, pointing to the narrow passage before him.

"We definitely didn't come from there!" Nathaniel dismissed.

"We are voting between these three," Sol explained, pointing towards a set of passages on the opposite side of the clearing.

"Trust me!" Rhys insisted. "This is the way!"

"Rhys, you are disorientated; we came from one of the passages on this side of the clearing— definitely not that one! We have to go this way if we want to go back."

"I know," returned Rhys. "I don't want to go back. I want to go to the henge. And that is this way!"

"Are you sure?" Sol asked, narrowing his eyes dubiously.

"No," Rhys confessed, "I'm not sure. But even still—will you come with me?"

The others stared silently back at him for a long while, contemplating his request.

"Okay. I will," Alkis agreed after a time. "Let's go," he added, striding across the gossamer glade to stand beside Rhys, turning back to await the others' decision.

"As will I," answered Cade, joining Rhys and Alkis.

Thia nodded. "If you believe the henge is that way, then that's where I'm headed."

"Well," Nathaniel sighed, "I insisted on joining you on your quest. I can hardly go back on my decision now!"

"Very well," Sol agreed lastly. "Further into the spiders' den we go."

"Thank you," Rhys smiled at each of them.

"Let's just take things slow," insisted Sol. "Keep your eyes peeled for any more of these things," he added, nudging the nearest arachnid carcass with the toe of his boot.

They continued their advance, delving deeper into the nest as the flanking walls of silk pressed closer together. After a time, the gossamer passages grew so tight that the company were forced to shimmy sideways through several chokepoints to avoid becoming ensnared. Arriving at a succession of forks in the path, Rhys led on, instinctively knowing the way, following the call of the henge ahead.

"Rhys!" Sol emitted in a low whisper, signalling the group to halt. The mage pointed ahead to a set of glinting eyes tucked deep in a funnelled recess in the branches above. Perfectly still, the spider continued to hide, laying in wait, ready to launch its ambush the moment that Rhys and the others drew closer.

"I hate these things," Cade uttered disdainfully.

"Me too," Rhys agreed, slowly raising his staff as he took aim for the arachnid. A blazing jet of flame licked out of the mages stave, the cone of heat swallowing the creature in a ray of ash and fire. The spider screeched, backing further into its hide as the webbing surrounding it smoked and withered away around it. The arachnids armour charred and shrivelled, its smouldering husk dropping to the floor of the tunnel moments later.

"I see they don't like fire!" Sol quipped as he caught whiff of the nauseating stench of burnt chitin.

"Do you know any creatures that do?" Rhys returned wryly, covering his nose with his cloak.

"I know a few," Sol replied seriously.

They stepped carefully around the blackened carcass and continued on. Eventually, the walls of webbing began to subside, and soon, the canopies reopened above to reveal the first gleams of moonlight. After a time, the gossamer had thinned to little more than a scattering of fraying fibres hovering in the wind.

"An expansive nest," Sol remarked, gazing back into the den of webbing.

"When we head back, we are taking a different route—one that avoids the nest all together," Thia insisted.

"It wasn't *that* bad," Rhys smiled. "I've always heard that spiders are more afraid of you than you are of them!" he chuckled.

"Somehow, I do not think that can be said for the giant variety," Cade shuddered.

"This way," Rhys urged, leading them on through the reassuringly cobweb-free woods ahead, the calls of the circle growing stronger with every step.

THIRTY-FOUR

Sleet descended through the misty air as darkness drew over Heartwood. Drawing his hood down further over his brow, Rhys listened to the pattering of rain and snow against wool, focussing his mind, concentrating on the beckoning call of the mystic stones ahead. Together, they trudged deeper into the darkling forest, until suddenly, the haze and trees yielded, giving way to a moonlit glade.

"This is it," Rhys declared under his breath.

Centred in the clearing stood a circular sarsen altar, its damp surface gleaming beneath moonbeams streaking out of the gloomy heavens. The mage stepped closer, the spongy, mossy ground underfoot hardening to sculpted stone. Channels etched out of the rock carved inward towards the altar, the ley lines of Cambria represented by grooves converging at the centre of the disc. Wind swirled in currents about Rhys as he stepped across the threshold onto the stone, the very elements around him seemingly reacting to his presence, drawing him inward, the altar demanding he approach.

Moving up to the altar, Rhys peered down at its surface. There, engraved across the sarsen, was inscribed the same sigil he had seen on the slopes of Arthest, the same sigil that head led him to this very place. Unlike the symbol carved into the altar of the Arthest henge, the lines and halos of this emblem were dull and lifeless, no ambient magic illuminating the carving. Centred in the shape, the heart of the sigil sank into the stone, tunnelling down into the altar as a cylindrical recess. Pulling off his right glove, Rhys ran his fingertips across the altar top, half expecting the markings to activate on contact with his skin, but beneath his touch, there was no stirring of magic, and the etchings remained dark and lifeless.

"I don't understand," Sol puzzled as he gazed around in confusion. "Where are the standing stones?"

"I can't see any of the runes you described," Thia observed.

"This isn't right," Rhys mused to himself, gazing around at the missing features of the henge. The shrine was obviously connected to the other circles in some way, but what was abundantly clear, was that this was far from the great central henge Rhys had imagined would lie at the convergence of ley lines throughout Cambria. He was missing something, but what?

Turning his attention back to the altar, he gently ran his fingers around the recess in the stone. Realising that he had approached from the wrong direction, Rhys denoted a set of steps rising to the altar top on the far side. Suddenly, the mage was transported back to the moment of his binding, and the answer seemed now obvious. Making his way around to the far side of the altar, Rhys ascended the steps to the top, and drawing his staff, he slowly inserted it into the recess.

A deep rumble tremored below ground, followed swiftly by the sound of grinding stone. The altar quaked underfoot, and a chorus of alarm rang out across the party as the ground beneath them began to drop. Leaping to safety, they flung themselves off the stone disc, back onto the mossy floor of the encircling glade, as steadily, seams began to open between the ley line grooves, sections of the disc sinking away at differing speeds. Rhys clutched his staff for balance, the altar beneath him continuing to shudder, and watched as the ground surrounding him opened up.

After several moments, the rumbling ceased, the forest glade returning to serenity. Rhys craned his neck to peer downward from atop the altar, seeing now the full effect of the transmogrification of the stone disc. What mere moments before had been a flat plateau, was now reshaped into a descending spiral staircase, curving around a central pillar that culminated with the altar.

"What in the world…?" Sol breathed as he rose back to his feet to peer down into the dark depths of the stairwell.

"I wonder where it leads," mused Alkis.

"To the circle," Rhys asserted with confidence. Drawing his staff out of the recess, he hopped down from the altar, onto the uppermost segment of the disc that served as the first step of the staircase.

"This is… different," Sol remarked in perplexity.

"I'll have to agree with you there," conceded Rhys.

"You think the circle lies underground? In a crypt?"

"There is definitely something down there," Rhys assured, his arcane senses continuing to tingle. "As to what we're about to find… well, your guess is as good as mine!"

"And you can feel the presence of this place? You were led here by the stones?"

Rhys nodded.

"Intriguing," Sol replied, turning his attention back to the way down.

A long silence elapsed as the group pressed closer together, all peering into the shadows with anxious anticipation.

"I guess I'll go first then," Rhys offered, sensing the other's trepidation.

The mage felt a firm encouraging pat

on his back from Alkis, the usually doughty knight shying away, happy for Rhys to take point. Suppressing his own niggling doubts, Rhys readied himself, drawing his wand and handing it to Thia. The witch wordlessly conjured several glimmering orbs of light, the hovering arcane lanterns ghosting silently through the air, before directed by a flick of the wand, Thia sent them into the depths to illuminate the way ahead.

His staff still drawn, Rhys tentatively lowered himself onto the next step. Creeping downward, he began his descent, following the glow of the mystic lanterns, stair by stair, his free hand tracing across the curving wall of stone as he guardedly kept his weapon aimed into the darkness beyond. As he climbed further down, the orbs ahead proceeded his descend, their dim light casting long shadows through the helical stairwell, as steadily and surely, Rhys led the others into the depths of the world.

The stairwell continued to cascade ahead, sinking fathom after fathom, storey after storey, until soon Rhys and the others could no longer make any real estimate as to how far they'd descended. The minutes quickly stacked up until close to half an hour of tentative descent had gone by.

"How deep are we?" Sol wondered. "Sixty... eighty... a hundred fathoms?"

"How much further do you think this goes?" Cade whispered, the hunter clearly unnerved by the extent of their depth.

"How much further *can* it go?" ruminated Thia.

"I think I can see the bottom!" Rhys exclaimed as a final step drew within sight.

Sure enough, Thia's arcane lanterns pulled into view, the hovering lights having come to a rest at the base of the stairwell. Beyond, a stone archway opened to a chamber cast in a cold sapphire hue. Thia extinguished the orbs and slowly their eyes adjusted to the dim lighting.

Rhys advanced. Stepping slowly beneath the arch, he found himself enter an immense cavern hollowed from the rock, the far side stretching over a furlong ahead. Azure crystals glowed in seams that crisscrossed the walls and ceiling, whilst rows of knife-like stalactites hung sixty feet overhead. The sound of trickling water echoed and dripped unceasingly, a constant rain dribbling down from the hanging mineral formations toothing the roof above to puddle across the floor of the cavern. High-pitched chirps pierced the air as bats roosted in amongst the stalactites, a thousand beady eyes glinting in the reflected light of the glowing crystals. The air inside the cavern was cool and damp, but surprisingly fresh, stirred by a gentle flowing current that descended from above. Despite their depth underground, the cave system was clearly open to the world above by some form of natural tunnel or chimney, allowing the air below to be recycled, and granting the bats passage in and out of the crypt.

"Wow," Thia breathed as she emerged from the stairwell with the others.

Before them, the ground rose in a series of natural rocky steps, smoothed by the erosion of water, culminating in a plateau, out of which rose a hand-sculpted table carved from mineral flowstone that had grown out of the cavern floor. Climbing the rolling steps, Rhys approached the limestone bench to find it strewn with a litany of esoteric materials. Crystals and gems were heaped in silver bowls, whilst arranged across a raised shelf, jars and pots were brimming with various salts and dried herbs. Empty phials sat in racks, and aged scrolls were weighted open, the parchment bearing glyphs and markings too faded to read clearly. A pestle and mortar positioned in the centre of the countertop sat next to a corroded copper athame, surrounded by the molten stumps of burnt-out candles.

Above all, one item amongst the clutter in particular caught Rhys's eye: a wand of unblemished white wood, the grain too fine to be anything other than elder oak. Out of the butt end of the wand curved a serrated edge of polished obsidian, forming a bladed knuckle guard that drew to a point just past the wand's tip. Unlike any wand Rhys had previously laid eyes on, it was unclear if the implement was created for ceremonial ritual purposes or designed with battle in mind.

"That's unusual," Sol remarked, sighting it himself as he came to stand beside Rhys.

"Crafted with healing magic in mind, no doubt," Rhys quipped as he continued to examine the brutal design. The mage grasped the implement from the stone tabletop to find that the instant his fingers clasped it, the wand transmuted within his grip. The white grain of the elder oak rapidly clarified, taking on the same crystalline diaphanous appearance as Rhys's staff. Emerald veins pulsed deep within the wand, thrumming in rhythm with Rhys's heart whilst the serrated blade jutting from the implement had transformed from black obsidian to a verdant ethereal edge faintly shimmering in the dimness.

"Whoa," Rhys breathed.

"Whoa indeed," Sol nodded in wonder.

"Look familiar?"

"It's reacting to you—to your unique arcane signature."

"Here," Rhys offered the wand to Sol, curious to see what would happen.

The moment the wand exchanged hands its form metamorphosed once more, now taking on the appearance of a singular forged length of burnished copper.

"The oak is plastic," Sol remarked, continuing to study the unique implement, "it can freely change—remaining unbound to the hand that holds it!"

"So, we know what happens when it is in the hand of a mage," Rhys pondered. "What about if someone else, a non-mage, takes it?"

"Easy enough to find out," returned Sol as he beckoned Thia closer and passed it to the witch.

In Thia's hand, the wand immediately returned to its original form of elder oak and obsidian. "This feels strange," she uttered, turning it in her fingers as she inspected it. "Wands normally feel conductive—magical energy flows unimpeded through the wood. But with this…" she contemplated. Taking a firm grip of the implement, she aimed the wand for one of the candle stumps on the table. A look of fixation struck her face as she focussed on the wick, but to both her and the others' bewilderment, the candle refused to light. "Nothing," she declared defeatedly after a moment. "The resistance in the wood is too high—it feels insulated. I'd have better luck trying to cast spells with a wooden spoon!"

"Let me try," Rhys suggested, receiving the wand back from the witch, marvelling as it transmuted once again to crystal and malachite. Mimicking Thia, Rhys turned his attention to the nearest candle stump, but unlike the witch's attempt, with barely a thought, flame birthed out of nothing, flickering suddenly from the wick in a puff of light and heat.

"Interesting," Thia pondered.

"I am keeping this!" Rhys declared, tucking the bladed wand into a slot in his belt, smiling as, having left his grip, it transformed back to its innate oak and obsidian configuration.

"I'd be cautious with that," Thia warned. "It's unlike any arcane implement I have ever heard of—it might have strange, perhaps even dangerous properties.

"You think it could be cursed?" Rhys surmised.

"I wouldn't rule it out," the witch returned gravely.

"I'll be careful," Rhys insisted.

"What is the rest of all of this?" Nathaniel asked, gesturing to the array of materials scattering the bench.

"Mostly just ritual components and alchemical ingredients," Thia returned, running her hands over the stone. "What is more noteworthy is the altar itself!"

"Altar?" Cade questioned.

"Look," Thia gestured, sliding her finger down a groove carved in the rock. Clearing away some of the clutter, the witch revealed several more gullies crisscrossing the stone, the channels all flowing into a broader canal that cut around the altar's perimeter, feeding a series of drainage holes.

"Is this...?" Sol asked in disbelief.

"A blood altar," she nodded.

"A blood altar?" Rhys repeated.

"An altar specifically created for sacrificial blood magic," she explained. "The sacrifice is slaughtered upon the altar—its blood spills onto the stone, collecting in the channels," she traced her fingers down the grooves, "and feeds into these holes." Thia walked slowly around the altar to its far side, where a spout protruded out of the rock, overhanging a font carved out of the stone beneath it. "And the blood collects here," she finished.

"Animal sacrifices... right?" Nathaniel asked hesitantly.

"Somehow, I doubt it," Sol murmured looking down from the plateau.

Rhys traced the mage's eye-line, following Sol's gaze to see nearly a dozen human skeletons sprawled out at the base of the stone steps.

"What a grisly fate to meet!" Alkis sighed as the others grimaced.

The skeletons were clad in brigandine, the leather laminate rotten by damp, whilst sections of exposed plate beneath were thick with rust.

"If they were sacrificed, it was likely willingly," Thia asserted, denoting the swords still sheathed in scabbards on their belts. "They are not bound, and their weapons were not taken from them."

"Volunteers probably weren't that hard to come by," Rhys remarked sarcastically, "they must have been lining up!"

"How could anyone ever willingly be sacrificed?" Nathaniel dismayed.

"If it were a religious offering to appease

the gods, then being sacrificed may have been regarded as an honour," Thia explained.

"The gods do not demand sacrifice!" Cade refused.

"*Your* gods don't," Alkis replied. "But worshipers of the Titan Pantheon in Iarbhaile and the northwest still produce animal offerings on their religious holidays, and in earlier times they would provide human offerings to the gods!"

"Do you worship the Titan Pantheon?" Cade asked the knight.

"I once did," Alkis replied.

"And now?"

"The Titan Pantheon is the old religion of Iarbhaile," he explained. "Each year, the number of those who keep the old ways diminishes. More and more, myself being one, are converting to the religion of the south: the faith of the One Creator."

"Not the pagan gods?" Cade questioned.

"No," Alkis smiled. "Sorry to disappoint you."

"Those who worship the One Creator once offered sacrifices too," put in Sol.

"They did," Alkis confirmed. "But not since before the time of the third prophet Sal Benrah, nearly four centuries ago."

"Well," Cade sighed, "if Joshua taught me anything, it is that everyone is entitled to believe in whatever gods they wish."

"Even if it leads to this?" Rhys derided, kneeling beside one of the skeletons, peering into the empty sockets.

"Which gods do you believe in, Rhys?" Alkis asked.

"None," the mage replied, stoically keeping his gaze locked with the skull in front of him.

"None!?" Nathaniel repeated in shock.

"But then how do you explain how magic and everything else in this world came into existence?" Alkis questioned.

"I don't know," Rhys shrugged. "But just because I do not understand the process of how this world came into being, does not validate the belief that Cambria's existence should be attributed to some mystical divine creator!" he reasoned.

"But… how else *could* the world exist?" Cade argued.

"Who is to say that it hasn't always existed? Or that it wasn't formed and shaped by a magical process that isn't fully understood?"

"But that makes no sense, Rhys," Alkis replied.

"To you three perhaps," Rhys smiled. "To me, the idea that an omnipotent being created everything seems somewhat more of a stretch. Who then created him? I am happy to say that Cambria's existence is an unsolved mystery that deserves a greater effort to be answered than simply surmising that it was the will of a creator, or multiple gods!"

The three of them fell silent.

"Do you really not believe in any religion?" Sol pressed Rhys. "Even after everything you and I have seen and been through?"

"You yourself Sol, said that those who have a poor understanding of magic often revere it, believing it divine. Would that not make you and I gods?"

"Some would think so," Thia agreed.

"But we are not!" Rhys continued. "Attributing what we don't understand about this world to the work of gods is, in my mind, the same as when those who are uneducated in magic choose to revere it!"

"I just have trouble imagining anything else," Sol sighed in disagreement. "And you Thia?" Sol asked.

"I don't know what to believe," she replied. "I'm agnostic—open to religion, but not fully won over by either the pagan beliefs, the Titan Pantheon, nor the Faith of the One creator. I do think Rhys could be right too—perhaps there aren't any gods. There are too many unknowns— too many unanswered questions to be certain of anything."

A long period of silence fell throughout the echoing cavern. Rhys seated himself on the stone shelf against which the skeletons were leant, taking a moment to sip from his waterskin. His eyes wandered about the cavern, glancing over the stone cast in the gentle glow of glimmering crystal seams. He peered through the gloom, to the far end of the crypt, and sighted a natural arch set in the end wall, though it was too far away and the light too dim for him to discern it in any great detail.

Whilst he continued to gaze ahead, something closer at hand caught his attention; it was faint enough against the backdrop of darkness, that at first, Rhys figured it merely a trick of the eye; yet the longer he stared, the more certain he became that it was not an imagined illusion. A dim wisp of amber swayed and rippled above the floor nearly two hundred feet away. It possessed no particular form, yet it seemed to cast a faint shimmering light across the stone beneath it.

"What is that?" Rhys asked, rising to his feet.

"What?" several of the others asked in unison.

"That!" Rhys replied, pointing to the faint orange haze.

"I cannot see anything," dismissed Alkis.

"That amber wisp some way ahead," Rhys reiterated.

"I think I can see it," declared Sol squinting.

"Come here," Rhys beckoned, gesturing the others to follow, figuring they'd likewise be able to make it out at a closer distance.

"Wait!" Sol urged. "Let us be cautious. There could be any manner of dangers lurking down here."

"You are right," Rhys agreed smiling. "There

could be cave spiders!"

"I hope not!" Cade shuddered.

Carefully, they made their way across the cavern, creeping through the darkness towards the unfocused form. The closer they drew, the brighter the shape began to ripple, as if it were awakening to their presence. In turn, the others each sighted the amber wisp as it burned more and more intensely with each step they took towards it.

"I don't know," Sol whispered warily. "It almost looks like a will-o'-the-wisp. But down here... underground!?"

"What do you mean?" questioned Rhys.

"Will-o'-the-wisps—they're found in marshlands, *exclusively*." The mage drew his staff as if to emphasise his unrest. "Be on your guard," he warned.

The others followed suit, readying their weapons as they crept closer, through the shadows, towards the ghostly ember quivering in the dark. Falling into rank behind the two magi, the party continued their approach, until, as they drew to within a dozen yards, the amber wisp condensed into the silhouette of a fiery spectre. A dark skeleton of smoke and shadows solidified within the flaming apparition, its infernal gaze directed the company's way.

Rhys and Sol halted their advance, beholding the burning spectre as its wreathing flames flared ominously against the intensifying preternatural darkness swirling about it. A momentary standoff elapsed as the black skull studied them silently from afar, before finally, Rhys braved a step closer, shielding his eyes against the glare of the flames.

"Halt!" a booming voice drummed. "Turn back. Leave this place!" the shadow commanded, the air shuddering with sinister reverberations after each word the spectre bellowed.

Silence descended and the company halted, not daring to approach any closer as the blazing skeleton continued to glower menacingly their way with its hollow gaze.

"Why?" Rhys challenged the spirit after a moment of hesitation.

"Turn back!" it thundered again.

"What lies ahead?" Rhys pressed, daring now to take another step closer.

"Turn back!" the terrifying voice repeated.

Rhys advanced closer once more. "What lies ahead?" he demanded coldly, gritting his teeth, and tightening his fingers around his staff.

"Turn back! Leave this place!" the being issued again. Its imposing voice bellowed louder than ever, yet shedding a portion of the preternatural distortion, the vocalisations now sounded more human than before.

"No!" Rhys refused. "Not without answers!"

"There are no answers to be found in these ruins," the spirit returned in an eerily familiar tone. "Be gone now, or you shall meet your end!"

"That voice..." uttered Sol in disbelief.

"I won't be turned away," Rhys insisted determinedly. "I have to know! What lies ahead?"

"For you, only peril!" the voice of Indus returned.

"Rhys!" Sol cried in alarm.

"Stand aside!" Rhys warned, squaring off against the flaming effigy of his nemesis.

"Rhys, get away from that thing!" Sol urged. "That is an avatar of Indus—It will kill you!"

A line of energy suddenly streaked across the floor between Rhys and the others. The rush of light swept around the mage in a wide arc, carving across the stone with blinding speed, encircling both him and the avatar. As the arcane ring completed, the lines of a vast glyph shimmered to life underfoot. Quivering bulwarks of flame erupted on all sides, a cage of conflagration enclosing around Rhys, trapping him inside the burning ring of fire with Indus's avatar, his friends sealed off outside.

The avatar of Indus blazed vigorously, and Rhys watched as the smoky darkness enwrapping the spectre condensed, solidifying into a length of charred wood and red-hot steel, taking form out of the air to become a staff identical to Indus's.

"Rhys!" the muffled cry of Thia pierced through the arcane barrier that separated them.

Daring to avert his eyes from the menacing spectre arming itself before him, Rhys peered back over his shoulder. Beyond the flaming walls of his infernal prison, the mage glimpsed a horde of animated skeletons clad in brigandine advancing on the others. The dead had risen, serving now as guardians of the crypt. Swords drawn, the undead protectors marched on Rhys's allies, ready to slay the intruding party.

Out of time, forced to turn his attention back to the immediate threat before him, Rhys was no longer able to watch the events unfolding outside the flaming arena. With its staff now fully formed, the fiery spectre of Indus's avatar began to march menacingly towards him. The glowing steel blade of the spectre's staff carved over the stone floor, sparks fizzling up from the edge as it trailed along the ground.

A ghostly howl rent at the air, verdant light shining from the tip of Rhys's staff as an ethereal blade unfurled. A blur of glowing steel whirred out of the shadows as the avatar lunged toward him. Rhys charged to intercept. Emerald energy and crimson heat clashed as the two weapons collided in a shower of crackling sparks. Their weapons bound, edges slicing across one another, popping and fizzling with raining embers as Rhys and the avatar twisted and countered their connected staves, pivoting against each other's parries as both man and spirit sought to manipulate the other's weapon to their advantage. The exchange broke and the blades parted. The outpouring of sparks ceased as Rhys twirled away, narrowly avoiding a slashing counterattack from the avatar.

Rapidly raising his staff in defence, Rhys blocked a hewing blow, deflecting the cleave as he backstepped away. Another lunge drove at Rhys, pushing him further back until he could feel the surrounding wall of fire scorching his nape.

A flailing counter gave Rhys the inches of space he needed to change direction, his adversary persisting to push forwards, the mage continuing to retreat, skirting now around the fringes of the ring of fire. Lancing and slicing at Rhys with unrelenting ferocity, the avatar repeatedly drove him back, assailing the mage with a continuous flurry of direct attacks. Still on the backfoot, Rhys locked blades again with the spectre, winding the bound edges across one another as he thrust forwards into a riposte. His jab sliced clear, narrowly missing the flaming spirit as it jinked aside of the lunge. Throwing too much of his weight into the drive, Rhys stumbled forwards, twirling clumsily to parry a vicious counterattack. Turning the blow with the shaft of his staff, the mage was knocked backwards during the disengage. Rhys winced as burning steel streaked across his inner elbow, a rapid reprisal strike cutting through the mage's broken defences, the heated blade slicing through flesh and cauterising the wound in a single foul lunge.

Staggering away, Rhys retreated in a series of awkward bounds, distancing himself as best he could from the still advancing spectre. A quick glimpse down at his elbow revealed the wound to be mostly superficial, but the brief glance was all he was afforded, as an instant later, the avatar lunged again, stave fully extended. Parrying the blistering steel away, Rhys countered, driving the spectre backwards for the first time in the fight. A redoublement from Rhys allowed him another advance, the mage pressing forwards as he unleashed an aggressive flurry of his own, reversing the momentum of the duel. The bout ended abruptly as the spectre broke Rhys's rhythm with a brutal deflection, sending the mage reeling away from the exchange.

In seconds, the avatar was on him again, but striking the ground with the butt of his stave, Rhys unleashed a shockwave that ripped outwards, staggering the spectres advance, causing the fiery apparition to stumble. Skipping clear of a flailing blow, Rhys launched a fist of silver energy from his staff, the missile of kinetic force taking flight in a blur of speed. The projectile smashed powerfully into the avatar, stalling the phantom's forward march, but after little more than a momentary falter of flames, the spectre's conflagrated form blazed hot again and stormed once more Rhys's way.

Sparks fizzled in the blistering air as crimson and emerald blades clashed again and again in rapid bouts, spirit and mage driving forwards and retreating in a deathly dance around the perimeter of the fiery arena. A twirling dodge landed Rhys on his foe's exposed flank, and with a forward jab, Rhys sliced glancingly across the spectres shoulder. A sharp deflection knocked his staff away before Rhys could inflict a killing blow, but as the mage recoiled from a corkscrewing counter, he watched black smoke begin to issue from the wound he had dealt.

Their weapons bound again, Rhys pivoting the hook of his ethereal blade to ensnare the avatar's edge, but as the mage attempted to turn the spectre's blade outwards, the phantom grappled his forearm with one of its flaming talons. Rhys screamed, breaking the bind and stumbling back as the wool of his sleeve charred away and the skin beneath blistered. Grimacing in anguish, Rhys staggered in retreat, narrowly stepping beyond the reach of the avatars next slash.

A feeble one-handed parry bought Rhys a few more seconds as he cradled his scorched forearm in tight to his torso, hoping the searing agony would subside. Adrenaline surging through his veins dulled the pain, and gritting his teeth, Rhys returned both hands to his staff just in time to block another overhead cleft streaking down at him.

Driving upwards, his staff raised horizontally, Rhys caught the edge head on across the shaft of his weapon, and twisting his body in a jarring pivot, he snagged the avatar's blade with his ethereal hook, renting the glowing steel away, opening up his foe's defences. Pirouetting with maintained momentum, Rhys dropped to one knee, stooping beneath a flailing slice from the spectre, reversing his stave and launching a battering ram of arcane impetus from the butt of the weapon. The air thundered as the bulwark of force drove outwards, slamming into the phantom's flank, knocking it sideways.

The abyssal spectre rapidly recovered its footing, turning ominously to march back towards Rhys with its weapon raised. But ready for his foe's advance, Rhys took aim, the veins inside his stave arcing blue with electricity. The air sparked as a fork of lightning connected Rhys's staff instantly with the avatar. Its black skeleton flashed and fizzled as the white bolt of charge grounded through its spectral form. The avatar's unrelenting advance finally halted, its spiritual body momentarily stupefied by the surge of electricity conducted through it.

Rhys watched as the dazed spectre began to steadily reanimate, bony fingers twitching as it once again tightened its grip around the charred shaft of Indus's stave. Lifting a foot clumsily from the ground, it took a step toward Rhys, then another, resuming its menacing forward march. The air around Rhys began to chill, and suddenly, bitter winds swept up, whistling around the inside of the ring of fire in an icy vortex. The avatar broke into a charge, storming the final few yards towards Rhys as the mage raised his staff. The veins inside Rhys's weapon chilled white, and suddenly, from out the end of the staff spouted a plume of frozen mist. Fire and smoke vanished in a cloud of freezing fog, the avatar swallowed instantly in an outpouring of frigid vapour as a blizzard began to churn inside the flaming arena. The elemental clash raged, fire and ice battling one another for supremacy. Rhys roared, tightening his grip as ice continue to gush from his weapon, his last reserves of strength dwindling, as through the white mist, he spied the faint gleam of red steel slowly edging toward him.

Unable to maintain the torrent of ice and fog, Rhys gave out. A thick freezing murk hung in the air as Rhys gasped for breath. Clutching his stave tightly, he raised his ethereal blade in anticipation, waiting for the avatar's skeletal form to emerge from the frigid haze. Steadily, the fog thinned, and Rhys caught sight of a dark skull looming inside the murk. The mist parted, revealing the spectre hunched over before him, flames quenched, leaving an extinguished black skeleton bent double, barely able to support itself as it leant over on a staff of singed wood and cold steel.

The immolated skull slowly rose, two vacant sockets meeting Rhys's gaze in defeat. Without hesitation, Rhys lashed out, his ethereal blade rending vertebrae, decapitating the spectre with a single blow. Before the lopped skull even contacted the ground, the avatar disintegrated to ash, blowing away in the vestiges of Rhys's blizzard.

The glowing lines of the glyph faded, the surrounding ring of fire petering out in the dying winds. Beyond the limits of the dispelled arena, the animated corpses harrying Rhys's companions collapsed, their arcane puppet strings severed, the curse that raised them broken. As the final embers of Indus's spiritual guardian scattered, all fell still.

THIRTY-FIVE

Clasping Rhys's head between his hands, Sol pressed their brows together, before embracing his fellow mage powerfully. "Well done!" he beamed.

"Thanks," Rhys breathed, smiling through his exhaustion.

"Are you alright?" Sol asked, noticing the charred and blood-soaked sleeve of Rhys's left arm.

Rhys shrugged. "A bit worse for wear—but you should see the other guy!" he grinned, glancing at the pile of ash that had moments earlier taken form as Indus's avatar.

"Thia," Sol summoned the witch over, allowing her to see Rhys's injuries for herself. "These wounds require a defter hand for healing than I possess," the mage explained.

"Is everyone else alright?" Rhys called out, looking around at the others.

For the most part, they appeared to have come away from the affray more or less unscathed.

"They fare a lot better than you!" Thia insisted. "Somehow you always manage to come away from these encounters the worst off!"

"Then it is a good job you are here," Rhys smirked, locking eyes with the witch.

"I need you to take your shirt off."

"Oh?" Rhys returned wryly.

"For the wounds..." she returned abruptly.

"Of course," Rhys replied, feigning disappointment as he attempted to undress. Managing to unfasten his cloak with one hand, he next turned his attention to the arduous task of wriggling out of his tunic. Across his forearm, the burnt wool had glued itself into the weeping burn beneath, whilst a little further up the same limb, a bloody gash across the inside of his elbow was already beginning to clot against the fabric. Furthermore, at some point in the duel, he had somehow unwittingly sustained a gash across the ribs, that though only shallow, stung viciously as he attempted to remove his garments. Wincing and grunting as he tried to doff the tunic, the mage struggled for a good moment before Thia and Sol intervened, gently stripping him until he was shirtless.

Without any hesitation, Thia rapidly closed the gash across his side, the skin weaving quickly back together until little more than a long scratch along his ribs remained. With the most minor of the wounds dealt with, the witch turned her focus to both the burn across his forearm and the partially cauterised cut running along the inside of his elbow.

"These are going to scar," she warned.

Rhys nodded silently, having expected nothing less, and watched as Thia rummaged through her messenger bag to produce a jar of black ointment. Uncapping the pot, she carefully spread the pungent salve over the exposed, weeping flesh of Rhys's forearm. The mage grimaced as the dark poultice smeared across his wound, but after a few moments, the balm had already begun to sooth the burn. With the wound thickly caked, Thia bandaged Rhys's forearm, turning her attention finally to the gash running up the inside of his elbow.

Drawing closed the puckered flesh once again by way of a spell, Thia emptied out the remaining contents of the ointment jar, liberally applying the last of the salve over the singed skin surrounding the cut, before enwrapping the joint in a second dressing. His arm tightly bound, the pain dulled, Rhys felt the arcane poultice quickly beginning to work its magic, a numbing tingle seeping into the muscle of his arm.

"Keep it bandaged for the next day," she instructed. "I'll inspect it tomorrow night and see if it needs any further attention."

"Thank you," Rhys uttered gently. Quickly redressing, his attention once again returned to the heap of ashes scattered across the floor of the crypt. "What *was* that?" he asked Sol. "You said it was an avatar of Indus?"

"That's right," Sol nodded as he strode over to inspect the ashes. "I have only ever read about them. I never expected to see one!" he expressed gravely. "Those skeletons that the others and I faced—they were thralls: mindless reanimated corpses. Once raised, their only aim was to kill any intruders. Beyond being able to follow a few basic orders expressed by the necromancer that raised them, thralls have no capacity for thought. Though still requiring blood magic to produce, they are in essence, relatively simple undead creations. An avatar on the other hand..."

"A different kettle of fish?"

"You could say that," Thia put in, joining the discussion. "An avatar is also an undead servant of its necromantic master, but unlike simple thralls, they possess a level of intelligence —sentience even. They are conscious to a certain degree, capable of independent thought, imbued with traits and powers of their master, and able to act with relative freedom within the confines of their domain. They can improvise, strategise, converse... An avatar believes itself an individual. It thinks that it is alive. That *thing* might well have thought it *was* Indus."

"And so what? The knowledge of how to create an avatar is hard to come by?"

"Well," Sol scoffed. "Until today, I thought an avatar was purely theoretical. I've not heard of anyone ever actually summoning one."

"I believe it has been done," returned Thia, "I've read accounts. But it's not simply a case of it being obscure magical knowledge—the power requirements... the number of sacrifices needed to create a being like that you faced..."

The three of them silently gazed around at the brigandine clad skeletons, then back to the blood altar at the far end of the cavern.

"This was potent dark magic indeed," Sol warned. "That being was bound to Indus's will. It possessed a portion of his mind—his power. I'm impressed you won out against it."

"If it was bound to Indus's will, does that mean he knows we are here?" Rhys asked.

"I wouldn't know," Sol returned shruggingly.

"It is possible," confirmed Thia.

"Shit," breathed Sol. "Looks like you were right about the importance of this place, Rhys."

Rhys nodded. "Not only has Indus visited this place, but he went to considerable lengths to keep whatever is hidden here a secret."

"And what is hidden here?" Alkis probed. "What could be so important that he was willing to perform human sacrifices to keep it a secret?"

Rhys glanced over to the archway set in the far wall of the cavern. "I don't know," he replied. "But I want nothing more than to find out!"

"Then let's do just that," Sol proposed, now finally as intrigued as Rhys.

Rhys led the others vigilantly towards the

cavern's far end, the stone walls and ceiling tapering to a natural archway that led through to a narrow passage. Pausing before the mouth of the tunnel, Rhys glanced back at the others, hesitating briefly as his sensed they were reaching a pivotal moment in their journey.

Running his fingers across the smooth walls of the passage, Rhys stepped into the tunnel, advancing slowly into the darkness until, up ahead, a teal aura began to radiate across the walls and ceiling. Thereafter, the light grew brighter with every step, the passage widening before suddenly it opened into a second cavern bathed in a turquoise luminance. The ceiling vaulted overhead, sloping down uniformly around the domed crypt. Suspended in the air above, millions of motes of light glimmered against the darkness, hanging motionless as they twinkled all around. An expanse of glassy water sheened throughout the cavern; beneath the unnaturally still surface, vast crystals radiated a spectral cyan aura that diffused softly throughout the crypt.

Centred in the water body, a circular sarsen disc sat as an island, etched with runes and markings akin to the carvings of the Northern Circle. Engraved into the heart of the island, Rhys could make out the sigil he'd traced over the map of Cambria; this time, the Northern Circle halo, and the eastern ring representing Arthest, shimmered faintly with arcane light.

"We're here," Rhys declared.

"How do we get across?" Sol asked, denoting the absence of a bridge.

"I'm not sure," Rhys hesitated, before attempting to dip the tip of his staff into the water. To the mage's amazement, the liquid resisted his weight, the surface tension holding firm against his staff, barely even undulating under the distortion. Wide eyed, Rhys slowly lifted his foot, raising it out above the water.

"Rhys!?" Thia cautioned hesitantly.

The mage gently lowered his boot until his sole was resting upon the water's surface. Tentatively, he shifted his weight forward. Rhys grinned widely as he stepped out onto the water, turning back to face the others as the turquoise light below flickered gently in soft ripples.

"Wow," the party all mouthed together, before one by one, they too stepped cautiously out onto the water.

Treading carefully, Rhys shuffled over to the sarsen disc, stepping off the liquid, up onto dry land once again. The others each in turn followed, gazing about in wonder at the mystical chamber. As Sol dismounted the water, following Rhys up onto the sarsen island, he stooped to examine the carvings etched across the stone. "There is another recess here," he declared, peering down at a cylindrical slot centred in the sigil.

"Hold on a moment," Cade exclaimed, peering up overhead at the suspension of light moats glimmering above them. "Those are the stars!"

Rhys raised his gaze, rapidly spotting several familiar constellations arranged in the lights. "You are right!"

"It's a map of the heavens," Thia remarked. "I wonder if they translate to the stars' current positions?"

"Nothing," Sol declared defeatedly.

Rhys turned back to see the mage withdrawing his stave from the recess in the stone.

"Not quite sure what I was hoping for," he added. "But I figured something would happen."

Rhys shrugged. "And still no standing stones."

"This must be it," mused Sol disappointedly gazing up at the celestial map glinting overhead. "I've had doubts this entire time," he admitted, "but just before now... I really thought we'd find some answers here!"

"There must be something!" Rhys insisted, crouching now to inspect the etchings for himself. He ran his fingers softly across the sigil, sensing echoes whispering from deep within the stone. There was something here. This circle was calling him, drawing him closer. Without thinking, his body almost acting under its own volition, Rhys steadily rose to his feet and lowered the end of his stave down into the receptacle.

When Rhys next looked up at

his surroundings, he was elsewhere. The subterranean crypt had vanished around him. Overhead, the celestial map had been supplanted by the true heavens, a countless see of stars glinting impossibly high above. Stretching across the surrounding horizons, the jagged snow-capped peaks of the Virminter Mountains gleamed beneath the moonlight.

Rhys was still clutching his staff, his weapon slotted into a receptacle pit carved into sarsen, but now, the island of stone beneath him had grown in size tenfold. Ahead, towering upwards from the northern rim of the henge, an immense bluestone monolith loomed dark against the night sky. Turning eastward, Rhys saw a second great standing stone, positioned in accordance with Mount Arthest's exact bearing. Heaped around the remaining circumference of the vast monument, positioned along the rim of the sarsen plateau, were nine cairns of bluestone, the remaining standing stones of the great circle lying in ruin.

Rhys gasped as memories of a half-forgotten dream came rushing back to him. He'd stood here before. He'd watched the Arthest monolith reassemble, forged anew from the rubble it had been reduced to. The vision had come to him that night in Wythe, shortly after he had visited the circle on Arthest. Rhys's touch had rekindled the stones, reactivating the eastern henge, and establishing its connexion back with this central circle. A sudden understanding came to Rhys, information hazily seeping into his mind, imbued to him by the henge in which he stood. This place was the convergence of ley lines throughout Cambria, the heart of the continent, the central focal point of all magic, the Nexus.

Rhys peered down at the vast sarsen plateau, gazing at the converging channels chiselled out of the rock to form the sigil that had led him here. The shape formed a map of the network of henges across Cambria, it was a chart of ley lines: the Atlas.

Releasing his staff, Rhys strode out across the plateau, following the Atlas's northerly ley line towards the Northern Circle menhir. Whispers cried out from the surface of the stone, beckoning Rhys closer. The mage gently rested a palm against the towering monolith, and in that instant, his mind was set ablaze with images and voices. An incomprehensible jumble of information flooded his mind, racing through his thoughts with dizzying speed and deafening tones. The visions and sounds were fragmented, scattered, incomplete. Rhys's head began to spin, overwhelmed by the indecipherable torrent of information streaming through his consciousness. Unable to endure the tide of visions, he drew away. Shaking off his disorientation, Rhys panted as his mind steadily cleared.

The stone was an archive; the entire Nexus

was an immense arcane library of knowledge and power, but whilst the circle lay in ruin, that knowledge, those ancient secrets, were inaccessible.

Turning back to return to his staff, Rhys froze still in his tracks. Indus stood ahead of him at the heart of the Nexus. The mage's form was spectral and translucent, flickering rapidly in and out of existence, and Rhys quickly understood that he was looking upon a projection created by the Nexus.

The image of Indus stood in the same spot Rhys had first appeared, clutching his own staff where Rhys's still stood. Gazing around, Rhys realised that the nine ruined menhirs of the henge now stood as illusory projections around the perimeter of the Nexus. He peered on with intrigue, watching as the vision of the past steadily began to unfold before him.

Indus drew a blade across the palm of his hand, spilling blood across the stone at his feet. He began to incant in inaudible mutterings. A crimson glyph steadily set alight, an intricate and extensive pattern of fiery lines and symbols burning to life as they extended outwards from the mage. Indus gripped his stave in bloodied fingers, and suddenly, the fire blackened. Dark energy swept outwards, tearing down the ley line channels of the Atlas, surging outwards towards the surrounding menhirs. The great monoliths began to fracture and rent, fissures tearing across the stones as they cracked and crumbled, collapsing under their own weight as one by one, they were reduced to dust, all except one: the Northern Circle.

The images faded, and once more Rhys was alone within the circle. A sudden series of revelations dawned on him. Indus's dark powers, his knowledge of forbidden magic and esoteric secrets, he'd learnt from the Nexus. Plundering the Nexus's archives, the power-hungry mage had acquired the knowledge he deemed useful in his pursuit to conquer Cambria; then, determined to prevent anyone from discovering what he knew, he destroyed the stones, reducing the Nexus to ruin. Indus had sought to keep his newly attained knowledge secret. In doing so, he'd severed the Nexus's links to the other circles across Cambria, rendering the knowledge contained within the stones unattainable.

Rhys cursed in frustration. He'd come seeking answers. Before Indus's desecration of this ancient site of power, the answers he'd sought would have been here for him to discover. But now, with the primal knowledge of the Nexus locked away, finding a way to stop Indus seemed just as impossible as ever. That was unless the Nexus could be restored.

Rhys slowly swivelled his head eastward. There in front of him, the Arthest menhir stood reforged. When the henge had been activated under Rhys's touch, its connexion with the Nexus had been re-established, the monolith rising out of ruin. Revolving on the spot, Rhys glanced over the nine cairns heaped around the fringes of the Nexus, each pile of rubble representing a stone circle in some distant region of the continent, its link severed from the other henges. But if one could be restored, surely the others could too?

The knowledge wasn't lost forever, it simply had been locked away. All Rhys had to do was to rekindle the network of henges throughout Cambria. If he could visit the remaining nine stone circles and activate them as he had done to the henge on Mount Arthest, the Nexus would be restored.

Clasping his staff, Rhys drew his weapon from the stone and was transported back to the crypt beneath Heartwood. Turquoise light glimmered upwards from the surrounding body of water once again, and overhead, billions of artificial stars glimmered across the ceiling.

The others were still staring up at the celestial map above them, chatting idly amongst themselves, seemingly oblivious to Rhys's disappearance. The mage glanced around at them in momentary bewilderment as they paid him little regard, before it quickly dawned on Rhys, that he had never vanished. At no point had he ever been transported out of the crypt physically; the journey had occurred solely in his thoughts. In his mindscape, several minutes had passed, but here in the crypt mere seconds had gone by.

Thia caught his eyes, seeing instantly the perplexed expression across his face.

"Rhys?" Sol smiled, likewise noticing the mage's consternation. "Is everything all right?"

Rhys met eyes with each of his companions as he processed all he had seen, before finally declaring, "I know what we need to do!"

Thank you for joining Rhys and his companions on their adventures across Cambria.

Reviews and ratings are extremely important to authors that are just starting out, but unfortunately, the vast majority of readers don't take the time to say what they think.

If you've enjoyed reading Rise of the Apostate, please let me and others know what you thought. I read every review and love finding out what people think of my work.

If you are interested in finding out more about my upcoming projects, please sign up to my mailing list on my website.

Leave a review:

*http://www.amazon.co.uk/review/
create-review?&asin=B092QYNKBM*

Mailing list:

https://www.drhillauthor.com/

BOOKS IN THIS SERIES

The Archmage Saga

Sole survivor of a dark curse, Rhys North meets a mysterious stranger amidst the ruins of his village: Arlas Al'Asim, leader of the Circle of Magi, an ancient order of arcane warriors sworn to the protection of Cambria.

Displaying a natural aptitude for magic, Rhys begins his training and undergoes an arduous pilgrimage to join the Order himself. But with tensions rising in the magi ranks and dark omens spreading across the land, he quickly finds himself thrust into the forefront of a conflict that has been building for centuries.

The first three entries in an epic fantasy series, this action-adventure saga is both brutal and heart-warming in equal measure.

Rhys's quest takes him across Cambria, from the frozen wastes of the north, to the bustling city of

Orthios, and the legendary lost island of Thule. To uncover the truth behind the fate of his village, Rhys hunts down an ancient network of stone circles in a desperate fight to save the world from a fanatical mage of unspeakable power

Dawn Of Tyranny

Rhys North and his companions find themselves in Orthios, the once capital of the Cambrian Empire, in search of another stone circle to restore the Nexus. But the so called 'City of the Gods,' is a dangerous place. Orthios is on the brink of revolt, and their presence has not gone unnoticed. In his attempts to seek retribution against the traitorous mage Indus Mark, Rhys finds himself caught at the heart of a long-brewing political struggle between the city's Council of High Lords, whilst targeted by a mysterious religious cult known as the Church of Ashes.

With war looming, and Indus's influence growing ever more powerful throughout the continent, Rhys once again finds himself at the heart of world changing events, unsure who to trust, yet determined to stand against the tyranny of his enemies.

Beyond The Brink

Rhys North's journey continues as he and his companions sail beyond the Brink of the World, into the heart of the perilous Wyrm's Triangle, to the mythical Stormy Isles.

Having narrowly escaped Indus and his followers in both Orthios and Westport, Rhys and the others set sail for Thule in search of the next conduit. Reaching the shores of the Stormy Isles seems an impossible task in and of itself, as past the Brink of the World, the laws of nature break down. But onboard the White Marlin, with the help of Captain Arne Anderssen and his sons, Rhys and the others stand their best chance of making landfall in a part of the world lost to time.

An eternal tempest, a leviathan of the deep, and a spectral cavalcade roaming the skies all stand in the way of Rhys and his task, but with the aid of his friends and the ancient inhabitants of Thule, he will ascend the slopes of Sumeru in search of the lost stone circle.

BOOKS BY THIS AUTHOR

Flight Through Infinity

The Nomad is alone. Midway through an endless journey across the stars, he must fight to survive. Equipped with little more than a small single-manned fighter, he must scavenge for what few resources can be found in a dead and decaying universe. His ship and equipment steadily breaking down, the Nomad is forced to rely on little more than his ingenuity in order to keep himself alive and the Fighter in the sky; all whilst being hunted by a race of mysterious sentient machines across the endless bounds of infinity.

A hard sci-fi survival adventure filled with emotional strife, deep introspection, and tense action.

Printed in Great Britain
by Amazon